PRAISE FOR CHRI*

The Season of Silver Linings

GOLD MEDAL WINNER READERS' FAVORITE AWARDS

FINALIST INTERNATIONAL BOOK AWARDS

"Charming and sincere, Jada's journey to reconcile the past left me with a smile on my face and hope in my heart. The idyllic setting only adds to the joy of reading this heartwarming tale of past mistakes and glorious futures."

—Heather Burch, bestselling author of *In the Light of the Garden*

"In *The Season of Silver Linings* we see love on every page. Each novel in the Sweet Lake series offers a special experience for the reader, and the third book may be your favorite yet."

—Grace Greene, *USA Today* bestselling author

Sweet Lake

FINALIST INTERNATIONAL BOOK AWARDS

"[This book] has such a charming small-town vibe and endearing characters that readers will find themselves falling in love with quirky Sweet Lake and hoping for a series."

—*Booklist*

"In this uplifting and charming story, each room of the inn is filled with friendship, forgiveness, and love."

—*Kirkus Reviews*

The Comfort of Secrets

GOLD MEDAL WINNER READERS' FAVORITE AWARDS

SECOND PLACE WOMEN'S FICTION, ROYAL PALM LITERARY AWARDS

FINALIST INTERNATIONAL BOOK AWARDS

FINALIST KINDLE BOOK AWARDS

"Welcome back to the Wayfair Inn, where discovering secrets and overcoming human frailty are the ingredients for finding love and happiness. Reading Nolfi's *The Comfort of Secrets* feels like coming home."

—Kay Bratt, bestselling author of *Wish Me Home*

"Poignant, honest, and filled with heart, *The Comfort of Secrets* has it all. With a natural talent for lyrical prose, Christine Nolfi sweeps you away."

—Heather Burch, bestselling author of *In the Light of the Garden*

Second Chance Grill

FINALIST PUT YOUR HEART IN A BOOK AWARDS

"Nolfi writes with a richness of heart that is incredibly endearing."

—Renee Fountain, *Book Fetish*

"An emotionally moving contemporary novel about the power that relationships have to transform lives."

—Susan Bethany, *Midwest Book Review*

Treasure Me

FINALIST NEXT GENERATION INDIE AWARDS

"A riveting read for those who enjoy adventure fiction. Highly recommended."

—Susan Bethany, *Midwest Book Review*

The Tree of Everlasting Knowledge

"Poignant and powerful, *The Tree of Everlasting Knowledge* is as much a saga of learning how to survive, heal, and forgive as it is a chilling crime story, unforgettable to the very end."

—Margaret Lane, *Midwest Book Review*

the

road

she left

behind

the

road

she left

behind

A NOVEL

CHRISTINE NOLFI

LAKE UNION
PUBLISHING

Published by Lake Union, Seattle

www.apub.com

Amazon, the Amazon logo, and Lake Union are trademarks of Amazon.com, Inc., or its affiliates.

ISBN-13: 9781542004213
ISBN-10: 1542004217

Cover design by Caroline Teagle Johnson

Printed in the United States of America

For my sister Trish

Chapter 1

The harbor cruise had devolved into a kidnapping.

Slipping past the revelers, Darcy inched toward the relative privacy of the boat's lower deck. *She* was the hostage.

That morning, Darcy had stopped in to clean out her office with a minimum of fuss. She'd rehearsed her goodbye to the staff, the usual pithy speech she trotted out whenever quitting the latest job. Just a few quick words about how much she'd enjoyed the year in Charleston as the assistant manager for Big Bud's Harbor Tours.

The plan went disastrously awry. The moment she'd hoisted the heavy box of belongings into her arms, her replacement—a tall brunette with the smooth gait of a racehorse—appeared in the doorway. A girl from accounting darted in behind her. Together, they wrested the box from Darcy's grip and pushed her into the corridor.

In their enthusiasm, they pushed too hard. Darcy stumbled head-first into the flock of assistants on three-inch heels. Southern women understood grooming like nobody's business, and a cloud of perfume accosted her. Darcy's flats skidded across the linoleum. Nose tingling, she shrieked. Caught between terror and a sneeze brought on by Lancôme, she pitched forward.

The assistants caught her a thin second before she face-planted.

Once they righted the shuddering plank of her body, Darcy attempted to bolt. She felt like an untamed filly hemmed in by a dozen silk-clad jockeys of varying ages. The women—stronger than they appeared—captured her.

During the last year, the stealthy ways of Big Bud's staff had become all too familiar. Oh, the women meant well as they bypassed common courtesy—and US law—to scroll through employee files, gathering information with the zeal of hostesses planning a gala. If they discovered an employee birthday on the horizon, the women brought in helium balloons and birthday cake. Anniversaries rated balloons, cake, *and* small presents wrapped in silver or gold. If a woman left on maternity leave, she would return to find baby gifts stacked on her desk and luscious platters of homemade baked goods lined up in the lunchroom.

Factor in a family pet, and these women pulled out all the stops. When Big Bud's French bulldog gave birth to a squirmy litter of pups, the enthusiastic staff paid for family photos. They even purchased a burnished-gold frame and hung the best photo in the lobby.

Overall, the niceness factor was sweet, even heartwarming. But these women from the land of Dixie weren't usually accomplices to a kidnapping. Darcy was still demanding an explanation when they began to circle her.

High heels clacking, they had pushed her out the back of the low brick building and down the gangplank. Before Darcy got a grip on their plan, they'd pushed her aboard the *Irma*, a two-deck party ship—and the fanciest vessel in Big Bud's fleet.

Bud, his belly jiggling and his beard flapping in the salty breeze, told the staff to return within the hour. At seventy-six, he was no longer seaworthy. Hugged close to his side, his wife—the real-life Irma—waved with merriment. The boat rumbled to life.

Officially kidnapped, Darcy surveyed the retreating dock with frustration. The staff, leaving her alone to stew in her own juices, clattered up the stairwell to the boat's top deck. Corks popped, and the cheap champagne Bud kept onboard during the tourist season began flowing.

With only an hour to get their groove on, the employees weren't about to waste time.

To the east, a container ship carved a ponderous swath as it lumbered toward Charleston Harbor. The sun, lazy on the fine June morning, lifted above the horizon. Golden light scattered across the foam-capped waves.

The solitude was nearly enjoyable.

The boat picked up speed, drawing cheers from the staff above. The shoreline retreated from view. Resigned to her fate, Darcy leaned against the railing. A one-hour delay didn't represent a major calamity. Even if it *was* the worst day of the year.

A voice came from behind. "Aren't you having a drink, honey?"

One of the secretaries joined her at the prow. Trista, or Trixie—a middle-aged redhead who worked the evening shift. Darcy rarely interacted with her.

"I'm fine, thanks."

"You're not celebrating at your own going-away party? There's nothing wrong with starting the day with a teeny glass of champagne."

The secretary meant well, so Darcy made an effort to scrape the irritation from her face. "Is there coffee onboard?"

"I'm sorry, there isn't. Should I find some orange juice? I'm sure there's some below deck. I'll make you a nice mimosa."

With misgivings, she eyed the champagne bottle. "Really, I'm good. I have to be on the road soon."

The redhead lowered the bottle. "Sure, honey. I don't want you getting behind the wheel if you're tipsy." She lifted her own glass and took a noisy sip. Leaning close, she dropped her voice to a whisper. "Where are you going, anyway? Everyone says it's a secret. I don't mean to pry, but I do love a mystery. Did one of Bud's competitors make you a better offer?"

The friendly curiosity echoed the comments Darcy had become proficient at dodging. The loss from eight years ago still festered like a wound that would not heal. She avoided chatty conversations out of fear that a well-meaning coworker might unearth the details.

Regret sifted through her. After years drifting from one job to the next, Darcy knew how to snuff out the tiniest flicker of friendship.

Only this time, she'd failed. At this particular job, she'd made a friend she'd miss.

The first time ever.

"I don't have my plans nailed down," she hedged. Despising the lie, she layered false cheer into her tone. "Something will turn up."

"Hold on. Did someone on the staff hurt your feelings?" A burst of anger rippled across the redhead's shoulders. "Is *that* why you're leaving? Sweetie, talk to Bud. He'll fix it."

"There's nothing to fix," Darcy assured her. She didn't wish to share details about the new job she'd accepted out of state. "I wanted to leave, and Bud's already found a new assistant manager. It's time to move on, that's all."

"Move on?" The woman stared at her, wide-eyed. "You quit without having something else lined up? Why'd you do a fool thing like that?"

The questions were beginning to feel like an interrogation. "I'll find something when I decide where to land. It's no big—" She cut off.

A funny sensation carried her attention to the upper deck.

Is someone watching me?

Employees milled around in small clusters, clinking glasses and gesturing at landmarks. Charleston's peninsula streamed by, the church steeples gathering sunlight on their pointed spires and the historic antebellum homes peeking out from behind ash-colored shadows. A school of dolphins kept time with the boat. Their sleek bodies slipped through the waves like mermaids welcoming in the day.

The dolphins began arrowing away from the boat. Darcy barely noticed. Shielding her eyes to study the employees above her, she replayed the moments when she'd been hauled down the gangplank to the *Irma*. She couldn't recall if she had seen Samson get onboard.

Then she saw him, and dismay snatched her breath.

On the metal stairs leading down to the lower deck, Samson wavered. He attempted a smile.

Fate was often cruel, and Samson Dray had suffered more than most. Shuttled through South Carolina's foster care system, he'd carried his biblical name into adulthood on a slight build. With skin the color of teak, and dreadlocks that swung across his narrow shoulders, he smiled often and with genuine affection that never failed to brighten the atmosphere at Big Bud's. The eighteen-year-old was newly released from foster care.

When tourists stood ten deep at the counter, grumpy from the Lowcountry's swamp heat and wilting in their bright vacation clothes, Samson handed out icy bottles of water. If he noticed an older couple in the crush, he would drag folding chairs from the storage room and invite them to sit near the wall, out of the general chaos. A fussy toddler in the crowd was soothed with a lollipop; boisterous children received bags of peanuts and a gentle request to quiet down. Given Samson's easygoing nature, they readily complied.

In between busy periods when tourists waited to board the fleet of boats, Samson dispensed with his role of cheerful butler and danced among the island of desks in the main office, happy to run errands for the staff or handle odd jobs for the elderly Bud and his wife.

The redhead caught the silent exchange between Darcy and the dark-skinned teen everyone at Big Bud's treated as a favorite. Smiling faintly, she excused herself.

The moment she'd gone, Samson climbed down the stairs.

Darcy swung her attention to the water. This wasn't how she'd planned to exit Samson's life. Not trapped a mile from shore without a rehearsed script at the ready.

As he loped across the deck, erasing the distance between them, she came to a depressing conclusion. She'd devised *no* plan for how to say goodbye.

Sparing her a recriminating stare, Samson rested his elbows on the railing. He gazed out to sea. Waves lapped at the side of the boat. Darcy followed his cue, pretending interest in the landmarks streaming past. Spidery threads of embarrassment crawled up her neck.

Proffer an apology? Or remain silent until he fires up the salvos I deserve?

The silence grew oppressive. Breaking it, he said, "You sure are ugly."

Relief spilled through her. "You think?" She hadn't expected his standard greeting on their last day together. An inside joke, really. Samson had come up with the gem last winter after she took him to Green Island Bar for shrimp po'boys and three men had hit on her in as many minutes.

"I hate to point out the obvious," he quipped, still refusing to look at her. "You're uglier than normal today."

"My special gift."

"Guess we all need a talent. Although I don't know how you go out in public without a sack over your head."

"I knew I forgot something." Gulping down the salty air, Darcy kept her eyes trained on the waves. "I did take special care with my ugly routine this morning. Seemed appropriate for my last day on the job."

"Time well spent. You could scare fish from the water."

"My intention, of course."

"Your office is all packed?"

"Don't ask what happened to the box of my stuff. Someone stole it. Right before they manhandled me onto this boat."

Tiny cowrie shells clicked on Samson's dreadlocks as he nodded with faint amusement. "Don't you worry none, Darcy. Theft is exactly what you need. I'm sure Irma herself is tearing through the box as we speak. Lord knows what Bud's better half will find inside."

No personal effects were hidden in the box—a minor point. The notion of anyone rifling through her things bothered Darcy. That was another inside joke—Samson liked to tease her about her paranoia. She detested sharing personal information for reasons never explained to her young friend.

Discussing the shattering events of the past was even more out of bounds.

"I hope Irma doesn't make off with my gel pens," she said, dismissing the thought before it triggered sharp, unwanted memories. "I'm partial to the ones with purple ink."

"Then you're out of luck. Irma likes anything purple."

"She does?"

Samson grunted. "Plan on buying new pens," he replied. There was no telling if he was joking. "Older ladies like Miz Irma wear dresses with big pockets. Haven't you noticed? She'll be filling hers."

"Nonsense." He *was* joking. Darcy laughed, releasing some of the tension brewing inside her. "Irma keeps a Bible on her desk, right next to her pot of African violets. No way does she steal."

"For a college-educated woman, you sure are dumb. There's larceny in every soul."

"Not yours."

"Like you know what's inside me. We haven't been friends very long."

"I know people." Darcy attempted to add something else. Words failed her.

Samson never borrowed a paper clip without asking. Considerate, decent—his raw goodness was hard to understand. A childhood short on love and long on disappointment should have tempted him to pitch his tent on the wrong side of the law. Some people were onions: peel back enough layers, and there was nothing underneath. A precious few were like apples. Life had bruised Samson, but he retained a solid core.

On the railing, his fingers stilled. "Darcy, do you want the God's-honest truth? I've been doing my best to channel meanness. Working real hard at it too. I just don't know how to get the meanness to bubble up inside me." He slid a glance in her general direction; it seemed more fearful than accusatory. An indication of distress, maybe anguish. With lightning speed, he returned his attention to the harbor. "So you're going. Farewell. It's been nice knowing you, and all that. I'm not dumb. I know you won't change your mind. Your stubborn streak is harder than stone."

"Samson . . ."

"I get it. You don't want some kid dragging his sorry ass behind you on a new adventure—extra baggage, and you like to travel light. All I'm saying is we make a good team. Almost like we're family. And I can pull my weight." He slid his elbows off the railing. Crossing his arms, he watched the gulls swooping past as the boat rounded the tip of Charleston Peninsula.

A pang of guilt struck her deep. Samson was still more boy than man. Yet he was man enough not to let her see him cry.

Helplessly, she splayed her hands. "I want you to forgive me. Not today—but someday. I don't want you feeling bad just because I don't think it's a great idea to bring you along." The plea for understanding brought no reaction as he continued to study the splashing waves. "Samson, I know you're feeling adrift now that you're out of foster care. But you've spent your whole life in Charleston. This is your home. I don't have roots. Not anymore. I never stay anywhere long. One year exactly, that's all. Then I move on."

"I'd still like to go."

"My lifestyle isn't a great choice for someone your age. You need a life that'll give you a sense of direction."

He weighed the explanation with suspicion—or doubt. It was hard to tell. Over the last months he'd begun to idolize her, and she wondered if he feared missing out on what he imagined would be a grand adventure. Little did he know the lonely future awaiting Darcy.

"One favor," he said. "That's all I'm asking."

"Anything."

"If you get on the road and change your mind, send a text. All I need is a time and place. I'll find a way to catch up."

A childish request, heartbreaking in its simplicity.

"You can't follow me. Big Bud and Irma rely on you. No one responsible quits a job without giving notice." She reached out to offer comfort, but she left her palm hovering above his shoulder for an uncomfortable moment. Lowering her hand to her side felt like the worst kind of retreat. "By then, I'll be four states away. Too far for you to catch up."

"Bud and Miz Irma won't mind if I quit right away. You know what they're always telling me."

"If you're patient, you'll find your North Star." The older couple went out of their way to encourage Samson's belief that his life's direction would reveal itself if he looked hard enough.

His dreadlocks clacked as he gave a sharp nod. "Everyone's got one," he said with fierce conviction. "Even if it's buried deep inside. Even someone like me."

"You'll find your star," she promised. "Just not with me."

Her frustration welled. What right did Samson have to assume she possessed the means to help him at all? She'd allowed a nearly maternal urge to bring him into her orbit. He was young and alone, and his sweetness reminded her of the sister she'd lost. But she never would have succumbed to the desire to protect him if she'd known he'd begin to view her as a guiding light.

Anger layered onto her frustration. He was not to blame. Months ago, she'd begun buying him dinner after work and allowing him to hang out at her apartment. As if treating him like a cherished little brother could fill the hole in her heart.

Or stopper the grief over all she had lost.

Laughter rang out from the upper deck. The new manager was flirting with a man from the accounting department, the one with a goatee and heavy brows. He grabbed her by the waist and whirled her around. The champagne in her glass sloshed out in a glittery arc. The scene provided a stark contrast to the emotions colliding inside Darcy.

Tears collected on her lashes. Brushing them away, she leaned into Samson. Even shoulder to shoulder, he kept his eyes locked on the waves.

She glanced skyward. "Most of time I'm just lost," she admitted. "I've been lost for a long time. Even if I believed in guiding stars—and I don't—I wouldn't recognize mine if it fell from the heavens and landed right at my feet."

Samson withdrew his arms from the railing. At last his dark, solemn gaze swung to hers.

"Someday you'll find your North Star," he said. "You've just lost the will to look."

~

Late-morning sunlight poured through the window. Checking under the bed, Darcy was satisfied she'd left nothing behind.

Only the wrought-iron bed and a simple pine dresser occupied the bedroom. The rest of the apartment had always felt equally severe, with angular Danish furniture in dull, uninviting gray. From the first day she'd moved in, the rental's lack of warmth had appealed to Darcy. It was easier to leave an apartment she'd never considered a home.

Still, she lingered. She dared the memory of Samson's disappointment to seize her again. Now that he'd aged out of South Carolina's foster care system, he needed to find somewhere to live. He'd been looking into group housing, but she knew he'd put off a decision in hopes of leaving Charleston with her instead. Aside from his job, there wasn't much tying him to the city.

Let it go.

Better to leave Samson here, with his idealism rooted in fertile soil. If he became familiar with the real Darcy, he'd learn the worst lessons.

Not that she allowed the heartache to cripple her or allowed herself to succumb to self-pity. She was too pragmatic to discount reality. Many people were knocked down by misfortune. Most people, in fact—if they loved deeply enough or lived long enough. A friendship became estranged, or a marriage led to divorce. Illness sent you into a tailspin, or financial hardship erased your self-confidence.

Or death took the people you cherished.

Tugging her long, wheat-colored hair into a ponytail, Darcy hesitated. She checked under the dresser for stray items and found only several dust bunnies. The box she'd packed this morning at the office—which Irma had *not* rifled through—was already stowed in the car.

Moving day. Always on the dreaded anniversary, always to another city chosen at random. This year it would be Cape May, in New Jersey. Thanks to an executive headhunter website, her new job started next week. An inside sales position with a national company specializing in flood insurance. A big change from the casual atmosphere at Big Bud's.

After Darcy dropped off the apartment key with the landlord, she wheeled her luggage into the parking lot. She was just settling in behind the steering wheel of her Honda Accord when her smartphone rang.

Reading the display, she frowned. It was Latrice calling.

For a fraction of a second, Darcy hesitated.

The middle-aged Latrice worked as the housekeeper for Darcy's mother. By mutual agreement, they only chatted on Christmas. More contact was too painful for them both.

Why is she breaking protocol?

Whatever the reason, it didn't bode well.

On a steadying breath, Darcy picked up. "Latrice. Hello."

"Hi, sweetie. How are you?"

"Fine, I suppose."

"You sound congested. Are you coming down with something?"

A painful image leaped before her eyesight. Samson, waving good-bye as she'd marched off the *Irma*. His disappointment was added misery on the anniversary of the deaths of her beloved sister and distant father.

"I'm all right." A falsehood. She'd cried ugly-girl tears all the way back to the apartment.

A silence rife with skepticism filled her ears. Latrice wasn't easily fooled. She'd been sneaking around the emotional terrain of Darcy's heart for years.

"You sure about that?" she asked. The loving timbre of her voice threatened Darcy's weak hold on her emotions. "From where I'm sitting, it sounds like you're talking through a nose filled with snot."

"My allergies are just acting up. I'm fine."

"You're not fine, but I'll give you points for bravery. You never were one for complaining. Remember when you ran the hundred-and-four temp?"

"Listen, I have a busy day ahead. Can this wait until we talk at Christmas?"

"That high temp got a hold of you in first grade," the housekeeper continued. "You were cherry red and sweating like a sumo wrestler. Worst case of strep throat I'd ever seen."

"Oh. Right. I do remember."

Latrice gave a low murmur of approval. "You never made a fuss. My brave girl," she said. "I'm still mad at myself for letting your little sister follow us into the examination room. Why didn't I leave Elizabeth with the nurse? I suppose we're all prone to making bad decisions, and I was young at the time . . ."

A double meaning was hidden in the story, one flavored with forgiveness and advice. As the housekeeper rambled on about poor choices, Darcy glanced at the dashboard clock. One minute spun into the next.

Curiosity snuck past her apprehension. "What did Elizabeth do?"

"When Dr. Johnson reached for the syringe of penicillin, she let out a howl like nobody's business. She thought he'd do you harm."

"Poor Elizabeth."

"What are you talking about? Poor *me*. Once she quit hollering, she threw up on my shoes."

"Elizabeth puked on your shoes? Yuck."

"Right next to the exam table. She'd had spaghetti for lunch. I thought *I'd* throw up. You were still comforting her when Dr. Johnson asked you to roll over for the shot."

Before her death, Elizabeth had been squeamish in the extreme. The sharp scent of antiseptic, blood oozing from a scraped knee, a glimpse of a snake slithering in high grass—it never took much to make her queasy. Darcy recalled a spring afternoon during their elementary school years when she found the half-eaten remains of a mouse on the mansion's circular driveway. Curiosity drove her to snap off a branch from her mother's expertly trimmed boxwood to examine the bloody remains. With fascination, she'd poked and prodded, unaware of her little sister standing close behind.

For weeks afterward, Elizabeth slept in Darcy's bedroom with her head burrowed beneath her big sister's armpit.

For sisters so close in age, they couldn't have been more different. When they were teenagers, Elizabeth would dash from the living room whenever Darcy turned on a horror flick. The vampire romances Darcy read until her senior year of high school made Elizabeth shudder. No matter how hot the guy depicted in the pages, Elizabeth couldn't square razor-sharp fangs with passionate love.

"I don't recall Elizabeth throwing up at the doctor's office," she admitted.

"I had to throw those shoes away."

"I'm sure she felt bad about ruining them."

Another memory rushed over Darcy. The arduous labor her sister had endured to bring her son, Emerson, into the world. How Elizabeth clung to Darcy's blood-starved fingers as each contraction gripped her. How Elizabeth, two days after Emerson's birth, had elicited a solemn vow from her big sister.

If anything happens to me, promise you'll look after my baby.

At the time, Elizabeth's worries seemed far-fetched. She was twenty years old, a young woman with her whole life ahead of her. Or so Darcy thought. Never could she have imagined that her sister would die soon after Emerson's birth.

Self-loathing coursed through Darcy. The broken promise haunted her still.

"Elizabeth made the cutest drawings to apologize," Latrice was saying, her lighthearted tone at odds with Darcy's sad thoughts. "The minute we got back to the house, she ran off to get her crayons. I still have the pictures she made—she drew a halo over my head." Latrice paused, clearly relishing how much she'd enjoyed tending to her young charges. Getting back on track, she added, "There's no shame in being out of sorts today, child. The anniversary is hard on all of us. Your mother most of all."

Darcy bit her lip. The falling-out with her mother was bad enough. Pondering the raw bitterness Rosalind endured every June was an agony not worth exploring.

"Did you go with her to the cemetery?" she asked, astonished by her curiosity.

"First thing this morning. The lilacs by the patio are blooming like crazy. I made two bouquets. Of course she complained the whole drive."

"About the lilacs?"

"About the car smelling like a brothel. The way she went on, you'd think I'd dumped a bottle of perfume in her Mercedes. I can't imagine why she prefers store-bought roses. All the scent is bred right out of them. She managed well enough at your daddy's grave. She broke down at Elizabeth's. She always does."

Bile rose in Darcy's throat. After the accident, Crowne Funeral Home had performed a miracle on her father. Their careful work allowed for an open casket during the calling hours prior to the service.

Not so for Elizabeth.

Latrice said, "I am sorry about breaking our rule and calling you today. There wasn't any choice." She paused a beat. "You must come home."

Chapter 2

You must come home.

Her keys slipped from her fingers. They jangled to the floor of the Honda.

"Baby girl, did you hear me?"

Darcy scrabbled for the keys. "I heard you."

"And?"

"Be realistic. I'm not welcome at my mother's house." Why Latrice thought otherwise was beyond comprehension. "It's been almost a decade since I last stepped foot in Ohio. I'm never coming back, although I do hope you'll take me up on my offer." At the end of each once-yearly call, they routinely discussed meeting one day in a vacation spot, Miami or Hilton Head. Even though Darcy couldn't recall Latrice ever taking a vacation, she kept extending the invitation. "I've moved on, Latrice. Built a new life on my own. I moved on because I didn't have a choice."

"You've stuck your head in the sand is what you've done. Living like a vagrant, wandering from one city to the next. You need to get unstuck!"

"I'm not a vagrant." Distracted, she held up the key ring. The tiny silver key, the one for her carry-on, was missing. "You know why I left."

"Darcy Angela Goodridge, your stubborn streak is a mile wide."

She peered at the floor for the missing luggage key. "You're not the first person today to mention my better qualities," she said, recalling Samson's nearly identical words. The key glinted, and she retrieved it from the toe of her canvas shoe. "What's wrong with standing my ground? Contrary to what you believe, some relationships can't be fixed. Like the one between me and my mother."

"I'm sick and tired of this foolishness. Don't you think she regrets what she said?"

Latrice was referring to their argument on the night of the double funeral. Darcy still wasn't sure how much of the blame rested with her. Refusing to accompany her mother in the limousine to the gravesite wasn't her most rational decision. Half-mad with grief and haunted by the events set in motion by her unforgivable behavior, she'd driven alone.

A familiar misery twisted inside her. "You don't want to believe my mother can be intentionally cruel. But she meant what she said that night. I've never doubted it."

In the days leading up to the funeral, whenever Darcy made the mistake of entering a room occupied by her mother, a formidable silence rained down on her. All those frigid glances and the tight anger thinning her mother's lips. The tacit accusations were an impossible weight on Darcy's heart.

After the caskets were lowered into the ground and the mourners drifted away—all of them, including her rigidly composed mother—Darcy had stood at the gravesite with her eyes blurry from tears and her thoughts hollowed out. She stood alone in the unforgiving air until the daylight retreated. A dark chill carried into her bones as she walked back to her car. For hours, she drove aimlessly through Geauga County's winding roads—sobbing as night stole the last sunlight from the hills, replaying the irretrievable mistakes that led to her father's and Elizabeth's deaths.

It was well after midnight when she finally returned. The lights were still on in the mansion. In the library, her mother was pouring generously from a bottle of Macallan Scotch. Clearly grieving, and needing to blunt the tragic reality that she'd lost her husband and the daughter she'd loved more than anyone else.

Her skittering, ravaged gaze caught Darcy. Setting down the bottle, she let loose a torrent of rage.

Darcy left Ohio the same night.

The memory sickened her. "Did my mother ask you to call?" Her voice nearly broke, but she reined in the emotion. "The truth, Latrice. Does *she* want me to come back?"

The impassioned query floated unbound. On the other end, Latrice made a small cry of distress.

Darcy jammed the key into the ignition. No, her mother didn't want her back in Ohio.

Not ever.

"Rosalind didn't ask me to reach out to you," Latrice admitted. "How could she? She doesn't know we stay in touch. At least I don't think she does."

"She'd have a hissy fit if she did."

"Child, she's upset you ran off. She's upset about lots of things."

"I didn't 'run off.'" Darcy threw the car into drive and pulled out of the lot. "I was a legal adult. I chose to move away."

"Running from the hurt is no badge of maturity. I swear. Running off must be a genetic trait."

"What's that supposed to mean?"

"You're not the only Goodridge to run from hard situations. Emerson does too. I don't blame the child. He's got a lot on his mind. We all do."

Emerson.

Darcy eased into the traffic on King Street with pinpricks of guilt scattering across her heart. Once she left Ohio, she'd trained herself not to contemplate Elizabeth's baby boy—or the promise she'd made to look after him. She'd left her nephew in the care of his prickly, career-driven grandmother and the same housekeeper who'd given more attention to Darcy and Elizabeth during childhood than their successful parents.

Emerson was eight years old now—a child Darcy no longer knew.

Latrice said, "For the record, one argument on the night of the funeral shouldn't have made you leave home."

"Thanks for lending an opinion. I don't agree, obviously. Just tread carefully, okay? I don't want her needling you if you slip up and mention we've been in contact."

"Sweetie, you *have* been gone a long time. You think I tiptoe around your mother? If she throws too many complaints my way, I stand up for myself. She never pushes me too far."

Darcy sensed the truth in the statement. As one of the most conservative judges in northeast Ohio, the Honorable Rosalind Goodridge made countless attorneys tremble in her presence—and sentenced many of their clients to long prison terms. Yet Rosalind wasn't getting any younger, and she did have Emerson to raise. After decades working in the mansion, Latrice was probably back to nanny duty.

Despite her dismal mood, Darcy chuckled. "Don't mention we've been in touch, okay?"

"What does it matter how your mother reacts? Once you come home, it'll take her no time at all to figure out who called you. Are you coming or not?"

"I'm still in South Carolina, but I'm on my way to the next job, in New Jersey. An eleven-hour detour to northeast Ohio is *not* on the agenda."

"Tell the company in New Jersey to find someone else. I'm serious, child. Emerson is lonely. This last year has been hard on him."

"In what way?"

"I can't go into the details long-distance. The point is, he's not a baby anymore."

Apprehension wicked the moisture from Darcy's mouth. "You mean he's started asking the big questions?" she guessed.

"It's natural for a child to be curious about his background. Oh, your mother does her best to avoid the conversations about his mama's death and why he doesn't have a daddy. It cuts me to the quick, watching how she disappoints him with her lawyer's dodges." Distress layered the remark, and Latrice paused to take a few rapid breaths. "He's been wondering why you never come around."

Darcy's heart thumped out of rhythm. "He asks about *me*?" She'd assumed she never crossed his mind.

A foolish assumption. She *was* his aunt.

"Your mother stonewalls him whenever he mentions you."

Recalling her mother's sharp tongue, she asked, "Do they argue?"

"I'd call their interactions more like swordplay than all-out war. Nothing like the way you and your mother used to firebomb each other with insults. Heavens, I don't miss those days. Your nephew is proper. He's too much of a little man to stoop to anger. Emerson pelts her with so many questions, he's sucking out what little gray matter Rosalind has left in her head."

"Doubtful. She can hold her own against an eight-year-old. I'll bet half the lawyers in Geauga County take antianxiety meds before appearing in her court."

"They don't know how to push her buttons like her grandson does. That boy latches on to a line of questioning like a terrier on to a bone."

"Well, he *is* eight. Old enough to expect real answers."

"Not getting any would explain his bad behavior." Latrice expelled a weary breath. "Emerson takes off on his own. He just disappears. It began last year—he'd come home from school but then walk right off the estate."

As Latrice went into detail about Emerson's habits, worry stole through Darcy.

How could an eight-year-old walk off a fifteen-acre estate without detection?

A landscape crew worked the grounds, and a cleaning service came in weekly to keep up the mansion. From the once-yearly phone calls, she knew that Latrice now spent most of her time in the kitchen. It was hard to imagine a boy slipping past so many adults.

A stronger emotion edged past the worry. "Doesn't anyone watch him?" She steered the car onto East Bay Street.

"We've been through a dozen babysitters, and I usually stay into the evening. Makes no difference. Some nights, Emerson doesn't come back until bedtime. There's a hundred acres of Metro Park forest behind your mother's place," Latrice said, referring to the system of lush nature preserves surrounding the city of Cleveland, including the posh Chagrin Valley. "I'll wager he's roamed most of the forest by now. And there's Nella's spread next door." She fell silent for an ominous beat. "That was before things got bad."

"You're scaring me."

"If a little fear makes you drive faster, then good."

Latrice paused, and Darcy's world shifted precariously. The traffic blurred. The sun felt too bright, like a spotlight trained on Darcy's transgressions.

Is Emerson in danger? How much of his troubling behavior is my responsibility?

She'd walked out of his life when he was just a baby. She'd left him to spend his childhood inside a cold, sterile home. Just like she had.

She was still assessing whether she was to blame when Latrice spoke again.

"I'm sure the anniversary has Emerson upset too," she confided. "Last night, he disappeared after dinner."

"But today is the anniversary," Darcy cut in. "Not yesterday."

"Yes, and your nephew has been feeling blue for days now. I assumed he was in his bedroom, reading. He hasn't come back."

"Call the police!"

"They're searching the forest now. One of the officers has a scent dog. Last I checked, they were walking the Chagrin River. Emerson likes to fish—he might be near the water. You should be here when the police find him. He needs you. Aside from Rosalind, you're the only family he's got."

Protective feelings for the boy collided with a thousand reservations. "He also has you."

"Yes, he does. Your mother wears through my patience on a regular basis, but that boy is special. There's nothing I wouldn't do for him. But I can't replace the mama he lost. *You* can."

Darcy wasn't sure how to respond. The possibility of becoming part of her nephew's life spun unexpected joy through her.

Unfortunately, there was a problem in the form of an unforgiving judge. She couldn't become part of Emerson's life with her mother standing in the way.

She appraised the traffic rising toward the Ravenel Bridge and the beach communities to the north. The answer was depressingly obvious. And clear as the blue sky above Charleston.

"Promise you'll text an update the minute Emerson is found," she said. "I'm sorry. I'm not coming back."

~

She hung up on a very upset Latrice. Within seconds, her smartphone rang again.

Groaning, she punched her Bluetooth and put Samson on speaker.

How long had it been, two hours since she'd last seen him? The close monitoring dredged up memories of high school and Principal Helmsley stalking her whenever she cut trigonometry class.

Dragging her emotions from the cellar, she greeted her young friend with a hearty dose of false cheer.

He mimicked her upbeat tone. "How's the drive going? You must be halfway to Charlotte by now." Barring a reply, he rushed on. "I shouldn't have laid on the guilt this morning. I ruined your going-away party."

"Relax. You didn't ruin anything."

"I swear I didn't realize you'd fall apart when I asked to come with you." Faltering, he filled the air with silence for a moment. "After you got off the boat and went out to the parking lot, you were a mess. Pitiful, really. If someone had told me, 'Darcy Goodridge acts like the ice queen, but she's the most pathetic soul you'll ever meet,' I would *not* have believed it. Now I feel like Grade A shit."

"Don't swear." She pressed a tissue to her running nose. "Respectable people don't use foul language."

"You sure are something," he said, chuckling. "Shouldn't you get a hold on your own behavior before you start fussing over mine? I'm not the one who was bawling like a baby in the parking lot."

"You saw me crying in the parking lot?" She'd marooned him on the gangplank after jumping ship.

"Everyone saw, Darcy."

"The whole staff?" Talk about a violation of the first order. Like discovering she wore nothing but her faded, sad-day panties while choreographing a dignified exit.

"We should've made popcorn. The redhead you talked to on the *Irma*? She squashed her face so tight to Miz Irma's picture window, I thought she'd suffocate. Big Bud tried to shoo everyone back to give you some privacy. Irma did too—she said it was rude for all of us to stare, even if a cool cucumber like Darcy Goodridge was drowning the parking lot in ugly tears. No one listened to her, though. With all the pushing and shoving, Irma nearly went down in the stampede. Bud got to her in time."

"Damn it."

"Don't swear." Samson released a breath layered with sympathy. "You *did* put on a show. Out there blubbering in the dirt, scrabbling around for the car keys you'd dropped. We were casting votes on who ought to perform the rescue mission when you finally hurled yourself into your car."

Humiliated, she prayed she'd misheard. "I was blubbering in the dirt?" She did recall dropping her keys. Repeatedly.

"Doesn't matter. You're on your way now. Off on a new adventure with nothing but good times ahead. How's the traffic? Google Maps says there's an accident near Columbia. I hope you're not stuck behind a row of fender benders."

"There are no accidents to report." Still embarrassed, she veered toward the Coleman exit with the awareness that the tremor in her hands was increasing. Continuing the journey before she pulled herself together wasn't prudent. "It took longer to finish up at the apartment than expected. I found stuff crammed in the back of the foyer closet."

"A careful woman like you doesn't usually forget anything. Good thing you checked twice."

"I walked back through the whole apartment. Even rechecked the shelves in the kitchen cupboards."

"Why is your voice shaky?"

"Good question." She decided to answer truthfully in yet another impetuous move. It was easier to confide in Samson now, with the endless highway ahead and her stay in Charleston over. "I got an unexpected call from an old friend. Well, not a friend exactly. More like a family member forced to wear a stupid gray uniform."

"You've got family in the military? I thought you were an orphan like me."

"I am, in all the ways that count." The disclosure lanced her with distress. "Latrice is a housekeeper. She's got a spicy side to her personality. Probably a defense mechanism to deal with her frosty employer. I've known her forever."

"She's here in South Carolina? How come you've never made introductions? I'd like to meet her."

"Latrice doesn't live here. She's in Ohio. She works for my mother."

"Slow down. You've got a mother too?"

The revelation seemed too much for Samson. He clucked into the conversational void, like he needed to reboot his brain.

Darcy was about to end the call when his brain powered back up.

"Why are you just telling me this now? Friends don't keep secrets, at least not the big kind. How many times did you invite me over to raid your fridge or watch Netflix? I know the walls of your apartment like the back of my hand. You don't have one measly photo of kin."

A public shaming wasn't necessary. Her late sister deserved a photo in any digs she occupied. As did her father, even though they'd never been close. Latrice and Emerson did too. It occurred to her that she'd never owned a photo of Emerson—a child now missing and presumably roaming the forest.

Keeping a photo of her mother was out of the question. Chewing glass was preferable to hanging a picture of the unforgiving judge anywhere Darcy might live.

"I move around a lot," she reminded him. "Do you expect me to haul family portraits from one city to the next? There isn't room in my luggage."

"What about your wallet?"

"What about it?"

"Don't you have photos of Latrice and your mama? You know, smashed in between the credit cards?"

"Does it matter?"

"It does if you want to get inside the pearly gates when you're called to meet your Maker." More clucking. She sensed his disapproval thickening like cement curing around her abundant regrets and mistakes. Confirming her suspicions, he added, "You're taking the wind right out of my sails. Maybe it isn't a big sin, Darcy, not keeping photos of your kin—not like stealing or doing murder. But you ought to show more respect."

Highlighting her faults managed to firm up her defenses. A situation unreliable at best. Continue chatting, and she knew she'd spout more ugly tears.

"Can we debate the finer points of family respect later?" she asked. "I promise to call you once I'm in New Jersey. I won't forget."

"Oh, sure. You're going to fill in the details now that you've left Charleston. According to Google, you're stuck in a bumper-to-bumper mess outside Columbia. Why not tell me about your family now?"

The traffic opened up. She took a side street toward the beach. Beyond the rasping fronds of the palm trees, the ribbon of ocean shimmered a deep blue.

"Stop worrying about accidents. While you're at it, log off Google." Zooming into a parking lot, she brought the car to a jerky halt. "Since I'm ridiculously off schedule, I'm going to take a walk. The conversation with Latrice didn't go well. Actually, it went badly. I need to blow off steam."

"You're at Isle of Palms?" Samson knew the beach was her favorite place to decompress. "You haven't left Charleston?"

The hope in his voice made her cringe. "I'm still here." She yanked the key from the ignition. "But only for an hour."

~

Tugging off her sandals, Darcy wove through the patchwork of colorful towels and lounging tourists. Seagulls screeched overhead. Heading into the surf, she walked north, away from the crowds. Walking fast, as if to outpace thoughts of Samson. She needed to focus on the more pressing concerns. With quick strides, she splashed through the surf.

Once her legs grew weary and she escaped the smell of suntan lotion, Darcy plunked down on an empty patch of sand to consider the upsetting facts Latrice had shared.

According to Latrice, Emerson had begun running away last year, near the end of the school year. He only returned home when hunger drove him back to the estate. Each time he reappeared, he had refused to provide an explanation. He would simply unpack his camping gear and trudge to his room on the mansion's second floor.

Yesterday was the first time he'd stayed out all night.

The reasons why he preferred spending hours alone in the forest were obvious. There wasn't a father listed on Emerson's birth certificate. He lived beneath the critical eye of his strong-willed grandmother, a busy county judge. The demands of the court meant Rosalind was surely absent too often. The deaths years ago of Darcy's father and her sister, Elizabeth—the mother Emerson had never known—also factored in.

During her once-yearly conversations with Latrice, the subject of Emerson rarely came up. The housekeeper never offered many details. A kindness, really. Judge Rosalind Goodridge had lost both of her daughters, one due to tragedy and the other due to her understandable rage. She didn't want her surviving daughter anywhere near the grandson she cherished.

Rosalind had made her opinion clear during their last painful quarrel. Darcy wasn't welcome in her nephew's life. The less she knew about Emerson, the better.

Digging her toes into the sand, she wondered if her nephew resembled the mother he'd lost. Had he inherited Elizabeth's freckles or her long, oval face? Did he play a musical instrument, or have a knack for art?

During her own childhood, Darcy spent idyllic days in the large swath of forest encircling her parents' estate with Michael Varano, her closest childhood friend. Together they'd climbed the steep banks of the Chagrin River in search of salamanders. Perched high in the massive, hundred-year-old oak behind the Varanos' acreage next door, they surveyed the Chagrin's churning waters, the fierce struggle between the stubborn boulders and the ever-moving river, the race between immovable objects and sharp currents.

Much as Elizabeth liked shadowing her older sister, she rarely agreed to explore the forest whenever Michael appeared at the front door. Happier indoors, Elizabeth dutifully practiced the piano at Rosalind's urging. On Saturdays she suffered through private lessons with a grim-faced tutor, a woman with dull gray hair and a fixed expression of faint impatience. Darcy, in faded cut-offs, would pad across the living room toward the outdoors.

Will the police find Elizabeth's son quickly?

Unsure, Darcy pressed her toes deeper into the damp sand. Her refusal to aid in the search left her sick-hearted, ashamed.

She hated disappointing Latrice.

On a sigh, Darcy recalled the last time she'd seen Emerson. A soft-fleshed newborn with a bad case of colic. The months after his birth had been complicated, but Darcy never complained. She shared responsibility for the newborn's care with her sister, Latrice, and her floundering parents. The Honorable Rosalind Goodridge and Dr. Jack Goodridge were embarrassed by their grandson's illegitimacy. The complication in their unblemished lives resulted in more arguments than Darcy cared to remember.

Having a newborn installed in the mansion seemed incongruous, like setting a tornado loose in a once-serene world. Or perhaps Emerson's furious bawling convinced Darcy the mansion was suffering a strange invasion. In her more self-centered moments, she had viewed Emerson as an imposition standing in the way of her own happiness.

Standing in the way of the unexpected and consuming romance she had sparked with Michael during her last spring in college. Like so many aspects of the life she'd once led, Darcy rarely contemplated the love affair that had ended on the night Elizabeth and her father died.

The emotions Darcy once harbored were still a source of shame. Emerson had been a defenseless baby; he was now a defenseless child. A boy wandering the backwoods of Geauga County unprotected.

He was out there with a backpack, a toothbrush, and a lightweight polyester tent. Emerson used his smartphone's GPS to travel the dense forest. Latrice assumed he'd learned basic survival skills in his Cub Scout troop—before he'd dropped out because the other boys picked on him. Emerson never ran off without bringing a flashlight and extra batteries. He never forgot to pack dental floss.

Or so Latrice said.

Despite the gravity of the situation, Darcy entertained a feeling of hope. Emerson prepared well for his unsanctioned forays into the forest. His organizational skills were excellent. How many kids thought to pack extra batteries *and* dental floss?

A slow smile crept across her face. At his age, she'd been scatter-brained, too busy having fun to even make her bed.

Chapter 3

A shadow fell across Darcy. The interruption pulled her from her thoughts.

Samson asked, "What are you grinning at? There's nothing out there but ocean."

Her jaw fell open. "What are you doing here?"

"Making sure you're all right." He sat down beside her on the beach. "How *are* you holding up? You were awfully low when we talked."

"I'm not feeling low."

Abysmal is more like it.

Samson tugged off his shoes. Wiggling his toes, he bumped her, shoulder to shoulder. "I didn't mean to give you a hard time when we talked, even if you *did* take the wind out of my sails. You've got the right to keep your family a secret. Doesn't mean you should've hung up on me—you've got better manners than that. But it did start me thinking. You might have lots of reasons to avoid talking about your family."

"I can't even imagine what you came up with."

"Nothing good, I'll admit."

"Samson . . ."

He held up a hand, silencing her. "Who've you got to confide in besides me? Now, come clean. There's no need for embarrassment between good friends. Your mama . . . did she beat you?"

A preposterous query. "Only at tennis," she said. "When it comes to competitive sports, she's vicious."

Relief washed over Samson's features. Then a strange fascination bloomed in its place. "You ever met the slapping kind of women?"

"Please tell me you're not serious."

"If you don't know what I'm talking about, you're lucky." He gave out a low whistle thick with wonder and an undertone of trepidation. "I've seen uncivilized women up close. Like at my second-to-last foster home. My foster mother was built like a tank. Solid, bigger than most men. She gave off a scary vibe like she'd steamroll over you if you put one toe out of line."

"Tank Lady had a short fuse?"

"Especially when it came to the next-door neighbor. You've never seen two women who hated each other more."

"What happened?" Darcy asked. Other than remarks about his need to find a new living arrangement since he'd just aged out of the system, Samson never talked about his foster care years. Now he'd captured her interest with the bizarre story of female aggression.

Her curiosity lit his face with excitement. "My foster mom and the neighbor lady both owned mangy dogs. You know the kind—flea-bitten mongrels with a taste for chasing mail carriers and small children."

"That doesn't sound good."

"It wasn't. Those dogs barked at each other from opposite sides of the fence, making all sorts of racket from dawn till midnight. One afternoon, the neighbor's mutt got loose. Eighty pounds of hostility racing all over the neighborhood, dropping poops everywhere, scaring the mail carrier when she hopped out of her truck, scaring children. Like little Jimmy, the kid who lived around the corner. When the beast charged down the sidewalk, Jimmy flew right off his bike." Samson twined a dreadlock around one long finger, his dark eyes rounding with sympathy for unsuspecting children and, Darcy presumed, mail carriers.

"You know what happened? Right before that rotten dog went home, he trotted onto our front porch and made a piss puddle."

"He *peed* on your foster mother's porch?" Darcy's knowledge of matters canine was limited. She assumed dogs preferred tree trunks, or the occasional fire hydrant.

"Right by our front door." Samson's eyes grew even wider. "I'm talking about a lake of pee with an ammonia stench like nobody's business. My foster mother should've smelled the foulness. She didn't—not until she was standing in the mess. She'd gone outside to collect the mail."

Alarm stiffened Darcy's spine. "What did she do?"

"After she soaked her shoes good and screamed to high heaven? Well, she went wild. Leaped down the front steps, hopped the fence, and slapped the neighbor lady silly. You wouldn't expect someone her size to move so quick."

"Rage will make anyone speedy."

Samson nodded in agreement. "I felt sorry for the neighbor lady— watering her petunias, paying no mind. She didn't have a chance."

The story finished, Samson began making lazy patterns in the sand. Darcy watched, her thoughts bounding forward. It was difficult to understand how someone with low impulse control slipped under the radar to become a foster parent. She wondered about the other homes the well-mannered youth had been shuttled through. Were they also bad? The thought made her queasy.

It also worried her to consider where he'd land next. At eighteen, his options were limited.

Samson patted her leg. "Now you tell me," he said, drawing her from her troubled thoughts. "Does your mama have a mean streak? I'd like to understand why you've never brought her up."

"God's honest truth, pal. The great and powerful Rosalind Goodridge never resorts to physical violence."

The proverbial light bulb switched on inside Samson's head. "Great and powerful . . . like the Wizard of Oz?"

"Believe me, you do *not* want to look behind the curtain. As for slapping people down, my mother can turn hardened lawyers into mincemeat with a few choice words."

The cryptic remark puckered his brows. "What's mincemeat?"

"Never mind," she said, content to leave him clueless. "Listen, I came to the beach to decompress. While I'm thrilled you stopped by, I won't sit through an interrogation. Will you please give it a rest? I'm asking nicely."

"Why should I?"

"It hurts to discuss my mother."

"But I'm your friend."

"True enough, but I'm still not going into it."

With a nod, he continued trailing his fingers through the sand to form a moon straddled by two stars. His North Star and hers, Darcy presumed. Guiding lights to carry her past the pain.

He said, "Suit yourself. I can tell you're hurting something awful. Talking can make you feel better, but I'm not going to push you." He looked away. He squinted at the sun, which seemed content to bake them to a crisp. "Got any water in your ugly purse? I'm thirsty."

"I should've grabbed a bottle from the car." She knew he meant well, and the prospect of hurting his feelings didn't appeal. "Look, if I give you the really short version, will you drop the subject?"

"Sure."

Darcy searched for a calm impossible to conjure. "There's a simple reason why I never talk about the past. My younger sister and my father were killed."

The disclosure halted Samson's doodling in the sand. He stared at her, hard.

"It's been almost ten years," Darcy forced herself to add. A spasm racked her face. She rushed on, determined to get through this quickly. "They died because of me."

"You *killed* them?"

"By making a series of incredibly stupid choices. If I'd been more responsible, they would've been home safe in their beds. They never would've been in harm's way."

"What about your mother?"

"We don't have a relationship. She can't forgive me. The mistakes I made . . . I've earned her loathing."

Sadness rippled across Samson's lean face. "People do lots of dumb things. They don't mean for their dumbness to bring disaster." He shrugged. "Want to tell me the whole story?"

"Not ever."

"Have it your way. I'll sit here minding my own business until you change your mind."

A gurgling laugh erupted from her throat. "Have I ever mentioned you're determined? Granted, you're nowhere near the size of a tank. But you're doing a decent job of steamrolling over my objections."

Oddly, the laughter brought a measure of relief. A small easing of the weight Darcy carried, a brief respite from the self-loathing and the shame. Absently, she wondered if Samson had been right all along. She *did* need a friend, someone capable of sifting through the wreckage of her past without casting judgment.

Together, they watched the surf roll in to lap at their toes. An old man strolled by with a Pomeranian on a leash. The Pomeranian wore knitted booties in an attractive shell pink. Apparently, the booties kept the pampered canine's paws free of irritating sand. They both chuckled at the sight.

Darcy said, "I forgot to ask how you got to the beach." Samson didn't own a car, and Uber was a luxury he couldn't afford. "Someone from Big Bud's dropped you off?"

"Miz Irma drove me."

"That was nice of her. Plus, I'm glad we got another chance to say goodbye." Much as Darcy hated ending their time together, she needed to get on the road. "Ready to head out? I'll take you back to work."

"There's no need." Samson darted a cagey glance her way. "Miz Irma doesn't mind waiting. She said to take all the time I need."

Darcy lifted her brows. "She's in the parking lot?"

"She brought along a book. She's catching up on her reading while I reason with you." The youth dug his smartphone from his pocket. "I'm supposed to send her a text after you make up your mind."

"Samson, hold on. We've already been over this—"

"I'm not a charity case," he broke in. "I've been in Charleston my whole life. I don't expect to find what I want if I stay here. Don't ask why I'm sure. I just am. There's something better waiting for me—I just have to go looking for it. Like that saying about nets and having the guts to jump off." He frowned. "What's the saying?"

"Leap, and the net will appear." It was one of her favorite maxims, although Darcy had yet to find a way to leap past the grief dominating her life. To bound forward and move on.

"That's the saying! I'm eighteen now. I'm ready to make the leap. Besides, look here what I've got."

Leaning sideways on one skinny hip, he produced a white envelope rolled into a fat tube. He unwound the rubber band keeping it closed. Darcy gasped.

The envelope was stuffed full of ten- and twenty-dollar bills.

"The whole staff pitched in," he announced, waving the windfall before her face. "Put your mind at ease, Darcy. We'll split everything down the middle—rent, food, even gas for the drive. Oh, I almost forgot. Miz Irma sent a message."

Darcy returned his cagey look with one of her own. "What's the message?"

"Set your prideful ways aside and take good care of our Samson. Everyone at Big Bud's will miss you both."

She stifled a groan. She'd already disappointed Latrice by refusing to drive back to Ohio. There was no telling when Emerson would reappear, or if the police were still searching the forest. Given Darcy's refusal to come back, Latrice might not call with an update anytime soon.

Now Samson believed his cash prize guaranteed a seat on the road trip. A trip she always took alone. Hands down, he'd become the thornier issue.

An air of resignation brought her to her feet. Overwhelmed, she trudged into the warm surf. She studied the Atlantic as if the solution to an unsolvable dilemma lay hidden among the waves. She doubted she had the stamina to look out for Samson. If she allowed the eighteen-year-old to tag along, he would become a permanent fixture in her life. Assuming the responsibility meant she must help him find a good job, decent friends his own age, and suitable roomies once he moved out of her apartment. It was a tall list.

Trapped on the emotional fence, she plodded back to shore. Still seated on the beach, Samson read her face with the breathless anticipation of a child hanging dreams on a wishing star. Doubt shadowed his eyes as he searched her face for a decision she hadn't yet made.

Darcy halted. Twenty paces off, a gray lump on the beach snagged her attention. A duffel bag.

One big enough to hold the scant belongings of a recent graduate from South Carolina's foster care system.

Her disbelieving gaze swung to Samson.

"Miz Irma helped me pack," he said. "In case you made the right choice."

~

In the green hills of North Carolina, Darcy exited the highway.

They were somewhere north of Fayetteville in a stretch of beautiful country. Her muscles ached from hours behind the wheel—a minor inconvenience compared to the hunger cramping her stomach. Between the morning's conversation with Latrice and Samson ambushing her at the beach, she'd forgotten to eat.

Curled up on the passenger seat, Samson continued to sleep. Reaching into the back seat, she grabbed the beige thigh-length sweater, an old favorite, wedged beneath his duffel bag. She layered the sweater over him as she came to a gentle stop at a light off the exit ramp.

An unconscious, nearly imperceptible grunt rose through the silence. He snuggled deeper beneath the wooly fabric.

Darcy let him sleep.

During the first hour of the trip, they chatted nonstop about nothing at all. When she flipped on the radio, he skipped the opportunity to give his vocal cords a rest and sang to every song. If the lyrics were unfamiliar Samson invented his own, adding references to the Gullah culture of the Lowcountry.

Darcy sang along. And why not? They were marking Samson's first trip outside Charleston—his first trip *anywhere*. His fizzy excitement made the air inside the Honda lighter than helium. Together, they filled the car with song until his eyelids began to droop.

She rolled down the window as she turned onto a dusty road. The drone of the interstate faded. Wending her way along, she searched for somewhere to eat.

For tonight, she'd booked two rooms at the Holiday Inn outside Cape May. The apartment search was tomorrow's main event. She'd need to find a place with a second bedroom for her young charge. A minor inconvenience. There was an entire week ahead before the new job began.

Peering through the windshield, Darcy mentally went over the items sure to occupy the coming days. Opening bank accounts for them both. Learning the streets of Cape May. Becoming familiar with her new job, new responsibilities, and the dozen or so employees working at the insurance agency where she'd been hired. Replacing her South Carolina driver's license with a new one for New Jersey. Replacing

Samson's license too, although she wouldn't encourage him right away to use his lottery winnings from Big Bud's staff as a down payment on a serviceable car.

Cape May represented her eighth move in as many years. She ticked through the list of chores easily.

She tried to dispel the worry over her missing nephew. It was still early afternoon. The police were out searching. Chances were, they'd bring Emerson home by nightfall.

There was nothing she could do. Nothing she *should* do.

Sadness feathered through her, along with confusion, as she recalled the lonely childhood Latrice had described. Emerson was growing up without siblings in his grandmother's elegant mansion. A privileged yet sterile life. And he'd spent last night outdoors, sensibly equipped with a flashlight and extra batteries.

Tapping the steering wheel, Darcy reflected on her own childhood. She'd been adventurous at that age—sometimes recklessly so. However, like most children, she'd cultivated a healthy fear of danger. Bad stuff happened if you couldn't see where you were going, especially in the sections of the forest cratering down steeply toward the Chagrin River. Walk too close to the precipice, and you risked falling to your death. She never would have stayed out alone.

Of course, she'd rarely been alone during childhood adventures into the woods. Michael Varano—one year older and nearly as intrepid— had often leaped the fence between their properties to follow Darcy on her latest escapade. They'd spent many afternoons exploring the forest together; during summer's hottest days, they'd donned swimsuits to splash around the deeper sections of the Chagrin River.

Darcy's sister usually stayed indoors. The marvels hidden in the forest's vast acres and the sheer freedom of being outdoors held no interest for Elizabeth.

On the rare occasions when Darcy talked her sister into camping near the green necklace of forest surrounding their parents' estate,

Latrice accompanied them. Elizabeth, never a fan of long nature walks or rugged evenings sizzling hot dogs over a campfire, spent most of the time complaining. The sleeping bag wasn't soft enough. The ground was too hard. The hooting owls made her jump. Latrice—a young woman back then and equipped with endless stores of patience—would point to the mansion's lights, blazing in the distance, in hopes of reassuring Elizabeth that there was nothing to fear in the dark. If Elizabeth took to whining, Latrice produced the butterscotch candies both of her young charges loved.

Once Elizabeth fell asleep, she would wedge herself like a skittish pup between Darcy and the stalwart housekeeper who was the stand-in mother for the Goodridge sisters.

Getting on now in years, Latrice was too arthritic for nights outdoors beneath the stars. Emerson camped alone. What if he'd trekked too far into the forest to find his way home? A chill flashed through Darcy as she steered the Honda down the dusty road.

Furtively, she glanced at the youth sleeping beside her.

Careful not to wake Samson, she retrieved the smartphone from her bag. The urge for an update tempted her to dial Latrice's number.

Is there any news yet?

Irritated by her waning self-control, she returned the phone to her purse.

Emerson hasn't been abducted. He walked off the grounds voluntarily. The police will find him.

Driving to Ohio was out of the question. Contrary to what Latrice believed, Darcy couldn't show up on her mother's doorstep—their relationship was beyond repair. Even the crisis of a missing child wasn't reason enough to cross enemy lines.

Would I like the opportunity to forge a relationship with my nephew? Yes, absolutely.

He was the child of Elizabeth, the sister she sorely missed. The child she'd promised to watch over and protect.

Beside her, Samson stirred.

At the edge of the sweater's soft folds, drowsy brown eyes flecked with amber blinked slowly. "Good morning, ugly lady," he murmured.

"Samson, morning is long gone."

"Where are we?" On a yawn, he struggled into a sitting position.

"In the middle of nowhere." She nodded at the trees bowing leafy arms as they drove by. Spirals of dust lifted from the road. "Hungry? I got off the interstate to hunt for somewhere to eat."

"I'm starving."

"Me too," she lied. Reflecting on her nephew's disappearance had dampened her appetite.

The sweater she'd draped over Samson clung to one lean shoulder. He eyed the garment with interest. "How long did I sleep? Feels like forever." He folded the sweater into a neat square and placed it in the back seat on top of his duffel bag. "I sure need something to help me wake up. Sweet tea, or coffee."

The traces of sleep made him look much younger. "Best guess, you slept for about an hour," she said. "Maybe longer."

"Want me to drive for a while?"

"I'm good." A red-shingled diner rose into view. Darcy sighed. "Finally."

Empty picnic tables surrounded the small roadside diner. Aside from a chubby brunette at the takeout window and a bearded man working the grill, the place appeared deserted. A country barbecue shack, miles from civilization.

Samson ordered a pulled pork sandwich and sweet tea. Darcy ordered the same, swatting him back when he reached for the wad of cash he'd received from Big Bud's generous staff. She made a mental note to suggest he let her stash the envelope in her purse for safekeeping once they returned to the car. It was doubtful Samson had ever possessed so much cash before.

They found a seat in the shade. Samson dug in. He made short work of his sandwich.

"Want another?" Darcy placed a ten-dollar bill next to his untouched napkin. "My treat."

"I already told you. I'm not indignant."

"You mean indigent." She smiled. "No one implied you're a charity case, pal. You *are* just out of high school. There's no shame in letting me spring for lunch."

"There's no pride in it either." When she pointedly stared at the napkin, he snatched it up to wipe away the barbecue sauce rimming his mouth. Lowering his elbows to the picnic table, he leaned forward. "Why don't you let me wake up properly before you get ugly?"

"You love when I get ugly," she teased.

"Not right now, I don't." Samson balled up the napkin. Playfully, he tossed it at her head. "For your information, I'm all grown up—just like you. We're traveling partners, that's all. I don't need you mothering me every minute of the day."

With that, he sauntered off to order more food.

The mouthing-off was impressive, like something she would've done at the same age. Darcy watched him go, her emotions lifting. Who knew what potential lurked beneath Samson's agreeable nature? An unforeseen element, something strong and worth cultivating. Once they settled in, she resolved to check out the universities in the Cape May area. Lots of adults earned a degree through night courses. It was worth lobbying Samson to consider the idea.

By the time he returned, Darcy's appetite was flaring back to life. Licking her lips, she pressed the plastic knife through the middle of the sandwich's doughy bun. The idea of her unexpected traveling buddy carving out a future of more than odd jobs and handouts from well-meaning coworkers made her giddy—and ravenous.

Samson slid onto the bench opposite. He nodded at the two perfectly equal halves she'd made. "Why do you do that?" He unwrapped his sandwich.

Darcy took a tentative bite of the half she'd reserved for herself. "It's not important."

"It's a weird habit. Before we ran off from Big Bud's, you always left half your sandwich growing stiff by your keyboard. Weirdest thing I'd ever seen. Tell me why you do it."

Stalling, she picked up her sweet tea and took her time sipping. "We didn't 'run off' from Big Bud's," she said, returning the beverage to the table. Under no circumstances would she reveal the meaning behind a private, and very painful, ritual. "I gave three weeks' notice, remember? You insisted Bud and Irma didn't mind if you quit on the spot."

"They didn't care. They want me to find my North Star."

"Let me eat in peace."

"What's wrong with discussing my star while we eat?"

"We'll chat about your star later on. We still have a long drive ahead of us."

"Why are you grumpy all of a sudden?"

"I'm not grumpy."

"You are. And you're looking for ways *not* to explain why you waste food."

Reaching across the table, he poked the untouched half. She swatted his hand away. Then she sighed.

"Fine," she relented, fearful he'd wheedle the truth from her. "Let's discuss your special star. How does hitching a ride to New Jersey get you any closer?"

"You're really interested?"

"My day won't be complete until you tell me."

"I hate when you get sassy." He bit into his sandwich, a gooey mess of pork and melted cheddar. Chewing thoughtfully, he added, "My North Star sits near yours in a pretty patch of the universe." He bounced a thumb skyward. Clouds scudded across the bright dome of blue. "Those stars are real friendly with each other. They might be best friends."

"Just like us?"

He grinned. "Now you're catching on."

There was no sense pointing out that stars didn't have emotions, or the fact that there was only one North Star. "Change of plan," Darcy said. "Hold off on your silliness until we reach New Jersey. My stomach has been twitchy since daybreak. I don't need indigestion before we get back on the road."

Samson harrumphed with mild disapproval. "Go on, now," he chided, grabbing up his iced tea with a flourish. "Get defensive. I can tell when I'm poking a bear with a stick. You're laying on the insults because you don't want to talk about it."

"My ritual?" she snapped. She crossed her arms. "No, Samson—I don't. Can we please talk about anything else? Mystical journeys? Or mean dogs? I'm too queasy for another discussion of female aggression but, hey, if you don't have a better topic, I'm in."

The outburst put a slow smile on his face. In record time, he wolfed down the remainder of his meal.

"Now we're getting somewhere," he said when he finished. "Wasting food is a ritual? You could've just clued me in. If you've got some weird beliefs, who am I to judge?" His expression veered from curiosity to mirth. "One question. Will I insult your religious beliefs if I eat the sacred offering?"

The suggestion put horror in her gut. A fleeting inconvenience, because anger chased it away. The habit *was* nearly sacred. It provided a means to remember Elizabeth, a reminder of all the food she'd gladly shared with her little sister. All through childhood, and even into high school, they'd shared sandwiches and summer pears and the crisp apples they'd both loved, all of which Darcy had painstakingly cut into perfect halves.

She pushed the uneaten half toward him, aware he didn't understand the odd form of grieving. "If you're still hungry, don't let me stop you. Enjoy." She rose in a fine fury. "I'm going to the restroom. If you need anything else, there's money in my purse. Get whatever you want."

The restroom possessed all the typical charm of a roadside stop. The scent of mold hung thick in the air. Graffiti marred every surface. Thankfully the main door had a proper lock, because the door on the stall was MIA. Ripped from its hinges, it leaned against the wall by the leaky sink.

Darcy put stock in cleanliness, and a pampered childhood had left her a wee bit phobic about germs. This didn't stop her from hiding in the restroom for long minutes, splashing water on her face and staring at her reflection in the grimy mirror. Distracted, she combed her fingers through her tangled hair.

Why do I continually snap at Samson? He's a good kid. I did agree to take him along to New Jersey.

Today marked her sister's and father's deaths—an event Samson knew nothing about. Granted, she usually experienced whipsaw moods on the anniversary. Lots of tears, and a bone-deep feeling of exhaustion.

Which is my problem, not his.

Determined to keep her emotions in check, she trudged back toward the picnic table. Several paces off, she froze.

Samson was chatting with great animation, the phone pressed close to his ear.

Her phone.

His phone was out too. He was scrolling through Google maps, sliding the image northward, peering at highways and state lines while sharing the information with the person on the other end.

Darcy neared, slack-jawed. He waved.

"It's Latrice calling," he announced. Then his eyes darkened with a mild rebuke. "Darcy, I can't decide if you take more stupid pills or ugly ones. The secrets you keep! Poking fun at my beliefs, and pretending our stars don't align. Why didn't you tell me your second mama is black?"

Chapter 4

Ornella Varano tugged on her rubber boots. She went out the mudroom door.

For a woman in her early fifties, Nella looked much younger. Only a few strands of silver glinted in the dark-brown hair fanning across her shoulders. She was still trim and energetic, and she strode around the side of her large stone-and-glass home at a brisk pace. The warm June air carried the scent of tomatoes ripening in the vegetable garden abutting the slate walkway. Beyond the rectangular patio with its abundance of clay pots brimming with summer flowers, the acre of mown grass smelled bright and green.

Grass crunched underfoot as Nella strode in the general direction of the forest. The trees rustled, as if in greeting. Shielding her eyes, she scanned the long sweep of lawn for her adult son and his scruffy rescue mutt. Birdsong drifted across the empty expanse of grass.

It seemed likely Michael was back down by the river, helping the police. At last count, six officers from the Hunting Valley and Chagrin Falls police departments were scouring the deep woods and a good mile of riverbank. Since Emerson's disappearance yesterday, officers from five jurisdictions had been taking turns working shifts in search of the boy.

Emerson was still missing.

In the past, when Latrice secretly called from the Goodridge estate next door, worried because Emerson was gone again, finding the boy had proved easy. The housekeeper—unlike her stern employer—understood *why* the normally obedient child went to great pains to slip out undetected.

The fatherless boy had discovered a father figure next door.

For Nella, the blossoming relationship between her son and Rosalind's grandchild was a source of joy—and trepidation.

Judge Rosalind Goodridge despised Nella, for long-festering reasons. If Rosalind learned her grandson had befriended Nella's adult son, she'd put an end to it. Such an outcome would crush Emerson.

Nella feared it would crush Michael as well.

Turning away from the forest, she tamped down the nervous tension cramping her muscles. Only last year, Michael had moved back into his childhood home. Scarred by a short, unhappy marriage and a recent divorce, he'd left behind Chicago's fast pace and a successful career in banking. In a pursuit of a simpler life, he now built cabinetry for upscale homeowners in Geauga County with rare, sustainably harvested woods. Until his return, Nella, long widowed and sharing the rambling mansion with her aging mother, Tippi, barely noticed how much she'd missed having a man around the house. She'd always been close to her only child, but now Michael—mature, even-tempered, and every bit the responsible adult—had become more like a trusted friend.

Soon after Michael had returned to Ohio, Rosalind's grandson began crossing the hilly terrain separating the two properties. Nearly twenty years of betrayal simmered between the Goodridges and the Varanos. Emerson traipsed across the dividing line as if it were the most natural thing in the world.

Unannounced, without an invitation—a lonely boy drawn by the sharp whir of power saws and the clatter of men on the barn roof as Michael redesigned the space for his new business. The rapport between the boy suffocating in a privileged life and the man determined to get past his personal heartache was instantaneous.

Since then, Nella had become ridiculously attached to Rosalind's grandson. The mannerly boy with the wheat-colored hair took over a space in her heart not yet occupied by grandchildren. He loved fireflies, her homemade lasagna, and helping her elderly mother, Tippi, pluck handfuls of basil and ripe tomatoes from the garden. Emerson peppered the patient Michael with a flurry of questions. When Nella had first lured the child into the kitchen to fill his bottomless stomach with spaghetti and Italian pastries, he'd informed her in his soft, polite voice that she was too young to have a grown-up son. In his bolder moments, he enjoyed showing off for Michael by mimicking birdcalls whenever they explored the woods together.

Sometimes, when Michael trudged into the house after a long workday, covered in sawdust, he'd share amusing bits of their conversations. Michael, Nella, even Tippi—all three of the adults in the Varano household were smitten with the child.

Still, Rosalind's animosity for her next-door neighbor was long established. Nella's thirty-one-year-old son knew nothing of the reasons—but he knew enough to persuade his young admirer to return home quickly.

Most of the time.

There were days when Emerson seemed especially troubled. Boys picked on him at school, and his grandmother's sharp tongue wasn't easy to bear. If Michael sensed the child's distress, he gathered up hot dogs, buns, and marshmallows from the kitchen. Then he led his young charge to the far edge of the lawn to build a campfire and talk while the hot dogs sizzled over the leaping flames.

Yesterday, Emerson had broken his usual habit. He'd marched off into the forest without stopping by first.

Worry crept into Nella's blood.

Is Emerson lying injured in the forest? Unable to call for help?

She wove her fingers into a tight knot until her knuckles sang out with pain. Nightfall was only a few hours off. The child might spend a second night outdoors.

Jasper's excited barking cut through the air. On a property ten acres in size, it took a moment to zero in on the dog's whereabouts. When she did, Nella veered away from the forest. At a jog, she went across the south lawn, toward the barn.

Before her husband died, they'd joked about owning a horse farm with no horses. The previous owner had built a big red barn, complete with a riding arena. When they tore down the original farmhouse to build the spacious, stone-and-glass palace they'd hoped to fill with children, Nella had insisted on keeping the barn.

The decision was purely sentimental. She liked the idea of owning a modern house on a country property, complete with a rustic barn. Now Michael, his carpentry business thriving, was putting the barn to good use.

More barking rolled across the property. Following the sound, Nella strode into the riding arena. In the far corner, the rescue mutt dug frantically in the soft dirt.

"Old fool, you'll never catch a possum." She stroked the dog's brindled coat. He stopped digging to give her a look of patient incomprehension. "Where's your master?"

Straightening, she called out for her son.

Michael's sharp whistle resounded through the riding arena.

A second, smaller barn hugged the back wall of the arena. Flecks of dust floated through the dim, slatted light. A scent reminiscent of mushrooms wafted up from the earthen floor. Nella strode past the four stalls, each brimming with supplies for her son's carpentry business.

Angling her neck, she peered up the wooden ladder nailed to the outer wall. "Michael, are you up there?"

"Thought I'd check one more time."

"Find anything?" She climbed the ladder to join him.

Once a storage area for hay, the loft was now a cozy nook for her favorite child. Board games from Michael's long-ago childhood were stacked in the corner. Adventure books were strewn about. Lately, Michael had been purchasing new books at the bookstore in Chagrin Falls as fast as Emerson devoured them.

The loft's ceiling angled sharply. Michael, over six feet in height, prowled the perimeter, taking care not to bang his head on the rafters.

He held up the shiny wrapper from a granola bar. "I found this."

"You're sure it wasn't here already?"

"Positive. I scoured the loft first thing this morning."

Hope sent a dizzying wave through Nella. "If Emerson stopped by earlier, he made it through the night without harm."

"Why do you doubt the kid's ability to make it through the night?" The loft's dim light shimmered through Michael's halo of dark curls as he scooped up a blanket. Finding nothing underneath, he tossed it aside. "He's fine. I've taught him how to stay safe when he's camping."

"Meaning you *condone* his unauthorized camping trips?"

"Meaning boys will be boys. Besides, I've given him lots of pointers. He knows how to stay out of harm's way."

The fatherly pride in his voice squeezed Nella's heart. Shame followed—the sort of deep, black shame reserved for a woman whose actions had unwittingly harmed her adult son.

It seemed yet more punishment for the sins of the past. Nella bore the blame for Michael's childhood friendship with Darcy ending when she was in sixth grade and he was in seventh. When they had met again, right before Darcy finished college, circumstances forced them to keep their relationship a secret.

Now Michael's growing relationship with Emerson was at risk. If not for Nella's blind choices so many years ago, the boy's affection for Michael would have been welcome, rewarded. Their special chemistry would have been celebrated, even by Rosalind.

Out of habit, Nella returned her regret to a hollow chamber of her heart. "There are countless dangers in the forest," she said, focusing on the present. "It's one thing for Emerson to spend a single night outdoors. Granted, he's smarter than most children. But he's been gone for too long now."

"Stop worrying." Michael picked up a throw pillow, tossed it onto a folding chair by the wall. "I don't agree with him taking off without Rosalind's permission, but he's not stupid. Emerson isn't hurt. He's hiding."

The comment pricked Nella with irritation. "Okay, Mr. Psychic. *Why* is he hiding?"

"Not sure, exactly. Something's bugging him."

"Are you forgetting the anniversary? *That's* what is bugging him."

Her son waved off the assessment. "The anniversary isn't the reason Emerson took off. There's something heavy on his mind."

The onset of summer vacation turned most children into carefree imps. Nella recalled how Michael, during his own childhood, had found more time for mischief than reasonable. If heavy thoughts plagued Emerson during the perfect month of June, it seemed unfair.

"What's bothering him?" she asked.

"Lately I get the sense he's worried about losing Rosalind."

"He *is* more familiar with death than most children," she agreed. "He's grown up knowing his mother died when he was just a baby. His grandfather too. It's a lot for any child to handle. At eight, most kids believe they'll live forever. They assume the same goes for everyone they love."

"Emerson isn't like most children. He worries about lots of things."

On the night of the accident, Emerson had been an infant—unaware of the brutal change sweeping into his world. Nella wondered if the deaths affected him in subtle ways. Even so, there seemed no logical reason for the boy to worry about losing his grandmother too.

"Rosalind is only sixty-seven," she pointed out. "She takes good care of herself. I'm sure she's in perfect health."

"You don't need to convince me. Reassure Emerson once we find him." Michael crumpled up the granola wrapper and shoved it into a pocket in his jeans. "Last week, he asked me the average expiration date for old people."

"Expiration date? Like on a carton of milk?" Emerson loved milk, preferably with chocolate syrup. Since his arrival in their lives, Nella had been buying gallon jugs. Most weeks, she would also toss chocolate syrup into her grocery cart.

"I have the sense he's concerned that Rosalind is curdling. Maybe he overheard her talking to Latrice about a medical issue and got confused. The kid *is* determined to learn every word in the dictionary. There's still some language above his pay grade, though."

Talk of expiration dates and Emerson's insatiable curiosity kindled her worry. "What if he's fallen out of a tree? Or been bitten by a snake? What if he wants to come home, but can't?"

Nella wasn't aware she'd begun rubbing her hands in a fit of anxiety until Michael grabbed them to make her stop.

"Mom, this isn't his home." He eased her hands apart. A grin teased his lips. He did his best to extinguish it. "Emerson isn't hurt. The kid has more agility than a monkey, plus the brains to avoid snakes. He also has a first aid kit. A nice, portable kit with all the trimmings. I bought it for him."

Given Emerson's penchant for traipsing off into the forest, she wondered why she hadn't thought to buy him one. Count on Michael to think of it.

"What if he remembered to pack dental floss, but forgot the first aid supplies?" His fixation on good dental hygiene mattered not a whit if he was lying somewhere, bleeding.

"I'm sure he remembered to pack the kit. He doesn't like blood any more than he likes visits to the dentist."

"Is this more information from your crystal ball?"

Michael leaned in for emphasis. "I know how Emerson thinks," he said. Protective lights glinted in his midnight-blue eyes. The evolution of their mother-son relationship made her grateful for his reassurance when he added, "You're forgetting his big-time obsession with preparing well. I'm sure he mapped out this foray into the woods for a week straight before taking off. He's also smart enough to dodge the police. He's probably found a fishing hole off the beaten path."

"Your confidence in his abilities is heartening. But he *is* just a child. One who's been on his own for over twenty-four hours."

The mild scolding started her son grinning. "You and Tippi both need to relax," he said of his grandmother. He glanced in the general direction of the house. "Is she still holed up in her bedroom?"

"Like a molting crow. She's moping."

"Face it, Mom. It doesn't take much to upset Tippi. If the Cleveland Indians or her poker games go on a losing streak, she hides out in her nest."

"True, but she loves Emerson. She's *very* upset."

At eighty-five, the once-beautiful Tippi had lost several inches in height. Thanks to arthritis, her back curved like a bent sapling. This disagreeable result of the aging process didn't amuse her. In an indirect way, it *did* please Emerson—he was catching up with her on height. Tippi remained inordinately proud of her long hair, which was now the color of ash. She seemed unaware of the bald patches sprouting across her scalp like tiny wildfires. Add in Tippi's penchant for black clothing, and she *did* resemble a crow—one molting feverishly by the day.

At least she'd come down for breakfast this morning, sparing Nella worry about her general well-being. While slurping oatmeal in a churlish silence, she fended off Nella's stabs at conversation. Then she shuffled back across the kitchen floor, scowling, her black knit shawl clenched across her bosom. With all the activity surrounding the search, her decision to spend the day in her suite wasn't exactly a bad thing.

By now, she was invariably lighting candles before her statue of Mother Mary. Or burning through the rosary in a vigil of prayer. She'd come to live with Nella shortly before Michael returned home last year. After nearly a lifetime in Cleveland's Little Italy, Tippi now used Uber to take her to church in Chagrin Falls. When she wasn't regaling Emerson with stories about the dance hall she'd once owned in Little Italy, she collected friends at church socials and the book club hosted by the assisted living facility in Chagrin Falls. Most weeks, Tippi hosted poker games for the geriatric crowd in Nella's family room.

But Tippi was no saint. A killer at Texas Hold'em, she never donated her winnings to the church.

Nella asked her son, "Best guess . . . when did Emerson stop into the loft?"

"Around noon. When I came back at eleven o'clock, nothing was out of place. Emerson was probably on the lookout. He must have waited until I'd left the barn before sneaking up here."

Michael combed long fingers through his dark-brown hair. Between the unkempt curls scattered across his brow and the heavy five-o'clock shadow, he looked exhausted. Given his determination to find Emerson, she doubted he'd found time for a quick shower today.

He said, "After I checked the barn, I went down to help with the search on the riverbank. I also walked through a section of the forest north of the river. Emerson's never been there, but it seemed wise to look anyway. I've lost track of how many miles I've walked."

"We should tell the police we've found something."

"Already done. I called the Hunting Valley PD right after I found the granola wrapper." Michael picked up a book and placed it carefully by the board games. He slid her a sidelong glance. "They'll tell Rosalind her grandson has been hanging out in our barn. Once they do, our little secret is out."

Nella shut her eyes tightly. "Rosalind won't take it well." She opened them, more distressed than before. "She'll be livid once she learns how long the visits have been going on. She'll wring the facts from Latrice."

"I'll go over, explain in person." Michael rocked back on his heels, a man uncomfortable with the mysterious war between his mother and the dignified judge. "In retrospect, I should've talked to Rosalind last year when Emerson began stopping by. The kid would've been upset, but it would have been the responsible thing to do."

"No, Michael." The prospect of Rosalind taking her wrath out on him made Nella queasy. "There's no reason to put you in the middle of this. I'll talk to her."

"*You're* going over?"

The incredulity on his face pricked Nella with embarrassment. "No, you're right. If I do, she'll slam the door in my face. I'll be reduced to shouting on her front porch." Frustrated, she started across the loft. "Maybe it's best if we let the police tell her."

Her son's eyes twinkled. "Gutless . . . ," he murmured.

He followed her down the ladder. Jasper greeted them with his tongue lolling and his tail thumping.

Ruffling the dog's ears, Michael eyed her appraisingly. "When Dad was alive, you were best friends with the Goodridges. I remember lots of times you got together with them when I was in grade school. Why did everything go south between the happy foursome? You've never laid out the real facts."

A good question, and one she never planned to answer. The errors Nella made during her son's childhood were too awful to share. Too shameful. Reveal the truth now, and she risked damaging their relationship. The possibility of losing Michael's admiration—even his love—sent fear rolling through her. He was her only child, the bright star she revolved around. She'd never manage the fallout if he learned the truth.

Stepping past, she walked through the riding arena. "Why dredge this up now?" Her voice sounded high and false, even to her own ears. She paused in a long band of light cutting through the barn. "I haven't been on civil terms with Rosalind since you were in braces. After so much time, her animosity is best categorized as ancient history."

Emotion darted through Michael's gaze. Not censure. More than anything else, he seemed injured by her inability to level with him.

His reaction illustrated yet another way she'd failed him. The trust he so freely offered was never fully returned.

The distressing observation made her reflect on Darcy as she'd once been, before trauma scraped off her innocence. Browned by the August sun, dashing into the forest like nature's original child. Always laughing, inquisitive, and bright—like Emerson was today. Darcy, bounding from the forest with an empty bird's nest or handfuls of colorful leaves or a lime-green salamander cradled between careful palms. Her sweet, little girl's voice calling out. An irresistible lure for the bashful Michael, a boy chafing beneath a childhood stutter, long-limbed and unaware of the dark beauty he possessed. During those idyllic days, he hadn't understood how his striking looks would soon captivate girls and, later, women. Yet he'd never held on to the one girl with a natural claim to his heart.

Dismissing the memory, Nella strode from the barn. Her belly souring with regret, she inhaled the fresh summer air.

"I have to start dinner." Faking a casual expression, she glanced at her son. "How do you feel about clam linguine? It's that or frozen burgers. With all the activity surrounding Emerson's disappearance, I forgot to stop by the grocery store."

"Clam linguine sounds great."

"I hope I can blast your grandmother out of her suite. Tippi needs to eat something. There's no reason she can't pray for Emerson's safe return over a bowl of pasta."

"Don't push Tippi. She'll come down when she's ready." Michael paused midway across the grass, his attention straying to the forest.

"Aren't you coming? You must be starving."

"Later." He started off. "If Emerson stopped by earlier, he might still be nearby."

Chapter 5

Shadows painted the winding driveway into the Goodridge estate.

Halfway up the wide band of concrete, Darcy brought the Honda Accord to a stop. In the semidarkness, the grand brick house with its wide circular driveway seemed to float behind a curtain of heavy dawn mist. Switching off the car's headlights, she listened to her skittering pulse. Birdsong drifted out from the stand of maple trees lining the drive. A hint of pinkish daylight brushed the treetops.

On the back seat, Samson remained asleep. Yesterday, he'd bonded with Latrice during the call at the roadside diner in North Carolina. Two against one—Darcy knew she didn't stand a chance. With the housekeeper egging him on, Samson convinced Darcy to decline the job in Cape May on embarrassingly short notice.

Once they reached the Ohio border, she caught a few hours of sleep at a rest stop. Then she drove the rest of the way north accompanied by a gently snoring teenager—and a bad case of nerves.

In the Honda's cup holder, pearls of condensation raced down the bottled water. Snatching it up, she took a quick swig. Then she sent the text. Latrice pinged back.

Five minutes later, a silhouette waded through the gloom.

Darcy leaned toward the windshield for a better view. Rarely did Latrice spend the night at the mansion, and her sleepwear came as a surprise. A shimmery robe of fire-engine red encased the housekeeper's generous curves. The gown underneath was equally sexy, a turquoise number with abundant lace. Latrice finished off the ensemble with leather boots. The boots were grungy, speckled with mud.

"I forgot to pack my slippers," she said, catching Darcy's expression. Sliding onto the passenger seat, she glanced at the sleeping youth in back. "Mind explaining why you're driving a chatty teenager around? He seemed awfully nice when we talked, but I still don't have a clear understanding. I got the impression he views you as a mother figure."

"Latrice, I'm thirty—nowhere near old enough to be Samson's mother. He's eighteen."

"He mentioned his age during our last conversation, when you were driving through West Virginia." Latrice studied his sleeping form. "He's small for an eighteen-year-old. Doesn't look much older than Emerson."

"Yeah, well, don't point it out when he wakes up. He's sensitive about that. I'm planning to keep encouraging him to drink milk. Who knows? There may still be time for him to gain another inch or two in height."

"Where's his family?"

"He doesn't have one." Darcy gave her a quick rundown of Samson's childhood in foster care and how she'd met him on the job in Charleston.

After the summary, Latrice said, "A boy his age is too young to be on his own. Teenagers walk around with skulls emptier than a hollow gourd and enough smarts to fill a thimble. Why, you didn't start growing brains until you left for college. I can't say the same for your younger sister. All she got from higher education was a baby she was too young to raise." Latrice rolled her eyes. "For a woman who never married, I've sure raised my share of children."

"I'm glad I was the first."

"The first *and* the most difficult. Did you know you bit your mother about ten seconds after your first tooth popped through?"

The story was unfamiliar. "Are you serious?"

"Rosalind was furious. You took a nip out of her finger, and that was it. She handed you right back to me. Let's not go into your toddler years—talk about a child with a mind of her own. I could get you to listen—most of the time. If Rosalind used her high-and-mighty tone, *no* became your favorite word." Dropping the subject, she gave Darcy an appreciative pat on the arm. "It's kind of you to look out for Samson, especially since he's got no family."

"If I'd known he'd help you gang up on me, I might not have agreed to let him tag along. What am I doing in Ohio? I should be in New Jersey, hunting for a new apartment."

"Forget about New Jersey. Plan on a nice, long stay. There's no better time to visit northeast Ohio than the month of June. Once Emerson turns up, he'll want to spend lots of time with you."

Apprehension shuttled through Darcy. Eight years ago, she'd broken a sacred promise to Elizabeth. She *hadn't* watched out for Emerson—she'd lit out of Ohio at the first sign of trouble. If Elizabeth's son greeted her with contempt, she couldn't blame him.

She dismissed the worrisome possibility as Latrice nodded toward the back seat. "Are you planning to wake him up?" she asked.

Wishing for a toothbrush, Darcy ran her tongue across her teeth. A toothbrush and a hot bath. With bubbles. She was also famished.

Reaching into the back seat, she pulled the blanket up to Samson's ears. "It's still early. Let him sleep." He snuggled in. "Besides, he's innocent to the ways of the world. If my mother goes on a murderous rampage, it's best if Samson doesn't watch."

Latrice landed her suddenly stern regard on Darcy. "How you carry on. As if Rosalind would do murder." One brown, one gray, her eyes sat within a starburst of wrinkles. Latrice called them her David Bowie eyes.

"There's a first time for everything."

"No pessimism. You're here now. You might as well stay positive." Latrice peered at the mansion. "What's the plan?"

The question took Darcy off guard. "I thought *you* had a plan."

"You did?" Her accomplice pulled the sexy robe tighter across her bosom. "Give me a minute. I'll come up with one."

"Latrice, you're unbelievable. I've had less than three hours' sleep. I've been driving since yesterday. I'd give anything for a decent meal and a long nap. You, on the other hand, had ample time to work out a strategy."

"Take a deep breath, child. You're hyperventilating."

"I'm not." Darcy gave her a mulish look. "I'm angry because we're flying blind. Here I am, working with a coconspirator who doesn't know how to uphold her end of the deal."

"Stop complaining and take a deep breath."

A wheeze emerged from Darcy's mouth. She *was* hyperventilating.

"Breathe," Latrice instructed. Leaning in, she plucked at Darcy's T-shirt. "When did you get so thin? I didn't raise you to turn into a scarecrow." She poked at Darcy's ribs, drawing a gasp. Then a smile broke across her ebony features. "It *is* good to see you. Now stop complaining and give me a hug."

Further prodding wasn't necessary. Despite the Honda's tight confines, Darcy managed to wrap her arms around the housekeeper. A well-worn habit took hold, and she lowered her head to Latrice's shoulder. The familiar scent of rosewater soothed her frazzled nerves.

When they drew apart, Darcy asked, "Is there any news?" During their last phone call at four a.m., Latrice had mentioned the granola wrapper found in the Varanos' hayloft. Why Emerson was hanging around Nella's barn Darcy couldn't imagine. Obviously, he didn't know his grandmother loathed her next-door neighbor. The reason for Rosalind's deep and abiding hatred of Nella was a mystery not even Latrice could unravel. And not for lack of trying.

"We haven't heard anything else. The granola wrapper is a good sign, though. If Emerson made it through one night, he can make it through two."

"How did my mother take the news?"

"I'd call her reaction mixed. She was glad they'd found something of Emerson's. The news that it was found in Nella's barn made her livid. The way she was stomping around the house, I thought she'd call the police back to demand they arrest Nella. Heaven above. That would've been something—slapping your neighbor in jail for feeding granola to your grandson."

A niggling sensation warned there was more to the story. "You're implying Emerson stopped by, and Nella gave him a snack?"

"Anything's possible."

It was a crazy theory. Nella wouldn't risk outright war.

"Emerson probably heard the police searching the woods and wanted to avoid them," she decided. "That doesn't mean Nella fed him snacks while he was on the run."

"Maybe." Latrice shrugged. She seemed about to add something else. Instead, she swiveled her meaty shoulders toward the passenger-side window. She watched the sunlight creeping down the driveway.

The niggling sensation increased, leaving Darcy at a loss. No question about it—Latrice was leaving something out. A fact, or an unsavory detail to illuminate why Emerson was snacking on granola in Nella's barn. Something she felt Darcy wouldn't take well.

Why doesn't Latrice simply explain? There's no obvious reason why she couldn't.

Given Darcy's unfamiliarity with her nephew's behavior, she felt clueless.

What if this latest disappearance represents the tip of the iceberg? Just another example of a boy's delinquent behavior?

A remote possibility, all things considered. As the grandson of a well-respected judge, Emerson surely had received countless lessons on ethical behavior. Darcy recalled her own childhood, when Rosalind droned on about the rule of law or mind-numbing topics like the Magna Carta. As a jurist, her devotion to ethics and rules was absolute.

"Question." She waited as Latrice turned from the window. "About my nephew."

"What?"

"I hate to ask, but . . . does Emerson get into trouble? Does he steal things, anything like that?"

"Now hold on. You're jumping to conclusions. Your nephew didn't steal granola from Nella's house."

"Forget the granola," Darcy snapped. "I'm trying to understand his motivation for hiding out for two days straight. He took off because of the anniversary, right? If marking the date when we lost Elizabeth and my father upset him too much, maybe he did something bad. Broke one of my mother's precious figurines, or lifted cash from her wallet. Kids act out when they can't process more volatile emotions. Might explain why he's laying low."

"Good job, Darcy. You've come up with the dumbest theory in all creation."

"I'm merely speculating."

"Listen up. Your nephew has goodness bred to the bone. It's one of the reasons he gets bullied at the hoity-toity school Rosalind makes him attend."

"Why do the other kids pick on him?"

"Lots of reasons."

"Name one."

"Last month, right before he finished third grade, he caught one of his classmates working from a cheat sheet during the math test."

"Emerson called another kid out during a test?"

"He told the boy cheating wasn't a good strategy for a successful academic career." Pity crossed Latrice's face. "Recess was *rough* that day."

The story troubled Darcy. "Those were his exact words? 'A good strategy for a successful academic career'?"

"You're surprised?" Latrice cocked her chin. "You aren't the only one who worries about coming up with good strategies. Your nephew does too."

A compliment lay hidden in the remark, one Darcy refused to accept. "Actually, it sounds like something my mother would say."

"She's raising him, isn't she?"

"Is she raising him, or molding him in her diabolical image?" Darcy shuddered. "There's something weird about a boy imitating an elderly judge. Especially a judge who's wound too tight. No wonder Emerson hasn't won the popularity contest at school."

Latrice rubbed her belly. "I knew there was a reason my tummy's bothering me this morning. I'd forgotten how you like to spout off about your mother. This is turning into an interesting day."

Darcy glanced at the house. "Is she awake?"

"She's been pacing in her bedroom all night."

"She hasn't slept at all?"

"Not that I could tell. In between chatting with Samson, I *did* catch a few hours of sleep—thanks for asking. Your mother won't rest until the police bring Emerson home."

Pity took a swipe at Darcy. "I wish there was something I could do."

"There *is* something. Strap on your big-girl attitude and drive up to the house."

An obvious solution, yet Darcy hesitated. In the back seat, a soft snoring commenced. She envied Samson's ability to sleep through a treacherous dawn she'd much rather skip.

"How am I supposed to waltz into the house after eight years? What's my opening line?"

"Stop fretting. You'll come up with something."

"Yeah. Right." Snatching up the bottled water, she fiddled with the cap. When it refused to come loose in her nervous fingers, she plunked the bottle down.

Putting the Honda into reverse was out of the question. After coming this far, she wasn't driving away. Dealing with her mother promised to be difficult, but there was Emerson to consider. Once he turned up, she at least wanted to meet him. No matter how the rest of the events played out, she'd assure her nephew that, going forward, she would become an active presence in his life.

"Okay, fine. I'm going up to the house." A tangy kick of adrenaline tensed her muscles. She felt like a sprinter in the starting blocks, unsure if cheers or catcalls would follow her down the track. "Name your poison, Latrice. Do you want to stay in the car or flee?"

The passenger door creaked open. Apprehension tripped through the housekeeper's David Bowie eyes. "I'll give you a few minutes alone with Rosalind before I walk back to the house."

"Jeez, Latrice. I thought you had *some* courage."

"Not today." She trotted to the edge of the driveway. Then she flapped her arms. "Go on, now. There's coffee brewing in the kitchen. It's sure to lure your mother downstairs. Stay on your best behavior. Everything will work out fine."

Having issued the dubious advice, the housekeeper planted her feet. She looked absurd, standing there in her grubby boots with the breeze flapping her sexy robe.

With a salute, Darcy hit the accelerator and sped off.

$\sim$

Brushing the sleep from her eyes, Nella left her bedroom. Whispered conversation floated down the hallway from her mother's suite. Which made no sense.

Tippi didn't entertain guests at dawn's first light.

Outside the suite, Nella hesitated. She pressed her ear to the door. Inside, a heavy silence fell.

Drawing back, she stifled the urge to knock. Footfalls padded near the door, a soft pacing that went on for a good ten seconds. Then more silence.

Was Tippi rooted on the other side, offended by the surveillance? Nella's higher angels gave a nod in the affirmative.

Count on it.

Dismissing her curiosity, she went downstairs. No doubt Tippi was embarking on another litany of prayer or lighting more candles for Emerson's safe return.

Leaving her alone was prudent. Tippi no longer slept much, and she guarded her suite of rooms like a feisty terrier. This territorial posture softened only when she summoned Nella's weekly cleaning service to spruce up the place or she deigned Nella worthy to pop inside for afternoon tea. On those rare days, Nella drank Earl Grey with a disapproving eye as Tippi splashed brandy into her own cup.

Last night, while Nella made clam linguine, Tippi briefly appeared in the kitchen. Too hungry to wait for dinner, she swiped the fruit bowl from the kitchen table and stuffed napkins into the pockets of her roomy black dress. Without a word of explanation, she had plodded back upstairs.

With luck, she'd stop hiding like a hermit crab once Emerson turned up.

In the kitchen, the coffee was already made. Morning light cascaded through the windows. Filling a cup, Nella went outside.

On the patio, Michael sat nursing a cup of coffee. Fatigue rimmed his eyes. Yesterday he'd been confident no harm would befall Emerson. Now a fog of unease surrounded him.

Nella pulled a chair close. "Taking another day off?" He'd begun scouting for a building to expand his carpentry business. Secretly she hoped the search didn't prove fruitful too quickly. Once he found the right building, he'd look for an apartment nearby.

"I was scheduled for an install in Chagrin Falls. Already canceled. The couple understands why I can't make it in."

"Are the police widening the search?"

Michael was good friends with several officers in the Hunting Valley Police Department. He'd also built new bathroom cabinetry for the police chief in Chagrin Falls.

"I haven't called our PD yet for an update." Setting his coffee aside, Michael studied the daylight cresting above the forest. "I'm sure they're expanding the search. They'll ignore Rosalind and all her demands about keeping a tight lid on this."

"Michael, she *does* want her grandson found. She covets her privacy, that's all."

"She told the PD this is nothing more than Emerson's latest stunt, another camping trip without her permission. She believes they're perfect idiots if they can't locate a boy out fishing for trout."

"She didn't call them idiots, did she?"

"*Perfect* idiots. Her exact words."

"Diplomacy never was her strong suit."

Michael lifted his coffee mug, took a swig. "Her opinion no longer matters." He set the mug down. "It's been too long. The PD will assume Emerson is injured and can't get home, or that Rosalind is off base about why he disappeared. They'll notify the media and bring in more officers from surrounding jurisdictions."

"But he took off voluntarily. Latrice said his camping gear is missing, and we found the granola wrapper in the loft. He's nearby. If Rosalind wants to wait before going public, the police should respect her wishes."

Michael glanced at her with disbelief. "You're defending her? If the situation were reversed, she wouldn't return the favor."

"I don't care. People call her Ohio's hanging judge, but she *is* human."

"Then she'd do better to stop issuing edicts from on high. The police know how to do their jobs."

His lack of compassion was stunning. A levelheaded man, he wasn't usually this harsh.

"You must understand why she wants to avoid media coverage," Nella said. "After Jack and Elizabeth were killed, the media treated the story like cheap entertainment. The press followed Rosalind to the courthouse every day and harassed Latrice whenever she went into Chagrin Falls to shop. Losing Jack was hard enough, but what happened to Elizabeth . . ."

The reminder washed the criticism from Michael's strong features. "I get it, Mom."

"Do you? Once the media is put on notice, half the journalists in Ohio will tie Emerson's disappearance to the anniversary of the accident. They'll dredge up old photos of Elizabeth and Jack and rehash the awful details. In print *and* on TV."

Looking away, Nella studied her lap with dismay. As a widow, she understood the bottomless grief Rosalind had endured when she lost her husband. Yet the heartbreak of losing a beloved child—especially in the hideous way Elizabeth had died—was unimaginable.

An indecipherable brew of emotion gathered in Michael's eyes. "I'm sorry, Mom. What happened to Dr. Jack—and Elizabeth most of all—it was a tragedy. But don't ask me to sympathize with Rosalind. I can't. She doesn't deserve my compassion. I've seen the results of her cruelty. Do you expect me to forgive everything she's done to Darcy?"

At the startling question, Nella lifted her head. Her son hadn't spoken to Darcy since the accident that destroyed the Goodridge family. Nearly a decade ago. Not once in all the intervening years had he mentioned her.

His closest childhood friend, the girl he'd rediscovered when fate brought her back into his life a few precious months before Jack and Elizabeth died.

Losing Darcy twice had surely left scars her son deftly hid. Michael had stepped past the worst months of his youth with built-in common sense and a pragmatic streak to guide him. Through marriage, divorce, and the reinvention of his career, he never seemed anything less than content. And now he'd brought Emerson into his life—a child who resembled Darcy so closely, his frequent visits surely brought memories of her to the surface.

But Nella understood the reliable compass of Michael's emotions. If he savored memories of Darcy, surely he focused on the happy childhood friendship that had molded them both—not the brief love affair that came later.

Does he still care for her?

Regret clouded his features. It was enough to make Nella wonder if the wild-hearted girl who'd dominated his youth still laid claim to his devotion.

Inside the house, glass shattered with a crash. Nella's head snapped up.

Swiveling in his chair, Michael frowned. "Did Tippi come downstairs?"

"She's dropped something." Given Tippi's arthritis, the simplest tasks were treacherous.

Nella sprinted to the kitchen.

Clumps of last night's linguine were scattered across the floor. The broken container lay in sharp chunks. Tippi stepped over them in a determined path for the door. In her arms, a jug of milk wobbled and a bottle of chocolate syrup nearly slipped free as she strove for a level of stealth her arthritic bones would not allow.

Leaning against the doorjamb, Nella tried to make sense of the heist unfolding before her.

"Mama, *what* are you doing?"

Tippi swung around. Guilt raced across her wrinkles.

She lunged for the hallway. In her haste, the cap popped off the bottle. Chocolate spurted wildly across the floor. With a shriek, she flung the bottle down.

"Mama—wait!"

Nella reached for her. A rash move. She skidded through the pool of chocolate like a car losing traction on ice. Unable to right herself, she went down with a bang. Pain sparked in her hip, but she hardly noticed.

Lying prone in the chocolatey mess, she watched in disbelief as her mother shuffled into the hallway in a slow attempt at a fast getaway.

Michael stormed inside. Unaware of the mess on the floor, he began sliding. He was a tall man, a tower of muscle. With a howl of warning, Nella shielded her face. If he plowed into her, she was toast.

He righted himself a skinny inch before he nailed her shoulder. On a growl, he demanded, "What's going on in here?"

Chapter 6

Leaving Samson asleep in the car, Darcy waded through the retreating shadows and ascended the front steps of the stately brick mansion. Her pulse jumping, she stepped back into the world she'd once known.

The elegant oval foyer rested in silence. The staircase curving to the mansion's second floor stood empty in the shadowy gloom. Was Rosalind still upstairs? If so, there was no harm in looking around. Taking the risk, Darcy tiptoed into the dining room.

Everything was the same, from the gleaming Henredon table to the satin drapes festooning the bay window. The formal living room and the library with its towering walls of books both seemed unchanged. The porcelain figurines scattered on end tables appeared recently dusted. The designer pillows on the Queen Anne chairs and the sleek couches were arranged as Darcy remembered. Only the office adjacent to the library escaped a quick inspection. The door, tightly shut, warned her not to enter.

In the rustic family room, she walked past the wall of photos with her gaze averted.

Adrift, Darcy circled back to the foyer. After eight years, she'd expected some changes. New paint on the walls, or a replacement for her father's lumpy recliner in the family room. Even the watercolor Elizabeth had painted during her pregnancy, an amateurish rendering of rain-streaked tulips, still hung above the living room mantel.

A heaviness accompanied her through the darkened corridor that led to the kitchen. Echoes from the past called out. Elizabeth, chasing after her in this very corridor. A Christmas morning—from so long ago, the image was hard to grasp—pedaling a tricycle out of the kitchen with chubby-cheeked Elizabeth chortling from the red wagon hitched on in back. Hiding in the corridor in junior high, sharing lip gloss and secrets. The brilliant day in May, Elizabeth's last of high school, her eyes dancing as Darcy adjusted the silky folds of her graduation gown. The images were pure and good. Darcy clung to them for strength before letting them go.

A long island occupied the center of the kitchen. At the opposite end, a jungle of plants framed the windows behind the oak table. Deep-green ivy and delicate ferns, the plants were Latrice's contribution to a home otherwise more formal than nurturing.

Numb from sensory overload, Darcy found her favorite mug in the cupboard, the one she'd bought at Ohio University right before graduation. Time again coasted backward as she poured the hot black brew, revealing more difficult memories: an infant bawling in her sis-ter's arms as she trudged bleary-eyed to the table; Darcy speaking in hushed whispers to Michael Varano on her phone as Latrice, sighing with dismay, flipped pancakes at the stove. Lost in the memories, Darcy lifted the coffee to her lips. The last time she'd stood here, she'd been a brokenhearted girl.

It felt like yesterday.

"Darcy."

The familiar voice prickled the skin on the back of her neck. She lowered the mug. It took all her courage to turn and face her mother.

The Honorable Rosalind Goodridge did not possess great beauty. Her cheekbones rose in chiseled peaks. Her face was slightly too long, and decidedly narrow. Yet the authority in her expression, combined with her regal posture, captivated anyone caught in her sphere. Deeper lines than Darcy remembered etched her forehead. Rosalind's hair, swept up in a loose chignon, still resembled spun silver.

Darcy searched for an opener. Her throat closed.

Rosalind stepped into the kitchen. The barest hint of pleasure skimmed her eyes.

Snuffing it out, she tightened the sash of her robe. If waves of confusion buffeted her, she hid the emotion well.

"What are you doing here?" she asked.

The dark emotion rising in her mother's eyes threatened Darcy's confidence.

"I heard about Emerson," she said, grateful to have located her voice.

"How, might I ask?"

When she remained silent, impatience crossed Rosalind's features. Taking care to keep her distance, she poured a cup of coffee, then reached for the milk. The teaspoon clattered against the rim of the cup. Stepping back, she slowly sipped.

Rancor brimmed in her voice when she spoke again. "So you've heard about my grandson. You still haven't explained how the current situation is any of your concern. Why has his latest escapade brought you here?"

"I thought I should come, to . . ." Darcy faltered. To help? Offer solace? The complex reasons precluded a quick summation.

"I've asked you a question. Answer me."

The chill descending between them made responding difficult. "When I heard Emerson was missing, I thought I should come back. I care about him too, and he's been gone too long. I'm worried something may have happened to him." She hesitated as her mother's eyes narrowed. Angry now, she put a hard edge in her voice. "Stop looking at me like every word out of my mouth is suspect."

"Isn't it?"

Wounded, she held her ground. "I didn't come to fight with you."

"How refreshing."

Trying again, she said, "How are you holding up?"

"What a ridiculous question."

"I'm merely asking."

"How do you think I'm managing? My grandson is out gallivanting in the woods. The police can't find him. An eight-year-old, evading a squad of officers in one of the wealthiest jurisdictions in Ohio. My tax dollars at work." Rosalind's eyes lowered to the coffee mug gripped tight in her fist. She took a long sip, her features dulling with irritation. "A study in incompetence, the entire police force."

"I can't speak to the competency of the PD, but I wouldn't characterize Emerson's behavior as 'gallivanting.' A child doesn't run off without good reason."

The observation brewed storm clouds around her mother. "Thank you for that piercing insight," she snapped. "You don't know the first thing about Emerson."

A direct blow, but Darcy tilted her chin. "You're still angry with me," she said with forced calm. An irony, since the muscles in her thighs were twitching and her knees felt loose. The desire to flee nearly started her feet moving. Squashing the impulse, she added, "I'm not here to rehash the past. I came because I'm worried about my nephew."

"How do you have the gall to refer to him as your nephew?"

"Because he is."

"Please spare me the fake concern. My grandson isn't missing. He's rebelling. An irrational pursuit *you* are more than familiar with. Yet another reason why I can't abide having you underfoot, pretending you're here to help me through a difficult ordeal. There is no difficult ordeal, only a stubborn little boy determined to get his way. This is merely Emerson's latest attempt to—"

The tirade halted. Rosalind pressed a palm to her forehead. On her pale skin, splotches of red began forming.

Was she concerned she'd revealed too much? Regarding what, Darcy couldn't guess. Her mother seemed to imply that Emerson's latest disappearance was a planned event. A calculated ploy, for reasons still hidden. She was still trying to work it out when her mother's voice lowered to a dangerous pitch.

"Don't insult me by pretending you care about Emerson. Your nephew indeed. How can you refer to him as anything except what he is—a child who is nothing but a stranger to you? If you thought he mattered, you would have shown up before this." With the skill of a seasoned jurist, Rosalind altered her line of attack. "Where *have* you been?"

"All over."

"Clarification, please."

"I've been moving around the East Coast."

"You're a drifter? Surely a woman with your level of education can find suitable work."

Another jab, but Darcy squared her shoulders. They were on familiar ground with the thrust and parry of Rosalind's line of questioning, the incisive drilling away for information as she wore down her opponent's defenses until there was nothing left but her empty victory.

Darcy found the resolve to stiffen her spine. She was no longer a newly minted college graduate, beaten down by her mother's accusations that she was careless and wild, a blemish on the Goodridge name. That she was indirectly responsible for the pregnancy that derailed her sister's dreams of completing a bachelor's degree and entering law school.

That she had all but committed murder on the night of the accident.

The stranglehold of regret never abated. Never faded or became manageable. She didn't need her mother's contempt as a reminder.

She was older now, with the emotional reserves to withstand the low punch. Darcy knew how to keep her temper in check. She never let people in, not with the wide-eyed trust of her stolen youth. Nor did she viciously push people away—not in the way her mother was driving her off now.

"I'm not a drifter." Setting down her coffee, she crossed her arms. "I work management jobs in various industries—whatever suits my mood. I work hard, and I've *always* cared about Elizabeth's son."

"Why wait until now to come back?"

"Is that a rhetorical question? You know the reason."

"No, Darcy. I don't. I haven't the faintest clue."

The rejoinder struck like a bee sting. "How can you say that?" Dumbfounded, she wondered if her mother had purposely forgotten the argument on the night of the funerals. Sealed away the awful, scalding words in a corner of her mind.

Is it possible? No.

She sputtered, "You know why I left. And you certainly remember what you said when I came into the library and found you drinking. Found you drunk, actually. Why stand there pretending you don't?"

With a bang, Rosalind set her mug on the counter. "Our memories of that night aren't remotely similar."

"You're lying."

"How dare you foist this on me? I haven't the least insight into your motives—then *or* now. I can't begin to guess why a young woman abandons her family. It's beyond my understanding why you left the same night Elizabeth and Jack were laid to rest. Has it occurred to you that you've *never* visited their graves? Not once, Darcy. Not once in eight years. Aren't you the least bit ashamed?"

"Of course I am."

"It's a little late for absolution. If you cared at all, you wouldn't have moved away."

"You didn't leave me a choice."

A brittle laugh escaped Rosalind, the sound hollow and irrepressibly sad. A light misting of tears glistened in her eyes, but she shook them off. Her pride had always been stronger than her heart.

"Are we back to blaming Mother?" she murmured. "I see. You're too irresponsible to assume blame for your own failings."

"That's not what I meant."

"*Now* who's the liar?"

"I'm not lying!" They were perilously close to an outright shouting match. Needing to bring down the temperature, Darcy added, "There's no gain in rehashing this now."

"Or ever, since we'll never see eye to eye."

"We're both exhausted." She glanced at the clock above the sink. "I've been driving most of the night. From what I understand, you haven't slept at all."

"Obviously not."

"I'm sure Emerson will turn up soon."

A hint of mockery slid across her mother's features. "I'm well aware my grandson will return soon. I don't need your reassurance."

Refusing the bait, Darcy grappled with her composure. She was unbearably close to tears. A display of weakness would invite another verbal attack.

"Are you in your chambers this morning?" she asked. Rosalind's docket was always full. Since she clearly viewed Emerson's disappearance as little more than a prank, she'd leave soon for the courthouse. An obsession with punctuality demanded nothing less. "I'll check in at the hotel in Chagrin Falls. Why don't we talk again when you get home tonight? Hopefully Emerson will have returned by then."

Rosalind's lips curved, but no joy marked her face. "Ah. I see," she murmured. "You aren't as well informed as I presumed."

"What do you mean?"

Her mother hesitated long enough for a sense of foreboding to steal through Darcy.

"I'm not in my chambers today," Rosalind said. "Or any day, for that matter. I've agreed to an unwelcome retirement."

Chapter 7

News of her mother's retirement struck Darcy like a tidal wave.

The devotion Rosalind held to the law was absolute. From Darcy's earliest memories, her mother had spent hours sequestered in the mansion's library surrounded by leather-bound tomes, her reading glasses perched on her nose. At odd hours she arrived home or swept out of the mansion, her heels clacking across the marble foyer with unmistakable purpose. Rarely would she spend more than a few minutes with her two daughters, choosing instead to hurry to her chambers at the Geauga County Courthouse to prepare for upcoming cases or to meet with the prosecution and defense lawyers scheduled to appear in her court.

The predictable absences had seemed natural. Darcy's equally successful father also worked long hours as a vascular specialist in Chagrin Falls. Elizabeth, younger than Darcy by a year, never complained if Dr. Jack Goodridge missed a school play or a recital. She barely noticed if he arrived home too late for dinner, which the girls shared in the kitchen with the doting Latrice. But the obedient and pliable Elizabeth—her mother's favorite—often whined if the busy judge worked past the bedtime hour.

Now Rosalind had abandoned the law at the pinnacle of her career.

"When did you retire?" Darcy asked.

"Recently. I took a leave of absence, which I am now making permanent. The news will be announced next week."

"That doesn't make sense. You love your job."

"It makes perfect sense. There are no cases on my docket, no meetings to attend. I've hung up my robes."

"You said this is an unwelcome retirement." As a judge in the court of common pleas, Rosalind served consecutive six-year terms. She always won reelection handily—or so Darcy thought. "Were you forced out because of politics?"

On the counter, tendrils of steam lifted from Rosalind's coffee. Her fingers tightening around the mug, she took a leisurely sip. "Bravo, my dear." From over the rim, she regarded Darcy with cold amusement. "You've held a line of questioning for ten seconds."

"Stop baiting me. Explain why you gave up a career you love."

"You're asking me to trust you, and I don't. You're not honorable. You never were."

The pronouncement scalded Darcy. Tears burned at the back of her eyes.

The front door slammed. Heavy footfalls padded down the corridor. Latrice entered the kitchen with her salt-and-pepper curls bouncing and her sexy robe billowing. She halted in the thick atmosphere brewing between mother and daughter.

Rosalind arched a brow. "Latrice, were you outside half-naked? You look like a lounge singer."

"I'm not half-naked." Latrice sized up her employer's sedate robe and matching slippers with something less than approval. "Some of us don't live our lives in monochrome. I like the color red."

"Why don't you get dressed?"

"Why don't you?"

A squeak of protest rose from Rosalind's lips. Eyes narrowing, she held her tongue.

Satisfied, Latrice swung her attention to Darcy. "Where's Samson?" Her satisfaction vanished. Sniffing the air, she appeared to detect a foul odor.

"He's still asleep in the car," Darcy said.

Rosalind frowned. "Who is Samson?"

The query sank into the muddy silence. With ill-concealed worry, Latrice took stock of her employer's pinched expression and the tight set of her jaw.

She pressed a palm to her heart. "What did I miss?"

"Nothing," Rosalind snapped. "In fact, the conversation is over. My daughter is leaving."

"Leaving? She just got here!"

"She's leaving. *Now.*"

The harsh command pinged off Darcy's brain.

Am I being ordered out? Dismissed, like a convicted felon?

Yes.

Every nerve ending in her body fired with the same message: *Leave now.*

It was impossible to follow through. The disbelief careening through her was stronger, an immobilizing force.

With a growl, Latrice leaped to her defense.

"I suppose we're getting somewhere." She squared off before Rosalind. "At least you're admitting Darcy *is* your daughter. You've spent the last eight years acting like her name was banned from the English language. In case you haven't noticed, she's here to help. Can't you be anything but mean to her?"

"Latrice, I suggest you refrain from questioning my personal decisions. As for how I behave, I don't welcome or need your advice," Rosalind said, waving off the attack as if her trusted housekeeper were nothing more than a bothersome fly. "My choices are none of your affair."

"That's where you're wrong. This *is* my affair. I love Darcy—I love her nearly as much as you do, even if you're too proud to understand your own heart. How much longer will you let your grief over losing Elizabeth twist inside you like a snake? I'm not sure you ever cared much about losing your husband, and Dr. Jack was a fine man. Not that you remember—not with all your grief stored up for our sweet, gentle Elizabeth." When her furious employer sputtered in response, Latrice held up a warning finger. "Rosalind, don't give me that look. I'll know when I've crossed the line. I'm not even close. Are you going to stand there and pretend you don't love your only surviving child? Shame on you!"

The outburst left the housekeeper trembling with emotion, her forehead glossing with perspiration. Rosalind fared no better. The splotches of color in her cheeks bled away.

Darcy rested a palm on Latrice's back. "Thanks for sticking up for me." A terrible thread of hope pulled her eyes to her mother's. Her voice reduced to a childlike whisper, she asked, "Do you really want me to leave?"

Silence overtook the room. The question, unanswered, left a bitter taste in Darcy's mouth, like smoke from an untended fire. Like ash sifting down on the carcass of a broken family.

Rosalind looked away.

The rejection hit with the force of a well-aimed fist. Numb with understanding, Darcy felt her world shift irrevocably. No love remained in her mother's heart. There was nothing left but contempt.

Fending off tears, she walked out.

She felt like a fool for having come. Her mother didn't possess the capacity to forgive. Rosalind Goodridge knew only how to hand down judgments. Unbending, willful—she didn't possess the flexibility to grant their relationship a reprieve.

Blindly Darcy raced through the foyer. She flung open the door.

And nearly fell headlong into Michael Varano's grandmother.

From the looks of it, time was marching right over Tippi. Wrinkles crisscrossed her leathery face. A black dress three sizes too large covered her shrinking bones. Beige support hose and low-heeled black pumps finished off the dowdy ensemble.

When Michael and Darcy were children, Michael had called his grandmother's outfits her "Viva l'Italia" costumes.

At the sight of her grandson's friend, Tippi's jaw hung loose. Darcy scrambled for something to say. A greeting, an explanation—anything.

Instantly, the desire melted away. Her eyes swung to the boy Tippi hugged to a bony hip. Only an inch or two shorter than his diminutive protector, he was a beautiful child.

Wheat-colored locks fell across his brow. His nose was slightly too long, his mouth full and well carved. Intelligence gleamed in his mossy-green eyes, lifting now to study Darcy with interest and a bold air of disbelief.

"Aunt Darcy?" When she stared at him, speechless, he beamed. "You *are* my aunt . . . aren't you? Latrice said you look like me. I thought she was kidding." He flung himself at her waist. "We're practically twins!"

The affection, coming on the heels of her mother's dismissal, sent gratitude surging through Darcy. She wrapped the excited boy in a fierce embrace. A warm, woodsy scent rose from his scalp. The lightest emotion cartwheeled through her. Emerson bore an uncanny resemblance to her, but he smelled remarkably like his late mother. It was as if Elizabeth had left a lasting imprint on his very skin. A delightful discovery—a gift. Tightening her hold, Darcy rested her chin on the top of his head.

Her mother's rejection didn't matter. *This*—this immediate connection with her nephew—mattered greatly.

Her vision blurring, she resolved to keep Emerson in her life. Permanently. Nothing Rosalind might say would lessen her resolve.

The strength of her reaction wasn't lost on her nephew. Giggling, he allowed her to lead him into a long embrace. Emerson clung to her with all his might. He was a shrimp, but he sure had some strength.

"It's okay," he said, misreading her resolve for worry. He pressed his nose into her rib cage. "Nothing bad happened to me."

The affection cresting in Darcy kept her voice from returning. Mute with gratitude, she pressed kisses across the smooth skin of his forehead. His skin was remarkably soft; a hint of baby fat rounded his jaw. He seemed nearly too feminine with his unblemished skin, rosy lips, and the thick fringe of lashes decorating his eyes.

He would become a man soon enough—why not enjoy his boyhood while it lasted? Grinning, she planted another kiss on his nose. She finished off with a loud, smacking kiss right between his brows.

Emerson wrinkled his nose. Although he welcomed the affection, a lovefest of this magnitude was probably too much for him.

A theory proven correct when he squirmed out of her arms. Beside him, Tippi laughed as she produced a handkerchief to catch the tears weaving down her weathered cheeks. The surprising events apparently left her addled.

Darcy barely noticed her distress. "Emerson, where have you been? Do you have any idea how many people are out looking for you?"

"Yeah, I know." Sheepishly, he shrugged. Then he threw off his embarrassment to hook an arm through Tippi's. "I didn't mean to scare anyone. I've been with Tippi." He propped her up as she finished drying her cheeks. "We were socializing."

It was a weirdly mature response. "You were *socializing* for two whole days?"

"Yesterday, mostly. And last night. Tippi has an air mattress. She hides it because she doesn't think Nella likes her to have sleepovers. You know—with the old guys Tippi dates. She knows *a lot* of old guys. She doesn't like them sleeping in her bed, though. Lots of old guys thrash in their sleep. Anyway, we couldn't figure out how to inflate the air mattress." Oblivious to the sexual content lurking beneath the disclosure, Emerson blew out a stream of air. He resumed talking with a child's effervescent flair. "Tippi's couch is pretty comfortable. Did you know she has her own suite in Nella's house? Three whole rooms, and her own mini fridge. Before I went over to socialize, I was out tracking cougars in the forest."

"This is northeast Ohio, not Canada," Darcy said. "There are no cougars in the forest."

He gave her a look that reduced her to three inches in height. "Right . . . ," he said with prickly irritation. "I was *pretending*. You know—using my imagination."

A common practice for a child, surely. "If you were tracking imaginary cougars, why didn't anyone see you?" He'd inherited more than her looks. He'd also inherited her stealth. A survival skill, in Darcy's estimation. The dull Goodridge estate was no match for the call of the wild.

"I heard two cops talking on their radios, real loud," he explained. "They were old guys—easy to ditch. Mostly they were looking down, like they'd find me under the leaves."

"Wait. How did you ditch them?"

"By climbing a tree. It was pretty funny. They kept walking in circles."

It was doubtful the police shared his amusement. "You should've called out to them," she said. "It was wrong to make them walk around in circles."

She winced. What right did she have to play sheriff to his outlaw? The reprimand was automatic, a protective instinct that seemed to surprise Emerson too.

Since she was on a roll, she added, "At minimum, you should've let your grandmother know you were safe. Seriously, Emerson. Do you have a clue how many police officers were called in to look for you?"

"A lot. They hunted through the whole forest." He gave her a winning smile. "I kept watch with my binoculars. Want to see them?"

"Later."

"How long are you staying? We have three spare bedrooms," he said, cheerfully unaware of her familiarity with her childhood home.

"They're all nice. The biggest room has a flat-screen TV. Latrice hides up there to watch ESPN."

"Well . . ." Darcy was loath to make a promise she was sure to break. "We'll see."

Tippi worked her gums. Either her dentures were coming loose or she was attempting to form a coherent thought.

The old woman thumped Emerson on the shoulder. He stepped aside. Without further ado, she dove into Darcy's arms.

"Where have you been? You're all grown up! Why didn't you write to your Tippi, or call?"

"I'm sorry."

"You're a bad girl."

"I'll do better."

"Oh, stop. You do just fine. You're my little piece of golden. You always were." From inside the nest of Darcy's embrace, she reached out to tousle Emerson's thick locks. "This one is too."

"She taught me poker," Emerson said. "But I lost ten bucks."

"I won fair and square," Tippi said. "Don't complain."

Darcy laughed. "Jeez, Tippi. Did you nab *all* his cash?"

"Only what he had on him."

"I'm afraid to ask if you seeded the deck."

Dropping the subject, Darcy brushed her chin across the thinning wisps on Tippi's head. The strands of coarse hair swirled around a few bald patches near the top of her head. She needed a wig.

Darcy swiftly dismissed the observation. Releasing Tippi, she landed her startled gaze on the silver Audi coupe parked at the far end of the circular drive.

Nella stood at the vehicle's passenger side. She wore hip-hugging jeans sure to make her the envy of every middle-aged woman in the county. A knit top of bold azure showed off her slender body. To outward appearances, she hadn't aged at all.

No doubt Nella presumed it safer to remain outside while Emerson was delivered home. When she noticed Darcy, she offered a wide smile. She appeared delighted—and not the least surprised. Which was odd, since Darcy had never intended to set foot in Hunting Valley again.

The Audi's driver-side door opened. A headful of dark curls rose into view, followed by wide shoulders.

Darcy's pulse scuttled.

Michael eased his tall frame from the car. He moved with the slow motions of a man suddenly confronted by a ghost.

If the years had been unkind to Tippi, they'd been glorious to Michael. The lean, rangy build of his youth was gone, replaced by the thick-muscled build of a man in his prime. His features carried an appealing fullness. The first hint of crow's-feet framed his eyes.

Blinking, he did a double take. Drifting forward on the balls of his feet, he caught Darcy's eyes with a bold, probing gaze that dared her to look away. The intensity of his regard snatched her breath away.

Recovering, Michael snapped upright. His hand lifted in a tentative wave.

Just as quickly, his fingers stilled. A warning. His expression shifting, he looked past her.

Following his line of sight, she discovered Tippi shuffling into the foyer with her brows drawn low. She looked ready for battle.

A burst of Italian shot from her lips.

"Donna cattiva!" She raised an accusing finger. "Bad, bad woman."

The hostile salutation froze Rosalind in midstep. Latrice, following close behind, nearly plowed into her. Latrice's sexy pj's were gone, replaced by her boring maid's uniform.

Rosalind folded her arms. "Tippi." She gave an elaborate sigh. "Go home."

"Do you promise to be good to my little piece of golden?"

Darcy wasn't sure if Tippi meant her or Emerson. An issue of little importance. The petite Italian withdrew a rosary from a pocket of her dress. She shook the beads at Rosalind like a voodoo priestess. The harassment was summarily ignored.

With focused calm, Rosalind appraised Emerson. "Finally, you're back. Would you like to explain yourself?"

"No."

"Why not?"

"I'm angry with you. Very much so."

Latrice, hovering on the sidelines, grunted. "Get in line," she muttered.

Rosalind maneuvered Emerson away from the simmering Tippi. She planted herself in the doorway with her claws firmly clasping his shoulders. Darcy nearly laughed. If her mother feared Emerson would bolt again, her worries were unfounded. He looked exhausted from his adventures.

Rosalind asked, "May I inquire *why* you're angry with me?"

"Not at the moment, no." He slipped out of her grasp.

"Enough of this nonsense. I deplore obstinacy."

"As do I."

"Emerson Goodridge, do not test my patience. This isn't chess. You won't checkmate *me*. Now. You're my grandson, and I've asked you a question. Answer me."

"No."

Darcy stepped between them. "Stop badgering him. Can't you see he's tired?" Taking the cue, Emerson darted behind her back.

Rosalind's eyes blazed. "Stay out of this. You have no right to intervene."

"Oh yes I do," she tossed back, astonished by her own bravado. She'd let Rosalind defeat her, but she'd fight for Emerson. "I have as much right as you."

"She does," Emerson agreed from behind her back.

The inquisition ceased. With a gasp, Rosalind looked outside. Venom turned her eyes to jet.

Tippi made the sign of the cross as Rosalind stepped into the sunlight streaming through the door and fastened her furious gaze on the woman by the Audi.

Nella. Her nemesis.

Tippi whispered a prayer. Then she surprised them all by smacking Rosalind soundly on the wrist.

"Donna cattiva!"

With fist raised, she marched out.

Latrice hurried past, running down the steps to help the fuming Tippi negotiate the driveway. Michael met them halfway. Taking his grandmother by the arm, he steered her into the Audi's back seat. Nella leaped in on the passenger side.

Michael looked back at the house. The pull of his gaze brought Darcy outside.

On the top step, Emerson's camping gear sat in a heap. She collected his belongings, aware of Michael's eyes lingering on her.

At last, he looked away and got into the car.

Chapter 8

As the Audi sped away, the full force of seeing Michael struck hard. Darcy was still recovering from the shock when she noticed movement inside her car.

She'd parked the Honda Accord in the shade to the right of the mansion. In the back seat, Samson stretched his arms with drowsy abandon. Dreadlocks swinging, he peered out the window. Noticing her on the top step, he got out and loped across the driveway. Amazement marked his features as he appraised the three-story Georgian mansion. He looked like a kid who'd woken up in Disney World.

Darcy hurried down the steps. Given that her mother had just fended off Tippi's evil eye—not to mention the old woman's spicy aggression—there was no telling how she'd react to another unsanctioned guest.

Samson craned his neck to study the house's roofline and arched, Palladian-style windows. "*This* is where you grew up? You never said you were rich."

"I'm not rich."

"Are you stupid? This place is bigger than a hotel. Biggest place I've seen outside of the convention center in North Charleston. You could park this thing next to all those mansions on Charleston's Rainbow Row and put the other places to shame. Does Latrice live here with your mama and Emerson?"

"Latrice pulls down a generous salary to tolerate my mother. All the gold in Fort Knox wouldn't bribe her into living here." Darcy stole a glance at Rosalind, who was gesturing wildly in Latrice's face. For her part, the housekeeper was doing a fine impersonation of a ticking time bomb. It was anyone's guess if she'd explode before Rosalind became aware of the new intrusion and went off like a Roman candle herself. "Unfortunately for Emerson, he can't move out until he grows up."

At the mention of his name, Emerson darted past the arguing women. Slipping out the door, he came down the steps.

Samson lit up a thousand-watt smile. "Little man." He took Emerson's hand and shook it heartily. "Glad to see you're home. Your Aunt Darcy was mighty worried."

"You're friends with my aunt?" Curiosity and surprise fought for prominence on her nephew's face.

"Best friends. I'm helping her find her North Star."

"There's only one North Star. No one gets to own it."

"You're wrong, little man. We've all got a star in the heavens, one made special just for us. I'm helping Darcy find hers 'cause it'll lead me to *my* star. We've got what you call a spiritual connection."

Emerson wrinkled his nose. "I like stars," he said, apparently unable to digest the strange explanation. "I've never heard of having a special one."

"Trust me, it's up there somewhere. Keep your heart open. That'll help you find it."

Emerson studied the tiny shells woven into Samson's dreads. "How do you get your hair to grow like that?"

"My dreads don't come out of my head all done up. A lady in Charleston does the styling. Took her hours to finish."

"She's your stylist?"

"I guess so. She made me pay fifty bucks for the look." Samson twirled a fuzzy lock around his finger, then let it swing free. "The sitting around is boring. By the time she got my hair all twisted up, I was itchy to leave."

"Are you in high school?"

"I graduated in May."

"You're really short." Emerson hesitated. Then he added, "But that's okay. Mr. Leonetti says boys keep growing for a long time. He's the gym teacher at my school."

"He says boys grow past my age?"

"Sure. You're not very old." Having dispensed the comforting advice, Emerson rose on the tips of his tennis shoes. "Want to see my bedroom? I have a new Nintendo Switch."

Darcy grinned. An undersized teenager and an eight-year-old awaiting his first big growth spurt: she wasn't fully on board with Samson's notions about special stars, but this was clearly a match made in heaven. She never would have guessed he'd bond instantly with Emerson.

"Do you have *The Legend of Zelda*?" Samson asked. "I like that game."

"C'mon! We can play."

Rosalind appeared in the doorway. "Emerson." She swatted at the silver tendrils coming loose from her chignon. "You are not allowed to socialize ten minutes after being on the lam. You're in trouble, young man."

The warning had zero effect on the boy's fizzy mood. "Why don't you let me out on bail while we're entertaining guests? Have you invited Aunt Darcy and Samson to stay with us?"

"They're leaving." Smiling tightly, she regarded Samson. "My apologies. We haven't been properly introduced."

"No, ma'am."

"A pleasure, I'm sure."

"Thank you, ma'am." The ice in her gaze made Samson stumble into a posture between a bow and a curtsy. Darcy resolved that if he decided to genuflect before the intimidating judge, she would drag him to his feet.

He was still quivering when Emerson thrust out his chin. "*Why* are they leaving? I want them to stay."

"Your aunt has a previous engagement, and I'm still waiting for an explanation. Should we discuss a suitable punishment? I'm leaning toward removing all electronics from your bedroom."

Amazingly, the threat of punishment didn't make Emerson back down. "Why can't they stay with us? I've got a whole summer vacation with nothing to do."

"Your aunt isn't welcome here. Please don't ask for the details. I will not share them with you."

At the rebuke, Emerson lifted high on the toes of his tennis shoes. He dropped back down. "Fine. Have it your way, Grandmother. Then I'm leaving with Aunt Darcy. She's my family too." He regarded Darcy. "I'm not bad all the time. You should adopt me."

She grinned. "I'd like that."

The ultimatum shuddered across her mother's shoulders. She looked like a panting bull trapped behind the gates of Pamplona. Emerson, it turned out, was a fine matador.

Darcy smirked. *Welcome to Spain.*

Rosalind's nostrils flared. "That's enough." For perhaps the first time in her long and distinguished life, she had been bested by a child—one she clearly loved. "You win, Emerson. Shall we all come into the house?"

A thorny silence followed them into the foyer. Latrice stood in the middle of the marble expanse, wringing her hands. Darcy trekked in behind Samson. She suffered the unheroic notion of finding the nearest window and jumping through.

Latrice asked, "What are we doing now?"

Rosalind inhaled with ill-concealed pique. "Ask my grandson. He's presiding over these strange proceedings."

The housekeeper wagged a finger. "Emerson, you scared me something awful."

"I didn't mean to."

"What a heap of nonsense. How do you think I feel every time you sneak off?"

"Bad?" The boy seemed to view the question as a test.

"That's putting it mildly. I worry myself sick every time you disappear. Don't do it again." She broke out a big smile. "Would you like blueberry pancakes? I'll whip up a batch."

"No, thank you. I'm not hungry. Tippi keeps all sorts of cookies in her suite at Nella's house. We finished them all."

Snapping up her wrist, Rosalind glanced at her watch. "You were eating cookies at seven in the morning? Sugar is *not* a breakfast food."

"I wanted clam linguine. Tippi couldn't sneak it upstairs. Nella caught her."

"How ridiculous. Linguine isn't a breakfast food either."

Darcy watched the interplay with rising agitation. Usually her mother was faster on the uptake.

At last, the full import of her grandson's remarks blazed in Rosalind's eyes. "You've been at the Varanos' *all* this time? In their *house*?"

"Not the whole time," Emerson said. "Yesterday Tippi saw me coming out of Nella's barn. She snuck me into the house."

"Were Nella and Michael privy to this?"

"Privy?" Emerson bit at his lips. "I don't remember that word."

"It doesn't matter," Darcy interjected. She offered an encouraging smile. "Grandmother wants to know if Nella and Michael knew you were in the house."

"We didn't tell them. Tippi didn't think they'd understand."

Rosalind said, "Tippi devised the plan to hide you in her suite? I'm astonished she possessed the mental capacity. At her age, most of the wiring in her brain has turned to pudding."

"Not all of it," Darcy put in.

Her mother lanced her with a vicious glance as Emerson said, "I didn't want to come home yet, Grandmother. Tippi said she didn't mind how long I stayed with her."

"I can't believe you stayed with her at all. *My* grandson," she said, releasing an indignant breath, "*camping* inside the Varano household. Haven't I told you to stay on our side of the fence? You are *never* to set foot inside Nella Varano's house again."

"I'm sorry. I thought if I stayed out long enough . . ."

The words died away. It was clear he didn't understand *why* the location of his hideout mattered. Darcy sighed with relief. He knew only not to stray onto the Varanos' property—an injunction he'd ignored.

She caught the thread of something else. "Emerson, what did you think would happen if you stayed out long enough? Were you trying to . . . I don't know . . . make Grandmother *do* something?"

He studied his feet.

Latrice inched past Samson with a look of worry. "Darcy, hold on."

"It's okay, Latrice. Let me handle this." Bending slightly, she went eye to eye with her nephew. "What did you want Grandmother to do? Don't be embarrassed. You can tell me."

"I'm not sure I should."

"Relax, kiddo. If she tries to slap more years on your sentence, I'll take the matter up on appeal."

"Oh, all right. I wanted Grandmother to let you come visit." He gave Darcy a bashful glance. "Latrice told me Grandmother wouldn't let you come home unless she got really scared."

"You disappeared so I'd come back?" Darcy whispered.

Her mother expelled a furious gasp.

With a shrug, her nephew lowered his eyes. "Latrice told me lots of stories about you. Like how you climbed trees almost faster than me when you were a kid. And that you were funny. She said you once made her laugh so hard, she spit Coke across the stove. I wanted to know if you were nice like she said." A fine blush crawled up his neck as he added, "I stayed hidden to see if Grandmother would get worried enough to let you come back."

"Of all the ridiculous—" Rosalind glared at her housekeeper. "What other ideas have you put in his head?"

Latrice frowned. "This is your fault, Rosalind. Don't you see? He wanted to meet his aunt, get to know her. I didn't expect him to come up with an actual plan to bring her home."

"Naturally a child with his intelligence would come up with a plan. I don't believe this. My unfaithful housekeeper egging him on, and Tippi getting in on the act." Stiffly, Rosalind turned back to her grandson. "Emerson, you are not allowed inside Nella Varano's house. Not today, or tomorrow. Not ever. How many times have I told you to stay *off* her property?"

Darcy growled with frustration. "You've made your expectations clear. He gets it." It was cruel to belabor the point. "He came back, didn't he? He's safe. What does it matter where he stayed?"

"It matters because I will not allow him to roam about at all hours. Nor will he associate with the people next door."

"Give it a rest, Mother. Tippi fed him cookies. It's not a crime."

"How typical. Egg him on."

"I'm not egging him on!"

The retort rolled across the foyer like thunder. Samson, wide-eyed, cleared his throat.

"Does anyone mind if I go with Emerson to play Nintendo?" He inched toward the stairwell. "If you ladies are gearing up for a catfight, I'd rather not watch."

The remark was perfectly timed. "I want to see Emerson's bedroom too," Darcy said, turning her back on her mother. She winked at her nephew. "What do you say, Emerson? Can I tag along?"

$\sim$

On the mansion's second floor, the excited boy raced into a bedroom once decorated in sedate browns and muddy grays for guests staying at the Goodridge estate. Now the room was more welcoming—a perfect refuge for a growing boy.

Large, phosphorescent stars covered the ceiling. They rained down an accent wall painted midnight blue, behind the queen-size bed. The other walls, lighter blue, showed off wooden shelves neatly filled with a boy's treasures—glittery rocks, an iPad, stacks of books, a pocket telescope, and a dizzying variety of board games. Approaching the large double windows, Darcy inhaled the summer breeze whispering across the room.

Beside the iMac computer, a crystal paperweight refracted light across the walls. Picking it up, Emerson tossed it from hand to hand. "Do you like my room, Aunt Darcy?"

"It's great." Aware that her opinion mattered a great deal, she spiked her voice with animation. "When I was growing up, this room was used for guests. I like what you've done with it."

"Latrice helped. We redid everything last year. I even got a new bed, a bigger one. We got rid of the toys I don't play with anymore."

"You needed a room for an older kid."

With pride, he nodded. "I'll be in fourth grade this fall."

Samson came inside. "Look at this place." Turning in a slow circle, he whistled at the bedroom's generous dimensions. "You've got this whole place to yourself?" His attention lifted to the ceiling and the glowing constellation raining down behind the bed. "How'd you get the stars up there?"

"It was simple. They're adhesive."

"Man, you did a good job. I like the design."

"It was Latrice's idea. We stuck the stars up together."

Darcy asked, "Grandmother didn't mind?"

"She wasn't happy. She said the stars would deface the ceiling. I didn't know what she meant." The boy tapped the intimidatingly large dictionary beside his computer. "I had to look up the word *deface.*"

"How did you get her to come around?"

"Latrice talked to her. I'm not sure how, but she made Grandmother change her mind." Emerson slipped off his shoes and placed them in the closet. There was something pitiful about the way he set the tennis shoes down, taking care to line them up. From over his shoulder, he cast a glance. "How are you and Samson friends? You're not very close in age."

"We met on a job, in South Carolina," Darcy explained. "We worked for a tourist company on Charleston Harbor."

Emerson noticed a stray baseball on the floor. "Why didn't you make friends with ladies your own age?" Picking it up, he tossed the ball from hand to hand.

The direct approach nearly made her laugh. She'd been just as direct at his age. "Annoyingly blunt," her mother used to say.

"I guess I don't make friends easily."

"Me either." He tossed the ball into the closet.

"Do you have *any* friends at school?" she asked, fearful of the answer.

"Not really. Most of the kids think I'm weird. Grandmother doesn't help. At school functions, she reprimands the PTO ladies or Mr. Paternic, the principal. She always finds something to complain about."

Samson shook his head. "You're both pathetic. There's nothing easier than making friends. Just put yourself out there and act nice. Most people will show you their good side if you lay on enough sugar. There's nothing to it."

Her nephew lifted his brows. A lonely boy, desperate for a primer on friendship. Given his stilted home life, no wonder he needed lessons.

Coming to a decision, Darcy sat down on the bed. She patted the thick comforter, an attractive dark-blue fabric with silver thread running through. With amusement, she made out the glittery design—more stars, like the ones on the ceiling.

When Emerson joined her, she said, "Walk me through this. I'm not sure what you meant downstairs. Did you believe Grandmother would ask me to come to Ohio if you scared her by hiding out?"

"You're here, aren't you?"

Thanks to his impressive cunning, she was. "Why did you want me to come back now? I mean, why didn't you pull this stunt earlier? From what Latrice says, you've been sneaking out of the house since last year."

The question feathered worry across his features. Then his expression closed. The reaction put Darcy on alert. She suspected he was hiding something.

This wasn't the time to press for the details. They'd only just met. Better to forge a relationship first. Once he felt safe around her, he'd spill. No one shared painful secrets with a stranger.

"Out of curiosity, how long were you planning to stay hidden?" She posed the question lightly. "I mean, what if I hadn't heard?"

"Tippi would've let me stay in her rooms. It's basically an apartment."

It seemed odd, the familiar way he referred to the Varano women. *Tippi, Nella*—as if a long acquaintance had put him on a first-name basis with neighbors his grandmother despised. With the women Darcy had cherished before they were removed from her life. An unexpected sting of loss pierced her.

"You would have stayed hidden for days?" She swept a lock of wheat-colored hair from his brow, delighting in the softness of his skin. His hair color was a perfect match for hers, another poignant example of the family connection. "That sounds pretty boring."

"I'm glad it didn't take too long. Tippi's nice and all, but I got tired of watching TV and playing cards."

"She didn't mind if you hung around?"

"Not really. She wanted you to come home too."

"Emerson, this isn't my home."

"Why not? Why is Grandmother mad at you anyway?"

The question floated between them, unbound. A dreaded query—one of many Darcy knew she'd confront in the coming days.

Her nephew waited, the curiosity on his face mixing with unease. She wondered how to begin.

Chapter 9

There was no simple way to boil down years of rancor for a child's consumption. Darcy had begun sparring with Rosalind long before the accident that tore their family apart. She couldn't recall a time when she hadn't felt like the thorn to Elizabeth's rose, the uncultivated daughter her mother tolerated but never loved.

"Emerson, there are lots of reasons why I don't get along with Grandmother." Darcy flopped her hands into her lap. "I wasn't a good kid like you."

"You were bad?"

"I was mouthy, for sure. I argued with her over the stupidest things. And my room was always a mess. Mud tramped across the carpet, the bed never made—I hated being indoors. One day, she came home from the courthouse and found three frogs sitting on my pillow."

Her nephew's eyes lit with glee. "You brought *live* frogs into the house?"

"Grandmother pitched a fit."

"What did she do?"

"Kiddo, I spent half of my childhood grounded."

More than half, she mused. Rosalind had characterized her behavior as "mindlessly delinquent."

The Road She Left Behind

"Back then, she worked long hours. There was always some major trial demanding her attention. Your grandfather worked a lot too. He was a doctor in Chagrin Falls. He had a big practice."

"In vascular medicine," Emerson supplied. "He took care of people's circulatory system—how your blood goes through your veins and arteries. Grandmother says everyone called him Dr. Jack."

"It's true."

"Were you always in trouble?"

"Not on purpose. Mostly I got tired of waiting for my parents to come home and say 'hello' before Latrice made us go to bed. I guess you know your mom was a year younger than I." When he nodded, she added, "Elizabeth was much more patient. She'd go right upstairs if bedtime rolled around and our parents still weren't home. Sometimes I'd sneak back outside to play."

"You snuck out of the house? Like I do?"

The observation felt like a trap—one she'd willingly strolled into.

"Your mother never did," she rushed on. "She always followed the rules. You should be more like her."

"I do follow Grandmother's rules . . . sometimes." In his lap, Emerson steepled his fingers. Then he lowered his voice an octave to mimic adult speech. "A boy my age should have a pet. Latrice suggested I request a hamster. I promised to clean its cage and everything. I'd very much like a puppy, but it's out of the question. Grandmother says a puppy will soil her Aubusson carpets. She bought those carpets in France, and won't let a mongrel destroy them."

"You strike me as very responsible. I'm sure you'd take good care of a dog."

"I love animals. Dogs are my favorite."

"Should I talk to her? Do some old-fashioned lobbying?" Darcy suspected he knew the word. On the nearest shelf, a tome in navy blue glared out: *The United States Congress: A History.*

"You can't change her mind. Not unless she stops being mad at you." With disconcerting maturity, he gave her knee a reassuring pat. "Thank you for offering."

"I guess I'm not the best person to lobby on your behalf," she agreed, wishing for the courage to enfold him in her arms. The combination of his baby face and feigned maturity was so darn cute. Heartbreaking too. A child practiced at mimicking adult behavior knew how to hide—and suppress—his emotions.

"It's okay. Latrice got me some magazines with pictures of dogs. I keep them in my desk." Dismissing the subject, he looked up. A gentle yearning crossed his face. "What was my mom like?"

Remorse pricked Darcy. There was no adequate way to summarize the kind, talented sister she'd cherished.

"You know what? You sure take after her," she assured him, lacing her voice with animation. She'd deprived Emerson of a mother. She'd do her best to salve the wound with beautiful images of the gentle soul he'd never have the opportunity to meet. "She also loved animals. When Elizabeth was your age, she wanted a bunny rabbit more than anything. I'm talking about a big-time obsession with soft, furry, nose-wiggling bunnies."

"She did? No one ever told me that."

"There was nothing she wanted more. A white bunny rabbit—it was all she talked about."

"Grandmother vetoed the idea because of the poops?" he asked. When she nodded, he sighed. "Why can't someone invent a pet that doesn't poop? It would solve everything."

Samson chuckled. "You Goodridges have a weird thing about cleanliness. If you don't want a pet dropping poops everywhere, keep it on a leash!"

"Tell it to the judge," Darcy said wryly. "The Honorable Rosalind Goodridge lives in fear of stepping on turds." Dropping the subject, she told Emerson, "You know, your grandparents used to have big parties on Saturday nights. They had lots of friends from the country club who would come over. Your mom and I used to sit on the stairwell together listening to the music until our bedtime." She declined to add that her parents' closest friends had been the Varanos next door. Mr. Varano's heart attack, and the mysterious feud that began after his death, changed everything.

"What else did my mom like?"

"Playing the piano. She was very talented."

"She also wanted to be a lawyer, right?"

"And a judge someday."

"Just like Grandmother," Emerson supplied. "And my mom liked to paint."

"She loved watercolors. I'm sure Grandmother has shown you Elizabeth's work." Darcy paused to inhale a steadying breath.

Staying away this long had been cruel. She was a living conduit to the mother Emerson craved, a walking history of Elizabeth's successes and mishaps.

How could I have been so blind?

She wondered how much of her self-loathing was rooted in the hasty decision she'd made to leave Ohio.

If I'd stayed to replace the mother Emerson lost, would I have found my own path to healing?

Catching his bashful gaze, she said, "Your mother would've loved your bedroom. She was very organized. Just like you."

"Did she keep a schedule?" Hopping off the bed, Emerson scampered to his desk. He pulled out a black vinyl DayMinder as weirdly mature as the book on the US Congress. "I keep all sorts of stuff in my organizer. What time to wake up, when I can play video games, how much time I'll read. Since I dropped out of my summer activities, Grandmother has me take tests."

Samson gaped at him. "She tests you during summer vacation, like a teacher?"

"On Tuesdays and Fridays."

"That ought to be illegal."

"Tell it to the judge," Emerson said, mimicking Darcy's smart-ass remark.

Samson crossed his arms in disgust. "A boy shouldn't do anything in the summer but sleep in late and goof off." He sent Darcy a look of irritation. "While we were driving here, why didn't you tell me about your mama's job? Is she a mean judge? With all the talk of summer homework and no pets for little boys, I've got a bad feeling. She put away a lot of black men in her time? Hit me with the truth. I can take it."

There was real fear in his eyes. "Relax." She rose from the bed. "She doesn't have you on her docket."

"I don't know what she's got me on, but it's not her good side."

"Welcome to my world."

With a grunt, he leaned against the wall. "There's too many black men in prison. Make one bad move and the system comes down on you. It's not right."

Emerson gave a sympathetic nod. "The judicial system *does* need reform."

"Start by telling your grandma to stop locking my people up."

"She won't listen to me. I haven't passed the bar."

Darcy slipped the DayMinder from her nephew's fingers. She glanced at Samson. "Let's keep our political views to ourselves, shall we?" She returned the DayMinder to the drawer. "While you're at it, don't spout any liberal opinions while we're in my mother's domicile. She'll evict us."

Latrice appeared in the doorway, a stack of linens cradled in her arms. "Darcy, why don't you help me make the beds?" She gave Emerson a warning look. "Don't even think about Nintendo. Your grandmother hasn't ruled yet on whether it's best to strip your room of electronics. Do yourself a favor and don't give her any ideas."

The boy's face fell. Samson looked equally disappointed.

"Has Emerson shown you his building set?" Latrice gave Samson a friendly smile. "The rods are magnetic—coolest thing you'll ever see."

At the suggestion, Emerson trudged to the closet. Dragging out a large box, he glanced at Samson. "Do you like to build stuff? We can make a skyscraper."

"Sure."

They were digging handfuls of multicolored rods from the box as Darcy followed Latrice from the room. Chuckling softly, Latrice started down the hallway.

Darcy gave her a quizzical look. "What's so funny?"

"Samson, acting like a boy your nephew's age."

"I worry about his immaturity. A lamb set loose in a world full of wolves. I wasn't a sophisticate at eighteen, but I don't recall being *that* innocent."

"You weren't. By eighteen, you had enough common sense to know how to protect yourself. Samson *is* a lamb." The housekeeper paused before the first guest bedroom. The sweet-scented linens she carried perfumed the air. "A child raised in foster care doesn't receive much in the way of guidance. I'll wager Samson lived in a dozen foster homes before he graduated from high school."

"He did, from what I've gathered. He's aged out of the system, which is how he ended up on a road trip with me. He's been feeling adrift and hinting about leaving Charleston with me for weeks now. At first, the idea didn't seem like a good one. But I changed my mind." She grinned. "I'm glad for the chance to help him out. Samson is a great kid. He's the only real friend I've made since leaving Ohio."

"You're doing the right thing. If you didn't lend a hand, when would he get the chance to learn the lessons we all need to become adults? Being dumped out of foster care must be frightening. No wonder he's clingy with you."

Darcy winced. They were close, but she wouldn't characterize his behavior as clingy. The word implied an unhealthy level of dependency. In fact, the possibility gave her pause. True, Samson *was* attached to her. Before they left Charleston, his visits to her apartment were a daily affair. When they weren't hanging out or working together at Big Bud's, he rang her more often than a robocall.

At her puzzlement, Latrice scowled. "Darcy, wake up. Samson views you as part mother, part big sister. I doubt he's experienced much closeness with anyone else. He's learning how to become an adult by emulating you."

"Shouldn't you save the psychological analysis until you're better acquainted with him? You only had a few phone chats while we drove here. You've really just met him this morning."

"I have eyes. I know what I see."

Troubled by the observation, she followed Latrice into the guest bedroom. The prospect of the dreamy youth viewing her as a role model didn't appeal. The abundant mistakes she'd made disqualified her for the job.

"I'll tell you something else about kids who grow up in foster homes," Latrice said. "Many have special needs of one sort or another. Tax dollars rarely trickle down to the neediest children."

"Since when do you know so much about the subject?"

"I know more than you think. When you were in sixth grade and Elizabeth was in fifth, I started looking into adopting a special-needs child. Not a baby—they usually find a home quickly. I was considering a toddler or a child close to school age."

The disclosure startled Darcy. "Why didn't you go through with the plan?"

"Water under the bridge."

"I really want to know."

Marching to the bed, Latrice snapped out the sheet. "Are you going to stand there, or help?"

Scrambling to the opposite side, Darcy grabbed the sheet's fluttering hem. "You would've been a great mother. The best."

"I *was* a great mother."

"You still are. Look at how you insisted on our yearly Christmas phone calls. It always made me feel better during the loneliest time of the year. And when I was a kid, I never would've survived my hypercritical mother and absentee father without your butterscotch candies and 'chin up' speeches. You're great. The best."

"*Mm-hmm.*"

"Tell me why you didn't go through with the adoption. I can understand why you skipped marriage—guys can be a major PITA. But any kid lucky enough to have been adopted by you would've hit the jackpot."

"Stop buttering me up. I don't want to talk about it."

A blanket lay on the dresser, neatly folded. Darcy hurried to fetch it.

"Yes, you do," she said, determined to wear the housekeeper down. Latrice had a long history of giving in with enough sugar-coated prodding. "C'mon, tell me. I want to hear."

When she handed off the blanket, Latrice stalked around the side of the bed. With swift strokes, she smoothed it down.

"After the falling-out between your mother and Nella, I couldn't bring myself to go through with the adoption," she said.

"Why would my mother's sudden hatred of Nella stop you from adopting a child?"

Pity competed with the affection brimming in the housekeeper's eyes. "You were twelve years old when your mother broke your heart. After she decided you couldn't remain friends with Michael, you sobbed for days. Puberty is hard enough for a child. You'd been through too much, and you needed me. So I dropped the idea."

"You didn't have a child of your own . . . because of *me*?"

"Oh, Darcy. You were crushed when your mother cut Michael out of your life. You'd been thick as thieves since you were in first grade and he was in second. Closer, at times, than you were with Elizabeth. Not that she wasn't also devastated."

"It's true. Elizabeth loved Michael as much as I did. He taught her to play Monopoly and ride a bike."

"He was like a big brother. Your best friend, and the brother she'd always wanted."

"I know."

Leaving Darcy adrift in the center of the room, Latrice went to the closet. She produced a comforter as sweet-smelling as the linens.

She rolled the comforter out across the bed. "I couldn't begin to understand why Rosalind suddenly despised Nella," she said, lost in the reverie. "It made no sense. They'd been close since you and Michael were babies. Then she came up with that rule out of the blue. Since she was done with Nella, you couldn't have Michael. My heart broke for him too. He'd lost his father, and racing around in the forest with you was the best medicine for his grieving heart."

"Mr. Varano was a nice man. He already had gray hair when we were kids, but his age never stopped him from playing with us. Michael loved his dad."

"Yes, he did. I doubt he ever thought twice about the age difference between his parents until that awful heart attack. Of course, Mr. Varano *was* a lot older than Nella. He'd been having heart trouble since Michael was a baby. Sad, those May-December romances. Rosalind should've been lending Nella a shoulder to lean on, not treating her like a pariah. She certainly shouldn't have taken her wrath out on you and Michael."

"No, she shouldn't have," Darcy agreed. "Michael's grandmother was still living in Little Italy at the time—I remember he was staying with Tippi for the weekend when my mother handed down the edict. He left for Little Italy on a Friday, and my mother told me on Saturday that I couldn't play with him anymore."

A bright flash of anger sparked in Latrice's eyes. "You weren't allowed to see him when he came home on Sunday? Just one last time?"

"That's right." At the housekeeper's dismay over forgetting the details, Darcy added, "You didn't always work weekends then. You weren't here when my mother told me."

"You're sure?"

The reason for Latrice's faulty memory was obvious. "The Friday Michael left with Tippi for Little Italy, you only worked until lunchtime," Darcy reminded her. "The root canal, remember? You came back on Monday with a tender jaw—and more trouble in the Goodridge household than you needed."

"I'd forgotten about my root canal. Not something I'd ever like to repeat." She shook her head, the lines on her brow deepening. "Poor Tippi—I'm sure she was just as upset as Michael when she brought him home and heard about Rosalind's decision. She had begun taking Michael some weekends to give Nella time alone to grieve. You didn't like it, and neither did he. You used to play together from dawn to dusk."

They were silent for a moment. Then Darcy said, "I hated my mother for taking Michael away from me."

"For all the good it did. You found each other again, didn't you? All grown up, and smart enough to keep Rosalind in the dark."

"Our timing wasn't great."

"No, it wasn't. Elizabeth had just become a new mother, and your parents didn't handle the change well. Between their arguments and your sister learning how to care for Emerson, this house wasn't the happiest place." With fierce energy, Latrice plumped up the pillows. "But I was glad when Michael came back into your life. I've always wondered if you would've fallen in love if there'd been enough time."

Even now, contemplating the secret romance that had ended on the night of the accident was painful. The "what if" questions were difficult to face.

"We didn't date long enough for the relationship to deepen." There was much that had happened during those months that she'd never shared with Latrice. During their brief yearly phone calls, the topic had never come up. Which made her add, "I'm sure Michael has never forgiven me. I left right after the funeral."

"Didn't you say goodbye?"

"I didn't."

"Oh, Darcy. I assumed you'd at least . . ." Latrice rubbed her lips together. Quickly, she composed her face. With an air of resignation, she reached for the pillowcases. "Let's put Samson in this room," she said in a businesslike tone, sparing Darcy further torment. "You're planning on a nice long visit, aren't you? Emerson could use the companionship."

"We'll stay for a week or two." She caught the pillowcase Latrice tossed over. Then she glanced around the bedroom. "Is this a good idea? Staying at the house instead of booking hotel rooms? My mother was in the process of throwing me out when Emerson made his grand entrance."

"For your information, your mother *asked me* to make up the guest rooms. She even instructed me on which linens to use. The good ones, in case you're curious."

No doubt as a gesture to Samson's comfort, Darcy mused. *Mother is nothing if not a gracious hostess.*

"Where is she now?"

"In her room, showering. She just got off the phone with the police department. After sounding the all clear, she informed me not to expect her home until dinnertime."

"She's leaving right after her grandson has relinquished his life on the run? Where is she going?"

Latrice heaved out a sigh. "How should I know? I'm in charge of everything inside these walls. When I spread to outside, I'll alert you."

"Question." Darcy tossed the last pillow to the top of the bed, her mouth suddenly dry. "A few questions, actually."

"Fire away."

"When did my mother retire? She always planned to stay on the bench until she was too deaf to hear cases."

"She came to a decision a few days ago. She was on a leave of absence before then." Latrice settled her hands on her hips. "I can't tell you why she quit. Every time I nudge her for details, she bares her teeth like a rabid dog."

"It's bizarre. She wouldn't quit without a good reason." One Latrice clearly wasn't privy to. Later, a Google search was in order. Setting the mystery aside for the moment, Darcy forced herself on. "When Tippi brought Emerson home, I saw Michael in the driveway." She swallowed. "He saw me too."

"The poor man. I should've given him some warning."

"You should've given *me* some warning. Last I heard, Michael was in Chicago, happily married, and moving his way up the ladder in banking."

"I don't know about the 'happily' part. Less than a year after he moved to Chicago, he married a woman just like himself. Career-driven, practical. Who wants to marry their clone?"

Michael, obviously.

That he'd married less than a year after her departure from Ohio struck Darcy as a rebound move—one she knew she was in no position to judge.

"How long is he here? Did he bring his wife?"

"He's not just visiting. After the divorce, he moved back into his mother's place."

"Wait. What?"

Waving off the question, Latrice said, "He has a new business. Custom cabinetry. He's set up shop in Nella's barn. There are so many orders coming in, he needs to begin hiring employees. I'll say one thing for Michael Varano: everything he touches turns to gold."

The news was overwhelming. Michael was divorced? And he'd given up a career in banking to build cabinetry? Perhaps that made sense. His late father, an architect, had taught him the basics of carpentry long ago. His keen financial acumen aside, Michael had always liked working with his hands.

"Why am I only hearing about all of this now?" she asked.

Latrice withered her with a look. "If you're going to roam the earth like the prodigal daughter, there *are* details you'll miss."

Chapter 10

A cacophony of electric saws and pneumatic nail guns punctuated the air. More than a dozen men, setting in stud walls and framing in windows, filled the expanse like bees.

Striding past, Michael entered the large, empty space that would become Carl and Lizbeth Tinley's kitchen. The Tinleys, presently living on the east side of Cleveland with their two young children, were looking forward to Geauga County's slower pace. They'd purchased a run-down duplex within walking distance of Chagrin Falls's picturesque town center. They'd torn down the old structure and planned to move into their new McMansion before the last apples were plucked from northeast Ohio's bountiful orchards.

Michael was still undecided about taking on a job of this magnitude. He was pacing around the generous space when Kyle Mandel, the contractor, shouted over the noise in the living room.

Despite Kyle's girth, he easily dodged two carpenters struggling with a sheet of plywood. Entering the framed-in kitchen, he gave Michael a quick nod.

"Can you do it?" Kyle's bulbous nose twitched as he waved at the sawdust filtering through the air. "My team will set in all the cabinets. All you need to do is build."

"How long?"

"To finish the cabinetry? I can give you until October first."

"Firm deadline?"

"I'm not missing the bonus, pal. The Tinleys are paying hand-somely to move in before the first snowfall."

Michael scraped back the curls from his brow. "When do you need a decision?" The job was tempting, if intimidating. From his estimate of the kitchen's dimensions, the Tinleys were looking at three full walls of cabinetry plus a center island approximately eight feet long. By far his biggest job to date. "May I have until the end of the week to decide?"

"You have until tomorrow morning. Keep your bid reasonable, and the job is yours. If you're not on board, I'm talking to a custom outfit in Pittsburgh. I'd rather give the work to a local guy, even if his grandmother takes my uncle Paulie at five-card stud on a weekly basis."

"Tell your uncle to stay away from Tippi. Honestly, Kyle—I'm positive she cheats. She'll steal his last dime."

The contractor's nose twitched again. "Too late." Pulling a handker-chief from his pocket, he caught a blustery sneeze. "She's already stolen his heart. A major crush in your eighties? Right? But what can I do?"

"Start by warning him," Michael joked. "Tippi's a heartbreaker with a gambling obsession."

His smartphone buzzed. He picked up before having the good sense to scan the display panel.

"Hey, buddy. No, I'm at a job site." Embarrassed, he held up a finger, which Kyle regarded with ill-concealed impatience. "Emerson. No. Not until I speak with your grandmother. It's only been three days. Sure, I miss you too. Listen, we'll talk later . . ."

By the time he hung up, the contractor's impatience had evolved into a mild sense of wonder. "Was that who I think it was?"

"Geauga County's favorite runaway? Yeah."

"You've got to be kidding me."

"Kyle, he lives next door to my mother. Not exactly a state secret."

"Why does the hanging judge's grandson have *you* on speed dial?"

When Michael shrugged, in no mood to explain his growing friendship with the boy, the contractor grinned. "Word to the wise, pal. Don't piss off Judge Goodridge. Some of the officers at the PD are still licking their wounds. Like it's *their* fault Emerson keeps running off. Get on Rosalind's bad side and she'll take a chain saw to your ego—or your permits."

"Thanks for the tip."

"Did you hear how she cussed out the PD in two jurisdictions? Chagrin Falls *and* Hunting Valley."

And the ditzy young receptionist in the Falls, Michael recalled. On day two of the Emerson drama, Rosalind had submitted the girl to a ten-minute tirade. After the judge stormed out of the precinct, the receptionist broke out in a case of hives.

Kyle, hungry for details, licked his lips. "Why is her grandson calling you?" Evidently, he was enjoying the discomfiture crowding in on Michael.

"I'm teaching him the basics of carpentry. No power tools, although he's itching to try them."

"Hold on. You're doing craft projects with Emerson? I thought Rosalind doesn't like your family."

"She doesn't."

"Man, this is good." Kyle landed a good-natured punch on his arm. "What are you building with him?"

"A bird feeder. For Rosalind. I don't want Emerson to keep having to sneak over to visit, but she won't take my calls. Hard to get the situation aboveboard when she keeps hanging up on me." Michael crossed his arms. He didn't need to defend his relationship with the child. Whatever had soured between his mother and Rosalind, it shouldn't affect an eight-year-old boy.

"How long has this been going on—the friendship between you and the kid?"

"Since last year, when I moved back. He started coming around after school and on weekends. We hit it off. Emerson is a nice kid. He's lonely. It can't be easy growing up without parents."

"The whole thing is sad, especially what happened to Elizabeth. There wasn't much left to put in the casket." Kyle fell silent for a long moment. Then he said, "The women over at the funeral home still go out sometimes and leave flowers."

"Nice of them," Michael murmured, wishing to drop the subject.

Within days of the funeral, he'd left for Chicago. Packed his bags and dispelled every question about Darcy taking off or where she'd gone. Under the circumstances, moving forward seemed the best option. The sad events in Ohio were quickly overtaken by the hustle of investment banking in a larger city.

Since moving back to Ohio, he'd discovered an unsavory truth. Although he'd packed up and moved on, the longtime residents of Geauga County were less fortunate. The accident on the treacherous curves of Chagrin River Road lingered in public memory like sediment no one thought to wash away. There was now a caution light at the bend in the road where the accident had taken place, and six new streetlights had been placed at intervals on the once-dark stretch of road.

After promising a quote by morning, Michael left the work site. He climbed into his truck with his emotions in flux.

Whatever Darcy had once represented in his life, she was now a stranger. The impish girl from his childhood with leaves tangled in the sunlit strands of her hair—the girl who'd pretended not to notice the stutter that beat down his ego until he quelled it in junior high—she no longer existed. Gone too was the slender young woman with a thoroughbred's gait and a million reasons why they shouldn't explore the relationship they'd ignited when they met once again, quite by accident.

A blustery spring day in Chagrin Falls and Darcy, a few months short of finishing college, had been roaming the streets in a skintight knit dress of cobalt blue, peering into shop windows, her lips rimmed in a pretty pink color. A full decade had passed since the abrupt severing of their childhood friendship. Michael was too busy scrolling through his phone to notice her blocking his path.

Walking too fast, he collided with her. He'd been hurrying back to First Ohio Bank, where he'd secured a job after graduating from Case Western.

Five inches taller and a good forty pounds heavier than Darcy, he almost knocked her off her feet. Pitching backward on her strappy sandals, she cried out. He swooped an arm behind her waist just in time. The cell phone crashed to the pavement. A minor loss.

He held her in an awkward imitation of a lover's embrace, her back arching beneath his palms. Heat crawled across his scalp as her mossy-green eyes sparked with recognition. When she realized the man holding her was the boy she'd once known, she'd laughed.

Michael dismissed the memory as the light before the ice cream shop turned red. Tourists in bright summer outfits began crossing the street. A vendor stood near the curb selling bags of popcorn, the savory scent of butter heavy in the air. Across the street, in the park, children swerved their bikes around adults strolling near the metal railing and the pounding thunder of the Chagrin River.

The light changed. Michael turned toward Hunting Valley—and home.

As the sounds of the mighty river fell away, he allowed his thoughts to wend back in an agonizing pursuit he rarely condoned. How he'd climbed over the park's railing at midnight with Darcy to watch the moon paint the churning Chagrin River a molten silver. Crickets sang in the dark. The melody was nearly drowned out by the rush of water leaping over rock. How he'd twined his hands in Darcy's long hair, eager for her neck to drift back and her lips to part.

The memory scorched him with regret. Like holding his palm over an open flame, the remembering.

He wondered if they'd both fallen in love during those short, stolen months. Or did he make the leap alone? If death hadn't broken their brief interlude, if the Goodridge family had remained whole, would his passion for Darcy have kept her in his life forever? In the bitter aftermath, he took the safest route away from heartache and built a new life. Through a marriage that was, more than anything else, a smart business arrangement for two busy professionals who enjoyed each other's company and the comfort of a steady sex life. Then came the divorce, a preordained event for a couple seeking convenience more than love.

Even after returning to Ohio, he held the conviction that he'd left Darcy solidly in the past.

Eight years later, he was no longer sure.

~

Tiptoeing past the guest room she occupied, Darcy hesitated outside her late sister's room. Since her arrival three days ago, the door to Elizabeth's bedroom had remained shut.

On the mansion's back forty, Emerson and Samson were tossing around a football. Yesterday, after her mother—apparently bored in her unwanted retirement—left for a massage at a local day spa, Darcy had taken her nephew and Samson into Chagrin Falls for ice cream and a stroll through the park. In retrospect, she should have cleared the excursion with her mother. When Rosalind arrived home, she made good on her threat to punish Emerson for running away. With Latrice's help, she removed all the electronics from his bedroom. Computer, iPad, laptop, Kindle Fire—Rosalind even removed the boy's Nintendo Switch and his camera. According to Latrice, the entire lot of devices now filled a corner of the master suite.

Last night, pity for her nephew encouraged Darcy to retrieve his smartphone. She undertook the operation while her mother sat alone in the living room, sipping a cocktail and watching the nightly news.

At some point, Rosalind would discover the missing contraband. Either she'd plunge Darcy into an icy hell of dark looks and silence or read her the riot act. There really was no telling.

Leave tomorrow's troubles for tomorrow.

Satisfied with the decision, she rested her hand on the doorknob to Elizabeth's room. Her heart thumped out of rhythm. Soon the boys would troop back into the house. Her mother was downstairs, in her small office adjacent to the library. If Darcy wanted a few minutes of privacy, she needed to go inside now.

Mustering up the courage, she opened the door.

She paused in the center of the darkened room. Her eyes drifting shut, she detected a lemony fragrance from a recent dusting. Then her heart stirred. Underneath, she caught the faintest whiff of cinnamon from the cheap drugstore perfume Elizabeth had often worn in college.

Feeling weightless, Darcy padded to the window and drew back the curtains. Bands of sunlight spilled across the familiar heart-shaped rug. Light pooled on the four-poster bed. Stuffed animals were neatly arranged on the ruffled pillows. Even when motherhood had forced Elizabeth to mature at lightning speed, she had refused to pack away the girlish accoutrements of childhood.

It was a sweet contrast to the bedroom directly across the hallway. In Darcy's childhood room, Rosalind had ripped out the wall-to-wall green carpeting and repainted the walls a soft blue. A sateen coverlet gleamed on the king-size bed. A chaise longue and an overstuffed chair were arranged by the window, as if waiting for the guests Rosalind no longer entertained.

Elizabeth's room was a clock stopped in time. Posters from the Harry Potter movies dominated the walls. On the dresser, a chubby pink jewelry box snuggled beside a photo album with half of the pages bare. Dust escaped from inside the album as Darcy turned the leaves. The photos commemorated Emerson's first months of life: in the hospital, pressed against his exhausted mother; sleeping in the bassinet in Elizabeth's bedroom; in the kitchen with his tiny face wrinkling as Darcy held him in an awkward embrace.

From behind, Latrice said, "It's a good sign."

Startled, Darcy flipped the album shut. "What is?"

"You, coming in here. I assumed it would take longer."

"Me too. I've been looking for a moment when no one was around."

Softly, Latrice shut the door behind her. "I'm glad you found one."

"This feels like a time machine transporting me back eight years. The only thing missing is the bassinet my sister used for Emerson."

"It's around here somewhere. In the attic, I'd guess." The memory of those difficult times deepened the lines around Latrice's mouth. "After you left Ohio, I moved into one of the guest bedrooms. I stayed here until Emerson started preschool. I didn't want him to go through another big transition. Once he started preschool, we filled out the schedule with babysitters. But I was still in charge most days."

"Who took care of the house?" With an energetic child to watch, Latrice couldn't have managed her original duties.

"That's when Rosalind first hired a cleaning service, to get the chores off my back. I was busy enough."

"What happened to your home in Chagrin Falls?" Latrice owned a sweet bungalow with yellow roses trailing across a white picket fence. "You found a renter?"

"The lady that owns the dry cleaners in the Falls. She rented the place until I was ready to move back in."

"I'm glad you didn't have to sell. I'm hoping for an invitation."

"Stop by whenever you'd like. Emerson loves to visit. It will do you both good to get out from under Rosalind's thumb."

"We will, thanks." Sliding open a dresser drawer, Darcy trailed fingertips across the neatly folded sweaters. Unable to resist, she withdrew a fuzzy purple sweater, one of her late sister's favorites. She pressed it to her face. Placing it back in the drawer, she asked, "Am I being silly?

Picking up Elizabeth's scent on her belongings makes me feel better. Almost like she's here."

"You're not silly, child. You miss your sister." With purposeful strides, Latrice went to the closet. She returned with a frayed sweatshirt, the old Cleveland Browns number Elizabeth used to sleep in. "Try this one." Her lips trembled as she held the sweatshirt out. "It was in the laundry room on the day of the accident. I hung it back up, unwashed, when your mother went to the funeral home to discuss the arrangements. I knew we'd need it someday."

"Oh, Latrice."

"Don't be shy." Eyes watering, she wagged the sweatshirt before Darcy. "I come in here sometimes just to hold this ratty old sweatshirt to my face. I can't seem to stop. It carries a brighter scent of your sister than anything else in the room."

The implication being that Latrice spent more time in Elizabeth's room than she preferred to admit.

Does she come in here to grieve privately? Does the ritual of running her hands across Elizabeth's belongings make the sorrow manageable?

Darcy hoped so.

Accepting the garment, she returned to the bed. She dipped her nose into the soft cloth. The act of breathing in her sister's scent was sacred. An undeserved reward, like a rainbow lifting above a summer storm.

The familiar cinnamon perfume wafted from the garment. Beneath it she detected the natural, woodsy aroma of Elizabeth's skin. The scent unlocked a dozen impressions in a tumbling rush. Elizabeth, climbing in beside Darcy in a sleeping bag as an owl hooted in the night; how their parents' long absences made their reliance on each other even stronger, an unbreakable bond that gave them both confidence. And the sweetest memory of all: Elizabeth on her seventh birthday, grabbing the biggest stuffed bear in a toy store and then throwing herself into

Darcy's arms. For months, Darcy had saved her allowance to buy the extravagant gift.

She doubted she'd actually saved enough. Latrice surely made up the difference while allowing Darcy to take all the credit.

The mattress shifted as Latrice sat down beside her. "Feel better?" she asked.

"And worse." Darcy placed the garment on her lap. "Does Emerson come in here?"

"Not often."

"My mother?"

"All the time." Lowering her eyes, the housekeeper rubbed at an imaginary spot on the flaring skirt of her gray uniform. "I can't bear to look at her when she comes out."

"What does she tell Emerson about his father?" It bothered Darcy that the question of her nephew's paternity was never resolved.

"Rosalind keeps the discussion simple. There wasn't any sense in keeping the truth from Emerson. A boy his age has questions in need of real answers."

"How simple? Does he know about the frat party and Elizabeth's one-night stand?"

"Your mother softens the story around the edges. She tells him Elizabeth drank too much and felt embarrassed about sleeping with a young man she'd just met. He knows she never saw the guy afterward, much less remembered who he was. She follows up with a lecture about the dangers of underage drinking and why Emerson should avoid liquor at all costs." Latrice grunted. "Like it's on his agenda to start bar-hopping anytime soon."

"Does he know Elizabeth didn't clue us in about the pregnancy until the fifth month? I wish we'd all known sooner. It's crazy how far along she was before we found out."

"He understands enough for a boy his age."

It seemed a small consolation—one that didn't halt the guilt needling Darcy. "I should've figured it all out. I could've helped her remember a few details about the party. What the guy looked like—anything." Reflecting on those complicated months sent frustration surging through her. "No one but my naive kid sister could skip her period all summer long before facing reality."

"She wasn't the first young woman in history to pretend a late period didn't amount to much. She was too frightened about what lay ahead. Facing unpleasant news was always hard for Elizabeth."

"Talk about a major case of denial." Darcy got to her feet to hang up the garment. Halfway to the closet she stopped, overcome by sorrow. "When we came home from college that summer, why didn't I notice something was up? All I remember are her mood swings and general grumpiness. When she wasn't working the waitressing job in Chagrin Falls, she spent most of her time moping. Like her whole personality had changed."

Rising from the bed, Latrice sighed. "She *was* moodier than usual."

"Why didn't I unravel the secret? We were so close. There were so many signs she was in trouble. I missed them all."

"If you're boarding the guilt train—don't." Latrice snatched the sweatshirt away. Without ceremony, she hung it back up. "You weren't to blame for Elizabeth getting pregnant."

"Easy for you to say. You aren't the one who took your kid sister to a frat party."

"She was an introvert. You were helping her make new friends."

"She didn't even want to go. She kept complaining about being a wallflower in a bunch of older students. I insisted on taking her along."

The decision, Darcy ruefully noted, was another black mark against her character—one Rosalind would never forget. It didn't matter if Elizabeth was the most bashful sophomore at Ohio University and spent most of her free time hiding out in the campus library. Darcy, more outgoing by miles, had simply wanted to break her sister's bad habit. What was the point of attending college if you didn't broaden your horizons?

Latrice scowled. "She was twenty years old," she said. "Elizabeth should've had the sense to watch out for herself. Did *you* hand her a bottle of whiskey and tell her to do shots? No, you didn't. It was her choice. Not yours."

"Why do you always let me off the hook? I was older. I should've been more responsible."

"Now you're being ridiculous. Or have you forgotten how you described that night after we *did* find out about the pregnancy? A huge party with hundreds of kids streaming in and out, blowing out their eardrums to rock music? Were you obligated to watch over your sister 24/7? How were you supposed to know Elizabeth went upstairs with a boy she'd just met? Weren't you down in the basement, shooting pool with some of the other students?"

She'd assumed Elizabeth was dancing, or talking with a dark-haired girl she'd bumped into, someone from her sociology class.

"After midnight, I went looking for her. She was passed out in the living room with two other girls from her dorm. When I woke Elizabeth, she never mentioned going upstairs with some guy. All she ever *did* remember was his sense of humor. Whoever he was, I guess he kept her laughing while he poured too many shots." Darcy sighed. "She'd promised not to drink. I got her a Coke before I went to play pool."

"You gave her good advice before going downstairs with your friends. Your mother can look at this any way she wants, but she's wrong to blame you."

"Tell it to the judge," Darcy said. The comment woke the heartache slumbering beneath her breastbone.

"Rosalind's opinion doesn't matter."

"Yes, it does."

Wandering to the window, Darcy surveyed the rolling lawn. Her attention drifted all the way to the forest. Emerson and Samson were nowhere in sight. Perhaps they'd come back inside to raid the fridge.

Behind her, Latrice released a muttering burst of anger. Her voice was still bright with heat as she said, "Are you *ever* going to take your sister off a pedestal? She was human, Darcy. A young girl who had too much fun at a party, and who should've had the good sense to get on birth control first. Especially since she wasn't a virgin."

Darcy spun around. "What are you talking about? Elizabeth dated a few guys in high school, but none of those relationships were serious. And her first year of college? She was so bashful, she hardly talked to guys."

The ready defense earned her a look of censure. "There you go again, putting her on a pedestal."

"I'm doing nothing of the sort. Elizabeth *was* a virgin before the frat party."

With consternation, Latrice fastened her hands on her hips. "Darcy, you became sexually active your last year in high school. You had the good sense to tell Rosalind and Dr. Jack. They sure weren't happy, but you *did* tell them."

"Hey, I wasn't happy about telling them either." For days afterward, she'd walked around the house feverish with shame. But the prospect of having a child before she was prepared for the responsibility proved more frightening than the public humiliation of telling her stone-faced parents that she needed birth control.

"Well, they got you a scrip for the pill. Elizabeth should've done the same when she started messing around with the young man in her music class."

"What music class?"

"Ohio University, first semester. Over a year before you took her to the frat party."

"Wait. Elizabeth met someone at college?"

"Remember when you girls came home for Christmas break? One morning, your sister cornered me in the kitchen," Latrice explained. "She wanted to know how late for a period was too late, and if she might be pregnant. How a young woman makes it all the way to college without understanding her cycle is beyond me."

Darcy fell against the wall, dumbfounded.

Elizabeth lost her virginity more than a year before she got pregnant with Emerson? This led to a more disturbing thought. *Why do I readily accept blame for my late sister's choices?*

It was easy for Darcy to pretend her mother's low opinion of her was the only reason. Knowing now that Elizabeth's decisions had been her own, she realized many of those decisions were made without bringing her big sister into the loop.

"That's right, child." Effortlessly, Latrice read the emotions racing across Darcy's face. "You suffer from the same fault as the other Goodridges, living and dead."

"What fault?"

"None of you ever view the others in a realistic light."

Chapter 11

"Mama, let me help you."

Darting across the lawn, Nella took the paper bag from Tippi's gnarled fingers. Inside, ribbons of fabric nested in a snowy white tangle.

There wasn't much Tippi didn't recycle. Worn bed linens were no exception. At dawn, her mother had padded downstairs with an old sheet tucked beneath her arm, intending to cut the fabric into foot-long ribbons. The garden's tomato plants were already four feet high, a leafy wall of tumbling growth. The plants encircled the tall stakes Michael had pounded into the ground last spring. It would take several hours to secure the sharp-scented vines to the stakes. All the bending and stretching would leave both women sore.

A fair trade, Nella decided, lifting her face to the sun's warming caress. It was a perfect June morning, breezy and not too humid. Michael was still in Chagrin Falls, discussing the kitchen cabinetry for a house renovation.

On the opposite side of the garden row, chubby basil plants waved leafy arms. Tippi crept past. A new layer of straw covered the path.

"I'll start with this one." She halted before the tallest tomato plant. "Give me the ties."

Nella carried a sturdy wooden stool down the path. "Sit down first." She plunked down the stool beside her mother's calves.

"I'm fine standing."

"Oh, I'm sorry. Did that sound like a request?" If she didn't insist, her elderly mother would topple into the plants after ten minutes of the sun beating down on her. "Mama, I'm serious. I'm delighted you want to help, but if you don't follow the rules you're going back inside."

"You and your stupid rules. Treating me like a child, acting like I can't make my own decisions—who put you in charge?"

"You did. When you began having dizzy spells and lost most of the sight in your left eye."

"Go ahead. Make fun of me."

"How can I resist?" Playfully, Nella plucked at the loose waistline of her mother's black dress. "Tell you what, I'll stop joking around if you'll stop dressing like a European peasant from World War Two. When you were younger, you loved fashion. You've been dressing like a woman in mourning since, well, Daddy's funeral. He's been gone a long time. Why don't you lighten up?"

"Why don't *you* shut up? Give me the bag."

Nella arched a disapproving brow.

"All right. I'm sitting."

With ill-concealed pique, Tippi settled her petite frame on the stool. The billowy folds of her dress fanned out, an oversize tent hiding the beat-up Nikes she wore to work in the garden. Beneath the last plant in the row, Michael's rescue mutt lolled on his back, his belly cleverly positioned to catch the sunshine.

Tippi glanced at the dozing mutt. "Jasper, why don't you bite my daughter? Just a nip on the ankle to make her stop badgering me?"

The dog's back paws twitched.

"If I had a treat in my pocket, you'd listen," Swiveling toward her daughter, Tippi smacked Nella's jean-clad thigh. "Hand it over."

Nella placed the bag in her lap. "I'll work on the tops, you tie up the bottom branches," she said, kissing her mother's forehead.

"Enough with the yapping. Let's get this show on the road."

For twenty minutes they worked in companionable silence. The tangy scent of ripening fruit coated their hands as they gently tied up the thick vines. Some of the tomatoes were already ripe. Taking care not to damage the vines, Nella plucked the dense ruby globes and placed them in a basket at her feet. A cardinal fluttered past, its vivid red wings beating the air. They'd moved on to the next plant when she detected a wisp of laughter drifting over the back forty. Curious, she went up on tiptoes to look above the lush wall of greenery.

Emerson came across the back lawn with a youth who didn't appear much older. They plodded forward with their backs hunched to avoid detection. Which was ridiculous—they were skulking around in plain sight.

Alerted to the commotion, Jasper sprang up and sprinted across the grass. Evidently, the boys were attempting to sneak into the barn to visit Michael.

Nella strode out of the garden and cupped her hands around her mouth. "He's not there," she called.

At the sound of her voice, Emerson looked up as if to say, *You caught me!*

Giggling, he tried to grab Jasper, now racing with canine delight around him.

The older boy, clearly less schooled in sneaky behavior, leaped to attention. He looked ready to salute when Emerson nudged him. Together they approached, Jasper bounding at their heels.

Nella met them at the edge of the garden. "You're wasting your time," she told Emerson. "Michael isn't working in his shop. He went into the Falls."

"He told me."

"You've talked to him?"

"About an hour ago."

Like Tippi, who rarely bent to Nella's will, her adult son wasn't malleable. The news that he was back in contact with Emerson so quickly after the boy's latest disappearance was a worrisome development.

"He's in town, quoting a job," she said. "He called you from the job site?"

"I called him. He promised we'd talk later." The boy released a plaintive sigh. "Is Michael coming home soon? I want him to meet Samson."

"I expect him in an hour or so." Nella smiled in greeting at his friend.

Her longing gaze swung back to Emerson. In the three days since she'd last seen him, she'd walked around with a hole in her heart. The desire to cuddle him nearly sent her forward. With dismay, she considered how furious Rosalind would be if she discovered her grandson's latest trip onto Varano property.

Emerson said, "Can we hang around until Michael gets back?"

"I *am* thrilled to see you, but it's not a good idea. You can't visit without permission."

"Oh, there's nothing to worry about. Grandmother won't find out."

"You're missing the point, sweetheart. You need her permission to visit. I promise, Michael will talk to Rosalind. He hasn't been able to get her on the phone, not yet. But he won't give up until she's given permission for you to come over."

Doubt creased the boy's face. "You're sure he'll keep trying?"

"I'm positive. He misses you too—although he wouldn't approve of you coming by without Rosalind's knowledge. Emerson, your disobedience will only make matters worse. You can't ignore your grandmother's rules every time she leaves for the courthouse."

"She didn't go to the courthouse."

"She's not in court this morning?"

"She's meeting a lawyer for brunch. Some lady she worked with a long time ago. Before she became a judge."

An old colleague from Brennan & Dooney? When Michael and Darcy were children and Nella considered Rosalind her closest friend, Rosalind had carved out a respected career as a trial lawyer at the law firm before winning a judgeship in Geauga County. It seemed unlikely the dedicated judge would alter court business for a brunch date.

Inexplicably, the disclosure worried her. "Rosalind took the day off?"

"And every other day."

A riddle, as if the boy wished to evade a difficult truth. "You've lost me." She tousled his hair. "Why would your grandmother take every day off? She's a busy judge. Her docket is never empty."

"She stopped working, and I know why. She thinks she's smart, keeping everything to herself, but I'm not dumb. I can figure stuff out. Even when adults lie to me."

Breaking off, Emerson left the cryptic remark hanging in the air. Then he lifted his eyes, allowing Nella to read the apprehension in his gaze—and the fear. Her stomach tumbled.

She was still trying to get a handle on the situation when he said, "I asked Michael a question, but he didn't know the answer. Samson didn't know either."

"It's a tough one," Samson agreed.

Emerson's fingers inched up his arms as if looking for someplace to hide. "Lots of questions scare people. If they're scared, they don't learn the answer. Learning multiplication was scary. It took me a long time." He paused. "I hope you can help me, Nella."

"Or course. What do you need to know?"

"What *is* the average expiration date for old people?"

"It's different for everyone. Most people live a long time."

"You're sure?"

"Sweetie, lots of people live into their nineties or longer. Tippi plans to celebrate her hundredth birthday, and that's a long way off."

Privately Nella wondered if he was mistaken. She couldn't imagine a plausible reason why Rosalind would retire at the height of her career.

There had been no mention of Judge Goodridge's retirement in the *Plain Dealer*. The article would have appeared at the top of the newspaper's Metro section. Nella would have seen it. Even if she'd missed the announcement, Michael or Tippi would have noticed it.

Behind her, the row of tomato plants rustled.

Tippi shuffled out of the garden and spotted Emerson's friend. The mapwork of wrinkles comprising her face deepened with scrutiny and delight.

The reaction was understandable. The quiet Samson was a polite youth with large brown eyes and a colorful array of tiny shells bound up in his hair. Given his delicate stature, guessing his age proved difficult. Fourteen? Fifteen, tops? Nella wasn't sure.

Tippi walked over. At her advance, Samson's ebony brows lifted. When she came within spitting distance, she looked him up and down. Her expression bloomed with fascination. Tippi never held much stock in respecting other people's space, and she boldly patted her hands down his accordion ribs. The youth snapped to attention like an undersize marine.

"Don't you eat?" She pressed a thumb against one of his ribs, testing the narrow plane. "There's no meat on your bones!"

"Oh, I have a good appetite. I just don't seem to keep the weight on."

"Do you eat breakfast? It's the most important meal of the day."

"Most of the time."

"You're not eating enough."

Tippi looked to Nella as if to say, *Fetch the pasta. We'll feed the skinny boy.*

Not the worst idea, Nella mused. She was contemplating packing up a carton of pasta for the boys to take home when her mother, intent on a thorough inspection, began fingering Samson's dreadlocks. Laughing, she tapped a tiny shell, then another. The patient youth plastered on an uneasy smile when she cradled his face between her palms.

Nella steered her mother back. "That's enough, Mama." To Samson, she said, "Please forgive Tippi. She has no boundaries."

"It's all right, ma'am."

Tippi patted his cheek. "You're a nice boy. Come back and visit when the nasty judge isn't looking."

"Mama!"

"Walk them back to the property line, Nella. If they stick around, that stupid judge will put a warrant out for your arrest." With a wink at the boys, Tippi went back down the garden path.

There wasn't time to savor relief. "Both of you—let's go." Nella took Emerson's hand and started across the grass.

"We just got here!" he protested.

"If Rosalind is out to brunch, she might return soon. Promise you'll stay on your side of the fence until Michael speaks with her. I'm sure they'll work something out."

In a childish pique, Emerson took wooden steps to slow their advance. "What if they *can't* work something out?"

"They will. Have patience."

Samson walked along beside them. "She's right," he said. "Let him take on the judge. We should lay low."

"I *hate* being patient."

At a quickening pace, Nella tugged him along. "You don't have a choice. Keep disobeying your grandmother, and she'll only become angrier. Trust Michael to get her to come around."

Ditching the childish pique, Emerson reverted to the more adult speech he'd learned by mimicking Rosalind. "Be reasonable," he said, his head bobbing as Nella took long strides. "Michael can send a million texts and call every hour. Grandmother won't listen. She's obdurate."

"Nice word choice." Affection for the frustrated boy surged through her. As they erased the distance between her property and the fence, she steered him beneath her arm. "Have you been reading the dictionary again? When we *are* able to schedule a real visit, I'm looking forward to hearing all the new words you've picked up. We'll break out the Scrabble and fight to the finish. You can show me who's boss."

"Please don't patronize me. It won't make me feel better."

"I hate seeing you upset. Will it help if I mention how much I love you? To tell you the truth, I haven't dealt with a meltdown since Michael was your age. I'm not sure what to say to make you feel better."

"I'm not having a meltdown. I'm enraged."

Nella suppressed a burst of laughter. "Don't get too enraged. We'll work something out."

They reached the property line. Emerson ground to a halt. Samson was slinging his leg over the fence when Darcy appeared on the mansion's front porch.

On the day of Emerson's return, Nella had sensibly remained by her car. From a distance, she'd only caught a glimpse of Darcy. Expectancy swirled through her as Darcy came down the steps. The warm breeze caught her long hair, fanning it out. Her attention danced across the green band of lawn sloping away from the front of the mansion before moving to the left to scan the circular driveway.

She noticed them, and relief darted through her expression. She veered past a cluster of maple trees to meet up.

Nella's exhilaration melted away as she neared. Pity tightened her throat.

Darcy was too thin. Her lightweight summer blouse hung from her shoulders. The skin beneath her wide green eyes looked bruised, a sign that insomnia plagued her sleep.

The girl ambling toward her was a mere shadow of the vibrant college student who'd once bedazzled a young and ambitious Michael. Nor did she resemble the fizzy child from his childhood, always moving and always smiling, a whirlwind of laughter and energy. Darcy approached with her shoulders curving inward, as if to fend off an unseen blow.

Nella hoisted the reluctant Emerson over the fence. "I believe this belongs to you," she said.

"Don't I wish." Leaning over the fence, Darcy gave her a quick hug. "How are you?"

"Great. And you?"

"Still getting my sea legs. There have been a lot of changes since I was last here. It takes some getting used to."

"I can imagine." Nella regarded the quietly stewing Emerson. "I'm sure you're enjoying getting to know this one. He's a great kid."

"Yeah—most of the time." Darcy gave him a quizzical look. "Really? Sneaking into the no-fly zone after Grandmother took away your electronics to prove she meant business? You promised to stay in the backyard. Are you trying to get all of us in trouble?"

Samson interrupted. "I made the promise—my bad. I thought it was better to stick by him. Once he decided to go next door, there was no stopping him."

Nella chuckled. "He *does* have a mind of his own."

"Samson, you're not responsible," Darcy said. Then she flicked Emerson's nose. "Give me a hint. Should I buy a leash?"

He swatted her away. "Like I'd let you," he replied, still trapped inside his little boy's anger.

"Yeah? Keep it up, and I will." She assessed his flushed cheeks and jutting chin with admirable patience. "Is there a pet store in Chagrin Falls? I can't remember. Wait. There's a hardware store. I'll bet they have everything I need to build a cage."

When he remained silent, she studied him with misgivings. They were at an impasse.

Breaking it, she poked him in the stomach. Not hard—just a light tap to jiggle the remnants of baby fat encasing his tummy.

A grin materialized on his face. "Better make it a strong cage," he warned. "I can sneak my way out of anything."

"What if I get a lock?"

"I'll pick it."

A lighthearted squabble broke out. Silently Nella assessed the physical similarities between the long-absent Darcy and her nephew. The same mossy-green eyes and fair complexion, the same pale-blond hair. The similarities didn't end there. They were both accomplished at running away from the difficult circumstances of their lives.

The sound of a car's engine purred up the drive. Stepping past the trees framing the property line, Nella watched the Mercedes's leisurely ascent toward the grand brick house.

Adrenaline spiked through her. Rosalind, her hands gripping the steering wheel, leaned sideways. She peered out the passenger-side window. At Nella.

By sheer luck, the trees obscured most of the fence. Rosalind couldn't see the boys lingering to the side, or Darcy.

Not yet.

The Mercedes came to a jerky halt. Rigid with fury, Rosalind climbed out. In her haste, she spilled the contents of her purse across the pavement. For a heart-stopping moment, she disappeared from view. In seconds, she'd reappear.

Nella pushed the boys toward the house. "Get going," she barked. Samson had also spotted the car, and he nudged Emerson forward. The boys darted between the maple trees. They dashed around the side of the house undetected.

At the engine's low rumble, Darcy tensed. Twenty feet away, her mother's car idled.

Rosalind, still scooping up the contents of her purse, remained hidden from view.

"Go inside, Darcy. I'll take care of this."

"Did she see you?" When Nella gave a stiff nod, Darcy planted her feet. "You're not facing her alone. I'm staying."

There wasn't time to argue. "Please go. I need to talk to your mother."

"Nella, you can't be serious. When was the last time you talked to her? When I was a kid? No way will she listen to you."

"Stop arguing. What I need to settle with her doesn't involve you." Nella made a motion as if to shoo her. "Let me handle this."

Relenting, Darcy pivoted away. She disappeared through the trees without a moment to spare. Nella's stomach pitched as Rosalind popped back into view. The car door slammed shut.

Despite the confines of her pencil-thin black skirt, she came around the hood of the Mercedes at an impressive clip. She had paired the skirt with a peach blazer, a matching silk blouse, and a long strand of pearls that swung wildly as she halted at the edge of the pavement. The grass was soggy from last night's rain. The issue was of no concern to Nella, dressed in jeans and tennis shoes, but Rosalind cared mightily about her expensive clothes.

Her thunderous gaze latched on Nella. She tugged off her heels.

She plunked them down on the hood of her car, then marched to the fence. "Why are you lurking near my house?" She pointed a finger due south. "Go home."

"In a moment." Anxiety buzzed around in Nella's stomach like a hive of bees. "We need to talk."

"There's nothing to discuss."

"Rosalind, it's been nearly two decades since we've had a civil conversation. For once, can't you withhold judgment and listen?"

"There's no reason I should." She turned back toward the drive.

"For the love of all that is holy—will you *please* let me finish?"

The shrill comment rocketed across the grounds. From the cluster of maple trees, a robin shot out into the sky.

Rosalind's back stiffened. She turned around. Lips compressed, she stalked back to the fence.

Her acquiescence was a stunning reversal. She would listen—for a moment, at least.

The moisture fled Nella's mouth. "After my husband died, I wasn't myself." She struggled to maintain her composure. "Joseph was so much older, already middle-aged when we fell in love. I should have considered the possibility that he might die long before I was ready to lose him. Even so, I wasn't prepared for him to die at a conference halfway across the country."

The barest glimmer of sympathy flickered in Rosalind's gaze. "Joseph's death was a shock for all of us," she murmured. "He was a good man."

"I miss him every day."

"I'm sure you do," Rosalind agreed.

The tiny softening of her stance gave Nella the courage to hurry on. "Losing him was like having the foundation of my life torn away. He took care of everything for us. I was frightened about managing our finances, caring for our home without his assistance or advice. I was frightened by the prospect of raising our son alone. Michael was only thirteen—too young to lose a father." Hesitating, she lowered her eyes. The millstone of remorse stole her ability to look at Rosalind. "I'm not making excuses. What happened afterward . . . it was a mistake. I don't expect you to forgive me. I don't deserve your forgiveness."

Rosalind bristled. "Your immorality is the *only* subject upon which we agree."

The retort blistered Nella's face with heat. "I'm sorry for the pain I've caused you," she said with all the good grace she possessed. "I never allow myself to forget how much I've hurt you."

"I'm glad you can't forget. I certainly haven't."

"Rosalind, I pray constantly to become a better woman. One moment of weakness can alter the lives of so many people. Friends and family—people I love and should never have caused so much pain." A black wave of shame rolled over her. "It was the worst mistake of my life. I never should have allowed it."

"Allowed it? You act as if you made one stumble on the road to sainthood. Stop twisting the facts. You *welcomed* the affair."

The accusation nearly dissolved her precarious hold on her emotions.

Is it true? Did I seek comfort after Joseph's death without understanding where it would lead? Or did grief drive me to welcome the moments of lust, to trade my honor and my self-respect for a mindless night of sex?

An unsolvable mystery. The truth laid buried with her younger self, with a woman she no longer recognized. A weaker version of the pragmatic adult molded from the wreckage of one impulsive act.

Unable to argue the point, she stared blankly at her feet. "I betrayed you in the most fundamental way. You were my closest friend. I wish I had the power to repair our friendship."

"You don't."

A harsh verdict, and one she readily accepted. "I understand. But this is no longer about us. There's Emerson to consider."

"This has nothing to do with my grandson."

"Yes, it does." She shut her eyes against the shame. "The breach I caused between our families . . . it's wrong to make him pay the price. He's such a good little boy, lonely and sweet. I can't bear to watch him suffer."

She heard Rosalind expel a mirthless laugh. "I can't imagine where you're going with this."

Nella had never earned a college degree. She couldn't point to the successes her opponent took for granted. But the sarcasm gave her the fortitude to lift her chin and look at Rosalind. To study her with the assessing eye that all women hone if they have raised a child well.

The signs of physical decline were apparent. Beneath the carefully applied cosmetics, Rosalind's skin resembled onionskin paper growing brittle in the sun. Tiny capillaries were visible, like a patchwork of delicate and artfully concealed bruises. She didn't look well. As if to demonstrate her frailty, she lowered a hand to grip the fence. She seemed unsteady on her feet.

Searching for other clues, Nella heard herself say, "Your grandson has been coming over to my house for over a year now. I'm sorry to tell you like this. I should have alerted you when the visits began."

In her mind, Emerson's worrisome question floated unbound: *What is the average expiration date for old people?*

"Now, wait one minute. My grandson has gone to your house *repeatedly?*"

"That's why Michael has been trying to contact you. He's struck up a friendship with Emerson. He understands how difficult it is for him, growing up without a father. No matter what you think of me, can't we find a way to allow *their* relationship to continue?"

"Absolutely not."

Snatching her hand from the fence, Rosalind stood blinking at the sun. Taking in all she'd learned, digesting the news with shallow breaths. When she spoke again, her eyes were dull with venom.

"I'm astonished you have the gall to mention Michael." Her fingers curled into fists. "I'm curious, Nella. The second time, when you started up again—the year after Michael finished college. Did you ever stop to think how *he'd* react if he'd learned the truth?"

Bewildered, Nella tried to make sense of the accusation. *The second time?* A full ten seconds passed before she processed the meaning.

When she did, the implication washed acid through her stomach. *Rosalind believes I carried on with Jack—for years?* Appalled, she readied a defense.

Too late—Rosalind cut her off.

"I'm not sure what to call a woman like you," she said. "After your son graduated, why *did* you and Jack continue meeting at your house? Wouldn't it have been more dignified to call my husband at his practice and set up a time to meet at a hotel? Or were you afraid someone on his staff would inform me? Ten years after our falling out, everyone knew how much I loathed you. Or was it more thrilling to set up the trysts at your house—and risk Michael finding out? Then again, he *is* your son. Perhaps he's amoral like you, and wouldn't have cared about your sexual exploits." When Nella backed away from the fence, repulsed, an awful sort of victory flashed in Rosalind's gaze. Then she frowned, adding, "Don't insult me by pretending you don't know what I'm talking about."

"I don't. There was only the one time with Jack. Just once. Right after I lost Joseph."

"Stop lying. Two weeks before Elizabeth and Jack were killed, I came home early from a benefit. Jack assumed I wouldn't return home until midnight. I went upstairs expecting to find him getting ready for bed. When I looked out the bedroom window, I saw him walking across the backyard, to your house."

"No—you're mistaken." Nella shook her head in fierce denial. "I don't know what Jack was doing, but he wasn't on his way over."

"Stop pretending. He was coming over for one simple reason. You'd resumed the affair." Rosalind paused long enough for hatred to glaze her features. "As for my grandson, he'll have nothing to do with any member of your family."

Chapter 12

Michael tugged off his work boots. A quick appraisal of the kitchen warned that something was wrong.

Breakfast dishes were heaped in the sink. On the counter, a puddle of condensation surrounded a jug of orange juice. At the table, his grandmother sorted tomatoes with the enthusiasm of a child trapped inside on a rainy day. Tippi had plucked a whole basket of tomatoes from the garden. Many were bright green and nowhere near ripe.

Worried, he patted her shoulder. "Where's Mom? Did she go out?"

"She was nosing around in the liquor cabinet."

"You mean dusting?" Her obsession with cleanliness was legendary.

"I mean drinking. Boozing it up. Getting snockered."

"Tippi, are you having an episode? Mom never gets drunk. Other than the occasional glass of wine, she rarely drinks."

A rumble of discontent rose from his grandmother. "There's nothing wrong with my faculties." Stabbing the air, she pointed toward the living room. "If Nella ran off with my Hennessy, she's in big trouble. Go check, Michael. Make sure she didn't take my brandy."

"Take it *where?*"

With moody disinterest, Tippi plucked another tomato from the basket. "She's out in the barn, skulking inside Emerson's loft. Getting toasted in a boy's playroom—who does that? I raised her to have more sense."

"Emerson isn't with her, is he?" Michael peered under the table, grabbed his tennis shoes.

"She made him go home."

"When?"

"Right before lunchtime. He came over with his new friend."

"Great. Emerson broke himself out of prison again. Just what I need."

Michael laced up his shoes in record time. He'd promised to call Emerson later. He should've laid down the law, told the kid not to leave his grandmother's property under any circumstance. There wasn't much point of trying to make his case before the ill-tempered judge if Emerson kept mucking up the works.

A minor concern at the moment. How a child's penchant for getting into trouble factored into Nella's drinking spree, Michael refused to guess.

Taking long strides past the vegetable garden, he wondered what could have upset his mother enough to explain the break from her normal behavior. He couldn't wrap his brain around the idea of her getting drunk.

In the small barn behind the riding arena, Jasper was panting near the ladder to the loft. The loyal mutt, keyed into Nella's distress, would guard his post until she came back down.

"It's okay, boy." Michael patted the dog. "I'm on it."

In the annals of strange sights, Michael had witnessed his share. The girl he dated in college, who once laughed so hard a trickle of pee ran down her leg. The surly boss at his first job in banking, who picked his nose during meetings. Tippi on the living room couch, getting handsy with one of her beaus.

This was something new. His mother sat against a wall with her legs flung out like a rag doll's. An endearing sight—if you ignored the plastic cup and the bottle of Ketel One propped against her hip.

Ducking the low rafters, he came across. "Doing shots?" Joining her, Michael examined the empty cup. "How many?"

"Three."

"Planning on more?"

"I'll get back to you."

He tossed the cup across the floor. "What is your opinion regarding friendly advice?"

"Not good." Blinking slowly, she frowned. "You're my son, not my spiritual advisor. I'm beyond redemption."

The pitiful remark made him smile. His mother attended church regularly. She let the local Girl Scout troop camp in the back forty every spring. During northeast Ohio's bitter winters, she dumped fifty-pound bags of corn near the forest to feed the deer. Once, during his senior year of high school, he found her seated on the back deck in tundra attire, cradling a sparrow between her thick mittens. She'd found the bird, which had flown into the living room window, stunned in a snowdrift. Michael would never forget the sight of the bird trembling back to wakefulness, then rocketing out of her hands.

He said, "I doubt you're beyond redemption, although it wouldn't hurt to deal with whatever is bothering you. A better choice than getting drunk. Speaking of which, Tippi will be pleased you didn't walk off with her brandy."

"I hate brandy. It makes my nose stuffy."

"Since when do you like vodka? Hard liquor isn't your thing."

"That isn't entirely accurate." With jerky movements, she brushed a strand of hair from her cheek. "I drank my first vodka martini at the grand old age of eighteen."

"You did not."

"Did too," she assured him. "Such a sophisticated adult drink. How could I resist? They went down so easily, I'd have two or three before the night was out."

He tried to form a mental image of his practical mother throwing back martinis. A daunting task. Michael prided himself on his ability to read people. Yet maturity didn't equip a man with the skills to apprehend the full nature of his own mother, especially not of the young woman she'd been long ago.

"It's hard to believe you were into martinis. Half a glass of wine, and you're tipsy."

"I got more than tipsy on the martinis. After your dad and I married, I switched to wine. It didn't leave me feeling smashed, but still made me feel all grown up. Not that I ever drank while pregnant."

He knew those first years of marriage were marked by a series of miscarriages. Michael wasn't sure of the sum total she'd endured in her desire to bring him into the world. He'd never had the stomach to ask.

"Those were difficult years," she murmured. "By the time I finally got pregnant with you, I'd lost the taste for vodka."

"Not the worst outcome."

"No, it wasn't."

He felt helpless, unable to quell the pain sifting through her features. Wishing to lighten the moment, he said, "If I ever have a daughter, remind me to watch her like a hawk. I don't want her wolfing down martinis like her grandmother. Not at a tender age."

"Don't blame Tippi and your late grandfather for my habits. They would've been horrified if they'd known."

"*Dad* turned you on to hard liquor?"

Her eyes were slightly glassy as she regarded him with amusement. "In your father's defense, he didn't expect to fall in love with the new girl in the secretarial pool. He was already in his forties, past the age when most people marry. One of Cleveland's most successful architects, but completely wrapped up in his career. It's a toss-up which one of us was more besotted."

"Is this about Dad? You're drinking because you miss him?"

She picked up the Ketel One, hesitated. Setting the bottle down, she folded her hands in her lap. "I saw Rosalind."

"When you walked Emerson and his friend back to the fence?" She gave him a questioning look, and he added, "Tippi gave me the rundown."

"Rosalind was pulling in when I walked the kids back. She didn't see them. I hate to imagine the sort of punishment she'd devise for Emerson if she had."

"You spoke with her?"

"And Darcy, but only for a minute. I sent her inside with the boys before the fireworks started."

Mention of Darcy sparked his interest. An inconvenient reaction he quickly suppressed. Aside from the brief moment on the day they'd brought Emerson home, he hadn't seen her. Michael wasn't sure how he'd react when they did finally come face-to-face. They had enough unfinished business for an hours-long conversation.

He said, "Tell me about the fireworks with Rosalind."

"There's not much to tell. I stood there while she railed at me." Wearily, Nella rubbed her face. "Son, I need to ask you something."

The worry threaded through the remark put him on alert. "Anything."

"When you and Darcy began dating, I assumed you only told me. There'd been no communication between our family and the Goodridges for ten years. I assumed you knew the wisest course was to keep your relationship with Darcy secret, at least until you were sure of your intentions."

"That *was* the best course."

"Did you tell her father? Jack couldn't have been pleased."

"I didn't tell him. We ran into him a few weeks after we began dating."

"Did he ever come over to the house?"

Michael nodded. "Yeah, a few days after we ran into him. You were out with friends for dinner. I didn't tell you when you got home—didn't make sense to upset you."

"*How* did he find out about you and Darcy? Seriously, Michael. Jack's medical practice was in the Falls, and everyone knew Darcy was his daughter. Please tell me you weren't foolish enough to walk around Chagrin Falls holding hands."

The remark irritated him. "Of course not," he said. "During daylight hours, we steered clear of the Falls. Darcy worried about her parents finding out. We started dating just a few months after her sister had Emerson. Not the best timing."

"I would imagine life on the Goodridge estate was awfully tense. An unexpected pregnancy, and Elizabeth dropping out of college. I'm sure it was a stressful time for the entire family."

"And you'd been on Rosalind's enemy list for a decade by then."

Nella frowned. "Darcy was afraid of rocking the boat?" she asked.

On impulse, Michael reached for the vodka. He took a swig, flinching as the alcohol burned his throat. Rehashing their short romance was an unwelcome task. He'd never shaken the suspicion that by chasing after Darcy he'd added to her troubles.

After a long pause, he said, "More than anything, Darcy worried about giving her mother another reason to come down on her. Rosalind already blamed her for Elizabeth's pregnancy, which was crazy. Darcy took her kid sister to a frat party—she didn't have anything to do with Elizabeth deciding to have a one-night stand."

"Rosalind never required much reason to come down hard on Darcy."

He'd always wondered why. "You were close with Rosalind when we were kids. Did they *ever* get along?"

"It's not that simple. It's more accurate to say that Rosalind wasn't prepared for motherhood. By the time she met Jack, she'd already built a successful law practice and was vying for a judgeship. He'd opened his practice in Chagrin Falls and didn't seem in a hurry to start a family. Darcy was an accident." When his brows lifted, Nella shook her head with bemusement. "Were you under the impression only teenagers have unplanned pregnancies? Rosalind took birth control pills for too many years. Her gynecologist had recently taken her off them. I have no idea what protection she *was* using. Obviously, it wasn't foolproof."

An unwanted pregnancy and a professional couple too focused on getting ahead. At least Elizabeth had wanted Emerson. Michael recalled how often Darcy, when they'd dated, had mentioned her sister's affection for her newborn son. All children deserved to be cherished, and Darcy was so incredibly special.

"Rosalind didn't want Darcy?" he asked with heat.

"You know how precise she is. She didn't want her schedule altered without her conscious permission. It didn't help that Darcy was a colicky baby, up every hour. I would've helped Rosalind through the transition if I'd had more time. You were only a year old."

"So Latrice stepped up to the plate."

"Gladly. She adores Darcy. She felt the same way about Elizabeth."

In silent agreement, Michael nodded. During his first years of friendship with Darcy, Latrice always hovered in the background, a loving presence. Baking cookies for them to take on their adventures in the forest, teaching them how to play croquet in the backyard. The rest of the time they were at Michael's house, learning to play the board games his mother bought for them.

"Everything was different with Elizabeth," his mother was saying. "A perfect baby, never fussy . . . I'm sure it helped that she resembled Rosalind."

"Darcy *is* the female version of Dr. Jack. When Emerson grows up, he'll look just like his grandfather."

"He will," Nella agreed. She studied him with misgivings. "When Jack came over to the house . . . what did you discuss?"

"He wanted me to stop seeing Darcy. I refused."

"How did he find out?"

"We ran into him at a restaurant in Beachwood. It was fairly late—ten at night, I guess. He wasn't with Rosalind."

"Who was he with?"

Not knowing had always bothered Michael for reasons he couldn't identify. Dr. Jack Goodridge had been a gregarious man, well liked. There were any number of professional associates or friends he could've been dining with that night.

"I'm not sure. Darcy was pretty upset when he saw us, and we left in a hurry." Dropping the subject, he studied his mother for a long moment. At last, he asked, "What did Rosalind say to you this afternoon? I'm not prying. I'd just like a sense of what I'm dealing with before I press my case to see Emerson."

"She won't let you see him. She made that much clear."

A challenge. He smiled grimly. He got to his feet.

Game on.

He reached out a hand, which his mother readily grasped. "This is only round one," he said, steering her to her feet. "If Rosalind won't return my calls, it's time for the direct approach."

His mother eyed him with dismay. "I know that look. Michael, what are you planning?"

He scooped up the vodka and the plastic cup. "To pay her a visit," he said, determined not to let Emerson down. "First thing tomorrow."

～

Stars twinkled across the inky black sky.

Darcy came down the slate steps leading from her mother's patio. With the onset of night, the grass unfurled toward the forest in a sea of charcoal gray. She tried to catch a glimpse of Samson. The moon was still low on the horizon, making it difficult to see in the murky darkness. Turning on the porch lights was the obvious solution—one she quickly

Christine Nolfi

dismissed. If Samson had wanted them on, he would've taken care of it himself when he slipped outside.

It took a full minute to locate him, seated on the grass. Given Rosalind's behavior at dinner, an air of unease surrounded him.

After Latrice set the dining room table, Rosalind had spent the dinner hour submitting them to snappish comments and chilly silences. Her argument with Nella over the fence—a conversation Darcy had nervously watched from a second-floor window—continued to simmer in Rosalind's expression as she took her place at the head of the table. The mood went downhill from there.

When she wasn't making Darcy or Samson uncomfortable with caustic remarks, she traded subtle barbs with her grandson. Emerson spent the entire meal getting under her skin. An unnecessary ploy, in Darcy's estimation. The topic of him visiting next door never came up. Yet there was no missing the subtext of the brittle conversation between the angry boy and his unyielding grandmother. Emerson wanted the visits to resume. Rosalind was having none of it.

While they argued in a roundabout way, Samson pushed bits of chicken marsala around his plate. After days of witnessing Rosalind's dismissive treatment of Darcy, he appeared terrified of becoming the judge's next target. Latrice, taking pity on him and Emerson as well, reappeared the minute dinner was finished. She asked if they would help clear the table. At the suggestion, Emerson pushed his chair back, grabbed the glasses, and marched off. Samson, filling his arms with dishes, hurried after him.

In the darkness, Samson pulled his knees up to his chest. Staring intently at the heavens, he didn't hear Darcy's approach.

"Hey," she murmured, pausing beside him. She glanced up at the star field glistening above. "Found it yet?"

"My North Star?" He rested his chin on his knees. "Not yet."

"Let me know if you see mine up there."

"You know I will."

The tension at dinner had left Darcy's muscles stiff with anxiety. Rolling her shoulders, she glided her attention across the sky. There was nothing more soothing than the natural world, and she breathed in deep breaths.

"Are you okay?" She sat down beside him.

"Not really."

"If I'd known my mother would be such a pill, I would've suggested we drive into Chagrin Falls for dinner. It would've been sad leaving Emerson alone to deal with her, but he knows how to hold his own."

"I bet he does. I don't think he's even scared of her."

"I'm sure he is, sometimes. But he's been dealing with her for a long time. You haven't. It wasn't fair to submit you to her bad behavior."

"It's not your fault." Considering, Samson lifted his chin from his knees. "I just don't understand. Your family is rich. You've got everything you could ever want. Nice clothes, nice cars, and a house big enough to keep a whole bunch of families safe and warm. You Goodridges have *everything*. I thought people like you were the lucky ones—happy all the time."

"The things you own don't bring happiness. In fact, owning too much stuff can get in the way. It becomes a wall between you and the people you're supposed to love. You spend your life stacking up more possessions and more professional success. For some people, those ambitions become the central focus of their lives. The *only* focus." It occurred to Darcy that she'd never believed her parents loved each other. Not with the gentle, unswerving devotion that should grow out of marriage vows. "I'm sure that's what happened to my parents," she added. "They put their energies into building their respective careers. Even their social lives were tied up with making the right friends, the right connections."

"I feel sorry for you. My childhood was bad—all the moving around from one foster home to the next. Your childhood was lousy too."

The sympathy in his voice pricked her eyes with tears. "Samson, you had it worse. No kid should grow up in foster care. At least I had my sister to lean on." Before she lost the nerve, Darcy slung her arm across his shoulders. She planted a kiss on his forehead. When his bashful gaze met hers, she let him go, adding, "You know, you're the baby brother I never had. I hope you'll always think of me as family . . . because that's how I feel about you."

Samson grinned, but his eyes watered. Too much emotion didn't sit well with the average teenager, and he lifted his shoulders with feigned nonchalance. "You're okay," he said.

"Just okay? C'mon. I'm the big sister you always wanted. Should I start nagging you about signing up for college courses in the fall? Find something else to nag you about?"

"Save the big-sister routine, okay? I'm not in the mood right now."

"Got it."

He was silent for a moment. Then he asked, "Was your mama always mean?"

"Not to Elizabeth."

"Your daddy? He was mean too?"

"Mostly he just wasn't here. Working late, golfing at the club—my parents were into the country club life in a big way. I guess I assumed most kids were raised by the help. I'm glad Latrice *was* there for us."

"I don't know what's more pathetic—you being raised like an orphan when your parents could've loved you, or me *being* an orphan and believing real families did nothing but love each other."

"Don't use my family as a measuring stick. The Goodridges have turned dysfunction into a high art form. I'm not sure we even knew each other." The admission weighed heavily on her. "I assumed I knew my sister better than anyone. And I didn't. Just today, Latrice told me a secret about Elizabeth I never would've guessed."

"What kind of secret?"

Sharing details of Elizabeth's sex life was taboo. "Put it this way," Darcy said. "She wasn't the angel I'd presumed."

"You thought your sister was perfect?"

"Pretty much."

Disbelief glinted in his eyes. "How are you supposed to love someone if they're perfect? Darcy, you've got to stop taking so many stupid pills. Don't you know we're *all* a mess? Dealing with our nasty faults, getting stuck on the bad stuff like jealousy and anger. You love someone in spite of their badness. It's the only way to help them do better."

His belief in the healing power of love was inspiring, if too optimistic. Love wasn't a magic potion. In families like hers, love was in depressingly short supply. Look at how she'd put her late sister on a pedestal. She'd missed out on knowing the real Elizabeth—she'd missed out on deepening the only relationship in her family she'd relied upon. It wasn't like there was much evidence that Rosalind and Jack Goodridge had genuinely loved either of their daughters. They'd cared about their careers and their active social life. The children they brought into the world were an afterthought.

At least Darcy had always been secure in Elizabeth's love—and Latrice's.

"If you'd known my sister, you would've thought she was close to perfect," she said. "Elizabeth was kind, with a generous heart—like you." Playfully, she bounced her shoulder against his. "And I don't take stupid pills."

"Yes, you do. Remember how nervous you were about coming to see Emerson? You thought he wouldn't take to you."

"He didn't have any reason to like me. His absentee Aunt Darcy. I shouldn't have waited until he was eight years old to become part of his life." She nearly mentioned the promise she'd made to Elizabeth, a promise broken when Emerson was just a baby. Guilt kept the words bound inside her.

"He's not all grown up. There's time to make up those lost years." Samson plucked a blade of grass, thinking. After a moment, he said, "Lots of your habits are dumb. Like moving from city to city. Whatever made you think roaming around was a good idea? Like a plant trying to grow with its roots torn off. We all need to plant ourselves somewhere good. Of course, there's nothing dumber than the way you leave half of your sandwich on your plate. Where I come from, you don't waste food." He bumped his shoulder against hers, his expression growing smug. "It took some pondering, but I've figured out why you do it. When you and Elizabeth were growing up, you shared everything, including your sandwiches."

"We did."

Satisfied with his powers of deduction, he stretched his legs out. He let the silence wind out as they scanned the night sky. At length, he cast her a quick glance.

"How did Elizabeth and your father die? I know it's hard to talk about. I'd ask Latrice, but her mouth starts quivering every time your sister's name comes up."

Darcy trailed her fingers through the grass. There was no simple way to skip the full, brutal details and give a basic accounting. She'd brought Samson all the way from South Carolina to the Arctic freeze of her mother's house. Submitting the good-natured youth to all the complications of her very broken family was hard on him. He deserved a basic explanation.

Near the forest, a swarm of fireflies sparked dots of light across the darkness. They looked like Fourth of July sparklers waved by unseen hands.

Without preamble, she began to explain. "I had an argument with my father and stormed out of the house. I ended up at Seasons Tavern— it's just a few miles from here. I was upset, drinking too much."

"Why were you arguing with your dad?"

"Samson, which part do you want to hear? The basics of the accident, or why my father wanted me to break up with Michael?"

The remark dropped out unchecked. Samson's eyes rounded.

"You were dating the guy next door?" When she heaved a sigh, he laughed. "In case you haven't noticed, Michael's your nephew's personal hero. A lonely kid like Emerson can get territorial. What if he doesn't like the idea of his aunt dating Mr. Superhero?"

"Oh please. I wasn't much older than you when I dated Mr. Superhero. Ancient history."

"So you fell for the guy?"

"We weren't in love, if that's what you're implying."

It occurred to her that she wasn't sure of the truth. Grief over the deaths of Elizabeth and her father had blotted out everything else. Whatever she'd felt for Michael lay buried beneath layers of remorse.

"How long did you date?"

"Just a few months. Being with Michael was a refuge during a stormy year." She gave a quick summary of their childhood friendship, which came to an abrupt close with the falling out between their mothers. Wrapping up, she added, "When we were kids, Michael was my touchstone. Always steady, loyal. I'm sure he's a great influence on my nephew."

"A boy needs a good role model." Letting the subject go, Samson tripped his attention across the sky. "Tell me about the accident."

"I ended up in the bar because I felt awful. Throwing back too many drinks, wondering how to break up with Michael. My father had insisted my mother would never forgive me if she found out I was dating Michael. I didn't need another black mark in her book."

Following Samson's cue, she lifted her eyes to the heavens. At random, she picked out a star. It was more brilliant than a diamond, winking alone in the southeast portion of the sky. She pretended the glittering dot would lead her true north, toward understanding, as she trod further into the memory of that night.

"When I left the bar, I got a flat tire on a winding stretch of Chagrin River Road. No streetlights, and it was raining like crazy. One of those summer downpours that seem like they'll never stop. The storm scared me so much, I pulled out my phone and called Elizabeth. Walking back to the bar would've made more sense. Someone would've helped me change the flat."

"Like you said, you were scared."

"Doesn't matter. Waking Elizabeth was self-centered. Why did I think it was okay to bug her at midnight? Emerson was just a few months old. The last thing she needed was an SOS from her big sister. But I knew Latrice was staying over and my parents were home. Emerson wouldn't be alone. She was already downstairs, pulling on a coat, when we hung up."

Samson's curious gaze flicked across her features. "Your dad came with her?"

She nodded. "I'm sure he felt bad about arguing with me earlier and tried to convince Elizabeth to stay home. She would've refused. It didn't take them long to reach me."

The memory wrapped Darcy in its cold embrace. She dared her heart to survive the images flooding her mind. The rain coming down in sheets. Her father reaching into the trunk and muttering a complaint. The jack clanging on the wet road before he hoisted it up and walked to the side of the car.

Elizabeth pivoting on her heel to glare at Darcy. *Are you planning to help, or not?*

"My father began working on the tire," she continued, a weight of misery pressing down on her. "By then it was pretty obvious I'd had too much to drink. My father knew why I was drunk, and kept his opinion to himself. Elizabeth blew up. When I started climbing into the back seat—I felt woozy—she grabbed my arm. We started arguing. Somehow, we ended up in the road. In the middle of the unlit road, about ten feet behind the car. The rain was pounding the crap out of us, and we just kept shouting at each other. We didn't argue very often, but she was upset. Really furious that I'd been driving while under the influence."

"She had a point," Samson muttered.

"I knew she was right. I just wasn't used to my younger sister coming down on me so hard."

"Like you'd switched roles and *she'd* become the big sister?"

The observation startled her. "Yes, exactly," she agreed. "It really upset me. When I got tired of her reading me the riot act, I stalked to the berm. I left her standing there."

A heartbreaking image, carved in Darcy's memory: Elizabeth shouting, the rain pelting her face. Unaware of death standing close behind.

The pity in Samson's eyes was unbearable. "Tell me the rest," he whispered.

Darcy shut her eyes, resisting the memory. The sudden glare of headlights. The pickup rounding the curve, too fast.

"I left her, Samson. She never saw the truck . . ."

The questions Darcy never fully escaped gripped her.

Why didn't I notice the truck sooner? Or call out a warning? One treacherous moment stood between the family I cherished and the ruined life to follow. In that terrible instant, why didn't I react?

More excruciating questions followed.

If I hadn't been drinking—if I'd been alert, in control—could I have reached Elizabeth in time? Pushed her out of the way?

"The guy driving the Ford pickup came around the bend too fast. Lightning quick, like he was in a hurry. He swerved wide, probably because he'd noticed my car and my father's parked on the berm. The truck skidded toward the hood of my car. My father didn't have time to react. He was crouched down, working on the flat." The memory unfolded in stark, terrifying detail. "He was killed instantly. The truck was out of control by then, swerving down the road. Toward Elizabeth . . ."

In agony, Darcy balled up her fists. She pressed them into her eye sockets. She was unable to ward off the memory.

Of five thousand pounds of hurtling steel dragging Elizabeth's precious, helpless body forty yards down the road.

Chapter 13

Sickened by the memory, Darcy struggled to her feet.

On impulse, she stumbled toward the house. A wave of nausea rolled through her. Fending it off, she took rapid gulps of air. Then she spun around and began running.

She went around the side of the house and ducked into the laundry room door. Samson came in behind her.

"Darcy, it's okay." With hasty swipes, he mopped at the sweat on her brow. "Are you dizzy? Tell me what to do."

"I'm good."

"Yeah? You're shaking."

He followed her into the kitchen. The spotlights above the table were dimmed. On the counter, Latrice's purse sat waiting for her to finish up for the night.

Darcy attempted a reassuring smile. "I don't like thinking about that night, much less discussing it," she admitted. "I guess it shook me up more than I expected."

"It sure did."

They walked into the foyer. She heard the soft clattering of dishes being stacked. Latrice, putting away the china in the dining room. A lucky break. Then she detected the low hum of the TV. Hopefully Emerson was watching a show with Rosalind.

"I'm going upstairs," she said. "Just give me a little while to pull myself together. I'll come back down when I have."

"Man, I'm sorry. I shouldn't have asked you to explain."

"Samson, you didn't do anything wrong. I've just never talked about it before."

Behind them, Emerson came out of the library. A bad break. Rosalind was watching TV alone.

"Why did you guys take off?" he asked. "I looked for you everywhere." Gone was the bravado Emerson had displayed while sparring with his grandmother at dinner.

Samson blocked his path. "We're cool, little man. Give us a sec, okay? We're talking about something private."

"Are you talking about Grandmother? Why can't I hear?" He looked torn between loyalty to Rosalind and curiosity about their private conversation. "She's not always mean at dinner. I'm sure she'll act nicer tomorrow."

"I'm sure she will," Samson agreed, stalling for time.

Darcy was grateful he'd taken the lead. The prospect of Emerson seeing her this upset sent her gaze up the staircase. She pressed a palm to her neck. Her skin felt clammy. She was about to excuse herself when her nephew darted around Samson.

"Aunt Darcy?" Unable to make sense of her silence, Emerson frowned. "What happened? Did you have another fight with Grandmother? I hate when she fights with you."

"We didn't have a fight." Another tremor shook through her.

"You look cold. You're shivering."

"She's coming down with something," Samson lied. He cleared his throat before adding, "Darcy, call a doctor in the morning. It could be the flu."

"Good idea. I'm sure someone can fit me in tomorrow."

Emerson watched the interplay with ill-concealed suspicion. He knew they were hiding something.

Eyes narrowing, he regarded Samson. "She doesn't need a doctor. What's going on? Tell me."

"Nothing, little man. She's just feeling poorly."

"I am," Darcy agreed.

"You're lying." The sweetness fled Emerson's face, replaced by scorn. "I hate when grown-ups lie. Grandmother lies too."

Darcy approached, but he stepped out of reach. "Oh, Emerson. I'm sure she doesn't." It was a bizarre accusation. Rosalind prized honesty.

They were at an impasse. From the living room, the murmur from the TV switched off. If Rosalind heard the conversation, it would take her all of ten seconds to reach the foyer.

"Everything's fine. Honest. Hey, I've got a great idea. Let's play Monopoly." She gestured halfheartedly toward the library. "Why don't you set the game up? I only need a minute to run upstairs. Then we'll play until bedtime."

"You're crying."

Panicked, she pressed a palm to her cheek. Her fingers slicked through the dampness.

"Did Grandmother make you cry?" Emerson crossed his arms. "She makes me cry sometimes. I just don't show it."

"You shouldn't hide your feelings. There's nothing wrong with boys crying."

"Adults hide their feelings all the time," he countered. "Why shouldn't I?"

There was no time to continue the discussion. Darcy's heart sank as her mother came into the foyer.

"What's going on in here?" Rosalind frowned at Emerson. "I found *Star Wars* on Netflix. Aren't we going to watch together?"

"Not until you tell Aunt Darcy you're sorry."

"For heaven's sake—*why* do I owe her an apology?"

"You made her cry." Emerson folded his arms in a disconcerting parody of Rosalind's stance. "Why can't you stop being mean? You shouldn't make her feel bad. You do it all the time."

Darcy gripped his shoulder. "Sweetie, you've got it wrong." Her words melted away as he shrugged her off.

The interplay put suspicion in Rosalind's eyes. Jaw set, she glared at Darcy. "Oh, I see. Is this a new strategy? Fake tears so my grandson will buy into your falsehoods?"

At the word *falsehoods*, Emerson's face lit with fury. "Grandmother, you're one to talk. You like falsehoods more than anybody."

"I deplore falsehoods. Did Aunt Darcy put this nonsense in your head?"

"Stop blaming her." He stomped his foot. "*You're* the mean one."

He sprinted across the foyer and clambered up the staircase.

"Emerson Franklin Goodridge, you are not excused!"

The reprimand caught him on the landing. He gripped the banister. Darcy's heart went out to him as he turned around. He was a brave little boy. Stiffly, he clomped back down.

A thunderous silence fell between the boy and his grandmother as they faced off. The sound of glass shattering echoed from the dining room. Darcy flinched. Samson began inching behind her for safety.

Latrice rushed into the foyer. "What's going on? I heard shouting."

Helplessly, Darcy raised her palms. Rosalind inhaled an impatient breath.

Emerson said, "I call the court to order."

Chin raised, he brushed past Rosalind. With confident strides, he disappeared into the living room.

Rosalind glanced skyward. "Of all the silly—" Defeated, she swirled long fingers through the air. "Let's go, ladies. Court is now in session."

Taking her sweet time, she strolled in after her grandson.

"Well, come on," Latrice whispered to Darcy.

"What are we doing?"

"Emerson plays a game of pretending he's a lawyer. It's how he gets your mother's undivided attention. They don't have many serious conversations. He gets one per year." The housekeeper smiled at Samson. "Why don't you go upstairs? These court proceedings can get dicey."

"Yes, ma'am." Samson darted for the stairwell.

When he was gone, Darcy grabbed Latrice at the threshold to the living room. "My mother only grants Emerson one serious conversation per year?" Grappling for her composure, she wiped the last tears from her face. "That's all?"

"Rosalind doesn't like the barrage of questions. They make her testy. Let's hope your nephew doesn't keep the court in session for too long."

Together, they sat down on the couch. Rosalind was already seated in her favorite Queen Anne chair like a smug defendant.

Not smug. Darcy studied her closely. A trace of anxiety inked her mother's gaze as Emerson began pacing before her. An eight-year-old mimicking a lawyer's movements, a child collecting his thoughts like pebbles on a riverbank. The scene would've struck Darcy as charming if she hadn't already sensed the doom leaking into the room.

"Grandmother." Emerson murmured the endearment with the sobriety of King Solomon. "You are under oath."

"I understand, counselor."

"Do you promise not to lie?" Resting his palms on the armrests of her chair, he leaned closer. "Or tell falsehoods?"

"I shall only tell the truth."

A small promise, fragile and frightening. Like the alarm no longer hidden in her mother's eyes.

I'm not ready, Darcy thought as the alarm, like a contagion, spread to Emerson. He looked ill, the color bleeding from his cheeks.

Blindly, Darcy reached for Latrice's hand. Together they waited with dread.

Emerson slid his palms up the chair's armrests. When his fingers grazed Rosalind's, he asked, "Are you nearing your expiration date?"

"I don't understand the query. Clarification, please."

Clarification—a word containing too many syllables. Emerson frowned.

"Please, Grandmother," he whispered, and his lower lip wobbled.

Rosalind sat transfixed. Her throat worked. Her eyes moved across his face, assessing the fear he failed to mask. The pride she usually carried with ease became a weight around her neck.

"Are you asking if I'm dying?" she said, and her expression collapsed.

Her reply seemed to swallow the light in the room. No one dared to draw a breath. A quiet descended, so chilling that it frosted the room with fear.

Emerson lowered his hands to his sides. His lips quivered, but his back remained arrow-straight.

The heartbreak he failed to conceal sent Darcy's fist to her mouth. Too late—a sob spilled out.

With bitter clarity, she understood. Emerson hadn't run away merely to bring her home. He'd sent up a flare, a warning for Darcy to heed.

Rosalind was dying.

Chapter 14

The blue comforter with its swirling pattern of stars was tented high in the center. A frightened boy hid underneath.

Closing the door with a soft click, Darcy hesitated. Some children preferred being left alone when upset. Others welcomed the reassurance of adult company. Leaning against the doorjamb, she watched a tight beam of light waver at the comforter's edges. A gentle clicking followed. Emerson continued playing whatever game he'd carried into his hiding place.

Once her mother had admitted the truth, he'd dashed from the living room.

She approached the bed. "How are you doing?"

The tented comforter shifted. The fabric stilled.

"Is Grandmother with you?"

"She's downstairs with Latrice." Darcy hesitated. "Do you want her to come up?"

"No." A tense beat, then he asked, "Why are you here?"

"Well, I wanted to check on you. To make sure you're okay."

"Do I have to go back down?"

Dread colored the question. The shock of Rosalind's disclosure would frighten any child. Darcy was frightened too. The news of her mother's condition left her emotions whipsawing between disbelief and shock. Amyloidosis. A protein disorder. A silent killer building up inside her mother.

There wasn't a chamber in Darcy's heart capable of accepting the dire news.

"Oh, honey. No, you don't have to go downstairs. Actually, it's better if you hang out in your bedroom. Definitely more fun to be had up here." She rubbed her running nose. For Emerson's sake, she needed to keep her emotions in check. "There's lots of stuff Grandmother needs to explain to me and Latrice. Do you want Samson to come in? He's in his bedroom."

"Not really."

"Mind if I join you, then?"

An indecisive silence. Then, finally, he said, "Okay."

Turning back the edge of the comforter, Emerson scooted over to make room for her. There was more than enough room for them both on the queen-size bed. Pulling the comforter back over their heads, Darcy followed his cue and sat cross-legged. Emerson handed over the flashlight.

At his knees sat an old-fashioned board game—marble solitaire. But these were no ordinary marbles. The small globes appeared hand-blown, with swirling designs of vibrant color inside the glass. The board of dark, burnished wood looked like an antique.

"Where did you get this?" She ran a finger around the glossy circle of wood.

"Grandmother bought it for me in Germany."

"She took you to Germany?"

"Last year, for spring break." Emerson hopped a blue marble over one filled with shimmering waves of gold dust. "She took me to France the year before that."

"Your mother loved Paris. Grandmother took Elizabeth for her thirteenth birthday." With misgivings, Darcy recalled the argument when she refused to accompany them. After Rosalind cut Michael out of her life, she refused to take any vacations with her mother. She'd stayed home with her busy father and Latrice. Her father skipped most family vacations due to his thriving medical practice; she'd rarely seen him during that lonely week.

"Next year, I wanted to visit Tokyo." Emerson placed the gold marble in the ridge at the outer section of the board. "The biggest fish market in the world is in Tokyo."

"I didn't know that."

"It doesn't matter now. I guess I can't take any more vacations with her."

"I'm sorry, Emerson."

A shudder went down the delicate curve of his spine. "Why is Grandmother dying?" Sorrow bloomed in his eyes. "She's not even close to seventy. Tippi is a lot older. Some of Tippi's friends are in their nineties. They're *very* old but they're not dying."

"Grandmother has a bad illness. I don't understand everything yet. I just found out too." She rested her hand on his knee. "I promise to explain once I have a better picture of what's going on."

"What will happen to me . . . after?"

He looked up then, the fear thick in his eyes. Pain gripped her throat. This was a test. Emerson wanted proof he could rely upon her. No matter the heartbreak they must encounter, he needed an assurance they would face it together.

She managed to steady her voice. "If there's nothing we can do to stop Grandmother's illness, we'll go on together. You and I," she emphasized. "But let's not get ahead of ourselves. She's still alive. We shouldn't give up hope."

"But she said she's dying."

"Yes, and I'm saying I don't have all the facts about her illness. Not yet. I refuse to believe there's nothing we can do. Maybe there's something out there, a medicine or a procedure, that can help. Something she's overlooked."

"What if there isn't, and she dies?"

A reasonable question—one she dreaded. The overload of the evening's disclosures had left her thoughts disjointed. How could Emerson grasp the possibility of death? She was still dealing with the first stages of shock herself.

"If there's nothing that can be done, you'll feel sad for a long time. I will too. But we'll have each other."

He eyed her warily. "You're sure?"

"Emerson, you won't be alone. That's a promise. I wish I'd never stayed away for so long, but I'm here now. I'll stay with you forever."

The night's events, too shocking for a child to digest, made trust a difficult proposition. "What if something happens to *you?*" he asked. "Nobody stays in my life. Everybody leaves."

His mother, Dr. Jack, and now Rosalind—the burden of losses was too great. No wonder he entertained doubts.

"Nothing will happen to me," she assured him. "I'm young, like you. I have lots of years ahead of me."

"Do you floss?"

"Every day." She reconsidered. "Sometimes I forget when I'm busy. From here on out, I'll floss every day. You have my word."

"Aunt Darcy?"

"Yes, sweetie?"

"Where do people go when they die?"

"Someplace better than here."

"You mean heaven." Emerson picked up a crimson marble, set it back down.

"I do."

A tear clung to his lashes. It fell onto the board. "I don't care if heaven is the nicest place in the whole universe. I don't want Grandmother to leave. I'll miss her too much. I'll miss all her stupid rules."

The slender bones of his shoulders quaked with sorrow. He was a brave boy, and he made a valiant effort to tame the feelings crashing inside him. But children aren't capable of managing the most difficult emotions. Their hearts are untested and easily battered. Darcy knew this; Emerson did not. Motherless, with a talent for faking mature behavior, he assumed he could circumvent the tidal wave of grief rolling through him.

Throwing off the comforter, she pulled him onto her lap. When she lay back against the pillows, Emerson curled against her side without prodding, his legs wrapping around her thighs, his head tucked against her breast, as if they had snuggled like this often in the past. Like a mother shielding her child from the harsh reality that life, a haven blessed with sweet beginnings, was also a battleground cursed with bitter endings.

Darcy smoothed a palm down his back. She tucked him tight against her ribs. A sob broke from his chest.

Then he gave his tender heart over to tears.

Chapter 15

Shrugging on a jacket, Michael glanced around the shop. Currents of brisk dawn air rippled the sawdust on the floor. During the short, bleary walk from the house, he'd managed to forget what he'd come out to fetch.

The satisfying aroma of wood filtered through the small barn. The space, attached to the western face of the much larger riding area, was outfitted with table saws, jigsaws, a router table, and all manner of sanding tools. On the nearest table, a stack of Brazilian canary wood snagged his attention. The bird feeder he'd helped Emerson build was tucked behind the lumber.

Slinging the bird feeder beneath his arm, he strode toward the Goodridge estate. It was a safe bet the early-morning visit would roust the honorable judge from sleep.

He didn't care.

Hopping the fence between the two properties, Michael put his game face on.

He refused to allow Rosalind's longstanding hatred of his mother destroy the relationship he'd forged with Emerson. Having lost his own father in seventh grade, Michael understood the difficulty of growing up without strong male guidance. Hard, mostly. He'd never forgotten the junior high basketball coach and, later, the high school guidance counselor who'd quietly stepped in to fill the void. Emerson needed the same adult male influence, something lacking until now.

Letting the kid down was out of the question.

In the trees surrounding the Goodridge mansion, squirrels chattered to greet the fast-approaching day. The windows were dark. Brushing past the boxwood lining the stone walkway, Michael put the possibility of running into Darcy out of mind. He wasn't sure how he felt about seeing her again. The riddle had plagued him throughout a sleepless night.

Swiftly he climbed the front steps. He placed the bird feeder to the left of the door, near the railing and out of sight. It was best to keep the peace offering hidden for now.

Once he cornered Rosalind, he'd set the ground rules. No doubt Emerson would make an appearance before the adults finished talking. After Michael said his piece to Rosalind, he'd encourage her grandson to give her the gift. The eager child had outdone himself, patiently fitting together the joints for the rectangular base and gluing dowels in place for the roof. Together, they'd painted the bird feeder a deep forest green.

There was no telling if the gift would placate the ill-tempered judge. For the boy's sake, Michael hoped it would.

Next weekend, he planned to take Emerson fishing. They'd visit their favorite spot on the Chagrin River, not too far inside the forest. Saturday or Sunday, whichever day Rosalind sanctioned. Michael would promise to bring her grandson home by nightfall.

He lifted his hand and knocked.

A few moments passed. The door opened.

Mouth agape, Darcy stared at him. "Michael."

Relief spilled across her features. She looked fetching in white shorts and a purple tank top, her features soft from sleep. She hadn't yet run a hairbrush through her long hair.

"Good morning." The electricity crackling between them snapped him fully awake. "On your way out?"

She brushed past him. "Want to tag along? I need to escape."

The familiar remark sent his thoughts spinning back to childhood. The boredom of life with absentee parents or a recent argument with her mother had predictably sent Darcy into the forest.

"Sure." Dazed, he watched her bound down the steps.

At a fast clip, she crossed the driveway and rounded the side of the mansion. She was halfway across the back lawn before he caught up. Fir trees clustered between the two properties, where the grass gave way to brushy undergrowth. She darted through the trees.

Rosy light painted the treetops. They ducked into the forest, taking the path they'd used during childhood when their friendship had led them on countless adventures. The ground rose up steadily. The rippling murmur of the Chagrin River filtered through the heavy necklace of trees. On the precipice above the river, moss blanketed the ground, softening their strides as they approached a magnificent tree.

The huge oak clung to the edge of the steepest section of the hillside. It stood like a sentry guarding the dangerous line between safe ground and the thirty-foot drop to the river below. Pinkish light slatted across its massive trunk. Ponderous limbs stretched into the churning air far above the bubbling river.

A stack of large gray stones leaned against the tree's craggy trunk. Devising the makeshift steps had been an arduous task Michael had undertaken in grade school to make reaching the lowest branches easier. Summer storms often wrecked the steps, making rebuilding them a constant task. At age eleven, he'd finally had the sense to drag a pail of cement through the forest to set the stones permanently in place.

Stooping, Darcy inspected the makeshift steps. "Is the top stone new?" She ran a finger around the diamond-shaped contours. "It doesn't look familiar."

"Added last April," he supplied. "Emerson helped."

"You bring him here? To our tree?"

Our tree. The possessive remark surprised him. It also, he realized with a start, pleased him more than was sensible.

"I hate to break it to you—from your nephew's perspective, this is *his* tree."

"How far up has he climbed?"

"Not far. He's still working on his tree-climbing skills."

Walking around the massive trunk, she peered at the limbs thrust over the steep overhang like giant hands. "You don't let Emerson climb over the river, do you?"

The question was ironic. When they were children, he'd silently quaked whenever the intrepid Darcy shinnied up the oak tree and out onto a limb. Back then, curiosity won out over risk.

"Emerson knows the rule. He's only allowed to climb on the forest side."

She came back around, ascended the steps. With the agility of a child, she caught the lowest limb and hoisted herself into the tree. Leaning against the trunk, she stared at the ground. "My mother is dying," she said.

"What?"

"She doesn't have long. At least that's what she says. I won't know what to believe until I talk to her doctor."

"You can't talk to her doctor without her permission."

"I know, Michael. She promised she'd take care of it."

"How long does Rosalind believe she has?"

"A few months. Maybe until Christmas—it's hard to tell. She has amyloidosis."

"I'm not familiar with the term."

"It's a protein disorder. Amyloid, an abnormal protein made in your bone marrow, gets deposited in your organs. Liver, heart, kidneys—in my mother's case, the protein is replacing heart muscle."

"There's no medical intervention to stop it?"

"There are lots of therapies." Frustration rippled across Darcy's brow. "From what I found online, this isn't the type of disease that usually leads to a death sentence. At least not if caught early. My mother ignored the symptoms. Tingling in her hands and feet, an irregular heartbeat. Lots of fatigue and weakness."

No wonder Darcy looked wrung out. She'd spent the night searching websites. "How long has your mother been having symptoms?" he asked.

"For a couple of years, at least. It was hard to pin her down."

"Hold on. Didn't she mention the symptoms to her doctor?" When Darcy frowned, he expelled a disbelieving breath. "She *didn't*?"

"Crazy, right?" Bright spots of color rose beneath the nearly translucent skin of Darcy's cheeks. Agitated, she hopped down from the tree. "That's the part I don't get. It's not as if the symptoms would disappear if she hid them long enough. Why hide them?"

He suspected they both knew the answer. Rosalind controlled every aspect of her life. She took rigorous care of her physical health. Given her strong-willed nature, she'd undoubtedly believed in her ability to outwit the symptoms. If she ignored them long enough, they would disappear.

She'd believed her tenacious hold on life was stronger than any threat.

Michael asked, "If she kept this to herself, how *did* she receive a diagnosis?"

"She blacked out in court. Slid right out of her chair and crumpled behind the judge's bench. The defense attorney arguing the case before her thought she was having a heart attack. A woman on the jury totally freaked out."

"Pandemonium in the courtroom."

"Basically. It takes hell breaking loose for my mother to face health issues she shouldn't have avoided." Behind the oak tree, a scattering of birds arrowed down to the riverbank. Grim-faced, Darcy watched their descent. "She was hospitalized for several days. A cardiologist did the biopsy of her heart."

"And gave the diagnosis?"

Darcy nodded. "She took an immediate leave of absence, which she's now making permanent. The only option left is to get on a heart transplant list. She informed me and Latrice in no uncertain terms that she won't consider it. A minor issue, since she's not a great candidate. Or so she says. I won't buy the explanation until I talk to her doctor."

"What happens now?"

"From what I understand, amyloidosis reduces the heart's ability to fill with blood between heartbeats. That's why she blacked out. She'll have more episodes going forward. More dizziness." Darcy grimaced. "Shortness of breath . . . and more pain."

"You'll have to stop her from driving," he said, imagining the arguments sure to follow. "Gird yourself for battle. Your mother won't relinquish her mobility without a fight."

"Tell me about it. Latrice and I are mapping out a schedule—we'll need extra help, including a visiting nurse later on. A home health aide even sooner. I'm not ready for the battles to come."

"Does Emerson know? He's been worried about her. I'll wager he's been worried about her for longer than he's let on."

"He's the reason the rest of us know *anything*. Last night, he cornered her with the strangest question."

"Let me guess. He asked if she was nearing her expiration date?" When Darcy looked at him swiftly, Michael added, "There's not much that gets past your nephew. He's known something was up. Maybe he saw Rosalind have a dizzy spell, or noticed other symptoms."

"All the more reason why he wanted me to come back." An air of regret followed Darcy's movements as she scrubbed her palms across her face. She was only beginning to process the changes sweeping into her life. "After my mother revealed the basics, Emerson ran upstairs. I stayed with him until he fell asleep."

"He'll need all the love you can give him."

"I won't let him down."

"I know you won't."

She hooked a tendril of hair behind her ear, her expression gaining an admirable level of focus. For a woman more adventurous than steady, the change was fascinating to behold.

"Michael, we'll need to keep Emerson busy this summer," she said.

He caught the bright pronoun: *we*. She believed his participation was important; the assumption warmed him. "That's a good plan," he agreed.

"Watching his grandmother's decline will be difficult. I don't want him obsessing about what will come. I wish he hadn't dropped out of all his summer activities."

"It's not his fault. Rosalind makes enemies wherever she goes. By extension, Emerson catches the flack."

"Is there anyone in Geauga County my mother *hasn't* antagonized?"

"I'm sure there are a few holdouts," Michael remarked dryly. Considering, he added, "Strange how things change. Before Rosalind put my mother on the blacklist, she had lots of friends. All those women on the country club circuit. I've always wondered if their falling out led those mutual friends to pick my mother over Rosalind."

"Don't waste your time attempting to unravel the secret." Darcy appraised the leafy dome above them. "I need to schedule a sit-down with my mother's doctor," she mused, switching track. "How quickly will she decline? Do I need to hire a visiting nurse immediately? And most important, are there any viable options to stop the disease?" Her eyes watering, she inhaled a deep breath.

A flurry of questions streamed through Michael's head. Was Darcy up to the task? And what about Rosalind? Her ability to accept help from her estranged daughter wasn't a sure bet.

Only time would tell. Still, Darcy seemed ready to shoulder the hardships. It seemed a selfless decision—little more than Rosalind's cruelty and petty grudges bound them together.

～

The conversation finished, they left the forest.

Darcy asked, "Do I owe you an apology for dragging you on a walk?" To her surprise, spending time with Michael was easier than anticipated. "I doubt you planned on traipsing through the woods first thing this morning."

"It's fine. I'm glad we had a chance to talk."

"Do you want to see Emerson? I'm guessing that's why you stopped over."

"Actually, I want to see Rosalind." Matching her pace, Michael explained about his plan to begin taking Emerson on scheduled outings. Summing up, he added, "Should I come back later? All things considered, this isn't the best time to argue my case."

"As if there *is* a good time." Darcy hesitated. "How will you change her mind? She's told Emerson to avoid all members of the Varano family."

"If Rosalind wants assurances I'll keep her precious grandson away from my mother and Tippi, I'll promise to follow the rule—for now," he clarified with a gratifying note of determination. Evidently, he'd given this a great deal of thought. "It's time for things to change. Rosalind has spent too many years building a wall between our families."

"A *big* wall. Don't expect it to come crashing down with one lobbying effort."

"Just watch me. I intend to dismantle it brick by brick. Not because I care to analyze what went wrong in the first place or have any interest in patching up our mothers' broken friendship. My interest begins and ends with your nephew. The war games *will* end—for Emerson's sake."

His sincerity threaded hope through Darcy. Could Michael normalize relations between their families? The coming months promised to bring many difficulties. Having Nella and Tippi nearby for emotional comfort would be a gift. Emerson would need their support.

Darcy knew she would too.

"You love my nephew," she said, moved by the knowledge.

"Growing up surrounded by women isn't easy for a boy. At least I had my father for most of my childhood."

"He was a nice man." Unlike her own father, Joseph Varano had been a hands-on dad, finding time in his busy schedule for Michael— and Darcy. Silently, she was grateful that the loving parenting Michael had known in childhood would now benefit her nephew. Which made her add, "Emerson does need you to lean on, now more than ever. He hasn't even begun to process what my mother told us last night."

"It will be hard for you too, Darcy. We aren't built to accept death without a fight—our own death or a loved one's."

"Which is why I plan to fight. I don't care what my mother says. There must be something we can do."

"I'm glad you're not giving up. She's agreed to let you talk to her doctor?"

"She has."

"Check out all the options. If you find something viable, don't back down until you get her on board." Michael gave her a knowing glance. "While you're navigating her care, try not to be too hard on yourself. You have a bad habit of beating yourself up. Or have you turned over a new leaf?"

"I wish," she murmured. They reached the patio, and she drew him to a stop. "Question."

"Anything."

"Going forward, how should I approach my mother's illness with Emerson? Wait until he's ready to talk? Draw him out? He's awfully precise for a kid."

Michael grinned. "And too smart for his own good."

"I don't want to scare him with too many details or seem evasive if he *does* want the facts. I've begun looking into support groups, and there's a good child psychologist in Chagrin Falls. But I don't want to leave everything to the professionals. I want to be there for Emerson."

Breaking off, she cringed beneath a sudden wave of embarrassment. Foisting all of this on Michael felt wrong. It was kindness enough that he appeared open to easing them back into the friendship they'd once enjoyed. He seemed willing to overlook the complications that had come later, when they began dating.

Which drew her thoughts to the thornier issue. She owed Michael an apology. Eight years ago, she'd left Ohio without the courtesy of saying goodbye. They'd been deep in a relationship back then. Yet she'd allowed grief to drive her from Ohio without giving him the slimmest explanation.

Wording the apology was the real problem.

Unaware of her dilemma, he offered a confident smile that nearly masked the concern darkening his eyes. "Go slow with Emerson," he suggested. "He's a bright kid, and he *has* suspected Rosalind's illness for some time. Wait until he starts asking questions. In a day or two, maybe longer. And stock up on dental floss."

The amusing counsel eased the tension thrumming inside her. "That's your advice?"

"He likes to floss when he's worried. One of his quirks."

"At least he's not doing heroin."

"Hard drugs aren't his thing. But toothpaste is. Consider stockpiling the stuff. Your nephew also likes to brush when he's working things out."

"This is freaky, how much you know about him. Should I be jealous?"

"Totally up to you," Michael said, and the mirth in his gaze eased her worries. "Fair warning, though."

Her brows lifted. "There's a warning?"

"Don't even try to push me off center stage. I've spent a year hanging out with the kid when Rosalind wasn't looking. I don't mind admitting I like him a lot."

"I can tell," she agreed, grinning. The easy banter gave her the courage to plunge into the more difficult topic. "Michael, when we were dating . . . I'm sorry about what happened. After we lost my father and Elizabeth, I was a mess. That doesn't excuse my actions. I should have called you before I left Ohio. I should have said goodbye."

"Maybe it's better you didn't."

It wasn't the response she'd expected. "How so?"

"What makes you sure I would have let you go?" A hint of sadness etched his strong features. Snuffing it out, he added, "I thought we agreed you'd stop being hard on yourself. Start now."

"I'm a work in progress."

"Yes, you are. I am too." He rubbed his jaw, apparently searching for the right words. "Listen, you were in a difficult situation. I understand why you left."

"You're not angry?"

"Eight years after the fact? Get real. When have I ever held a grudge?"

She sighed with relief. *Never.*

Sobering, he added, "I am glad you came home, although I'm sorry about everything on your plate. If you need anything in the coming months, I'm here for you—and Emerson."

They went inside. The coffeepot sat unfilled, an indication that Latrice wasn't yet at the house. None of the lights were on in the living room, and the foyer rested in a peaceful quiet. Darcy peered up the staircase. On the landing midway down, Samson had taken a seat. Dressed in long johns and a threadbare T-shirt, he was thumbing through his smartphone.

He looked up. "Where is everyone? Emerson isn't in his room, and I haven't seen your mama yet."

"I'm not sure. We're still looking for them." She strode to the bottom of the stairwell. "Why don't you come down and meet Michael? He stopped over to talk to my mother."

When he came down, Michael said, "You're Darcy's friend from South Carolina? I've been looking forward to meeting you."

"Samson Dray." He stuck out his hand.

Clasping it, Michael smiled. "How old are you?"

"Eighteen, sir."

"You're here all summer?"

"I'm here permanently. Unless Darcy throws me out."

She chuckled. "I'd never throw you out. I consider you family."

"What are your plans?" Michael prodded. "Do you have work experience?"

The youth threw an uncertain glance at Darcy. She refrained from offering a lifeline. If this was a job interview, Samson should stand up for himself.

"Yes, sir," he said. "I've worked three jobs. I met Darcy at the last place."

"I could use an extra set of hands in the shop. My business is expanding faster than I'd expected. Are you interested?" When Samson brightened, Michael added, "You have a good work record? Showing up on time and all that?"

"The boss has liked me at every place I've worked." Samson squared his shoulders. "I'm always right on time."

"Can you start this week? I've taken on a new project, with a tight deadline to finish the cabinetry. I could use an assistant helping around the shop."

"You're offering me a job?"

"Let's meet at my shop in thirty minutes. We'll discuss your wages and work schedule."

"Sounds great!" Samson dashed upstairs.

Once he was out of earshot, Darcy said, "Word of warning. He's the sweetest teenager you'll ever meet, but he's awfully dreamy. More like a kid starting high school than a recent graduate. He grew up in foster care."

"When we get the chance, I'd love to hear why you brought him to Ohio."

"You'll enjoy the story—it's fascinating. Especially the parts about special stars and spiritual connections."

Michael quirked a brow. "Interesting."

Ending the discussion, he began strolling the perimeter of the circular foyer. He poked his head into each room. "Where *is* everyone? Did your mother take Emerson out for breakfast?"

"Good question." Perhaps there was a note in the kitchen. She began retracing her steps as Michael wheeled toward the front door.

"Darcy, check this out."

He stepped out onto the front porch. In the center of the wide sweep of lawn, Emerson darted from one tree to the next. Trailing behind, Rosalind murmured words too far away to decipher.

Darcy's eyes misted over. Despite last night's difficult conversation, her mother looked serene, nearly happy. Her makeup was carefully applied and her silver hair expertly styled. She'd gone to great pains to resemble the vision of health for her worried grandson.

She spied a pretty green box in Rosalind's hands. "What is she carrying?"

"The bird feeder? Call it a child's successful attempt at lobbying. I helped Emerson make it for her. I left it outside the front door this morning." Satisfaction spread across Michael's features. "Looks like Emerson found the bird feeder before I put the master plan in motion."

"You taught my nephew woodworking?" The gesture was incredibly kind. Then her heart lurched. "You didn't let him near power tools, did you?"

"Why not? Small boys and power tools are a match made in heaven," he quipped. "Next, I'll let him try out a chain saw. Let him do serious damage to the brush growing behind my barn."

"Very funny." Her nephew was a pipsqueak. The thought of him wielding power tools gave her the willies. She shivered.

At her reaction, mischief darted across Michael's face. He leaned close. "Got any other dumb questions?"

When she shrugged, he flicked her nose. The spontaneous affection startled them both.

They leaped apart like teenagers caught trading kisses. Michael's eyes delved into hers. The intensity of his gaze arrowed warmth to her belly.

He cleared his throat. "If you'll excuse me, I need to speak with Rosalind. Why don't you stay here? There's no reason to put yourself in the line of fire."

"I can take it. Besides, there's safety in numbers." Darcy trotted down the steps. "She *will* give you a hard time. Two against one. Let's keep the odds in our favor."

"Deal, but keep your mouth shut. I'll do the talking. If memory serves, you can't joust for thirty seconds without losing your balance. I'd rather not watch your mother draw blood."

"Hey!"

"Fear not, fair lady." He winked. "I shall slay the dragon on your behalf."

Taking the lead, he strode onto the lawn. Ten yards beyond, Rosalind had selected a tree for her new gift, on a branch low enough for a child to reach. Emerson swung his arms side to side as she slid the bird feeder into place. The branch wobbled as she let it go.

The sound of approaching footsteps caught her attention. When she swiveled around, anxiety slowed Darcy's gait. Michael continued forward at an even pace, ready to confront the woman now growing rigid at his approach. Rosalind's mouth thinned in disapproval.

He glanced at Emerson before pausing several paces from his opponent. Darcy waited behind him as he regarded her mother.

"Mrs. Goodridge, hello. Beautiful morning, isn't it?"

"Yes, it is."

"I've been meaning to talk to you. You haven't returned my calls."

The accusation's matter-of-fact tone deftly cornered Rosalind. At her side, Emerson watched her closely. He seemed no more certain of the conversation's outcome than she was.

"I have not," she finally agreed. "We have nothing to discuss."

"You're wrong. Emerson and I have become good friends. Your animus toward my mother shouldn't spoil it."

"He's my grandson. *I* will decide what is in his best interest."

"You're making a mistake. What are you trying to protect him from? I'm not the bad guy here."

The invective she prepared never left her lips. Emerson bolted from her side, abandoning her for the good-natured man trying to reason with her. His disloyalty startled her into silence. But children possess the sensitivity of a psychic, and the boy stopped short in Michael's long shadow.

A battle raged on Emerson's face. His dilemma brought Darcy a step closer.

They formed an uneasy circle, the three adults and the boy. Rosalind looked apoplectic with rage. In a subconscious bow to her feelings, Emerson shifted into the adult mannerisms he'd learned too well.

"Michael, I'm so very glad you're here." Too intimidated by his stern grandmother to venture closer, he mimicked Rosalind's stance. "We've received bad news."

"You have," Michael agreed. "How are you holding up?"

"As well as can be expected."

"Don't expect too much, sport. You have every right to feel bad."

"I suppose." A sob broke from Emerson's throat. The proof of his sorrow crumpled Rosalind's great fury like autumn leaves crushed on the wind. She was pressing a palm to her heart when he added, "It's quite difficult."

"I know." Lowering his large body, Michael planted a knee in the grass. "Come here, buddy."

His expression collapsing, Emerson raced into his arms.

Chapter 16

As June's breezy warmth gave way to July's blistering heat, the Goodridge household settled into a new routine.

Michael became a frequent visitor. He stayed long enough to share a few pleasantries with Darcy and Latrice before taking Emerson for the day's outing. Rosalind planned her schedule accordingly. She managed to avoid being downstairs whenever he arrived. Surrendering in the matter of sharing her grandson did not mean she liked the change.

In a bow to her enmity for his mother, Michael never took Emerson next door to visit with Nella. Instead, he planned outings in Chagrin Falls or farther afield. They visited the Cleveland Zoo and found new fishing holes on the Chagrin River.

On Sunday afternoons, they rented go-karts at a nearby track or visited the carnivals that popped up every summer in the towns scattered across Geauga County. They rode the Ferris wheel and competed at bumper cars. They consumed so much cotton candy, Darcy found sticky flecks in her nephew's hair when he returned home.

Often, Michael invited Samson to join them. He was one of the guys, after all, and every male needed days when he could avoid female companionship and simply horse around. Samson usually refused the invitations, choosing instead to man the phone at Varano Cabinetry or sweep the mounds of sawdust from the floor. He organized shipments of lumber as they came in, freeing up much-needed space in the shop.

He quickly proved himself indispensable and graduated to full-time status. In the evenings, with Darcy's encouragement, Samson began checking out colleges. He was planning to enroll in several courses in the fall.

Like Michael and his young companions, Darcy eased into a new schedule. She felt gratitude on the days that flowed by uneventfully. She hid icy bolts of fear whenever her mother walked with a slight limp. On some days, Rosalind took long naps unannounced. On the worst days, the progressing amyloidosis sent pain whipping through her extremities. She never uttered a complaint. Even so, Darcy and Latrice watched over her like mother hens. If Rosalind believed they were out of view, she rubbed her tender arms and calves, wincing with pain.

The symptoms of the disease tested her ability to endure. They did not break her spirit. She remained brittle and short-tempered with the two women tasked with her care. Yet Rosalind did make allowances. Even the battle Darcy had dreaded over banning her mother's driving privileges never materialized.

One rainy Friday in July, Darcy found the keys to the Mercedes by the coffeepot. Beside the keys was the title to her mother's car, signed over to her.

With her illness no longer secret, Rosalind succumbed to sullen acceptance. The independence she once took for granted was slowly curtailed. Darcy now ferried her to the salon and to the gym, where her declining health restricted her regimen to the seated elliptical trainer or working out with five-pound weights.

After much discussion regarding the responsibilities involved—and much badgering on Darcy's part—her mother finally gave her medical power of attorney. It was a cold triumph. Since the stubborn judge refused to add her name to a heart transplant list, few options remained for her care.

"She wants to die with dignity," Dr. Ruth Tanaka told Darcy. They were seated in Tanaka's Chagrin Falls office, waiting for Rosalind to return from the lab. With cropped silver hair and a no-nonsense style, Tanaka had been Rosalind's primary care doctor for decades. Rosalind insisted on coordinating all treatment ordered by her specialists through the offices of her seventy-year-old physician.

"What about options other than a heart transplant?" They'd been over this before. Darcy refused to accept that they were in a holding pattern, with death as the only destination. "What about experimental drugs or clinical trials? There must be something we can try."

"The Mayo Clinic in Minnesota is conducting a trial. The drug protocol looks promising, but your mother isn't an ideal candidate. A minor point. I mentioned the trial to her right before you came back to Ohio. She wouldn't consider leaving Emerson."

"What if I accompany her? I can fly home frequently. Latrice and Samson will help with Emerson on the days I'm with her in Minnesota."

"It's too late to enroll, Darcy. The trial commenced in June. As for experimental drugs, there are no medications available that we haven't already called into service to alleviate some of your mother's symptoms."

"Meaning we're at a dead end." Her own poor choice of words made Darcy wince. She held up a hand. "Sorry. I'm still trying to wrap my head around this."

Tanaka regarded her with sympathy. "I'm the one who is sorry. I wish there *were* more options. Your mother's disease has progressed significantly in the short time since she received a diagnosis." The doctor drummed her fingers on her desk. "You can't influence her to change her mind?"

"About going on a transplant list? Believe me, I've tried. Every time I broach the subject, she leaves the room."

"Then we're at an impasse."

Darcy's heart lurched.

When she remained silent, Tanaka said, "Aside from continuing the regimen of steroids and the various pain medications, there is no magic bullet. Frankly, I'm amazed your mother is doing so well. Rosalind has an uncommonly strong will. Bear in mind that hereditary amyloidosis is a rare disorder, and unpredictable. As more proteins aggregate in her heart, she'll present symptoms she can no longer control."

"Hereditary . . . should Emerson and I be tested?"

"Your nephew was tested soon after your mother received her diagnosis. He doesn't carry the mutation." Tanaka smiled reassuringly. "I can schedule the test for you, but you needn't worry. Most patients who inherit the mutation never present symptoms of the disease. In your mother's case, there were therapies we might have called into service if we'd found the disease sooner. I'm sorry we didn't."

The quietly compassionate words poured fear through Darcy. "What comes next?"

"Rosalind's neuropathy will become extreme. She'll experience more dizzy spells and difficulty breathing. She'll present many of the classic symptoms of heart failure. My nurse has literature you can read to become better acquainted with the symptoms."

It was a laundry list of horrors, none of which Darcy wished to face. "The neuropathy . . . she'll lose feeling in her arms and legs?"

"The tingling she now experiences will become more pronounced. She'll have increased weakness. I suspect she already has instances when her skin is distressingly itchy—I wrote a scrip that should help." Frowning, Tanaka added, "She will lose the ability to walk."

"When?"

"A few months, perhaps longer. We will continue to monitor her closely. Start thinking about moving her bedroom to the first floor. Knowing Rosalind, she'll fight you tooth and nail. Ease her into the idea slowly."

"Easier said than done." Overwhelmed, Darcy balled her hands in her lap. "Give me a timeline. How long until I need to move her downstairs?"

"Wait until the end of summer, when Emerson returns to school," the doctor said. "How is he managing?"

Considering, Darcy combed her fingers through her hair. "Great, most of the time. He's a lot like Rosalind—taking everything in stride. I have a child psychologist on standby. So far, Emerson doesn't appear to need the help. I'm keeping him busy, and a neighbor helps out. He's been a godsend. Several times a week, he takes my nephew out for adventures. Total 'guy time,' which Emerson needs."

"I'm glad you're keeping your nephew busy." Dr. Tanaka rose. "Your mother's labs should be finished. If you need anything before her next appointment, don't hesitate to call."

As Darcy left Tanaka's office, a low, heated conversation drifted into the corridor. With a groan, she slowed her pace.

In the outer office, she found her mother arguing with the receptionist. The nervous brunette clacked madly on her keyboard.

"Problem?" Darcy asked her mother.

"When is there *not* a problem? I schedule a morning appointment, then Dr. Tanaka's staff moves it to the afternoon. I've had this problem repeatedly."

"Is it possible you're overreacting? Lab days never leave you brimming with sunshine."

"Don't patronize me."

"I'm sorry. I didn't mean to patronize you. But you *are* retired. You're available whenever her staff wants to poke you with needles or make you pee in a cup."

"*Why* must you resort to vulgar language?"

"Habit?" When Rosalind glared, she tried the reasonable approach. "Why does it matter when you come in? I'm happy to drive whether you have a morning appointment or one in the afternoon."

"Don't be obtuse. It matters, Darcy."

The zinger hurt, but she took care not to react. "Okay, then explain it to me."

"I'm a morning person, not a night owl," Rosalind snapped, as if Tanaka and her browbeaten staff, working with malign intent, planned to haul her into the office at midnight. "Why schedule appointments if my physician's inept staff can't follow directions? Why not show up whenever I please?" She stabbed a frosty glance at the receptionist. "This isn't physics. No one has asked you to split atoms. Why aren't you done yet?"

"One moment, ma'am."

Rosalind expelled an elaborate breath. "By all means, take your time. Take all the time in the world. I love nothing more than standing here growing moss while you master basic clerical skills."

"Give her a break, Mother." Darcy offered the receptionist an apologetic smile. "Please forgive her. She's not always this rude. Sometimes she's asleep."

"You must live for those moments." The receptionist handed Darcy the new appointment card.

In the elevator, Rosalind plucked at her nubby yellow blazer. "Warn me now if we're having one of those days. Darcy and her comedy routine. Should I avoid you until dinnertime? Or would you prefer I book you on Comedy Central?"

"If I've offended your delicate sensibilities, I am sorry."

"No, you're not."

"Okay, I'm not. You love giving people a hard time. It's cruel. I don't have to like it."

"The world isn't up to snuff. Earbuds and text messages—I shudder to consider how the abundant diversions are lowering IQs across America. I'm doing the world a service by pointing out ineptitude."

Darcy grunted. "More like you're getting a cheap thrill by pounding harmless strangers into submission. What *is* the definition of aggressive behavior? It's been a decade since my last psych class."

"Darcy!"

"Well, it's embarrassing. When Elizabeth and I were kids, we dreaded parent-teacher conferences. You never made it through one without insulting the teacher or casting aspersions on the state of modern education. The minute you got on a roll, I ditched for the girls' room."

"I was a concerned parent. I paid good money to send you and Elizabeth to private institutions. If one of your teachers wasn't up to par, I made my displeasure known."

Yes, you did—while terrorizing the entire staff, Darcy thought. From what Emerson had described in their private conversations, he fared no better. Rosalind continued to browbeat educators far and wide.

Letting it go, she appraised her mother. "How were your labs?"

"I 'peed in a cup,' and gave my last drop of blood. Same as usual." Rosalind's discerning gaze swept across her. "Why don't you schedule an intervention with a stylist? You're beginning to resemble Joni Mitchell after her second divorce."

"I'm not into primping. That's your thing. Give me a bottle of mascara and a tube of lip gloss, and I'm good to go."

"Having your hair styled properly isn't 'primping.' When did you last visit a salon? Before or after that last psych class?"

"A week before I left South Carolina. I've been a little busy since then."

"Poor hygiene is a sign of a disordered mind."

"I *have* showered." Darcy lifted her hand to her mouth, blew out. "And my breath is minty fresh."

The elevator slid open. Rosalind marched outside at a brisk pace that belied her poor health. As she rounded the side of the building, Darcy hunted for signs of the progressive neuropathy Dr. Tanaka had described. Her mother's gait appeared balanced. She wasn't favoring her left or right foot. In a bow to looking her best, she'd even selected two-inch heels in a darker shade of yellow to complement her natty blazer.

"Darcy, hurry up." Rosalind veered across the parking lot in the direction of the Mercedes. "If you can't pick up your feet, I'll call an Uber. Did you get *any* sleep last night?"

"I'm coming!"

She was sprinting across the lot when a woman in a clingy pink dress got out of a black SUV. She sashayed into the aisle between the rows of cars with her purse flapping open as she rooted around inside the large bag. As she came forward, Darcy realized her plump features and curly brown hair were familiar. She was trying to place the woman's face when a strange thing happened.

On a gasp, the woman spotted Rosalind. She halted abruptly.

Her chunky gold necklace leaped off her bosom. It clipped her jaw. Spinning around, she raced back toward her SUV. In her haste, a sandal flew off one pudgy foot. Darcy watched in stunned disbelief. No danger lurked in the empty lot. It dawned on her that the woman was frightened of . . . Rosalind.

The startling deduction sent Darcy's glance winging to her mother. Rosalind's eyes lasered the woman's back.

In a gesture astonishingly out of character, Rosalind cupped her hands around her mouth. "That's right, run! You're a coward *and* a harlot."

The gibing sent the other sandal whipping into the air. The woman, picking up speed, cast a frantic glance over her shoulder. A mistake.

She rammed into the side of her SUV.

Rosalind shot a fist into the air. Triumph! She slid into the Mercedes's passenger side. "That'll leave a goose egg." She snickered. "Justice prevails."

Darcy gaped at her. "What is wrong with you?" Through the windshield, she watched with relief as the woman slapped a steadying hand onto the hood of the SUV. One of the straps had broken loose on her clingy dress. At least she hadn't been knocked out cold.

"There's nothing wrong with me. I feel good. Better than good."

Darcy's synapses lit, and the name fell into place. "Wait. Isn't that Morgan Harbert?" Thirty pounds heavier and older than she remembered. She jammed the key into the ignition. "That *is* Mrs. Harbert, right? You and Dad used to play doubles with the Harberts."

"I'm shocked you remember her."

"Well, I'll never forget her now!"

"She laughs like a hyena. I dreaded inviting her to cocktail parties. The minute someone told a joke, it was like listening to fingernails screech down a chalkboard."

"Care to explain what that was about?" In the rearview mirror, Darcy glimpsed the injured Mrs. Harbert with her hand pressed to her brow. A goose egg, indeed. She hobbled across the lot in search of her sandals. "Why did she run away when she saw you? She was *scared*."

With an enigmatic smile, her mother gazed out the window.

"Fine. Keep your nasty secrets. I'm not interested." Prickly with curiosity, she pulled onto the street. "I'll just stay shocked. If she hadn't run away, would you have put up your dukes?"

Her mother chuckled.

Not the response Darcy expected. "Word to the wise, sister. Get thrown in jail for assault and battery, and I *won't* bail you out."

More silence. At least her mother had stopped chuckling. If she'd kept it up, Darcy would've been left speechless.

"Do you have any errands before we head back?" she asked. "Latrice told me she's all set on ingredients for tonight's dinner, but maybe there's something else you need from the store?"

"Lilies."

"What?"

Snapping open her purse, her mother retrieved a lipstick. "Do not order lilies for my funeral. Or gardenias. There's nothing more depressing than huge drifts of sickly sweet bouquets festooning a casket."

Darcy swerved toward the curb, righted the Mercedes. "What *are* you talking about? You almost wrestled Mrs. Harbert in a parking lot, and now you want to discuss flowers?"

"I've given this a lot of thought. Order colorful bouquets. Ideally scentless." Rosalind flipped down the visor, uncapped the lipstick.

She rimmed her mouth in shell pink. "Something fresh and lively, for Emerson. I don't want him overly upset."

"If you're aiming for a happy event, stop overreaching. He's eight. He *will* be upset."

"I suppose I shouldn't worry. He won't let me down."

The conversation's morbid turn made Darcy suddenly defensive. She wasn't ready for talk of endings, or the goodbyes they would entail. "In point of fact, you've molded your grandson into your diabolical image. That doesn't mean he won't cry an ocean of tears."

"I'm not diabolical."

"You were to Mrs. Harbert. Did you send her a psychic message? Something really scary? I'd like to know why one mean look from you made her take off in a hurry."

"Oh, leave it alone. You're fathoms out of your depth."

"Apparently." Darcy forced her unwilling heart to approach the more upsetting topic. "If you want my opinion, Emerson is too young to attend." Rallying, she added, "If I mention the better option, you won't jump out of the car, will you? Every time I bring it up, you head for the exit."

"I'm not going on a transplant list. Stop bringing it up."

"The Tin Man got a new heart. Look what it did for him."

"I'm nothing like the Tin Man. If you're in the mood to watch a classic, tell Emerson when we get home. He loves *The Wizard of Oz.*" Rosalind studied her fingernails, frowned at a chip in the beige polish. "At my funeral, please seat my grandson by Judge Mandelbaum. He has a lively wit and a fondness for children. He'll keep Emerson in good spirits."

Darcy snorted. *Judge Isaiah Mandelbaum?* The portly jurist possessed a stern demeanor and a fondness for cigars. During childhood, Elizabeth had been terrified of him. Darcy had mostly been wary. The stench wafting from his severe black suits had made her sneeze.

"Mother, please. Must we discuss your funeral?" Pain shifted through her chest at the words, an agony she wasn't prepared to feel. "You're doing great. We have to begin making some changes on the home front, but nothing crazy. Let's put off the heavy stuff until later."

For once, her mother's eyes were free of rancor. "We have to talk about it at some point," she said.

"Not yet. There's still lots of time."

The road wound higher, past a hilly section of Metro Park and a subdivision of attractive homes. Darcy planned to take Emerson to a craft show in Cleveland Heights tomorrow, Handmade Heaven. When she and Elizabeth were in high school and, later, home during the long summer breaks from college, attending the fair had been a favorite July pastime. Tomorrow she'd bring Emerson home with his arms loaded with funky, handmade toys.

July was a carefree month, not a time to ponder the uncertain future.

She asked, "Are you scared?"

Rosalind dropped the lipstick into her bag. "Not yet."

She clicked the purse shut.

～

Darcy hurried back into the kitchen. The others were already in the dining room. Bending over the platter, she breathed in the delectable aroma.

"The turkey smells heavenly," she told Latrice. The expertly carved slices were drizzled with Latrice's famous gravy. "I can't believe you went to this much trouble."

"It was no trouble at all."

"Roasting a whole turkey *and* making all the trimmings?" True, people dealt with life's speed bumps in various ways. For Latrice, that meant devising lavish dinners more common in the holiday season. "If I haven't told you lately—you're incredible."

"Your opinion, not mine." A note of distress laced the housekeeper's voice. She began scooping mashed potatoes into a china bowl. "How was Rosalind's appointment with Dr. Tanaka?"

"Okay, I guess."

The housekeeper gave her the once-over. "You look frazzled. Mind explaining why?"

"It's been a strange day." An image of Morgan Harbert face-planting into her SUV flashed through Darcy's brain. "I'd rather not go into it."

"Fine by me. Did you get a chance to bring it up?"

"We only talked for a minute, on the drive home. She still won't consider the procedure."

The news slowed Latrice's movements as she finished scooping potatoes. The spoon clattered into the porcelain holder by the stove. She gripped the edge of the counter.

"What is it?" Worried, Darcy rushed over. Latrice wasn't usually quick to tears. She appeared ready to break the habit now.

"I'm mad at myself. Furious, to tell the truth."

"About what?"

"How could an eight-year-old boy pick up on his grandmother's symptoms, and I never noticed them? Oh, I made comments when your mother seemed tired, and she's seemed tired a lot since last year. It's not like she's getting any younger. When she took the leave of absence from her judgeship, I believed her ridiculous lies. Needing a few weeks' rest—what a heap of nonsense. Why didn't I ask more questions? Why didn't I make her tell me the truth?"

"Because you couldn't. The great Rosalind Goodridge seldom brings anyone into her confidence."

"I should've been quicker on the uptake. If we'd found the disease sooner, she'd have better options."

"Fair enough, but that doesn't mean you're at fault. If it's any consolation, she loves you. Even if she doesn't know how to show it."

There was proof enough in Rosalind's will. The lengthy document left the bulk of her estate to her two surviving heirs. The will was also chock-full of bequests to charities and foundations, generous gifts the wealthy judge continued to fuss over—and it also contained instructions regarding her loyal employee.

Darcy was to pay off the mortgage on Latrice's house in Chagrin Falls. She was to provide her with a monthly stipend for the rest of her life. The money to fulfill both provisions was already deposited in a fund at Goldman Sachs.

Rosalind had even penned a note thanking Latrice for her years of service—and terminating her employment. She'd never have to work again.

Latrice, oblivious to the largess, stared absently at the fragrant bowl of potatoes.

"I can't bear this," she said. "Your mother needs to get on the transplant list. There's so much to live for . . . why does she dig in her heels?"

"When I figure it out, I'll clue you in." Darcy resisted the urge to offer a long, rocking hug. If she did, they'd both start crying. They never allowed themselves to fall apart when Emerson was in the house.

Instead, she hoisted up the platter of turkey.

Latrice picked up the mashed potatoes. "Don't you give up, child. There's too much at stake. I'm putting my trust in you to wear her down." On the way out of the kitchen, she shook the sadness from her features. From over her shoulder, she whispered, "There's still time to change her mind."

They went into the dining room. Samson and Emerson had already carried in the side dishes of freshly baked bread, cranberry sauce, honeyed yams, and tossed salad. From opposite sides of the table, they gazed rapturously at the good eats.

At the head of the table, Rosalind frowned. "At last. What were you doing in the kitchen?"

"Nothing, Mother."

"You're no help to Latrice if you delay her in getting dinner on the table."

"Relax. We were just talking." She set down the platter. "You're hungry?" It was a good sign. "You hardly ate yesterday."

"I'm happy to make up for it today. I love turkey and all the trimmings." The judge regarded her talented housekeeper. "I do appreciate this. Thank you for going to the trouble."

"My pleasure. If you want turkey again next week, just say the word."

"You're too kind."

Darcy hovered behind the chair to her mother's right. "When Elizabeth and I were kids, Latrice ate dinner with us in the kitchen. It would've been stupid to set the dining room table for two little girls. Why doesn't Latrice dine with us now? We're all family here, and I'm tired of feeling like a cast member in *Driving Miss Daisy*."

Listening intently, Latrice placed the bowl of potatoes in the center of the table. She made no attempt to hide her smile as her eyes met Darcy's. Quiet affection flowed between them. To Darcy, it seemed the perfect reward after a very strange day.

Rosalind, her fingers poised above the bread basket, froze.

Emerson pulled his ravenous gaze off the turkey. "Aunt Darcy, what an exceptional question! Why doesn't Latrice dine with us? I've been pondering the same thing *for ages*."

"Please stop imitating my speech." Rosalind smoothed the napkin across her lap. "You can't have pondered anything 'for ages.' Not until you have a passing familiarity with compression socks and proof of membership in AARP."

"But it *is* a good question. What do you think, Samson?"

"This is your grandma's house." Swallowing, he gave her a respectful nod. "Ma'am, I believe the decision is yours. Where I come from, whoever pays the bills makes the rules. Plain and simple."

"What a sage observation. You have a great deal of common sense. A rarity these days."

"Yes, ma'am."

"Hold fast to your beliefs, dear," she added with genuine affection. The endearment startled everyone in the room. "You'll need those rock-solid beliefs once you have a family of your own. Children will chip away at your control like nasty little miners. Don't let them."

"I won't," Samson promised.

"Thank you for weighing in." With simmering impatience, she regarded Darcy. "Are you planning to eat while standing? Dinner is growing cold."

"The jury is still out." Change was never easy for her mother. Even one so obvious, it should have occurred long ago. "Will you answer my question?"

"Fine! I'll answer. I've never given much thought to our dining arrangements. Until my retirement, I was rarely home at the dinner hour. I usually worked late."

"Emerson had his dinner with me," Latrice told Darcy. Impish lights flashed through her David Bowie eyes. *"In the kitchen."*

"Wow." Darcy laughed. "Some things never change."

Rosalind fell back in her chair. Her irritation melting away, she regarded Latrice. "If I've offended you in any way—"

"You haven't," Latrice cut in. "I work for you. I understand." The emotionally charged discussion nearly stole her composure. With jittery strokes, she smoothed down her gray dress, the silly maid's uniform that Darcy despised.

When the housekeeper spoke again, her voice was hoarse and unsteady.

"Rosalind, things *are* changing around here. Most of those changes won't be easy. I feel awful about that, and want you to know I'm here for you. Through thick and thin. No matter what comes our way, you can always count on me. You're the prickliest woman in God's creation, but that doesn't mean I don't wish all the best for you."

In the days to come, Darcy would never know if the heartfelt monologue loosened her mother's famous hold on propriety. Or perhaps the dignified judge, having made the fleeing Morgan Harbert ram into her SUV, was still privately enjoying the triumph. There really was no telling. Whatever the reason, a welcome change arrived in the Goodridge household as Rosalind, with an air of great occasion, rose from the table.

She swept a gracious hand toward the chair to her right. The chair that Darcy, her throat now tight with gratitude, had refused to occupy. "Will you join us, Latrice? And please—join us for dinner in the future whenever your schedule permits. We'll wait while you change into your street clothes."

The housekeeper disappeared.

She returned wearing brown slacks and a yellow blouse. But she didn't sit to her employer's right. She gestured for Darcy to sit by her mother. Darcy gladly complied.

When Latrice's intent became obvious, Emerson and Samson picked up their plates and moved down the table until they were in the exact center. Latrice sat at the other end, facing Rosalind with a smile.

By the time the meal commenced, dinner was cold. Nobody cared. They feasted on turkey and all the trimmings like it was Thanksgiving in July.

When they finished, Latrice reminded Emerson they needed to leave soon. "Pleasant Valley Dentistry has evening hours," she explained to Darcy. "Your nephew has a cleaning at seven o'clock."

Darcy took a last sip from her glass. "Should I take him?"

"Don't bother. This is our annual July affair. Mind taking care of the dishes?"

"No problem."

Latrice regarded the boy. "Should we go shopping for new tennis shoes afterward? Your summer pair are getting scruffy."

"Can we get ice cream after we shop?"

"If your teeth don't hurt too much. But they never seem to."

They left the dining room.

Darcy, feeling adrift, watched them go. The cleaning and shopping was an annual event, long established by the housekeeper and Emerson. It was silly to feel left out.

Rosalind folded her napkin beside her plate. To her left, Samson trailed a last piece of homemade bread through the gravy on his plate.

"Do you have plans for the evening?" she asked him.

"No, ma'am." Her curiosity pleased him. "Do you?"

"I haven't, actually. I was wondering if you would like to learn how to play chess."

"I'd like that a lot."

"Wonderful." She rose. "I have a beautiful chess set in my office. Let's play in the living room. We'll be more comfortable there."

Darcy watched the interchange with her heart in her throat. She hated chess. The game took hours to play, and moved at a snail's pace. Before her death, Elizabeth had loved playing in the spare hours when Rosalind found the time.

Chatting quietly, Rosalind and Samson left. In the silence they left behind, Darcy collected up the dishes. The evening was her own.

For the first time since returning to Ohio, there was nothing but time on her hands.

The problem with having the evening to herself? It lent too much time to think.

Chapter 17

Needing a break, Michael left the barn and headed toward the house. Between frequent afternoons spent with Emerson and the sheer volume of cabinetry needed for the Tinley job, burning the midnight oil tonight wasn't a bad idea. A shower first; hours of toiling in the shop had left his muscles stiff. He wondered if he could raid the fridge on his way back outside without sparking an argument.

He slipped past his mother, plucking handfuls of summer lettuce from the garden. The savory aroma of beef stew—one of his grandmother Tippi's favorite meals—wafted through the house. Warning lights flashed in his brain.

A quick glance in the dining room confirmed his worst suspicions. Tippi was setting the table while singing Italian ballads off-key. Four place settings, which meant she'd invited one of her prehistoric suitors for date night. Michael hated abandoning his mother to deal with Tippi's latest romance alone. And missing out on Nella's mouthwatering stew would be a tragedy. But the prospect of watching Tippi and some old codger gumming food while leering at each other wasn't a great choice either.

No contest. Burn the midnight oil.

Michael went upstairs. When he stepped out of the shower, feeling marginally better, he trailed water across his bedroom. Shrugging into jeans, he decided his mother would forgive him for skipping dinner. Tippi? Not so much.

The Road She Left Behind

Resigned to the decision, he grabbed a T-shirt from the laundry pile he'd left on his unmade bed.

On the dresser, his smartphone buzzed.

R U busy?

He'd given Darcy his number weeks ago. If he took Emerson for an outing, sometimes she checked when they planned to return. The calls were too brief, although the motherly concern she displayed for her nephew was surprising and sweet. Michael hoped her newfound devotion would help her to finally put down roots.

This was their first text. When they'd dated years ago, they'd owned flip-top phones and used cars.

No. Why?

Spring me from prison? Martini bar in 15?

Flinging down the T-shirt, he strode to the closet. A button-down shirt—definitely. Grabbing a blue oxford, he started back toward the bed. He considered breaking out the cologne, a real date-night move. Immediately he ditched the idea.

This wasn't date night. Getting tangled up with Darcy wasn't on the agenda. There was too much on her plate. Besides, he needed more distance from his passionless marriage and a divorce that had come too easy. Letting Darcy tangle up his emotions yet again made no sense whatsoever.

Hello? If you're busy . . .

Michael nearly fell over his feet. She was waiting for a reply.

See U there.

In the center of Chagrin Falls, the martini bar sparkled like a Christmas ornament. The popular venue featured a glass wall facing the cobblestone patio in front, brass fixtures throughout the interior, and subdued lighting in shades of violet, green, and blue. On the patio, people milled around in small groups. Their animated conversations nearly masked the bluesy notes of the background music.

Inside, the leather booths and the tables were packed. Behind the long bar, four bartenders raced to fill orders.

Michael felt a tap on his back.

"You beat me here." Darcy appeared at his side.

"Only by a second."

"What are you having?" She squeezed past several women to reach the bar. "My treat. I'm in desperate need of an appletini."

"Long day?"

Darcy toyed with the ribbon of pale-yellow hair falling across her shoulder. "It's been a long month." She reconsidered. "Today wasn't *all* bad. Latrice joined us for dinner."

"Doesn't she usually?"

She chuckled. "You're remembering when Elizabeth and I were kids and we ate with Latrice in the kitchen. Tonight she joined us in the dining room. She'll continue to do so, from here on out."

"Sounds like a good deal." With the advantage of height, Michael lifted a confident hand. A bartender hurried over. "An appletini for the lady, and a whiskey sour." He handed over a credit card.

"Meeting was my idea. Why are you paying?"

"My treat." When the bartender returned with their order, he eyed the appletini with curiosity. "A new habit? You were into whiskey sours when we dated." On their second or third date, he'd turned her on to them. They became her go-to drink—with extra maraschino cherries.

"Tastes change." Mirth sparkled in her eyes as she nodded at his glass. "Aren't you tired of same old, same old?"

"Not even a little. I'm a man who knows what he likes."

Balancing their drinks, they went outside. He led her to a table in the corner of the patio, away from the din. Darcy looked pretty tonight, in a lacy top and jeans, her glossy hair tumbling down her back. She'd even done up her eyes with mascara and a shimmery eye shadow and rimmed her mouth in lipstick.

After she'd seated herself, he asked, "What's the occasion?"

"For tonight's jailbreak?" Absently, she trailed a finger around the rim of her glass. "Would you believe lilies and parking lot aggression?"

"Come again?"

"You don't want to hear. It's a long story."

One, apparently, she preferred not to share. There was a lot on her mind, surely. A host of new responsibilities—including a seriously ill parent and a young nephew now becoming a permanent fixture in her life. If she felt overwhelmed, it was understandable. Sure, Darcy possessed an adventurous spirit. But underneath lay a fragility she'd never understood—a need to assume burdens no matter the personal cost.

Searching for a neutral topic, he asked, "What have you been doing to keep busy?" He winced. "Did that sound judgmental? Caring for your mother must be a full-time job."

"It's not, at least not yet. But I *am* busy. Turns out the house isn't in as good a shape as I thought. Last week we had a minor catastrophe in Emerson's bathroom. One of those slow leaks under the sink that turns into a major flood. The mansion is nearly a century old. Most of the plumbing hasn't been upgraded in years."

"Hire a plumber to check the entire house," he suggested.

"Already done. There's also an electrician lined up. I'm also bringing someone in to check the foundation. Remember all the storage rooms in the basement?"

They'd often played adventure games in the cobwebbed spaces, daring each other to look into dark corners. One particularly embarrassing afternoon, Darcy had snatched away his flashlight. She'd let him howl in the dark for a good ten seconds before flicking it on again.

Not one to be outplayed, Michael returned the favor later the same week. While they were hunting for salamanders by the riverbank, he snatched her tennis shoes. Darcy was forced to walk all the way home barefoot.

"There's dampness in three of the rooms and a weird moldy smell," she was saying. "I'm worried there's a crack in the foundation. I can't find the source of the odor or the dampness. Latrice went down with me last weekend to check. She's also stumped."

"Have you mentioned the problem to Rosalind?"

"Why bother?" An air of resignation slumped Darcy's shoulders. She raised her glass and stared absently at the contents. "My mother has enough on her mind. Whatever is going on, I'll take care of it."

"Check for decay in the rafters. Wood rot can lead to lots of headaches. If you need a carpenter, you know who to call."

The well-meaning remark put an attractive gleam in her eyes. "I've been wondering about your new line of work. Why *did* you give up banking?"

"Long story," he quipped, stealing from her playbook.

"I'm sure you're happy. I'm simply curious."

They were straying too close to sensitive topics. If Darcy meant to steer the conversation toward a discussion of their ill-fated romance, there was nothing to gain by playing along.

"The short version? I didn't like who I'd become. I no longer felt grounded."

"You've always been grounded. It's hard to imagine anything throwing you off-balance." She looked at him fully then, in the way he remembered—boldly and without feminine artifice. "You were so driven back then. You had your whole career planned out. One more year working at an Ohio bank, then you were leaving for New York and Wall Street. You thought the Big Apple was the only place worth living. You nearly had me convinced to follow you there."

The admission took something vital from her features.

"Why bring this up now?" he asked. He was aware of the heat crawling up his spine, prickling across his scalp, quickening his pulse—the automatic responses of a man in the first stages of arousal. This wasn't about him, or flirting in some pretense to reignite what they'd felt when they were young and untested. Searching for clues, he watched her drain her glass.

"I'm not sure," she admitted. "I'm sorry."

"Tell me about the lilies." Despite his discomfort, he grinned. "And the parking lot aggression."

"My mother doesn't want lilies at her funeral. Or gardenias."

"She's planning her funeral?"

"Complete with a guest list."

The news didn't surprise him. "Can't the grim conversations wait a few months?" A precise woman like Rosalind would map out every detail.

"You'd think. I mean, it's only July. We have lots of time." A long sigh drifted from her. "I'm not ready to think about planning a funeral or saying goodbye. Dr. Tanaka believes there's a good chance my mother will celebrate Christmas. One last Christmas with Emerson—it would mean so much to him."

Five more months. Given Rosalind's fierce willpower, she'd likely circumvent death until after the holiday season, if only for her grandson's sake. Despite his low opinion of her, Michael knew her affection for Emerson was deep and unswaying.

"Have you begun looking into hospice facilities?" He declined to add that he'd done his own digging regarding congestive heart failure. Late at night, tooling around on the internet when Darcy invaded his thoughts. The end game wasn't pretty. Feeding tubes and unrelenting pain. "There are several good facilities in Geauga County. One of Tippi's friends was in hospice at a facility about ten minutes away. Nice woman—they kept her comfortable until the end. I can get the information for you."

"Don't bother."

"You've already begun looking?"

"I'm not planning on hospice. She'd like to die at home, surrounded by family. I want to give her that gift. It's the least I can do."

He caught the hesitation in her voice, the anxiety. The tiny thread of fear that made him want to protect her.

"What if Rosalind lingers for weeks? Are you prepared to outfit the house like a hospital?"

"I'll do whatever it takes."

"Death isn't pretty—or cheap. It doesn't arrive on a predictable schedule."

"Meaning what? Once my mother reaches the lingering stage, I should dump her in a cold, sterile facility?"

The defiance glossing her features gave him pause. But the decision she'd come to was the wrong one.

Resting his forearms on the table, he tried to reason with her. "Darcy, I can't pretend to know what you've been up to for the last eight years. I'll wager your life has been in a holding pattern since the accident, and you've never mapped out a way to move on. It's great you've come back. It's commendable how you've tried to convince Rosalind to get on a heart transplant list, even if she won't listen. If you can build a semblance of a relationship with your mother before her time ends, I hope it will help you get your life back on track. You don't need more hardship. You've had more than your share."

"You're implying I'm weak?"

"Your family has caused you enough burdens. What sort of toll will this take on you, and Emerson?"

"I shouldn't have brought this up." She splayed her fingers on the table. "Let's move on. What have Nella and Tippi been up to? Is Tippi still breaking hearts in town? I need to schedule a lunch date with them when my mother isn't looking."

"Stop deflecting. I'm lending good advice."

"And I ought to listen? Michael, I know you mean well." She exhaled a frustrated breath. "Let's not argue. Can we just enjoy a drink together? I've missed you more than I realized."

To emphasize the point, she leaned across the table. The curtain of her blonde hair glided forward in an enticing wave.

"I'm not arguing with you," he said, hoping to calm her down.

"Good. I have enough to deal with right now. I need to relax. For just an hour. Then it's back to the grind and the worry and the million debates I must have with my mother every single day. One hour," she repeated. "That's all I'm asking."

"You've got it."

"Thanks."

She rested her hand on his wrist. The gesture startled him, but he'd already noticed her expression growing distant.

Lost in her own counsel, she coasted her fingers across his skin. Wrist to elbow, the strokes long and languid. The heady assault teased his senses. During their short romance, they'd spent hours on hot, unsatisfying foreplay. Long hours fumbling in the dark on the banks of the Chagrin, their skin damp and their hearts thundering like the untamed river.

They'd never been lovers.

"Tell me about the parking lot aggression." He set his jaw in an unsuccessful attempt to blot out the sensation of her meandering caresses.

She gave a bizarre accounting of Rosalind shouting at popular Morgan Harbert. Morgan ran an insurance agency in the Falls.

Catching the story's more salient bits proved impossible. He couldn't clear his head, not with Darcy's fingers weaving indulgent circles across his skin. She seemed unaware of her actions, her voice gaining animation as she described her mother's odd behavior earlier in the day. Michael realized he didn't care about another one of Rosalind's feuds with yet another woman. Not at the moment.

Her caresses moved higher. They circled the sensitive patch of skin at the base of his upper arm. He'd rolled up his shirt sleeves before leaving the house and Darcy, her eyes still distant, seemed unaware of her warming touch slipping beneath the fabric.

He laid heavy fingers atop her roving hand. Clarity snapped into her gaze.

She read the warning on his face. At a nearby table, a chair scraped back. A slender brunette rose to greet a friend. Their voices seemed a million miles away.

Embarrassment flashed through Darcy's eyes.

She began to pull away. Michael caught her by the wrist. Their gazes meshed. His predatory instincts ticked through the reasons he should let her go. She didn't understand the crushing shock he'd experienced when she disappeared from Ohio. She didn't know he'd continued to want her, the craving strong and irrepressible—a need that drove him to self-disgust. He'd thirsted for Darcy like a man in the desert, even after he entered into a dry marriage of convenience. Now self-loathing crowded his mind. It led him to a painful truth.

A man craved what he couldn't have.

Surrendering to the greedy impulse, he glided his free hand through her hair, savoring the silky texture. Taking his time, he steered the heavy locks over her shoulder. When his fingers brushed her cheek, she trembled.

The reaction felt like triumph. He wasn't the only one she'd put at risk.

"Do us both a favor, Darcy. Stop flirting." With a self-deprecating smile, he added, "Why bother? I've been attracted to you my whole life. That doesn't mean I want to pick up where we left off. We did enough damage the last time."

"Forgive me. I didn't mean . . ."

The apology drifted into a muddled silence.

He let her go. "We have a natural attraction," he said, glad they were getting this out in the open. "We always have. Doesn't mean we should let it pull us off course."

"You're right." Tipping her head back, she sent her anxious gaze across the night sky. The stars were out, a canopy of twinkling light. "I need a friend, and you've been so good to us. Switching your schedule around to help with Emerson and giving Samson a job. Answering my SOS tonight. I'm sure you had more interesting plans for the evening." She covered her face with her hands. "I *was* coming on to you. What's wrong with me?"

"Nothing. It was just a mistake."

She flopped her hands into her lap. "Gallant to the end. You never change, do you?"

"I guess not."

"Even when we were kids, I had a major crush. Losing you when I was twelve . . . I didn't think I could bear it. I cried for weeks." The admission came at a price, and she looked away. "When we found each other again, right before I graduated from college, it felt like a miracle. As if we'd survived a divine test and proven ourselves worthy. I was sure everything would work out, somehow."

"I felt the same way." Pride lanced him, sure and swift. "I loved you, Darcy."

The words struck her with more force than he intended. He didn't want to hurt her.

Stricken, she searched his face. "You never told me."

"I never got the chance. I woke up one day, and you were gone."

Speechless, she stared at him. She looked fragile, her features creasing with regret. The urge to take her into his arms nearly overrode his common sense.

"Let's walk," he announced, pushing out of his chair. Having waded this far into a painful conversation, they might as well discuss the rest.

They darted across the street to the park. In the shadows, an older couple chatted quietly at a picnic table. Behind the brick walk leading deep into the park, the Chagrin River bubbled and leaped.

Michael said, "Will you clear up the stuff I don't understand? For starters, why were you out drinking on the night of the accident? We were supposed to meet for dinner. I called repeatedly from the restaurant. You never picked up."

It was the better part of valor not to mention the rest. Pacing in the lobby of the four-star Beachwood restaurant. His confusion switching to anger as the minutes wound out. The diamond solitaire tucked in a blazer pocket. Earlier in the week, he'd purchased the ring in the starry bliss of a man deeply in love.

"I'll tell you everything," Darcy said. "Just promise not to judge me too harshly."

A weight pressed his unprepared heart. Judgment was the last thing on his mind. But he did want answers.

"I'm listening," he said.

Chapter 18

An unexpected calm stole through Darcy.

She was tired of running. From the guilt she wore like a second skin, and the fear over the difficult tasks sure to darken the coming months. What point was there in running from past guilt or future trials? Doing so only made it harder to appreciate the blessings in her life. In the last, precious weeks Emerson had become the bright center of her world. And there was still time to build a semblance of a relationship with her mother before death took Rosalind.

And Michael? As she listened to the river's tumbling song, Darcy confronted just how much she'd hurt him. More deeply than she'd understood. If the unvarnished truth provided the means to bring healing, she would tell him everything.

"After I left Ohio, I rarely let you into my thoughts," she began. "I couldn't, Michael. My guilt over Elizabeth and my father crowded out everything else. That's why I traveled from one city to the next. Keeping people at a distance made handling the grief easier."

"What did you do for work?"

"Temp management jobs. Finding work was never a problem."

"How many cities?"

"Eight."

"You moved once a year?"

"Moving around kept my emotions in deep freeze. I didn't know how else to survive."

He gestured at a park bench. They sat down, and he lowered his elbows to his knees. "The night of the accident—tell me about the bar. When you went out drinking . . . who were you with?"

The intensity of his tone surprised her, but not as much as the subtext to his question. He assumed she'd been cheating on him.

Quickly, she checked her outrage. With no clear understanding of the reason for her disappearance, why wouldn't he question everything?

Needing to put him at ease, she said, "You were the only man I cared about. There was never anyone else. I was so upset, I forgot we'd made dinner plans. I went out alone."

He shut his eyes tightly. With regret, or relief? There was no telling, and the pain etching his features drove sorrow through her. With the sorrow came the question she'd avoided for too long, beating a miserable tempo against her heart. By leaving him, what had she given up?

Everything.

He asked, "Why were you upset?"

"I'd argued with my father. A real shouting match. Our first, ever." Grimly, she stared into the darkness. "It was ironic on so many levels."

"Why ironic?"

"Other than the occasional small talk or question about my academics, we rarely talked."

"Dr. Jack Goodridge, the original absentee father. When we were kids, his disinterest hurt you. I remember."

"After Elizabeth's pregnancy upended the status quo, he became even more distant. Drumming up reasons to work late or meet with colleagues after hours. Anything to avoid dealing with the changes at home. In fairness, none of us were prepared for the changes a baby would bring. My parents were entrenched in their careers and their country club life. And I'd found you again." She paused for a beat. "Don't get me wrong. I *did* fall in love with Emerson. How could I resist? But the household was thrown into turmoil by his bouts of late-night crying and Elizabeth's mood swings. Some days, she cried more than the baby did."

"You never mentioned the problems at home. I knew your home life was tense, with Elizabeth dealing with a newborn. I had no idea it was really bad."

"My home life wasn't a compelling topic at the outset of a romance." She shrugged. "I would've told you, eventually."

He gazed at her steadily. "The argument with your father. What was it about?"

"He told me to break up with you. Not a request—an ultimatum."

"Hold on. You agreed?" Betrayal thickened his voice.

"I didn't have a choice!"

"Why not? I sure as hell don't understand. You'd better explain."

No easy task, and she failed to quell the nerves batting around her rib cage. "After my sister came home from the hospital with her baby, my parents began arguing day and night. It was unnerving, listening to them go at it in their room late at night or shout at each other in the kitchen before they left for work. The house became a war zone." Her shoulders slumped beneath the weight of the memories. "My father insisted I break up with you for the sake of our family."

"Because of the fight between our mothers?"

"He said it was a lot worse than I'd ever understood. If I kept seeing you, I'd dredge up all those hard feelings. It would be more than my mother could handle. My parents didn't need another upset—with a new baby in the house, they were already on edge. My father warned me that another mistake could make our family fall apart."

A heavy silence fell between them. Michael scrubbed his palms across his face.

At length he said, "Your father told me essentially the same thing. Break up with you, or I'd destroy the Goodridge family."

The disclosure snatched her breath away. "When?"

"A few days after we ran into him at the restaurant in Beachwood. He showed up one night at my mother's house. She'd gone out to dinner with friends. My conversation with your father was pretty heated. He didn't go into the details about dealing with Elizabeth and a new baby, but he made his desires clear."

"What did you tell him?"

"I dug in my heels and refused to stop seeing you."

Overwhelmed, she pinioned him with a look of disbelief. "Why didn't you tell me? On our next date, or when we were sneaking in phone calls at midnight? Why did you keep this to yourself?"

"You were nervous enough about dating. All the bad blood between our mothers—you worried constantly about Rosalind finding out about us. Why would I add to your concerns? Your father's opinion didn't matter. Not to me, at least."

He nearly added something else. Instead, he held his tongue.

An unnecessary kindness. She knew what he'd declined to add.

Her father's opinion should not have mattered to her either. She should've ignored the threats. Like Michael, she should've held fast and refused to give up a relationship that was pure and good.

But she wasn't like Michael. She wasn't strong. Eight years ago, she'd caved beneath her father's demands.

On rubbery legs, she got to her feet. "It's getting late."

There was nothing left to discuss. She'd failed Michael.

She'd failed herself too.

He nodded. "I'll walk you back to your car."

∼

In a giddy arc, Emerson swung the bags at his hips. "Aunt Darcy, what about jewelry? Should we buy earrings or a necklace for Latrice?" After an hour of looking through the booths at the Handmade Heaven craft fair, they were still in search of the perfect gift.

The sky was overcast and dreary, the crowds thick. Emerson hardly noticed. After filling four bags with handcrafted toys and various gifts, he was the vision of sunny skies.

Veering into the next booth, he selected a garishly bright necklace. "What about this? I like the colors."

The moon-faced teenager working the booth drifted off to help another customer. Darcy lowered her voice.

"I don't know, Emerson." She studied the necklace's neon green and orange beads. Naturally, Halloween colors would appeal to an eight-year-old boy. "Isn't this necklace better suited for a girl? Latrice is a mature lady."

"What's 'mature'?"

"You know, grown-up. Latrice likes bright colors, but neon isn't her thing."

Emerson returned the necklace to the rack. "Can we keep looking? We found nice gifts for Samson and Grandmother. I don't want Latrice to feel left out."

"We won't stop looking until we find something fabulous for her."

"What about Nella and Tippi? Should we buy them gifts? We don't have to worry about Michael. He told me not to get him anything."

If the generous boy returned home with gifts for the Varano women, Rosalind would blame Darcy. Lately, they had been getting along fairly well. Why rock the boat?

She glanced at her watch. "It's already after two o'clock, kiddo. Why don't we find Latrice a gift and call it a day? We should head back soon. You're supposed to study this afternoon for at least two hours."

"Boys shouldn't have to study in July. Summer vacation is supposed to be a *vacation*."

"That's Samson's opinion." Despite her poor health, Rosalind continued to design elaborate study plans. She clung to the established routine as if her diagnosis wouldn't soon alter their lives. "What's on today's agenda?"

"The branches of government. Judicial, legislative, and executive. I have to read three boring chapters." Emerson hung his head. "Grandmother will ask lots of questions about the judicial branch. She loves anything to do with judges."

"No worries. I'll help you ace the test. We'll read the chapters together."

"You'll help me study?"

The expectancy on his face brought a twinge of guilt. She should've offered to help weeks ago. With all the other tasks occupying her days, doing so had never crossed her mind.

"Count on me as your study partner for the rest of summer," she promised. "As a matter of fact, I'm on standby if you need help when the new school year starts in August."

"Thank you, Aunt Darcy!"

He tugged her toward the next booth, and she tried to ape his enthusiasm. It was no mean feat. She'd felt blue since daybreak. Despite her best efforts, her thoughts kept stubbornly wending back to last night's conversation with Michael.

She still wasn't sure why she'd followed the mad impulse to ask him to meet at the martini bar. Granted, Rosalind's altercation with poor Morgan Harbert and the subsequent conversation about funeral plans left Darcy feeling out of sorts. Add to that Latrice joining them for dinner, then everyone scattering from the dining room afterward. But none of yesterday's surprises explained why she kicked off a night out with Michael by flirting.

She hadn't meant to reignite their romance. Not consciously.

For too long, guilt over the accident had blotted out everything else. Everything, including the affection she'd once felt for Michael.

Before meeting him, she should've prepared for their attraction to come flaring back to life. She should *not* have encouraged it.

A second worry nudged into her thoughts. She'd spent precious little time reflecting on the argument with her late father. During all the intervening years, she'd avoided the memory.

Why had my usually even-tempered father become furious when he demanded I stop seeing Michael?

At the time, Darcy assumed he meant to spare Rosalind further pain.

Now she wondered whether his reaction was more self-serving than she'd understood. She couldn't recall a time in her parents' marriage when her father had behaved protectively toward Rosalind. He was respectful and courteous. Never outwardly affectionate, and certainly not protective of the accomplished judge.

Drawing from her reverie, she heard Emerson say, "Aunt Darcy, look in here! There's lots of stuff for mature ladies."

Her nephew ran into the next booth. Racks of embroidered peasant blouses hung in attractive displays. In the back of the booth, dozens of pretty scarves were laid out on a table.

"What about this one?" Emerson selected a shimmery black scarf with dashes of crimson thread knit through.

"This is beautiful!" She dropped a kiss on the crown of his head. "Kiddo, you did good. Latrice will love it."

Emerson beamed. "Aunt Darcy?"

"Hmm?"

"Can we visit the Grand Canyon?"

In response, she cupped the side of his face. Questions regarding future vacations were becoming part of the daily routine. Yellowstone, Yosemite, Disneyland, and now the Grand Canyon—it didn't escape her notice the destinations involved miles of walking or required hiking boots. The sort of vacations that Rosalind, well into her sixties, would never suggest. She also suspected Emerson wanted reassurance she would remain in his life for the long haul.

"The Grand Canyon is a great idea," she said, wishing there were a simple way to steer him toward other, more difficult topics. Since the night when they learned of Rosalind's prognosis, he'd shied away from the subject. "Hey, if we plan a trip to the Grand Canyon, we should visit Sedona at the same time."

"What's Sedona?"

"A city about two hours south, in Arizona. There are cool rock formations in Sedona. I've always wanted to see them."

"Can we stay for a couple of days?"

"Sure." She withdrew a crisp twenty from her wallet and pointed at the cashier near the front of the booth. "We'll talk about it on the drive home. In the meantime, why don't you pay for Latrice's scarf? I'll meet you outside."

When he ran off to pay, she wandered out of the booth. Her smartphone rang. She scanned the display panel.

Michael.

"Darcy, hello. Am I catching you at a good time?"

Seeking privacy, she walked to the caramel apple stand across the way. "I'm at the craft fair with Emerson," she said.

"Having fun?"

"My nephew is buying out the place." A bee swooped out of the stand and flew toward her head. Swatting it away, she nearly dropped the phone.

"Darcy? Are you there?"

"I'm here."

"I wanted to thank you for last night. For answering my questions." Michael hesitated. "It wasn't easy for you, but I appreciate your willingness to talk things out. You cleared up a lot of my questions."

"The least I could do." The sincerity in his voice gave her the confidence to add, "I am sorry—for everything. Especially for leaving Ohio without getting in touch. Not my best move."

"Hey, I didn't call to wring another apology from you. In fact, I'm the one who should apologize. I didn't mean to grill you. Rehashing the past . . . it's hard. Anyway, I hope you can forgive me."

"There's nothing to forgive. You were upset. For good reason."

"Thanks for understanding." He let the silence draw out. "Anyway, I wanted to thank you."

"You did."

"Great. Let's put this behind us."

"Already done."

"I don't want to lose my friendship with you, Darcy. I hope that's okay. Remaining friends, I mean."

"It's more than okay," she said, unable to conceal the pleasure in her voice. A ridiculous dose of elation spun through her veins. "I want the same thing. I'd hate to think I'd completely botched our relationship."

"Not a chance. I'm glad we cleared the air."

He didn't appear ready to hang up. *Neither am I,* she thought ruefully.

"I'm glad too, Michael," she agreed, happy to prolong the moment.

At the tap on her waist, she nearly jumped out of her skin.

"May I say hi?" Emerson handed back the change from her twenty.

The request froze her smile in place. "Sorry, kiddo. Grandmother has to go," she stammered, praying he hadn't overheard the conversation. "She only called to check when we're coming home."

Prickly heat bled across Darcy's face. Lying was a coward's way out. But she couldn't rustle up an explanation on the fly for *why* she was chatting with his personal hero.

Emerson sniffed out the deception with the skill of a hound dog. "You're talking to Michael—you just said his name. Why are you pretending it's Grandmother?"

Great. He's caught me dead to rights.

At a loss, Darcy shrugged.

"And why is your face all red?" He wrinkled his nose. "You look funny."

"Ha-ha funny, or guilty funny?" A ridiculous query. She'd obviously stumbled out of door number two. "Please don't answer."

"Why? Because you're guilty?" His eyes narrowed. "Did you do something bad?"

"No!"

Michael, catching the play by play, chuckled in her ear. "Darcy, you'd never survive the Grand Inquisitor. Let me talk to him."

She handed over the phone. Emerson walked off.

At intervals he glanced back, his feathery brows climbing his forehead with consternation. Strolling past the caramel apple stand, he spoke rapidly into the phone. It was just as well he'd walked out of earshot. From the looks of it, he'd switched from chatting with his personal hero to a full-on interrogation. How Michael was handling the dicey conversation was impossible to tell.

While she awaited her nephew's return, Darcy put her nervous energy to good use by purchasing a trove of sugary treats from three carnival booths. Cotton candy, peanut butter fudge, the biggest caramel apple in the display. There was no harm in allowing Emerson to spend the drive back to Hunting Valley chowing down. If he did, there was an outside chance he wouldn't pepper her with questions about her bumbling attempt at deception—or her beet-colored complexion.

A notion she quickly abandoned as Emerson, kicking up dust with his tennis shoes, trudged back across the crowded avenue. At least there was no mystery with kids, she mused. If they weren't happy with you, they made their feelings plain.

"Michael told me," he said. He handed back the phone.

The cryptic announcement hung between them. There was no telling if Michael had simply mentioned having drinks with her last night, or had given her nephew a rundown on their long-ago and star-crossed romance. She was still attempting to muster up the courage to ferret out the details when a toddler with pigtails and a fistful of cotton candy lumbered into her nephew's legs. The tot was scooped up by her apologetic mother. Emerson seemed oblivious to the assault.

"What did he tell you?" Darcy heard herself say.

"About the lovey-dovey stuff." Emerson shuddered with boyish disgust. "You were Michael's secret girlfriend?"

So Michael had come clean. "A long time ago." Her mouth felt drier than the Sahara.

"He said you kissed him. Lots of times. When you were his girlfriend."

"Well, I could reasonably argue that *he* kissed *me*. It's hard to tell who starts the monkey business when you're dating."

"Kissing is disgusting. I won't kiss girls until I'm really old. Maybe not even then."

A smile toyed with her lips. "You might feel differently once your hormones kick in."

"What are hormones?"

She chastised herself. Why drag biology into this? Skirting a discussion of sexuality until he entered junior high sounded like a good deal.

"Never mind," she muttered. "Can we discuss something else?"

"No, we cannot. I'm disappointed with you." Donning his adult persona, Emerson crossed his arms. "Why didn't you tell me about the gross stuff with Michael?"

"Gee, thanks. Dating isn't gross. People do it all the time. Besides, there's nothing to tell." At her wits' end, she held out the treats. "Your choice. Take whatever you want."

Licking his lips, Emerson leaned closer. Then he snapped back. "Why do grown-ups use candy to make up with kids?"

"Because it works?" Cluing in to his meaning, she dredged up a more serious tone. "I never mentioned dating Michael because it *was* a secret, and it no longer matters. You were just born when we dated. That's how long ago it was. More important, I'm not obligated to share every detail about my life. There's lots of personal information adults don't share with children. Nor should they." She sighed. "I am sorry you're upset."

"Thank you."

"For what?"

"Apologizing. Grandmother never says she's sorry, even when she should. I really hate that." He patted Darcy's arm. "I'm proud of you. Michael says a boy doesn't become a man until he has the guts to say he's sorry."

She wasn't a boy or a man, but she caught his drift. "So we're good?"

"I guess."

Hoisting the bags up, he started toward the entrance gate. They were halfway across the parking lot when he came to a standstill.

"Aunt Darcy?"

"Hmm?"

"Michael is *my* friend. You know there's lots of fish in the water, right?"

"You mean 'fish in the sea.'"

"Whatever." He tapped his foot with the impatience of scholar instructing a dull student. "You know what I mean."

Unfortunately, she did. Emerson needed a father figure, and Michael was happy to fill the role. There was also Rosalind's care to consider. Darcy needed to prepare for the worst even as she continued lobbying her mother to consider a heart transplant.

Romance? Not now.

Her life required the focus of warrior pose.

Still, it seemed wrong to make an ironclad promise. Granted, no one sensible reignited a romance that had ended badly the first time. But forever was a long time.

She gave the thumbs-up. "Right. If I go fishing for a boyfriend, I won't cast my net anywhere near your buddy."

With relief, her nephew smiled. "You're the best, Aunt Darcy."

Plucking the cotton candy from her arms, he resumed walking.

Chapter 19

Pausing at the front door, Darcy made a quick count of the bags. "Emerson, there were four bags in the back seat. You missed one."

"I'll get it." He started back down the steps, then hesitated. Climbing back up, he grabbed the green container tucked against the railing. "Might as well check the bird feeder. I forgot to add seed this morning."

"Need help?"

"No thanks."

Darcy tossed the car keys on the table in the foyer. She detected the low murmur of the TV. No one in the Goodridge household watched TV in the middle of a Tuesday afternoon. At this hour, Latrice was usually preparing dinner. Rosalind was either reading or sequestered in her office by the library, sorting through paperwork and bills.

The cozy scene in the living room brought Darcy to a standstill. On the couch, Samson and her mother were drinking mugs of hot chocolate and sharing a bowl of popcorn. She noticed the fluffy blanket tucked around Rosalind. Worry darted through her.

"Your mama is feeling poorly," Samson explained. "She told me not to make a fuss, but I didn't like the way she was shivering. I found the blanket upstairs in the hallway closet."

"You left work early?" Most days he worked for Michael until dinnertime, Monday through Friday.

"Michael went to a meeting in Chagrin Falls. I came home a couple of hours ago."

Home.

The contentment in Samson's voice warmed her. She doubted he'd ever felt a sense of belonging until now.

Are we both settling into my mother's house? Darcy realized that they were.

Rosalind snuggled deeper beneath the blanket. "Did you enjoy the craft fair?"

"Emerson brought home tons of stuff. Toys, lots of gifts, and a goofy craft piece to hang in his bedroom." She described the art fashioned from brightly painted coat hangers. "Where is Latrice?"

"She popped a casserole into the oven before she left. She's running errands for the party. They're expecting a large crowd this year."

Every year, the homeowners on Latrice's street held a block party on the first Saturday in August. The Chagrin Falls Police Department had set up a permit for them to cordon off the street until nightfall. Over time, the party had expanded to include families on nearby streets, in the pretty development east of the town center. Samson was keen to meet teenagers his age. Emerson planned to spend part of the day hanging out with him and the rest of the time with Nella. No doubt the energetic Nella would spend the bulk of the afternoon taking Emerson from one street game to the next.

Rosalind would be none the wiser.

When Darcy had begged off, Latrice hadn't faked disappointment. By silent agreement, they no longer felt comfortable leaving Rosalind alone in the house. Her dizzy spells were becoming more frequent. She often felt weak. Like Emerson—who rarely discussed his worry over his grandmother's declining health—Rosalind pretended the frightening symptoms were a passing inconvenience.

Emerson came into the living room, his arms laden with bags. "We bought the place out, Grandmother. You won't believe all the stuff I found!" He grinned at Samson. "There was a lady at the fair who makes stars. They have glow-in-the-dark paint, and squiggly wires to hang them. They're big! I bought ten stars for you."

"Samson can't wait to see everything." Rosalind waved them off. "Go on upstairs. Spread it all out on your bed."

"Don't you want to see what I bought for you?"

"Surprise me at dinner." She smiled fondly at him, but Darcy noticed the weariness in her tone. She wasn't having a good day. "I'll savor the anticipation."

"Okay." Juggling the bags, he trotted out.

Samson waited as she took a last sip of cocoa, then handed him the mug. He hesitated. "Do you need anything else, ma'am?"

"I'm fine." She tugged the blanket higher up her waist. "You're very thoughtful. Thank you for spending the afternoon with me."

"My pleasure, ma'am."

After he left, Rosalind placed the half-eaten bowl of popcorn on the coffee table. "Your young friend is a treasure, Darcy."

"He is." It was heartening that her mother had noticed. Samson *was* special, and he went to great pains to please Rosalind.

"He reminds me of Elizabeth. Bashful and considerate. And engaging. While we were watching TV, he shared an amusing story about finding his North Star."

"His favorite topic." Darcy smiled.

"He was so animated! Why are people bred in the South such fine storytellers? I suppose he meant he's in search of his destiny. A realistic enough pursuit for an eighteen-year-old." The furrows on Rosalind's brow deepened. Then she surprised Darcy by adding, "Do you remember when Elizabeth found the four-leaf clover while you were camping in the backyard? She believed it would bring her good luck."

They rarely discussed her late sister. The topic was too painful. Darcy knew her mother would never forgive her for Elizabeth's death.

Yet she'd brought her up now, in a manner than appeared sincere. Without judgment.

Gingerly, Darcy took a seat on the couch. "She hated whenever I convinced Latrice to camp with us in the backyard. Listening to the owls hooting at midnight scared her." Treading carefully, she added, "She found the four-leaf clover the next morning. She couldn't wait to show you."

"How old was she? I can't recall."

"Eight," Darcy said. "Latrice let us sleep outdoors the first week of June, to celebrate the end of the school year. Father was at a week-long medical convention in Florida. You were busy with a murder trial."

"A murder trial in June, and your sister was eight . . ." Rosalind's voice drifted away as she sifted through her prodigious memory. "Of course. The Ganley trial. How could I forget?"

"Was the trial difficult?"

"Upsetting, more than anything. Such a horrible business. The defendant was convicted of murdering his pregnant wife. He believed she was unfaithful. She was four months pregnant."

The disclosure chilled Darcy. "That's horrible."

"I presided over a depressing number of murder trials with sexual jealousy at the root. There is no passion more dangerous." She gave Darcy a meaningful look impossible to decipher. "Thankfully, most people are less inclined to lash out. When betrayed by their beloved, they choose to die a little instead."

"I wouldn't know."

"I pray you never do." Her expression growing distant, Rosalind smoothed a hand across the blanket. "I was right in the middle of the Ganley trial when Elizabeth left the four-leaf clover on my desk in the library. I was preoccupied with the trial, working long hours, coming home late most nights exhausted. I don't recall tossing it into the garbage. She was heartbroken. I was too, once I understood what I'd done."

"It was an accident."

The forgiving remark lifted her mother's eyes. "I've been wrong about you, Darcy. In many ways. You're making a real difference in Emerson's life. I didn't think you had it in you."

Darcy wasn't sure if she should laugh or cry. Even when her mother edged toward a compliment, she couldn't resist adding a dash of criticism.

"I'm sorry you don't have more confidence in my abilities." Hurt competed with the defiance swelling inside her. "You've always underestimated me."

"Only because I don't understand you. I never have."

"We're nothing alike."

"No, we're not. You're impulsive, and more carefree than I can easily comprehend. You've been home for almost two months, and I don't have the slightest idea of your plans for the future. Do you have ambitions?"

The habit of pushing and prodding was so well ingrained, her mother seemed unaware of the injury her judgments inflicted. But they were having a real conversation, perhaps their first ever. Losing the opportunity to connect didn't appeal. She feared they wouldn't receive many more chances.

"Just because I didn't follow you into a legal practice or choose a career in medicine like my father doesn't mean I don't have ambitions. My dreams are more life-centered. I want to earn a decent living, but I don't view work as the end-all. It's a means to an end, nothing more. After the accident, when I moved away . . . I didn't have much but the nine-to-five and an empty apartment."

"You were unhappy?"

"I was isolated, cut off from people. I didn't know how to stop grieving and move on. I'm still learning how." The disclosure made Darcy's heart lurch. Ignoring the bruising pain, she added, "I want to reestablish the friendships I left behind, and make new ones. Find a good job, with flexible hours. Mostly, I want to raise Emerson. I love him so much."

"He loves you too."

"I hope so."

Furtively, she studied her mother. It was a risk to pose the question dogging her for weeks now. Did she dare? Doing so might spark an argument.

The desire to learn the truth overrode her fear.

"There's something I've been wondering about." With a bravado that didn't quite reach her bones, she caught her mother's imperious gaze. "What would you have done if Emerson hadn't run away? About me, I mean. You must have known Latrice had my number. It was a reasonable enough assumption. And you'd received the diagnosis. You knew the amyloidosis would progress quickly. How long would you have waited before getting in touch?"

"I'm not sure." Rosalind sank against the sofa's deep cushions.

"Would you have . . . waited until things were really bad, and then let me know? How would *that* have played out? Me, trying to get acquainted with my nephew while you were in the battle of your life." Pity for her mother wasn't strong enough to dampen the anger flaring inside her. "Emerson is not handling this well, in case you haven't noticed. He's pretending you'll bounce right back. I don't want him devastated when we're forced to move your bedroom downstairs and he can no longer avoid the realities. We need to guide him toward difficult realities *now*. We need to prepare him."

"You're right, of course. He's pretending I'm fine."

"This must be a first. You're agreeing with me?"

Rosalind pursed her lips.

Undeterred, Darcy forged ahead. "Mother, there *is* another option."

A muddy silence fell between them. Darcy knew not to break it.

At length, her mother said, "Please don't start. I'm comfy here on the couch. If you go into another speech about a heart transplant, I'll be forced to leave the room." She patted Darcy's hand. The rare display of affection was stunning. "Your sister would be proud of the way you've put yourself wholeheartedly into Emerson's life. You're doing a fine job upholding the agreement."

"You know about the agreement?"

"Elizabeth told me. Just a few days before she died. We were arguing about her mood swings. High, low, energetic, despondent—I was concerned about her instability affecting the baby. Then she announced that if anything ever happened to her, *you* would raise her baby. I don't mind admitting I was furious. How could she pick you over me?"

"It wasn't a contest, Mother. I'd just graduated from college. You were always wrapped up in another court case."

The wrong thing to say. A muscle in Rosalind's jaw twitched. Ceding the high ground wasn't something she did easily.

"It doesn't matter now," she said. "You've proven yourself up to the task of raising your nephew." With an air of resignation, she lifted her left hand. Grimacing, she slowly bent and then straightened her fingers. "The pain is maddening today. My fingers are on fire. I suppose this means the end of my dignity. Ruth says leather gloves will help."

Darcy winced. No matter how much she argued with her mother, she didn't relish seeing her in pain.

"Dr. Tanaka wants you to wear gloves?"

"Don't ask if I'll wear them outside of the house. I won't. There are some humiliations I won't condone."

Pain in the extremities was an awful result of her mother's disease. Anti-inflammatory drugs helped, but the pain would become severe in the coming months.

"Should I go out tonight, buy a pair?" Darcy asked.

"Don't bother. I'll have Gwynn pick them up."

"Who's Gwynn?"

"My new home health aide. I hired her this morning, after you and Emerson left for the craft fair."

"What? I wasn't even aware you were considering the idea."

"I contacted a service last week. Gwynn's first day is Saturday. I have her scheduled to come three days a week after that." At Darcy's surprise, Rosalind chuckled. "Why are you and Latrice convinced I ignore *all* your suggestions? We need another able body in the house. I can't have you and my loyal housekeeper curtailing your lives. You're afraid to leave me alone for ten seconds. As if I can't manage."

"We worry about you."

"Worry less, and invest your energies in your own lives—and Emerson's. Speaking of which, go to the block party on Saturday. You spend too much time cooped up in the house."

"Why don't we go together? We can watch Emerson play cornhole and wolf down too much junk food. Whenever you're tired, we'll leave."

"No thank you. There are too many women in the Falls with whom I *don't* associate."

"Like Morgan Harbert?"

"Morgan doesn't attend the block party. Children's baseball games and hot dogs aren't her thing."

"Good to know." At the craft show, Darcy had spotted the insurance agent. The goose egg on her brow was an angry red. "May I lend some advice? Don't be so hard on everyone. You might make some friends."

"Darcy, you amaze me. You believe *my* behavior is at the root of my unpopularity?"

"You're saying it's not?"

Rosalind tipped up her chin, a clear sign the discussion was over. Then she frowned at her daughter's hands.

She tapped Darcy's wrist. "Do the world a favor and visit a manicurist before Saturday." A foolish move, and she winced. The pain didn't stop her from adding, "Your nails are more ragged than a chain saw. If you refuse to use polish, can't you at least file them?"

Wearily, Darcy rose. "I'll check on dinner."

~

Nella ducked in the nick of time. Tippi hurled a bag of dinner rolls into the shopping cart.

It was Wednesday, and her elderly mother had been in a lather since Monday. Gossip about Rosalind's altercation with Morgan Harbert had reached the geriatric crowd, including Tippi and her friends.

At Monday's poker game in Nella's living room, gossip rang out at the table faster than the quarters tossed out to make bets. Who would the prickly judge assault next? With Rosalind now retired, would she use her abundant spare time to settle old scores? Given her legal connections, she could assault whomever she liked and never spend a day behind bars!

The theories were ridiculous, but Nella held her tongue as she ferried out pots of tea and gingersnaps for Tippi's gambling pals. News of Rosalind's life-threatening illness wasn't yet part of the rumor mill. Michael had told Nella in confidence; she had no desire to share the terrible news.

Not that her decision mattered. Tippi's friends were still in the dark about *why* Rosalind was now settling old scores—but Tippi knew the truth.

Beside the shopping cart, Tippi growled. "Do no harm. Isn't that the main gist of the Hippocratic Oath?"

"Mama, I wish I'd never confided in you back then. If I'd known you'd still be bringing it up years later, I wouldn't have."

"Nonsense. I would've found out . . . about you, and the others. I have lots of friends too, you know." Tippi reached for a loaf of bread, hurled it into the cart. "A woman scorned has a long memory, especially in a town the size of Chagrin Falls."

"He's been gone for eight years now. There's nothing to gain by rehashing his exploits."

"Tell it to Morgan Harbert. I'm sure it felt just like yesterday when she ran into Rosalind in the parking lot."

"No, that was just bad luck," Nella insisted, although from what she'd heard, the goose egg on Morgan's brow *was* impressive.

"Wake up, Nella. Some hurts don't heal without a good dose of sunshine. You think Rosalind won't confront someone else? Just you wait. She's no longer at the courthouse every waking minute. She's got lots of time now to get some payback. When she does, the gossip will reach more ears."

"You're overreacting."

Her mother waved off the remark. "If Darcy had never come home, none of this would matter. But she's here now. Sooner or later, someone will speak out of turn when she's within earshot. If Morgan hadn't almost knocked herself out cold running from Rosalind, she might have blabbed right there in Dr. Tanaka's parking lot. Imagine how much this will hurt Darcy if she learns the truth through the grapevine."

"I know you want me to tell her. I can't."

Nella wouldn't know where to begin. Broaching the subject promised to upend every notion Darcy held about her parents' marriage. There was nothing to gain by correcting her misconceptions. Dr. Jack was gone, and Rosalind was dying. The betrayal that had eroded their marriage no longer mattered. It wasn't a burden Darcy should carry.

Tippi said, "If you don't have the stomach to discuss this with Darcy, then tell Michael. He's a grown man. He'll make sure no one says the wrong thing if she's nearby."

"I can't tell him either. He'll never forgive me."

Tippi latched her hands on the cart, began pushing. As the fury melted from her face, her gait slowed. In the bakery aisle, she eased the cart to a standstill. Brett Long, the new pharmacist at the drugstore, wheeled past. Faking cheer, Nella waved at his three-year-old daughter. The toddler was tucked in the cart's seat with a teddy bear.

Nearing tears, she regarded her mother, studying her with the unconditional love that formed the bedrock of Nella's life.

Tippi dug a tissue from the pocket of her dress. "Find the courage to tell your son. Michael won't judge you." She handed over the tissue to catch the tears pooling in Nella's eyes.

"No, Mama." Nella swabbed at her eyes. "I'm not burdening my son. I'll deal with my sins privately."

Tippi thumped her on the arm. "Sin? What sin?" She patted Nella's cheek. "You're human. You made a mistake . . . like all the other women who fell for that dishonorable man."

Chapter 20

Dust spun through the air like planets in a lonely universe.

Wielding a broom, Darcy took an awkward swipe at the cobwebs hanging in silvery threads on the basement's cinderblock. She'd checked all the storage rooms. The source of the dampness remained a frustrating mystery. If there *was* a crack in the foundation, she'd never find it without assistance.

"Darcy? Are you down here?"

The basement was a maze of forgotten boxes and musty rooms. "Hold on, Samson," she called. She wended her way past the row of storage rooms. "I'll come to you."

In the main area of the neglected basement, naked light bulbs glared from the rafters. The wall beside the stairwell was packed waist-high with boxes, ancient steamer trunks, and wooden crates. She found Samson peering into a cardboard box.

"What is all this stuff?" he asked.

Withdrawing a musty textbook, he flipped through the pages. Puffs of dust exploded beneath his nose. He sneezed.

Darcy examined the cover. "It's a medical textbook—my father's. I doubt either of my parents ever threw anything away, including all their stuff from college." She gestured at the cluster of steamer trunks and wooden crates. "You're looking at Goodridge family history."

"Your daddy inherited this place?"

"That's right. If you're ever game for a real treasure hunt, sift through my grandparents' belongings. They were bigger pack rats than my parents. Some of my great-grandparents' belongings are also down here, in the storage rooms. They built the house."

"Your daddy's whole family sure was rich."

"The winning streak would've ended if my parents hadn't married. My father was a talented doctor, but he didn't have much sense about money. My mother handled everything, including their investments. When Elizabeth and I were kids, we weren't allowed to bother her on Sunday nights. That's when she took care of the bills and reviewed the week's stock trades." Dropping the subject, she led him up the stairwell. "Are you here to grab lunch? This is a first. I thought you were hooked on Nella's Italian cuisine."

"Most days, I am." He looked around the empty kitchen. "Where is everyone?"

"My mother is having a good day. She took Emerson to the science museum. The new school year begins in three weeks. She's been meaning to take him."

"Your mama is driving? Darcy, why didn't you take them? She was feeling poorly yesterday."

Touched by his concern, she kissed his cheek. The easy affection they now shared brightened his expression.

"It's all good. Latrice insisted on going. She's driving."

"Great. Then you're not busy."

"Not really."

"Michael is taking me to check out a used truck. The contractor he's building the kitchen cabinets for, Kyle Mandel? He's got a Ford pickup he wants to sell. It's old, but Michael promised to help me fix it up. He said he'll teach me the basics of car maintenance. I won't waste money on a mechanic."

Excitement peppered the explanation. Samson's first set of wheels—a milestone for any teenager.

"Will you come with us?" he asked. "I want your opinion before I make an offer."

"I'd love to tag along."

The heavyset contractor lived three blocks over from Latrice's home in the Falls. His tidy ranch house sat well back from the street. Children's outdoor gear covered a long, rectangular lawn in need of a mowing. At the top of the driveway, Kyle was pacing before a blue Ford F-Series truck in remarkably good condition.

Michael parked at the curb. "You go on ahead," he told Samson. "Kyle wants to show you the truck before we talk money."

"Yes, sir!" Samson sprinted off.

Climbing out, Darcy whistled softly. To her eye, the gleaming blue vehicle was in mint condition. "The truck looks brand-new. Are you sure Samson can afford it?"

"It's five years old. But, yeah, he can. Kyle will give him a great deal."

"Is Kyle giving him the great deal, or you?" She knew Michael had a soft spot for her young friend, and he was generous by nature. "This transaction has your fingerprints all over it."

"I kicked in a few hundred bucks and new cabinetry for Kyle's downstairs powder room."

"You're too kind."

He shrugged off the compliment. "Do me a favor. Don't tell Samson I pitched in. Making a grown-up purchase is an important milestone for a teenager. Besides, he banks every paycheck. He deserves a break. He's almost nineteen, Darcy. Time for him to spread his wings."

"Emerson, and now Samson." She leaned against the front grill of Michael's pickup, savoring the pleasure on his face. "You missed your calling. You should've become a father years ago."

"I like kids. I always have."

Hooking his thumbs in the pockets of his jeans, he joined her. With silent amusement they watched Kyle lift the Ford's hood to discuss something they couldn't hear. The eager Samson flitted beside him, his hands jumping across the engine block. A kid in the proverbial candy store.

His smile broadened when he spun around. "We'll be right back," he shouted. "We're going for a test drive."

Michael gave the thumbs-up. "Have fun."

Kyle got in behind the wheel. The engine rumbled to life. Grinning at the teen's enthusiasm, he slid back out. He lumbered to the passenger side.

Samson climbed in and shut the driver's door. Darcy watched his every move. She became dimly aware of a ringing in her ears. A metallic taste filled her mouth.

Adrenaline.

The truck started down the driveway.

The memory of Elizabeth standing in the road caught Darcy by surprise. Panic drilled into her. Sprinting forward, she flailed her arms through the air. She was across the grass in an instant.

"Samson, don't drive too fast!"

The truck slowed a fraction. He turned onto the road.

A plume of exhaust hung above the road as the truck disappeared from sight. He was fine. Perfectly capable of handling the vehicle. She pressed shaky hands to her temples. Beneath her fingertips, her pulse danced erratically.

Michael approached. "It's okay, Darcy." He studied her with concern. Then he gently led her back to his truck. "Kyle won't let him drive too fast."

Perspiration sprang onto her brow. "Samson pulled out of the drive, and before I knew it—"

"I know. You remembered the accident."

"Right." She wiped the perspiration from her brow. Then she laughed. A sudden, spontaneous release of emotion. "Am I a complete idiot? Screaming at the top of my lungs—it's a miracle I didn't make Samson drive into a ditch."

"You're not a complete idiot. But, yeah, screaming at a new driver isn't the best move. Not unless you're willing to spring for the truck repairs."

The mirth in his eyes made her laugh again. "Thanks. You're making me feel so much better." In truth, the humor *did* help.

He cocked a brow. "You missed your calling. You should've become a mother years ago."

"I like kids. I always have," she said, stealing his line.

"You like kids because you *are* a kid. Emerson shares lots of details. Like how the two of you play Monopoly while hiding under a blanket."

"We now have matching flashlights. I bought them last week."

"And you built a contraption to keep squirrels out of the bird feeder?"

To her merit, the squirrel baffle *was* inspired. "All it takes is a roll of twine and peanut-butter-covered bird seed for bait. Oh, and an old tennis racket. Emerson helped me devise the pulley system. The squirrels go for the bait, and the racket swings down. Easy peasy."

"The furry critters are keeping their distance from the feeder?" Michael asked, grinning.

"Yeah, but they *do* get a consolation prize. We toss out handfuls of seed at the tree line—away from the bird feeder."

"Face it, Darcy. Your inner child has morphed into an outer child. One of the many reasons you've never meshed with Rosalind. I'm sure she was born with her strict code of ethics and brittle personality fully developed. No assembly required."

A fair enough observation. "I suppose I am the whimsy in the Goodridge family tree. Footloose and fancy-free," she added sarcastically. Nothing was further from the truth, but she appreciated his notice of her creative side. "And here I thought I'd lost the talent."

"During your time wandering the earth? Not a chance."

"Good to hear you're confident I haven't."

"So." He offered a pirate's grin that nearly took her hostage. "Do you want *all* the nasty details about my conversation with Emerson?"

"The cozy chat when I took him to the fair? I'm afraid to ask."

"In my defense, I didn't expect him to drill me with questions about my relationship with you. It's your fault that I spilled. He wanted to know why you'd gone red-faced while talking to me." Michael leaned in, cornering her against his pickup. "Actually, you're blushing now. Am I making you nervous?"

Their gazes merged. Dredging up a suitable retort proved impossible. Warmth crested in his deep-brown eyes in a mesmerizing display. The way he looked at her made Darcy breathless.

"Why are you flirting?" she finally got out. "We agreed it wasn't a good idea."

"Did we?" He rocked back on his heels. Then he moved back in. He threaded his fingers through the strands of hair caught on her cheek. "I've always loved your hair," he murmured. "Like spun sunlight. Don't ever cut it. You look great with long hair."

"Thanks."

A sweet yearning drifted through her as she lingered on the five-o'clock shadow darkening his face. It was unsettling how the stubble on Michael's chin made him altogether too attractive. She'd take him unshaven any day.

Banishing the thought, she focused on the greater concern. "Whatever it is we're doing to each other, we have to stop. Emerson needs both of us—just not together. He's more frightened than he's letting on. If we're not there for him, he'll never make it through the next months."

"What about *our* needs?"

"They're secondary to my nephew's."

"What if we're discovering what we once felt for each other isn't gone?"

The heartfelt rebuttal arrowed through Darcy. An attraction stronger than gravity spun between them. When had it not?

Michael stepped back. He raked a hand across his scalp, as though coming to a decision. Then he plunged forward quickly. "I wasn't looking to get involved, not after striking out in marriage. I took it hard when you left. But I'm not one to wallow in self-pity. I thought I'd play it safe by marrying a woman who was your polar opposite. Someone too practical, like me. Those vows never took, for either of us."

"Why not?" she asked. The conversation was clearly difficult for Michael. She was grateful he trusted her enough to discuss his divorce.

"We were both wrapped up in our careers. Over time, we drifted apart. We didn't even realize we'd missed our most recent anniversary until a week afterward."

"Oh, Michael . . ."

Pride hardened his jaw. "It's okay. She did me a favor by asking for a divorce. You were still under my skin, although I didn't understand how deep until you came back. I didn't expect to feel the way I do for you, not after so much time." Pausing, he let his attention trip across the empty road. Then he looked at her again. "I'm not saying we shouldn't keep Emerson's needs in mind. Of course we should. Always."

"What *are* you saying?"

"A child shouldn't dictate our future." For proof, he cupped her face in his hands. A fine urgency colored his voice as he asked, "Is there something between us? Everything we felt for each other the last time . . . Do you still feel the same way? Because I do."

His touch sent pleasure quivering down her spine. "Yes, I feel the same way." She rested her forehead against his chin. "That doesn't mean we should follow through—not while I have so much going on in my life. I can't."

"I'm not losing you a third time."

"Then wait for me."

"For how long?"

The question hung between them. With the lightest touch, Michael lifted her chin. He searched her eyes.

She didn't have the answer. The fire in his gaze dimmed.

Then he rallied against the doubts and brushed his lips across hers. Tentative, testing, a request he waited for her to accept. He tasted like liquid heat, and she sighed. At the sound of her pleasure, he coasted his mouth across hers, harder now, teasing her senses until she leaned close, dizzy beneath his lovemaking. She bunched her hands against his chest.

Why won't he stop tormenting me and kiss me deeply?

The thought brought a moan from her throat. The husky sound put satisfaction in Michael's eyes.

He took her mouth fully with a kiss that left her spinning.

She was still spinning when he broke it off.

"I'm not as strong as you think," he whispered against her lips. "Don't make me wait too long." When she began to object, he pressed a finger to her mouth. "You're not the only one who wants what's best for Emerson. We'll find a way to ease him into the idea that we're a couple. He might feel jealous at first. Later, he won't. He's a lonely boy afraid of losing his grandmother. Isn't it better for him to have us together, to guide him through?"

The sweet, sensible explanation stole her voice. Mutely, she nodded.

We'll work everything out. Won't we?

In the distance, the sound of an engine cut through the quiet. Michael's attention veered above her head. He released her.

A horn blared. With a wave, Samson turned the Ford into the driveway.

Chapter 21

At the bottom of Grove Hill Lane, cars were parked at the south end of the field that local kids used for impromptu baseball games. Darcy found a spot at the end of a row.

Hopping out of the back seat, Emerson studied the tree-lined street. "Whoa. The block party is bigger than last year."

All the way down the lane, adults milled in happy groups. Children dashed about. The Chagrin Falls PD had already cordoned off the street, and four men were placing tables end to end for a buffet line. Farther down, a group of boys with a snaking hose were filling balloons with water and stacking them in large silver tubs. There was also a beanbag toss, a photo booth, and an area with card tables for games—Darcy even spotted a woman, far down the lane, setting up an obstacle course. Two girls, evidently the woman's helpers, were dragging tricycles from nearby garages.

Darcy waited for Samson to slide out of the passenger side, then locked the car. "Ready, everyone?" she asked.

They started down the street. On the front lawn of a white colonial-style house, a gaggle of teenage girls shared whispered conversation and tubes of lip gloss. A petite black girl in a scalloped jean skirt and a gauzy blouse looked up. She regarded Samson with unmistakable interest as he walked past.

Emerson smirked. "Samson, you have a secret admirer by Mrs. Olson's house."

"Be quiet," Samson muttered. From over his shoulder, he darted a glance at the girl.

When he did, Emerson rolled his eyes at Darcy. Then he pretended to gag. A totally inappropriate response, but at least he was acting like a normal kid. Progress, in her estimation.

She rapped her mischievous nephew on the head. "Hello, anyone in there? Don't make fun of teenagers. It isn't nice. And have some respect for karma. Mock Samson now, and he'll return the favor when you're thirteen."

"He will not."

"Yes, I will." Samson smoothed down his dreads. "Darcy, how do I look?"

He'd spent the morning burning a trail in and out of her bedroom, seeking advice on what to wear. She was fairly certain the nervous teen had tried on everything in his wardrobe—twice. With her assistance, he finally settled on gray jeans and a new white Nike T-shirt.

"You look fabulous. Total eye candy for every girl at the party."

Emerson snorted. "Eye candy? That's dumb. There's no such thing."

"Stop talking so loud." Samson studied him closely. "What's wrong with you today?"

"Nothing!"

Darcy intervened. "Both of you—chill. This is a party. We're here to have fun. Samson, go meet some other kids. I need to help Latrice with the cooking."

"Should I take Emerson with me?"

"And have him embarrass you in front of the girls? No way. When you're ready to play baseball, circle back and round up Mr. Obnoxious. The game usually starts by midafternoon." She pointed due south, at the kids heaping bats and mitts in a pile before the rows of parked cars. "I'll keep him until then."

Samson walked off. In a remarkable show of confidence, he veered toward the cluster of girls. Darcy was still admiring the spectacle when Emerson made a small noise that sounded like anger.

"I'm not obnoxious." He glared at her. "I'm eight."

"Yeah, and today you're acting your age." All morning long he'd been testy, his usual polite behavior nowhere in evidence. "Mind sharing why you're in a bad mood?"

"You wouldn't understand."

"Try me."

In response, Emerson deflated like a pricked balloon. His shoulders curved inward and his gaze flitted across the ground. The disconcerting reaction put Darcy on alert. There was more going on here than readily apparent. She wondered if the testiness was a ruse. Behind it, she sensed fear.

"Seriously. Tell me what's wrong." She gave his shoulder a reassuring squeeze. "I can't help if you won't level with me."

"I don't want to talk about it."

"Why not?"

"It's embarrassing." Stepping out of reach, he raised his slender arms in disgust. "Why am I so puny? Most boys my age grow fast. I wish I'd get bigger. Then no one could push me around."

He *was* frightened. Alarmed, she caught the edge of his T-shirt.

"Emerson, you're scaring me." She tugged him closer. "Has someone threatened you? I want the name. *Now.*"

"It's Noah."

"Who's Noah?"

Eyes rounding, her nephew listed slightly to peer around her. "He's standing in the driveway over there. The boy with the black hair. He's lived across the street from Latrice since I was in kindergarten." Emerson lowered his gaze. His voice paper-thin, he whispered, "Noah calls me a weirdo twerp. He hits me. Please don't tell Latrice. She's friends with his parents. Noah is mean, but his parents are nice."

"How long has this been going on?"

"Oh, I don't know. Forever?"

A finely tuned fury raced through Darcy. The last thing Emerson needed was stress at a block party. His grandmother was dying. He needed to have fun. Goof off, act like a kid. Forget his worries for one afternoon.

"Go inside," she said with forced calm. "Nella is helping Latrice in the kitchen. She's eager to see you."

"Aren't you coming?"

When she pressed her lips together, his brows scraped his hairline. He'd reached the obvious conclusion.

She'd protect him at all costs.

"No, Aunt Darcy. Noah is fifteen. He's got lots of muscles. He'll hurt you."

"Not a chance." Clasping his shoulders, she aimed him toward the brick walkway and Latrice's front door. "Go on. I'll be inside in a sec."

He ran inside.

Darcy appraised her opponent. With jeans slung low on his hips, Noah appeared more man than child, a muscular youth towering over his friends. He was chatting with a posse of less-attractive boys. One of the boys made a crude gesture at the girls across the street.

The boy, a skinny redhead, blushed darker than his hair when he noticed Darcy striding past the men setting up tables in the street.

She cupped her hands around her mouth. "Hey, Noah." The challenge in her tone drew the posse back. She came to a halt before him. "You *are* Noah, right?"

The other teens understood the danger a livid adult posed; Noah grinned.

"Who's asking?"

"Darcy Goodridge."

She caught a whiff of something acrid on his breath. *Tequila?*

"You've been bullying my nephew, Emerson?"

"The twerp? Bullshit."

She jabbed him in the chest. "Ever go near him again, and I'll report you to the police. Assault is a serious crime." She leaned closer. "You got that, asshole?"

Stunned, he stared at her.

She turned away. Behind her back, someone in the posse laughed. A typical reaction. The sort of mistake teenage boys made every day.

One that should have put her on alert as she strode across the lawn.

"She sure told you, Noah."

What happened next took Darcy off guard. A hand clamped down on her shoulder. Before she could react, she was pushed forward.

She fell hard on the grass. The impact kicked the air from her lungs. Dizzy, she began to get up. The vertigo increased, and she dropped back down on her bottom.

The flash of someone running full bore streamed past.

The street was filling up with partygoers and noisy chatter. None of the adults nearby caught sight of Samson. An underweight teen with more heart than muscle, he cleared the grass in three seconds flat.

Emerson's tormentor never had a chance. With one well-aimed punch, Samson knocked him to the ground. Two girls around junior high age ran up, their smartphones out to record the event. Other children playing nearby followed.

Samson didn't notice. Fists at the ready, he stood over Noah in a threatening pose.

"Were you raised by swamp pigs? You no-good white trash—why hasn't anyone hauled your sorry ass to the nearest landfill?" Anger brought out the natural Southern twang Samson worked hard to disguise. "You don't *ever* hit a lady. Am I making myself clear?"

Flat on his back, Noah raised frantic palms to shield his face. "Yes. Crystal!"

"Good. You keep it in mind."

Blinking the stars from her vision, Darcy watched in awe. She chuckled as Noah scrambled to his feet. He dashed around the side of his house with the posse on his tail.

Samson, approaching with a newfound swagger, missed the show. He helped her to her feet. "Damn," he muttered. He rubbed his sore knuckles. "That hurt."

"Don't swear." Her elbow, having taken the brunt of the fall, throbbed something awful. "It's unbecoming."

"*You* swore. At that lowlife, trailer trash boy."

"I did not."

"Did too. When you were—"

Breaking off, Samson looked past her shoulder. A hint of shyness coasted across his features. The emotion quickly gave way to joy.

Over what, Darcy wasn't sure. Until she turned around.

The girl in the gauzy blouse sauntered across the street toward them.

◠

The sweet fragrance of simmering barbecue sauce wafted through Latrice's house. Trudging in through the mudroom, Darcy paused to savor the aroma and pull herself together. After the confrontation with Noah—and Samson's impressive heroics—her pulse beat a jangly rhythm.

In the kitchen, Latrice and Nella leaned against a counter heaped with dishes in various stages of preparation. Beside them, Tippi gingerly climbed down a metal two-step ladder. Evidently, she had needed the ladder to watch the show from the window above the sink. With a wink at Darcy, she fist-pumped the air.

Latrice asked, "Having fun outside?"

Darcy noticed a few blades of grass on her shoulder. "Don't start." She brushed them off. "This isn't like my juvie stint at the jail. Didn't

Emerson tell you about the kid bullying him?" She grinned. "The score is now settled."

Nella chuckled. "From the cheap seats, it looked like Samson did the score-settling."

"Hey! I did my bit too."

At the table, a fork clattered down. Behind a plate of spaghetti, Emerson's face registered shock.

He swiped at the sauce ringing his mouth. "Juvie . . . juvenile detention? Aunt Darcy, you did jail time? You were *incarcerated*?"

"Nice word choice," Nella said.

Darcy smiled. "It's a joke, sweetie. I've never been incarcerated. Grandmother asked the Chagrin Falls PD to leave me stewing outside a jail cell. I was thirteen. The scare tactic was meant to make me behave." It was an unnerving experience Darcy never repeated. "I got into a fight outside the roller rink. Grandmother was furious."

"Why did you get in a fight?"

Latrice bustled to the table. "There was a boy at the rink a lot like Noah." She handed Emerson a napkin to wipe his face. "Jackson something-or-other. Nastiest boy in Chagrin Falls. He was making fun of a girl with a developmental disability."

Emerson sighed. "That's sad."

"It is," Darcy agreed. "She was trying hard to skate well. Jackson was badgering her so much she kept falling back down. When he walked out of the rink, I was waiting for him."

"You took on *a boy*?"

"I was tired of him picking on her. Every kid in the skating rink knew she had trouble at school, and her mother was stuck in the bathroom with her little brother. I'm sure if she'd caught Jackson bullying her daughter, *she* would've beaten him to a pulp."

"Gosh, Aunt Darcy. I didn't know you were a fighter when you were a kid."

Nella came to her defense. "She wasn't, Emerson. What she did to Jackson wasn't her usual behavior. At the time, there was a great deal of . . . tumult in Darcy's life."

"What's *tumult?*"

"Upsetting times. Sometimes kids act inappropriately when bad things happen to them." She gave Darcy a meaningful look. Mentioning Darcy's childhood friendship with Michael—or why it ended—wouldn't be appropriate. Changing the subject, Nella added, "Emerson, why don't you show your aunt the surprise? She'll get a kick out of it."

"Sure!"

Latrice removed his plate as he reached for two mason jars. Darcy hadn't noticed them on the table.

"Aunt Darcy, look what Tippi did. She's the best."

At the counter, Tippi gave the thumbs-up. "I am," she agreed.

Unscrewing the lid of the first jar, Emerson pulled out a fistful of bills. The loose change mixed in tumbled across the table.

Darcy scrambled to catch the coins. "Be careful!" She caught a handful of quarters. "What *is* all of this?" Each jar was packed tight with wrinkled bills and shiny coins.

"Tippi's poker winnings. Hers, and the winnings of the old folks who play with her. Mostly old guys. A few ladies play too. They're giving their winnings to Samson."

"Why?"

"To pay for his truck insurance."

"They're all pitching in?"

Approaching, Tippi reached for the jar. "This is enough to cover his first year of insurance. Michael got the quote for coverage." She began stuffing the money back inside.

"Wait. Your gambling buddies agreed to this?"

Truck insurance didn't come cheap. It was a generous gift.

"What else are we going to do with our money? Take it with us?"

"They aren't the only ones contributing." Latrice removed a package of celery from the refrigerator and set it beside the potatoes on the counter. "I did too. So did Nella and Michael."

"Count me in," Darcy said. She beamed at Tippi. "A full year's insurance is a boon for any teenager. As we speak, Samson is outside flirting with the cutest girl. I predict he asks her out by sundown."

"Gross," Emerson muttered.

Latrice grinned. "I've got my own prediction."

"What's that?" Darcy asked.

She handed Darcy a paring knife, then nodded at the potatoes. "That you'll have these spuds ready for the pot in record time. I'd like to relax soon. Get over here and start peeling."

Chapter 22

By late afternoon, the block party was in full swing.

Noah's parents, after hearing about his bullying of Emerson—and their son's altercation with Darcy and Samson—had banished him to his bedroom. His removal from the party gave Emerson the confidence to join the baseball game with kids of all ages. Adults lingered by the card tables, sipping wine and catching up with neighbors. Younger families helped their children navigate the obstacle course, where every child received a prize at the finish line.

By the picket fence before Latrice's house, Samson flirted with the girl in the gauzy blouse.

Darcy wandered the crowd alone. It was hard not to feel out of place. Most of Latrice's neighbors were strangers now. There were as many new faces on the street as people missing—neighbors who had moved away during the years she'd been gone from Ohio. She'd expected Michael to make an appearance. When the sunlight began to slant across the street, she realized the assumption was a foolish one.

Disappointed, she retraced her steps to the buffet table. She mulled over the idea of grabbing a slice of cheesecake while Emerson finished the ball game. She was still deciding when a group of adults, three houses down, drew apart. A familiar-looking woman stepped between them and into the street.

Blunt-cut, sable hair framed the woman's sultry features. Darcy paused by the buffet tables. She knew her somehow. As Darcy resumed walking, she attempted to dredge up her name.

Then it came to her. *Ellen. She's a CPA.*

She specialized in small business accounting and payroll.

Thrilled to have pulled the name from memory, Darcy quickened her pace through the crowd. Ellen Caraway. She'd managed the accounting for Darcy's late father's medical practice.

When she was one house away, Darcy waved.

Ellen spotted her. And frowned.

She glanced left then right, seeking an exit. She looked like a cornered animal.

At her reaction, Darcy ground to a halt. Ellen pushed through the wall of people behind her and hurried down the sidewalk.

Blinking, Darcy watched her disappear into the throng. Confused, she tried to work out what she'd done to upset the woman.

I didn't upset her. Ellen Caraway had seemed . . . frightened.

Like Morgan Harbert, on the day she got a goose egg on her brow when she slammed into her SUV. The day she caught sight of Darcy's mother in the parking lot. When Rosalind, with uncharacteristic heat, had shouted at her.

An odd coincidence?

A clammy awareness sprouted goose bumps on the back of Darcy's neck.

No. This is something more.

～

Dousing the lights in the shop, Michael stifled a yawn. Since daybreak, he'd been assembling the nine-foot-tall pantry for the Tinley job.

Outside, the late-afternoon sun painted the acres in shades of crimson. At his calves, Jasper panted.

"Ready for dinner, boy?"

It promised to be a lonely meal. Nella and Tippi wouldn't arrive home until after dark. Each year, they refused to leave the block party until they'd helped Latrice put her kitchen back in order. Michael wondered if Darcy would stick around to help. Missing the chance to see her was a loss. After their conversation the other day, she probably needed time to think.

Michael went inside and filled Jasper's bowl. He watched the mutt chow through the kibble as his thoughts wended back to Darcy. For reasons he couldn't identify, he was worried about her. Which made no sense. She was at the party, reconnecting with old friends.

The dog trotted off to find a cozy spot to sleep off his food coma. It occurred to Michael that he wasn't hungry. He couldn't shake the feeling that something wasn't right.

The hunch carried him back outside. Without making a conscious decision, he strode across the lawn. Ahead, the forest seemed aflame as the sun dipped closer to the horizon. He loved this time of year, when the balmy air held nightfall off until well past eight o'clock. Taking the path to the oak tree, he wondered if he shouldn't have brought dinner along. Eating with the river serenading him in the distance was an enjoyable pastime.

In the fallen leaves near the great oak, he noticed a bright flash of color. A purse. Darcy's.

"Darcy, are you out here?"

Birds chirped in the leafy canopy above. Peering over the ledge, he wondered if she was down by the river.

The precipice behind the tree was a sheer thirty-foot drop. Five paces to the left of the tree, however, the incline wasn't as steep. The path wound down in a curving pattern, with saplings sprouting across the rocky ground. Making his way down, Michael reached for one sapling, then the next, to keep his footing steady.

Darcy was sitting on a boulder, staring into the bubbling waters. He called out, and she waved.

When he reached her, she nodded at the section of the river below the oak. "Still the deepest spot?" She scanned the flowing water, her eyes quick and assessing.

"Yeah, it still is. Emerson wants to swim there."

"Like we did as kids?"

"He's still working up the courage."

She pulled her knees up tight to her chest. "Don't let him swim there after a heavy rain. He'll be swept downriver."

"He never goes in unless I'm with him. He's careful. So far, he's only gone in up to his knees."

"I should take him swimming. We could both use the diversion."

"Let me know when you do. I'll join you if I can spare the time."

"That would be nice." She sighed. "I loved swimming here when we were kids."

"We never got your sister to go in with us. Elizabeth wanted nothing to do with the river. In retrospect, it's amazing we ever got her to come down here."

"Yeah, and only a few times each summer." Darcy offered a faint smile. "My sister was definitely an 'indoor girl.'"

Michael surveyed the tightness at the corner of Darcy's eyes. "You came home early from the block party?" She *was* upset about something, confirming his hunch.

"Latrice dropped me off. I left Samson with the car. He met a girl, and Emerson is playing baseball."

"Who's with your mother?" He knew Darcy wouldn't leave Rosalind unattended.

"The new health aide my mother hired. Her name is Gwynn. Nice woman."

"She started today?"

"She did. She'll begin coming three times a week."

Darcy returned her attention to the river. Her eyes faraway, she appeared to be sorting something out. She hugged her knees tighter to her chest, as if the thoughts streaming through her mind posed a danger.

At last, she said, "Remember the night we ran into my father at the restaurant?"

It wasn't something he'd ever forget. "Yeah, I do."

"Before he walked up to us, a woman left the restaurant. She went out fast. Right as we came in—you bumped into her."

"I don't remember bumping into anyone." He wasn't sure where she was going with this.

"She was tall. Black hair, athletic build. She wore a slinky dress. Dark green or blue—I can't recall exactly. Don't you remember?"

Michael searched his memories. Nothing came to mind. Nothing but the alarm he'd felt when Dr. Jack saw them, and was instantly furious. An instinctive, automatic need to protect Darcy took over. Michael had blocked her father from getting into her face. Darcy had cowered behind his back as the two men exchanged heated words.

Brushing off the memory, he said, "Other than the short argument with your father, I don't recall anything else."

"I guess it doesn't matter. I'm sure the woman was Ellen Caraway."

"The CPA in the Falls?"

"I've been mulling this over for an hour. I'm positive."

She slid off the boulder, agitated. Or angry. Michael tried to decipher which as she tugged off her tennis shoes. She flung them away.

"You know what, Michael? I'm the one who ran away eight years ago, but I'm not the only Goodridge who ran from painful realities. My parents were running all the time. They used their careers as cover, but they spent their lives running—from each other, mostly."

"Slow down. Ellen Caraway was at the restaurant that night, with your father?"

"Forget it." She stared at the ground, her shoulders trembling.

He strode forward. "That *is* what you're saying." He brushed his fingers across her arm, waited until she looked up. "If your father was running around with Ellen Caraway, I'm not surprised. It's just another example of how you and Elizabeth got a raw deal. Honestly? I hardly remember Dr. Jack when we were kids. I sure as hell didn't like him when you and I were dating. If he was cheating on your mother, I feel bad for her—and it's taken me a *long* time to feel anything but contempt for Rosalind."

"She's not a bad person. We have our highs and lows. Sometimes we even like each other."

"I know," he said, suddenly aware he was cupping her face, his skin warming against hers. She leaned into his palm as he added, "Which brings me to my next point. Focus on what you're building with your mother—a genuine relationship. Maybe it'll never be perfect. But you're making headway. You might even get her to come around and get on the transplant list. Forget about whatever your father did. He's gone. It doesn't matter."

"Michael, you don't get it. This isn't just about my father running around with Ellen Caraway. What he did back then, what he did to *all* of us . . ."

Her voice drifted off. Sorrow rippled across her features. Then anger.

She spun away. "I need to cool off."

With bafflement, he watched her splash into the river. Blue water rushed past her calves. Then her thighs, as she waded in deeper. His heart clenched as she began swimming toward the deep center of churning water. She was beautiful, gliding through the river, her strokes powerful as she swam harder, working off her fury. He still wasn't sure what had set her off. Dr. Jack's apparent infidelities, her mother's disease—there was too much on her mind. With a start, he wondered if she was in the right frame of mind for a swim in churning waters.

He shouted a warning for her to turn around. She glanced back at him with devilish glee. Then she dunked under the water.

During childhood, her impulsive behavior had frightened him. Daredevil antics that pushed him to take risks. Stupid dares he couldn't resist. He never failed to follow along, to prove his courage equaled hers. It seemed miraculous that the antics had never led to broken bones or stitches.

He was a man now. His fears were more realistic. Of letting passion draw him into a relationship that wasn't ready to evolve. Of letting Darcy take the reckless lead, like she'd done so often before.

Mostly, he feared losing his heart before she was ready to offer hers.

Pushing the fear aside, he yanked off his shoes.

She broke the river's surface like a bullet. Keeping his attention locked on her, he splashed a determined path through the shallows. When the water reached his thighs, he muttered a few choice words. Then he dove in and swam to her.

Laughing, she read the irritation on his face. "You're sexy when you're wet," she teased, swimming a fast circle around him. "Word of advice: don't follow me in when you're wearing jeans. You'll sink."

"Next time, give me a heads-up. I'll wear shorts." He kicked through the swift undercurrents, came closer. "It'll be dark soon. How long are you staying out here?"

"Until I cool down."

Her wet blouse was plastered to her skin, her bra visible. "This isn't just about your father. Is it?" He tried not to stare.

"Not really." She glided backward, her strokes slowing. She glanced at the sky, burning crimson with the approaching night. "All I have are theories and supposition. I need to think it through."

"Can't you think on land?"

"In a minute." She swam closer. "Michael, why were you so . . . proper? When we were dating?"

"Stupidity?" He didn't like this side of her, the Darcy that toyed and teased. A defense mechanism.

"We should've had sex. It would've made me bolder."

"You don't need any help in that department."

"I mean with my father. If I'd already been in deep with you, I wouldn't have backed down so fast—when he told me to break up. Maybe I would've told him to piss off. That my life was my own. That it was none of his business."

She looked exhausted suddenly, her strokes uneven.

"If I'd stood up to my father, I never would've gone out drinking alone. Never would've called Elizabeth after having too many drinks, or put my sister in danger."

Playing a game of "what if" was a futile pastime. He refused to allow her to take it any further.

Taking her hand, he steered her into the shallows. They were wet as seals, but the air was balmy. Giving in to temptation, he thumbed the moist skin of her temples.

When his touch drew her closer, he said, "You have to stop doing this. Rehashing the past. Blaming yourself. Acting as if one different move would've changed the entire game. The truth, Darcy? You can't judge the person you were. Not with the wisdom you now possess. You didn't have that wisdom back then."

"I should get a therapist. I went to all this trouble putting a child psychologist on standby for Emerson. Fully covered sessions if he needs them, compliments of my mother's superb insurance coverage." She sighed. "*I'm* the one who needs help. There's lots of stuff I should work out."

"No kidding."

"How much is therapy, anyway? For adults. My coverage is fairly crappy."

He grunted. "I'll pay," he said. "You need a good year of counseling. Or two. If we can't find a decent therapist to fix the wiring in your head, I'll hire an electrician."

The quick retort started her eyes flashing. Then she grinned. She appraised his sopping wet T-shirt and the jeans sticking uncomfortably to his thighs.

"Swimming in jeans is *not* a good choice. Are you cold?" She pressed her hands to his chest. "Nope. Hot to the touch."

"And getting hotter by the minute."

"You're still too proper." She noticed his eyes tripping across her breasts. Playfully, she peeled the blouse from her skin, making the fabric opaque. "For the record, I wouldn't have objected if you'd gone faster back then. Sped up the timeline significantly."

"Give me a hint, Darcy. Do you want to talk, or make love?" He swiped a strand of hair from her cheek. "Word of warning. Stop looking at me like that, or we're going for the latter."

"*How* am I looking at you?" she asked coyly. He wasn't fooled. Her breathing was as shallow as the cool water tickling their calves.

"You're undressing me with your eyes."

"I am." The rich, throaty confession prickled heat across his scalp. "I want you, Michael. More than anything. But I need to do what's best for Emerson."

"We won't tell him right away."

"He'll sense the change between us."

"We'll be careful," Michael promised, his voice growing ragged. Her fingers were making a gentle exploration of his collarbone. He resisted the urge to pull her in tight against his hips.

His resolve nearly slipped when she brushed her lips against his. "Tell me," she whispered. "Why *were* you so proper?"

There was no reason to prevaricate now. Whether they took this further or waited, he'd already decided. He was committed to Darcy in every way that mattered.

"I meant to put a ring on your finger first," he admitted. "The night of the accident, when you canceled our dinner. I'd bought you an engagement ring. I wanted to make it official before we were intimate."

The revelation stilled her fingers.

She looked up at him with an exquisite blend of wonder and sorrow. "I would've said yes," she whispered.

Her declaration brought the rest tumbling out. "I've loved you my whole life," he said, steering her arms across his shoulders to bring her fully into his embrace. "You've been bound up in my life from the beginning. Sometimes I'm sure we're opposites, like earth and sky. The rest of the time, I'm not sure where I begin and you end." His heart thundered as the feverish lights in her eyes leaped higher, a tacit agreement—an understanding. "Isn't that how it's supposed to be?" he added, hungry for the taste of her mouth.

She nodded. "Two people so deeply in love, they're not complete without the other. I'll never be whole without you. I never was." She pressed her forehead against his cheek, adding, "Why did I allow my grief over losing Elizabeth to bury everything I felt for you?"

"It doesn't matter now. You're here." He hesitated. "Promise you'll never leave me again."

"I won't. Not ever." For proof, she dragged her mouth across his jawbone until they both shivered with delight.

He captured her lips in a hungry kiss. The needy whimper rising in her throat increased the tempo of his mouth on hers. With hasty steps, he led her away from the riverbank, his head spinning, his hands trembling as he molded her closer to the hard contours of his body.

Moss curved against the hillside like an emerald blanket. Drifting down onto it, they never broke off the kiss. They peeled off their wet clothes, laughing against each other's lips—playful, the way they'd been as children when they'd roughhoused together, too young to understand the significance of an attraction they'd taken for granted. The attraction meant to lead them here.

Raspy breaths broke from Michael's throat. Ending the kiss, he eased himself on top of her. Darcy held on to his hips, her teeth grazing his shoulder.

Unbound, he caressed her neck, her breasts. He groaned again. The sound—deep, nearly animalistic—made Darcy's eyes drift open. Her gaze hung on him like stars pinned to a night sky.

He entered her with a deep thrust. A slick jolt of consuming pleasure, and Darcy gasped. Her eyes remained locked on his. He found his rhythm, and she joined him, racing fast alongside him with anticipation and a greedy sensuality as they rose to the summit. Her eyes never left his face.

They were twin lights, calling him home.

Chapter 23

On Sunday, Darcy awoke to the rumble of thunder.

A quick glance at her phone confirmed her suspicions. She threw off the blanket. She had overslept. Given her habit of rising early, it was a striking development.

She padded across the chilly floorboards and drew back the curtains. Slate-colored clouds skimmed the sky. Pressing her forehead against the window's cool glass, she watched the sky churn and flash.

Yesterday, she had remained with Michael on the riverbank until the last glimmers of sunlight retreated from the forest. Professing their love, vowing to never again allow circumstance to break them apart. Later, they were slow and tender, savoring the fit of their bodies as they took exquisite care in bringing each other pleasure.

The memory was pure and beautiful. Yet doubt rimmed its fragile edges. Michael had discovered her alone by the riverbank yesterday—but she hadn't gone there in hopes of seeing him. She'd gone to sort through her awful theories about her father.

When they left the forest, after Michael pulled her close for one last, lingering kiss, why didn't she tell him the rest? If she was correct—and an awful certainty was lodged inside her like a stone—the secrets she'd uncovered affected him too. They explained why Rosalind despised Nella.

It would have been wiser to lay the facts at his feet. She wasn't sure how he would have reacted, but he'd deserved a full accounting. As he strode away in the waning daylight, why didn't she call him back?

She dressed quickly. There was no sense worrying about what she'd hidden from Michael. She'd find the courage to fill him in later. For now, it was best to get to the bottom of her family's secrets and lies.

In the kitchen, pancake batter resembled spatter art on the counter. At the table, Emerson swung his legs back and forth. A book sat near his elbow as he stared out at the storm clouds.

Darcy counted three dishes in the sink. "Did Samson make pancakes for you and Grandmother?"

"I had seconds. Grandmother didn't want any."

"Where's Samson?"

"In the living room. It's gross, how boys his age like to talk to girls on the phone. They've been talking for a long time."

Despite the tension centering inside her, Darcy grinned. "As in plural? I'll bet he's only talking to *one* girl on the phone. The girl he met yesterday."

"Her name is Makayla. She's a senior at Chagrin Falls High School." Emerson's nose wrinkled with disgust. "Samson is in love."

"If he is, it's none of your business. And no making fun of him, okay? He's old enough to have a girlfriend." On autopilot, she filled the coffeepot with water. Changing her mind, she poured the water down the drain. Apprehension over the upcoming discussion knotted her stomach. "Grandmother hasn't come down yet?"

"She's still in bed, going through the newspaper."

Reading the *New York Times* in the master suite was a Sunday habit. Usually Rosalind didn't come downstairs until late morning. All the better. It was best to have the conversation out of earshot of Emerson.

"I'll be right back. Stay here, okay?"

He looked up. "Where are you going?"

"To talk to Grandmother."

"You shouldn't bug her when she's reading. She doesn't like it."

"No one does. But yes, I get it." Darcy palmed away the perspiration beading on her neck. She hesitated. "Did you have fun yesterday at the block party? I'm sorry I left early."

"It was okay."

"Just okay?" His attention was back on the window, and the storm brewing outside.

He paused for a long moment. Then he looked at her. "Question," he said, mimicking her oft-used opener for tricky conversations. "When you came home in June, Grandmother was very angry with you."

"That's a statement, Emerson. Not a question."

"She still gets angry at you a lot."

"Still a statement. And I'm making progress with her. At least most of the time."

"Can you try harder? *Persuade* her to become real friends with you?"

"Nice word choice." She sat down beside him. With dismay, she noticed the worry curving his spine. A mother-daughter friendship was clearly an important topic to him. "What's going on, sweetie? You look awfully serious."

"I *am* serious. If you don't make Grandmother like you all the time, she won't trust you. If she doesn't trust you, how will you save her life? I heard Samson ask Latrice why Grandmother won't get a new heart. Latrice said the only way she'll agree is if you talk her into it."

The explanation—not to mention her nephew's poignant logic— was impossible to refute. This *was* on Darcy. If she didn't break down her mother's resistance, Rosalind was facing a death sentence.

There was a second issue, one Darcy tackled first.

"Is there anything about heart transplants you need to know?" she asked. They'd all agreed not to tell Emerson about the procedure unless Rosalind changed her mind. Why get his hopes up? But since he'd brought up the topic, it seemed wise to jump in fully. "I'm guessing you've already been prowling Google."

"Not really. I don't like stuff that's got to do with blood. I thought I should talk to you instead."

"Smart boy."

"If Grandmother has the operation, will it hurt?"

"She'll be sedated. She'll sleep through the entire procedure."

"Can I visit her?"

"Not for the first day or two. Once she's moved out of critical care, you'll be able to see her."

"The Tin Man got a new heart." Emerson laughed at his own joke. A nervous reaction, one Darcy recognized. It was also embedded in her own DNA.

"Weird," she muttered. She'd made the same joke to her mother, weeks ago.

"What is?"

"The way your mind works." *Like mine.* "You know. The crack about the Tin Man."

"That was inappropriate."

"No worries, kiddo. It was also kind of funny."

"Thanks." Lowering his chin to his knuckles, Emerson got back down to business. "Will you work harder at making Grandmother your friend? So we can get her fixed up?"

"Starting tomorrow," she promised. "I can't bring it up today. There's something else I need to discuss with her."

Emerson looked marginally better. Less worried, nearly hopeful. "You won't forget?" he asked.

"I won't." She rose. "Do me a favor. Stay downstairs until I finish talking to her."

"Okay."

"Want to go into the Falls this afternoon? The forecast calls for non-stop rain, but we can take a spin through the roller rink." She frowned. "You *do* know how to roller skate, right?"

266

"I'm a pretty good skater."

"Great. We'll hit the rink this afternoon."

After giving him a quick kiss, she left the kitchen. From the living room, Samson's murmured conversation drifted out. Marshaling her thoughts, she ascended the stairwell.

The spacious master suite, like its occupant, was subtle and elegant. Plush ivory carpeting softened Darcy's footsteps. A chaise longue in a deeper shade of cream sat near the French doors, which led out to the private balcony. The dressers, as well as the two nightstands on either side of the king-size bed, were golden teak. In the bed, her mother lifted questioning eyes.

"Darcy." The newspaper rustled to her lap. "Can I help you?"

A faint reprimand. Darcy swallowed against the dry spaces in her throat. Rarely did she enter her mother's suite. The infrequent visits made her alert to the changes. A new photograph on the dresser, of her playing with Emerson out back. A pair of supple leather gloves, folded on a nightstand.

Pivoting, she surveyed the long expanse of wall beside the French doors. The room was nearly spartan in design, with the exception of this one wall and its horizontal arrangement of photographs. All in matching teak frames—photos of Darcy and her late sister during childhood, more recent images of Emerson as he raced through the stages of childhood development. A decades-old portrait of Rosalind in her judge's robes, taken soon after she'd been elected to the bench. Surprise lifted Darcy's brows.

"I've never noticed before," she murmured. "There's not one photograph of my father in your bedroom." Given her upsetting conclusions, she now understood why.

"Does it matter?"

"Not to me. Not anymore."

Unable to quell the tension invading her muscles, she began pacing. Tossing the newspaper aside, her mother watched with growing impatience.

"What is wrong with you this morning?" Rosalind asked. "You look absolutely . . . frenzied. It's not your best look."

"I need to ask you something. You won't want to answer."

"Thank goodness you didn't pursue a law career. Your courtroom manner would not have swayed a witness."

"I need the truth." She stopped at the base of the bed. "Was my father unfaithful?"

Silence filled the room. Rosalind sat up straighter.

Her features unreadable, she motioned to the door. "I'm not having this conversation in front of the entire household. Where are Emerson and Samson?"

Darcy shut the door. "Downstairs. Emerson is in the kitchen, and Samson is chatting on the phone in the living room." She returned to the bed with her heart pulsing out of rhythm.

"Why are you asking about your father?"

"I saw Ellen Caraway. Yesterday, at the block party."

"The CPA?"

She gave a tight nod. "When I started walking over to say hello, Ellen looked alarmed. She ran off, like she couldn't get away from me fast enough. She reacted exactly the same way as Morgan Harbert the day you confronted her in the parking lot. So I'm asking. Did the 'good doctor' play around on you?"

"Stop with the cynicism. It doesn't suit you. He *was* a good doctor. One of the finest."

"And he was also unfaithful?"

Surrendering, her mother expelled a weary breath. She reached for the leather gloves. Darcy hurried forward to help her put them on. Rosalind lifted a hand, driving her off.

"Your father was unfaithful." Wincing with pain, she slipped on the left glove. "Repeatedly." Injured pride raised her chin. "Why do you care? It was a long time ago."

"Because I have the right to know if my parents raised me in a sham marriage." Darcy couldn't keep the anger at bay. "When did it start?" A terrible intuition warned she already knew the answer. But she wanted proof.

Which her mother, slipping on the second glove, quickly supplied. "When I was pregnant with you." She stabbed Darcy with an assessing glance. "Ah, I see. You've put most of this together on your own. Yes, Darcy—he was unfaithful even then."

"I'm not surprised. Everything about him was a lie."

"And now you're curious as to *why* I tolerated his behavior? Or are you merely appalled that a woman of my caliber did so? Yes, I let my love for him blind me. I spent years believing every lie. I believed him every time he promised never to stray again. When my safe delusions no longer worked, I realized it was too late to even consider divorce."

The explanation sickened Darcy. "You made the wrong choice. No woman should put up with a husband like that. You should've kicked him to the curb."

"I had you and Elizabeth to consider. I didn't want you growing up in a broken home."

Stunned, Darcy stared at her. Did her mother actually believe she'd done the right thing? That her great and tragic sacrifice had benefited her daughters?

"We did grow up in a broken home." Heartache threatened to steal her composure. As did the sob rising from her throat. "We grew up believing we were second best. That we didn't measure up, not against your stellar careers. The famous judge and the talented doctor."

"Stop this. You're attacking me."

"For good reason," she tossed back, the pain of betrayal too strong to tamp down. "You and my father hid inside your careers because you hated each other. Your hate became a prison for you both—and for me and Elizabeth. You trapped the four of us in a crucible."

"Not intentionally."

"What about Nella? He seduced her after she lost her husband, didn't he? That's why your broke off my friendship with Michael when I was twelve. Isn't it?"

"I didn't want you around that family. Not after what happened between Nella and Jack. I couldn't bear the reminder. Your father respected my wishes."

"Oh, I doubt a man like my father had your best interests in mind—or mine. He had the perfect arrangement, didn't he? The ideal home life, and a wife who quietly accepted his infidelities. The veneer of respectability gave him cover for his exploits."

"This conversation ends now. I won't allow you to stand there and judge my life."

A low growl of frustration escaped Darcy. "Yes, you will. I'm not going anywhere until I have all the answers." When her mother stared at her, apparently stunned by the demand, she added, "Nella was your closest friend. How could you let a . . . predator get to her? Because that's what we're talking about. A man who sleeps around repeatedly, relentlessly—a married man, one who uses his status and his wealth to get what he wants—he *preys* on women."

Rosalind got out of bed. She moved with the care of a woman no longer sure of her balance, which amyloidosis stole at inopportune moments. At last she steadied herself.

"The younger women your father targeted were arguably his prey," she conceded. Her mouth tightened. "Nella was different. She continued on with your father. It wasn't a short affair."

"I don't believe you. Where's the proof?"

"Darcy, you're nearing the line. *Don't* cross it."

"You don't have proof. You're angry at what he did to you, and she's an easy target. You've kept your hatred burning for Nella because he's dead, and you can't take it out on him. Should I ask *her* what really happened?"

"Don't you dare!" her mother shouted. She snatched up her robe. "You can't march into my bedroom and start digging into my past as if my private life is yours to inspect. Stay out of my business! If you discuss any of this with Nella, I will never forgive you."

The full brunt of Rosalind's misguided hatred struck like a fist. Darcy had lost Michael thanks to her father's abhorrent behavior. She'd lost her beloved sister on a rain-streaked night because she'd gone out drinking alone, cowed by her father's demands that she break up with the only man she'd ever loved.

Michael. Elizabeth. Eight years spent away from Ohio. Spent away from Emerson, a little boy I now love like a son. All of the heartache a result of my father's lust and my mother's unrelenting fury.

"You win, Mother. I'll let you keep your pathetic rationalizations." Darcy choked off a sob. "I won't talk to Nella. There's no point. You've spent so many years consumed by hate, you're unable to change."

She spun for the door. She left her bewildered mother rooted in the middle of the suite.

At the bottom of the stairwell, Samson paced in a tense circle. The sound of her footsteps lifted his gaze.

"What's going on upstairs? Were you fighting with your mama?"

Darcy scraped the hair from her brow. "I guess so."

"Is Emerson allowed to go over to Michael's house?"

"What? No."

"He just took off—without a raincoat. It's pouring."

Outside, thunder cracked. They both flinched as the sound rocketed through the house. Then Darcy felt sick as understanding dawned.

Her mother appeared at the top of the stairwell. "What's going on? Where's my grandson?"

She'd dressed in a hurry, the leather gloves no longer on her sensitive hands.

Ignoring the question, Darcy gripped Samson's arm. "Before Emerson went out, was he in the kitchen? Please tell me he was at the table, reading."

"He was upstairs."

"He heard the shouting?"

No.

The conversation was hurtful, brutal. Too sordid for a child's consumption.

Samson blanched. "I was in the living room. I only saw him for a second. When he came down. He shot out of here fast."

Yanking open the foyer closet, she grabbed a raincoat. "I'm going over to the Varanos'. I need to talk to him."

Rosalind came down the stairs. "I'm coming too."

"No, Mother. Stay here." Thunder rolled closer, rattling the windows. "He's upset. Let me talk to him."

Samson frowned. "*I'm* going with you."

"Stay with my mother. She needs you."

"Wait!" Rosalind rushed across the foyer. "Let's all go together. We'll find Emerson faster." She whirled on Samson. "Are you sure he's with Michael? He's not in the forest? He hides in the forest when he's upset. What did he tell you?"

Darcy never heard the rest. She dashed out the door.

Rain pelted her in heavy sheets as she climbed over the fence. The scream of blades whirring sent her past the house. Michael was in his shop, working.

Is Emerson with him?

On a wave of hope, she reached the door.

"Where is he?" She swung her gaze across the shop. Her heart fell.

Michael switched off the table saw. "Are you looking for Emerson?" He removed his safety goggles. "He's not here. I haven't seen him this morning."

"Michael, call the house! Ask Nella if he's inside."

A quick call revealed the worst. Emerson wasn't there.

Darcy's breath stuttered. Above the long stretch of lawn, lightning streaked the sky.

She bolted toward the forest.

Chapter 24

Darcy was halfway across the back lawn when the sky opened up fully. Sheet after sheet of rain pounded her back.

Behind her, Michael screamed for her to slow down. To her left, she glimpsed Samson jogging down the property line, his arm hooked through Rosalind's. Willing her body forward, Rosalind took uneven strides.

Darcy ran faster. *Don't wait for them. Emerson has a five-minute lead. There's no time to waste.*

She dashed into the forest. Forgoing the winding path to the oak tree, she bolted in a straight line. Heavy brush tore at her arms. Overhead, the canopy of leaves held off the worst of the storm—until she reached the clearing before the great tree. The lashing rain fell hard through the patches of open sky.

"Emerson?" She swiped at the droplets pelting her face. He was nowhere in sight. "Are you here?"

"Go away," he said from somewhere near the tree.

She slipped on a patch of mud, nearly fell. She righted herself. "Tell me where you are." She took careful steps forward, arms out for balance.

"Leave me alone. I don't want to see anyone right now."

From behind, heavy footsteps crunched through the underbrush. Then mingled voices. From the sound of it, Michael was circling around to help Samson lead Rosalind into the forest.

"Emerson, talk to me. We'll go inside. You'll feel better."

"No!"

Overhead, thunder exploded. Thirty feet below, the river churned beneath the assault of the whipping rain. Darcy scanned the sloping hillside and then the steep drop behind the tree. She bit down on her lip, frustrated. There were too many places to hide. The storm was increasing in billowing gusts, making it nearly impossible to spot the upset boy.

At last she saw Emerson behind the tree. He stood just a few treacherous paces from the sheer drop where the stable ground ended. In the pouring rain, he was unaware he'd stepped nearly to the edge of the precipice.

Terror sank her to her knees.

"Emerson, listen closely. Start walking toward me. Don't run." Her commanding tone glittered like steel. She rose back to her feet and sidled to the left. "I know you're upset. We'll deal with it later. It's not safe where you're standing."

His eyes widened. "What?"

He was a careful child. He'd never intentionally put himself in danger. But he'd done so now.

At her side, Michael halted. Sucking in an unsteady breath, he latched his startled attention on her nephew. Then he caught Darcy's gaze with a nearly imperceptible nod. Better for him to remain silent and let her talk Emerson to safety.

"That's right, kiddo. Start walking. *Slowly.*"

He took a tentative step. The terror mixing with Darcy's relief didn't stop her from lifting an encouraging hand. "Come on now."

Another step, as carefully placed as the first.

"I hate rain," he muttered. He squinted against the droplets batting his face. "I'm cold."

"You'll be warm and dry in the house."

He paused, his tennis shoes sinking into the mud. Darcy's stomach clenched.

Why has he stopped? He's still too close to the edge, too far away for me to risk bolting forward and scooping him up.

Her confusion was short-lived. Footsteps clomped through the forest's undergrowth. A soft gasp—her mother's. She glanced over her shoulder as Samson pulled Rosalind to a stop.

The youth stared wide-eyed at Emerson. "Oh shit," he blurted, the fear thick in his voice.

Rosalind broke free of his grasp. Panic tripped across her face as she assessed the situation.

"Emerson, come here," she barked. "Do it, sweetheart. *Now.*"

A faint command—a miscalculation.

Anger brightened the boy's face. He was already scared. The anger cut through his weak hold on his senses.

"Don't tell me what to do!" he shouted. "You don't make the rules!"

"Emerson—"

"Shut up! I'm not listening to you, Grandmother. You boss everyone around. I hate it. Stop making rules—you're not a judge anymore!"

"That's true," she agreed. "I'm not a judge anymore. I shouldn't make all the rules."

"You don't listen to anybody. Why don't you listen to Aunt Darcy? She's smart too, you know."

"You're right." Rosalind didn't like eating humble pie, but she made the effort now. "I should listen. I should listen most to the people I love."

"You don't know how! Why won't you let Aunt Darcy get you a new heart? You're being stupid."

"I am. I'm *very* stupid." Rosalind hesitated. Slowly, she blinked. Her eyes went glassy.

She listed sideways. A dizzy spell. Her knees began to buckle.

Darcy charged toward her, arms out. She caught her before Rosalind's knees scraped the ground.

With Michael's help, she steered her mother into a sitting position. Samson hurried over, unsure how to help. It was a bizarre sight, Rosalind sitting in the mud with the rain slicking down her face. There wasn't much to be done about it.

"Stay there," Darcy whispered. Her mother gave a tight nod. Rising, she regarded her nephew. "Emerson, let's do this," she said. "Take your time walking over."

He nodded.

A gust of wind barreled through the forest. The oak tree trembled against the blast. Handfuls of leaves showered down, a waterfall of bright green. High in the tree, a limb shook loose. It came down fast and struck Emerson on the shoulder.

He cried out as he was knocked backward. Dread gripped Darcy's throat as he rolled toward the precipice.

The ground beneath him gave way.

$\sim$

With horror, Michael watched Emerson plummet thirty feet to the river.

Rosalind screamed. Darcy, her attention trained on the hillside with a hawk's precision, sprinted to the left. She scrambled down the steep incline.

In the deepest section of the river, Emerson's head popped up. Then his arms, flailing. Fear lanced through Michael—the boy wasn't a good swimmer. Emerson slapped his arms against the water, searching for purchase on anything that would keep him from being swept away.

The wind howled, a demonic song to welcome the boy to his death. Michael sprinted for the hillside. Slipping, sliding, his fists grappling for saplings that snapped under his weight, he climbed his way down. Samson followed, bumping into him twice as they raced for the riverbank.

Darcy was already in the water, diving deep. Emerson screamed, the water rolling over him. He managed to swim to a rock and grab on.

Michael reached the riverbank. "Emerson—hold on!"

Darcy resurfaced not far from her nephew. A moment too late.

High above the boy, the storm pulled another limb from the oak tree. A heavier limb, fatter than the one that had sent Emerson spiraling off the precipice. A whoosh of threatening sound, and it hurtled down with ferocious speed. Emerson looked up, his eyes dark with understanding. He let go of the boulder to ward off the blow.

And was swept downstream.

Michael watched with his fists clenched and ice beating through his blood. He made the dreadful calculation. Darcy knew how to swim. She was safe for the moment, taking swift strokes to beat back the current.

Emerson would drown.

The decision sent Michael racing down the riverbank. The water rushed by viciously fast, yet he managed to gain speed. Ahead, an outcropping of rock jutted into the river. He threw himself down as Emerson's head popped up once again in the churning waves.

He caught the boy's arm with so much force, he feared he'd dislocated his shoulder. A sliver of relief darted through him as Emerson, his eyes filled with terror, reached up for him.

"Michael, I'm here!" Samson flung himself down and began hoisting Emerson to safety. "Catch Darcy!"

Michael rose to his knees. Frantic, he scanned the river.

There.

Darcy knew the river better than her nephew. She'd beaten a path to another outcropping. Spitting out water, grappling to hold on—the sheer force of the oncoming water slammed her against the unforgiving surface.

Michael leaped to his feet.

"Darcy, I'm coming!"

He dove in. His knuckles scraped across the riverbed. Legs pumping against the current, he took long strokes, beating the river back with all the power his muscles could supply and the pure, clean rage centered in his mind.

I will not allow the river to take what is most precious to me. I will not.

Spitting out a mouthful of water, he swam to her side.

Hard currents rolled over her shoulders as she held fast to the boulder. "This sucks," she announced. A rivulet of blood snaked down from her mouth. She didn't dare brush it away as she searched Michael's gaze. "You caught Emerson?"

"He's fine. Samson's with him." He scanned her face. "Anything broken?"

"No."

"Can you swim?"

Her teeth chattered. "I hit my head on something. When I dove in."

"You can swim, Darcy. You've always been a great swimmer."

"Right." She rested her cheek against the boulder, the currents washing away the rivulet of blood. "I feel woozy," she admitted.

Adrenaline coursed through him. He'd be damned if he'd let the river take her. Even if she passed out and became dead weight in his arms, he would get her to safety.

"We'll do this together. We're only twenty yards from shore." Icy currents pounded his back. Carefully, he maneuvered around the side of the boulder. With his right arm, he gripped her tightly. Kicking off his shoes, he planted his feet against the rock. "When I push off, you swim as hard as you can. Got it?"

"You won't let go?" Despite the peril, she laughed. "To be honest, I'm not sure I can make it on my own."

"I won't let go."

∽

In the third-floor corridor of the children's wing, a male nurse smiled faintly as Nella hurried past.

The alarming text from Latrice had arrived less than twenty minutes earlier. Immediately, Nella drove to Geauga County's Saint Jerome Hospital. She'd left a confused Tippi alone in the laundry room, folding linens. Nella resolved to call her mother once she knew Emerson was fine.

She paused in the doorway of the two-bed hospital room. The bed closest to the door was empty. A green privacy curtain separated the two halves of the room. If Rosalind was on the other side, the chances were high that she'd ask Nella to leave at once.

Rosalind's longstanding enmity no longer matters.

The fear scattering through Nella's blood would never abate until she was certain that Emerson wasn't badly injured.

With newfound determination, she stepped behind the privacy curtain.

On the other side, Latrice and Rosalind were seated near the wall, a few inches from the bed. Emerson was fast asleep. Nella's stomach lurched. Gauze encased his left wrist. A series of bruises peppered the side of his face.

"Nella. Hello." Appearing strangely embarrassed, Rosalind produced a welcoming expression. "It's good to see you."

The greeting left Nella speechless. Brows lifting, she assessed Rosalind's silver hair, plastered in wet clumps around her face.

"Were you in the forest?" she blurted. It was definitely something Latrice should've mentioned in the text.

"I wasn't much help. If your son hadn't followed Darcy to the oak tree, I can't bear to imagine what might have happened." Strong emotion rippled across her face. Fending it off, she motioned at the cramped space beside her grandson's hospital bed. "We seem to have run out of seating. Is there a chair on the other side? I can look, if you'd like to sit down."

The conciliatory remark took Nella aback.

Is Rosalind extending an invitation for me to join them?

Absurdly, she felt like Alice being dropped down a rabbit hole in a strange Wonderland.

Her confusion wasn't lost on Latrice. Beside the proud judge, the housekeeper allowed her head to drift back toward the wall—and out of Rosalind's line of vision. With a grin, she rolled her eyes skyward.

Amusement tickled Nella. Concealing it, she said, "I'm fine. Thank you. I don't mind standing."

Affection and worry pulled her toward the bed. Taking care not to wake the sleeping child, she feathered the lightest caress across the soft tufts crowning his head. Rosalind's gaze followed her with interest as she kissed his brow. She was thankful for his deep slumber after the terrible ordeal.

"How is he?" she asked.

"Nothing broken, thank goodness." Leaning forward, Rosalind smoothed a hand down the white blanket tucked around him. "His legs are badly scraped. He won't be running around for a few days." She hesitated. "Where's Darcy? I'm embarrassed to admit I haven't gone looking for her yet."

"Still in the emergency room, arguing with the doctors. They insist on admitting her overnight for observation. Michael is with her. Samson is too." Nella's phone buzzed. Reading the text, she chuckled. "According to Michael, Darcy just lost the battle. She's filling out the admitting paperwork now. They're sending her to a room on the fifth floor. Once Michael has the room number, he'll let us know."

"He saved my daughter's life—and my grandson's."

"Yes, he did."

"I must thank him." Rosalind blinked rapidly, her eyes moist. Latrice produced a tissue, and the shaken judge dabbed at her eyes. "I should go to find Michael, but I can't make myself leave Emerson just yet."

"Stay here, Rosalind. I'll convey your message when I see him."

"Thank you."

"My pleasure."

Latrice eased herself to her feet. "Will you both stop fancy-footing around each other? This is going to be a long night. I need coffee. Do either of you want anything from the cafeteria?"

They both shook their heads.

To Nella's astonishment, the housekeeper offered a parting zinger from the doorway.

"You behave, Rosalind. This is the perfect opportunity to kiss and make up. I expect you to do most of the kissing. Don't let me down."

She left, and the silence grew full. Nella wasn't sure how to break it. At the foot of the bed, she wavered.

Rosalind patted the chair Latrice had vacated. "Get off your feet, Nella. I'd much rather beg your forgiveness while we're sitting together."

"You want to apologize?"

"I've been pondering where to begin. Chronologically, or by degree of offense?"

"Rest your case, please. I have no interest in convicting you for past crimes and misdemeanors." Immensely relieved, Nella squeezed past and sat down. In the cramped space, their knees almost touched. "May I ask what brought on this change of heart?"

"Darcy. This morning, she shared a host of facts I should have discovered on my own. I am sorry, Nella." She glanced at her sleeping grandson. "What happened between you and Jack, I assumed—"

Nella laid a comforting hand on her knee. "There was only the one time. Just once, Rosalind. I will carry the shame to my grave."

"I'd rather you didn't." Rosalind inhaled a timid breath, her expression fluid. On the exhale, she said, "Darcy wants me to get on a transplant list."

"I know. My son mentioned it."

"As did Emerson. In the forest . . . right before I nearly lost him."

"Are you considering it?"

"The odds aren't good."

"They're good enough. Get the heart transplant."

Rosalind sighed. "I'm not sure how I feel about it. I need time to think." She studied her hands. Frightening blotches of red were sprouting across the skin. "I left my leather gloves in the house when I ran into the forest. This blasted pain. I'm miserable."

Nella was fearful of touching Rosalind's hand and making the situation worse. Instead, she pressed a kiss to her own fingertip. Gently, she pressed the kiss to Rosalind's cheek.

"What can I do to help? Name it. I'm at your beck and call."

"At the moment? Give me a thorough talking-to. Why did I leave my gloves in the house? And *why* am I exhausted this early in the day? It's barely noon."

"You're exhausted because you're in pain. Should I find a nurse? Can you take OTC meds?"

"Stop, will you? I don't require a nurse."

Pride, Nella mused, *is an exceptional hardship. Like carrying a block of cement on your back for all your natural-born days.*

"Fine," she decided. "I won't get a nurse. Give me your house key. I'll drive over and fetch the gloves. I'll be back in thirty minutes."

"Don't bother. I should leave soon, take a nap. By dinnertime I'll be as good as new." Rosalind plucked at her sweater. Mud stippled the fabric from her ordeal in the forest. "I've had two dizzy spells since Emerson and Darcy got to the hospital."

"Let me drive you home. No arguing. I'll stay with you tonight. Camp out in your living room. Latrice can go home and sleep in her own bed."

At the suggestion, Rosalind angled her neck. "Nella, you amaze me. We're both too old for a slumber party."

"Guess again. After today's excitement, we both need to blow off some steam."

"Must we invite Tippi? She'll root through my liquor cabinet, then sing Italian ballads off-key. I'm afraid I have no desire to hear your mother sing 'That's Amore' while she's liquored up. Or has Tippi given up her penchant for brandy?"

Nella giggled like a schoolgirl. She'd forgotten how much she enjoyed Rosalind's wit. "Tippi still drinks," she said. "But she's cut down with age. We won't invite her."

"We won't?"

"These days, she breaks into song after a tablespoon of brandy."

"Leave her home." Rosalind looked up hopefully. "You don't mind staying the night? This afternoon will be an awful bore. I do need a long nap."

"I'll read while you sleep. I miss your wonderful library."

"Those dusty old books miss you too." Rosalind let the silence wind out. In her lap, her hands stilled. At length, she said, "I'm losing sensation in my legs. It started last week. I've been too bullheaded to tell Darcy."

"You should be in a wheelchair." Nella placed another finger-kiss on Rosalind's cheek. "We'll go tomorrow, try out the latest models. Do you have a color preference?"

"In wheelchairs? Aren't they all a dreary gray?"

"Not all. I saw one online in a snazzy steel-colored blue. It will go beautifully with your complexion."

At that, Rosalind laughed. "Nella, you are too much."

Chapter 25

Darcy rose from foggy dreams. She dragged her eyes open. Shadows draped the hospital room. The corridor outside was quiet.

Wincing, she became aware of the throbbing in her arms. Then her legs. Tiny fire bursts of pain from being knocked around the river. With a start, she noticed her mother seated beside the bed.

She lifted her head from the pillow, groaned. "What are you doing here?" She flopped back down, a headache pounding at her temples.

"*Shhh!* I'm not supposed to be here." Her mother winked. She appeared positively giddy.

Flabbergasted by the rare display, Darcy gave her the once-over. Rosalind's silver hair was a puffy tangle, her eyes too bright. Which wasn't the worst of it. Beneath a beige knit top, she wore plaid pajama bottoms.

Flannel pajama bottoms.

Following her gaze, Rosalind said, "It's late. It didn't seem worth the bother to get out of our comfy clothes." She hesitated. "How do you feel?"

"Like I've been through a meat grinder. I have an impressive number of bruises on my legs. But they'll heal." She switched topics. "Latrice drove you here?"

"Nella did. We're having a slumber party. We were chatting over glasses of wine when *voilà*! The idea popped into our heads: let's sneak into the hospital."

"You . . . what?"

"If you're curious, Nella is hiding in the restroom. The one near the elevator."

Which meant her mother and Nella were back on speaking terms. More than that—they were in the midst of a slumber party in their pj's, devising late-night escapades, including slipping into the hospital. For two mature women, it was an interesting state of affairs. When had they made up? And why? The questions bouncing through Darcy's skull urged her to sit up.

A bad idea. Her temples pounding, she guided her head back to the pillow. The mystery would have to wait.

"How did you slip past the nursing station?" she asked instead. "Visiting hours end at nine o'clock. Michael tried to stay longer. They made him leave."

Her mother smiled. "Nella says Michael loves you."

"I love him too."

"The year you graduated from college . . . I didn't know you were dating him. I've been such a fool."

A remarkable admission—one bright enough to alert Darcy to a change in the air. Her mother wasn't visiting in the wee hours on a whim. She had a reason for coming.

"How *did* you sneak into the hospital?"

"At three in the morning?" Rosalind craned her neck, peered toward the corridor. "Most of the staff is asleep at the switch. We waited until the coast was clear and jumped in the elevator. When the man at the nursing station went to check on a patient, I made a dash for your room. Well, I didn't exactly 'dash.' In my present condition, I moved with the grace of an old sand crab scuttling down a beach."

"Mother, you're becoming absolutely delinquent."

"Marvelous, isn't it? I spent most of today sleeping—I have energy to spare." Rosalind shimmied her shoulders. "Are there any fruit stands nearby? I'd like to knock one over."

Darcy gaped. Was her mother cracking jokes?

Yes, she was. And superbly, at that.

"You *do* know the hospital will release me in the morning. We can probably spring Emerson by early afternoon. What do you need to discuss that can't wait?"

"I've changed my mind."

"You mean . . . ?" Darcy hesitated. It was foolhardy to get her hopes up.

"Yes, dear. I'll go on the list."

"You will?"

"I'll call Dr. Tanaka tomorrow. The news will make her day."

Darcy laughed. "Hell, it's already made *my* day and it's only three a.m."

"Don't swear. It's unbecoming."

"Right."

Her upbeat expression dimming, Rosalind dredged up her pricklier sensibilities. "Bear in mind, putting my name on a transplant list may lead exactly nowhere. They may not find a match in time. If they do find a heart, I may be too weak to survive the procedure. I've been such a stubborn fool. It will serve me right if they *do* find a heart but I don't make it through surgery."

Gratitude tightened Darcy's throat.

Mother will go on the list. We might actually beat the disease.

No. Not maybe. We will. *She'll come through this with flying colors.*

Darcy poked her hand out from beneath the blankets. "Stop worrying." She clasped her mother's hand. "You'll get through surgery, no problem. I'm sure of it. I don't have a smidgen of doubt."

"Don't be ridiculous. How can you guarantee I'll survive?"

The tears came too fast for Darcy to suppress. "You must survive," she said, blinking them back. "I'm not ready to lose you."

Chapter 26

Scanning the text message, Darcy wandered into the living room. After sending a reply, she looked up. She came to a contented standstill.

One week after the ordeal in the forest, everyone in the Goodridge household was still in "nesting mode." Although it was past eleven o'clock on a bright Sunday morning, no one—except Latrice, whipping up pancakes in the kitchen—seemed in any hurry to get dressed. On the couch, Samson clacked away on a laptop. Beside him, Emerson appeared bored with his Nintendo. Rosalind, camped out in her favorite Queen Anne chair behind the *New York Times*, looked comfy in a light-apricot nightgown and a beige robe.

"Breakfast will be ready soon," Darcy said to no one in particular. With triumph, she glanced at the napkin on the end table beside her mother's chair. The three orange slices she'd deposited there were gone. "Mother, would you like another nibble?"

"I'm not a cat, dear. Stop luring me with small bites."

"Well, it *does* get you to eat." According to Dr. Tanaka, she couldn't afford to lose weight. Darcy was determined to keep her fit and hale until they found a heart and scheduled the surgery.

"I'm fine for now," Rosalind assured her. "Is there yogurt in the fridge? I'm not sure my stomach will approve of pancakes."

"There is." Dropping the subject, Darcy glanced hopefully at the couch. "Anyone feel like setting the dining room table?"

Emerson tossed his Nintendo aside. "Go for it, Aunt Darcy. We don't mind."

"Ha ha. Got any other wisecracks you'd like to share?"

"Not really."

She began to retrace her steps. Then she halted. Out of the corner of her eye, she caught Emerson rolling up his pajama bottoms to his knees. Wrinkling his nose, he studied the cuts and bruises on his shins. The wounds were healing well. Yet, despite his aversion to blood, he was constantly tempted to pick at the itchy scabs.

Samson—his attention still trained on the laptop—batted Emerson's hand back.

"Leave them alone." Resuming his work, Samson peered at the screen. "Keep picking at them, and Darcy will put the bandages back on."

"I will," she warned.

"But my legs itch!"

The *New York Times* rustled. "Emerson, last warning." Rosalind balled up the napkin and took aim. The napkin popped her grandson on the head.

"Hey!"

Darcy noticed something else. "Samson, did you buy a laptop?" The one he was using didn't look familiar.

"This was Michael's. It's old, but still works. It'll do for now."

On Wednesday, Samson had come to a decision. He'd enroll at Lakeland Community College. Three classes, three days a week. Michael planned to switch him to a flexible schedule, allowing him to choose when to work and when to study.

"We should get you a new laptop before classes begin," she decided. "Let me spring for one. My gift to the new college student."

"I appreciate the offer, Darcy. But I'm saving up for a new one."

Her mother rustled her newspaper with faint irritation. "Samson, how many times must I offer to buy you a laptop . . . *and* pay your tuition? College is an important step for a young adult. This isn't charity. It's an investment in the future—one I'm happy to make. The world needs ambitious young adults."

Emerson snorted. "Yeah, right. Samson's big ambition is the girl he's dating at the high school. Makayla told him *she's* going to Lakeland next year."

Samson threw him a warning look. Then he rolled his eyes as Emerson returned his attention to his scabs, the temptation to scratch gleaming in his eyes.

Darcy moved in. Steering her nephew's hand back, she rolled down his pajamas.

When she finished, he folded his arms. "Aunt Darcy, should I learn Mandarin?"

A non sequitur of the first order. She laughed. "I don't know, kiddo. Should you?"

"I want to work in e-commerce. Do you think the Chinese would mass-produce the squirrel baffle we built? I could sell them online."

"Some advice: get a patent before talking to the Chinese."

"What's a patent?"

"Well, it's a kind of protection. For inventors."

"I don't understand."

Samson's fingers danced across the laptop's keyboard. "I'll show you a website that'll explain," he said. "Here you go. A patent gives you protection so no one can steal your invention. When I was in junior high, Big Brothers in Charleston got me signed up with a nice guy for about a year. He worked on the docks of Charleston Harbor, and he had an idea for a new kind of back brace for guys who do a lot of heavy lifting. I'm not sure if he ever got a patent, but I remember him showing this site to me."

"Why would someone in Beijing steal my stuff?"

"To make money on your idea. Look here." He swiveled the laptop toward Emerson. "This is the US Patent Office. Do you want me to send you the link? If you get a patent and someone tries to steal your stuff, you can sue them. At least I think you can. I'm not sure how you take someone to court if he lives in another country. Is there a World Court for things like that?"

The newspaper fluttered to Rosalind's lap. "We have international laws to govern affairs between countries," she told him.

"Do they work?"

"Sometimes. Not always. Countries find devious ways to steal intellectual property—patents, copyrights, and the like. It's a difficult issue."

"Then someone ought to make better laws." Samson rubbed his lips together, working it out. "How do you pass a law in your country but make someone in another country obey it?"

The question brought a dreamy sigh from Rosalind. "We have a lawyer in our midst," she murmured.

Her momentary bliss allowed Darcy to slide the newspaper from her lap. "Slow down, Mother." She found the section she wanted and tossed the newspaper back. "Let Samson get his feet wet at college before you steer him toward a career."

A knock sounded at the door. In a habit recently established, Michael let himself in. He came into the living room with a platter in his hands that trailed a delectable scent. Homemade *pizzelles*. The heavenly, wafer-thin cookies were Nella's specialty.

"Your timing is lousy," Darcy joked, although she certainly hadn't objected when he'd sent the text. "Maybe I'll have just one before we sit down to breakfast. Can you join us?"

"For Latrice's pancakes? Sure."

They exchanged a glance of longing—one Darcy quickly cut off. She recalled the promise she'd made to Emerson at the craft fair. If she went fishing for a boyfriend, she wouldn't cast her line toward Michael. A promise already broken, obviously. Michael had reluctantly agreed to allow her to decide when they'd tell Emerson the truth.

"Pizzelles!" Approaching, he surveyed the platter. "Grandmother, how many may I have before breakfast?"

"How about one? You can have more later."

"Only one? But Nella just made these!"

"Emerson—no. Cookies are not a breakfast food."

He glared at Rosalind. "Maple syrup has sugar in it," he said reasonably. "Why are pancakes a breakfast food, and *pizzelles* aren't? They're made with eggs."

They began to debate the merits of homemade Italian confections versus pancakes. As they did, Michael again caught Darcy's eye. Lingering, loving, his gaze traversed her face. She found she couldn't break off the connection—or stanch the warmth coasting through her veins.

This, she mused, *is the problem with intimacy. Now that we've uncorked the bottle, we can't put the genie back inside.*

Which explained why Michael unwittingly made a mistake next. Lowering the platter to his waist, he drifted toward her. Just slightly— an inch. Enough for Emerson, his nose hovering above the platter, to sense that something was afoot.

"Hold on." His brows lowering, he regarded Michael. Then Darcy. "What's going on? Aunt Darcy, you promised you'd pick another fish. *Any* other fish!"

The accusation threw the room into silence. But only for a moment. A fizzy sort of irritation spun through Darcy.

"Emerson, stop it." Taking the platter, she placed it on the coffee table. Choosing her words with care, she faced her nephew. "I'm not taking Michael away from you. He's not choosing between us. As a matter of fact, it's wrong to presume you have the right to decide what another person will or will not do. He loves you."

"And I love Darcy too," Michael added. He clasped the boy's shoulders. "Understand? Love isn't something you parcel out to just some people. You spread it around. The more people you love, the more people you're capable of loving. Does that make sense?"

It did, but Emerson didn't appear fully on board. "You're *my* friend," he said. "What if you start liking Darcy more than you like me?"

"I'm way past the 'liking' stage—in both instances. And I don't want to be your friend." Michael paused a dramatic beat, long enough to ensure Emerson hung on his every word. "I want to be your father. Which is a discussion for another day. I haven't asked Darcy to marry me yet. No offense, but you won't be around when I do. That's a private matter for me and your aunt to discuss."

Rosalind slipped on her leather gloves. "Thank goodness that's done. Keeping the secret was tiring. I'll admit, I wasn't invested in doing so for weeks on end." She got to her feet, then smiled at her grandson. "Chin up, dear. You'll get used to the change. Oh, and Michael—please thank Nella for making the *pizzelles*. I haven't enjoyed one in ages."

She swept up the platter. "Cookie, anyone?"

Chapter 27

In the Goodridge household, Christmas arrived in October.

Darcy lugged the pumpkin she'd bought for Halloween—a holiday now stripped from the calendar by unanimous vote—to the base of the tree where the bird feeder hung. Setting it down, she took stock of their handiwork. Michael was still high on the ladder, trimming the roof with lights. A fat Santa stood at the top of the front porch. The boxwood framing the house was trimmed abundantly with colored lights.

Michael glanced down from the ladder. "How does everything look?"

"Great. Now, come down. We're on a schedule."

"One sec."

"We have to leave soon," she warned. "Let's not keep my mother waiting."

In the two months since the ordeal in the river, life had rapidly returned to normal. Once Rosalind put her name on the transplant list, they all avoided the topic. The waiting was nerve-racking. Nella came over daily to boost Rosalind's spirits. Darcy continued knocking around the basement, finding dry rot to repair and other home improvements to occupy her worried mind.

Emerson was the real problem.

With the academic year underway, he became moodier by the day. When he trudged in from school, he clomped up to his bedroom to study. When he finished with schoolwork and grew bored with Nintendo, he flossed his teeth for long minutes before performing the habit that was now a nighttime ritual.

Emerson would sit down at his computer, find another image of the Tin Man, and set his laser printer whirring. The wall behind his bed was plastered with Tin Man images. Three days earlier, when Rosalind—during a rare afternoon when her stamina allowed her to climb the staircase—stepped into his bedroom and glimpsed his latest project, she decided an intervention was needed to bolster the spirits of a frightened boy.

Christmas. Immediately.

And so, three days ago, they'd begun decorating the house. Every last box of decorations in the basement was dragged upstairs. Samson—with a teenager's boundless energy and a keen-eyed determination to lift Emerson's spirits—insisted on leaving nothing behind. His curiosity led him into each of the storerooms like a kid on a scavenger hunt. Large boxes, small boxes, wooden crates layered in dust with antique ornaments peeking through the yellowing tissue wrapped around them. By the time he finished scouring the basement, every bit of holiday cheer packed away by a long line of Goodridges had been lugged up the steps.

Tippi helped Emerson sort through the haul; Darcy took her mother to Lowe's for the largest imitation tree in the place. The staff was just beginning to stock the aisles for the holiday season when the Goodridge women arrived.

All the wintry merriment proved lucky. That evening, at precisely seven o'clock, they'd received the call. Finally.

The transplant team was en route to Cincinnati to pick up the precious, lifesaving cargo. Rosalind would be admitted to the Cleveland Clinic within the hour.

Michael climbed down from the ladder. "Done." He kissed her briefly. "Is your mother packed?"

"Nella helped her finish twenty minutes ago." They were all driving to the hospital together. One big, happy—and nervous—caravan.

"Sounds good."

They went inside. Gwynn, the home health aide, was pulling on her coat.

"Where's my mother?" Darcy asked her.

"Already on the patio." Gwynn smiled. "Keep me posted regarding her schedule."

Darcy nodded. Given the progression of her disease, Rosalind would undoubtedly require a long hospital stay. Two weeks, minimum. Perhaps a month. Once she was released, they would need Gwynn's help—probably until past the *real* Christmas.

"Nella is in the kitchen helping Latrice with the dinner dishes. Tippi is with them," Gwynn added. She pressed Darcy's hand. "I'll keep your mother in my prayers."

"Thank you, Gwynn."

"Call me tomorrow when you have a chance. I want to hear how Rosalind is doing after surgery."

"I will."

After she left, Michael went into the kitchen. He came back out with the three women.

They all went outside. On the patio, they spotted Rosalind in her wheelchair. A heavy blanket was tucked around her legs. A fluffy down coat, zipped up to the neck, ensured the brisk October night wouldn't start her shivering.

On the lawn, Emerson and Samson were conducting an animated conversation. A dash of wind blew Darcy's hair away from her face. Michael, noting her coat flapping open, buttoned it up.

"What *are* they doing?" Darcy started across the patio.

Michael caught up to her. "My guess? Debating which star is best."

"But they aren't the ones choosing!"

Tippi and Nella hurried past. Latrice, pausing by Darcy, cupped her hands around her mouth. "Boys! Stop arguing. Let Rosalind pick her own star."

Darcy chuckled as the boys dashed toward the patio. It still tickled her that Rosalind had consented to choose. She'd grown fond of Samson—including his beliefs about finding your very own North Star, the one meant to guide you.

Bending over the wheelchair, she brushed a wisp of hair from her mother's eyes. "We have to leave for the hospital soon."

The news pleased Rosalind. "Good. I'll nap on the way." She appeared tired, her skin pale.

"Well, hurry up," Darcy prodded. "It's getting cold. You look like an ice cube."

"Oh, hush. I'm trying to choose. There are so many interesting possibilities." Hesitating, Rosalind waved Michael over. When he neared, she said, "Fetch Samson. I want to pick from the yard. All the light from the house is making this impossible."

"Good thinking. There's less light out back." Michael whistled to the boys. When they trotted up, he told Samson, "Grab the other side of the wheelchair—carefully. We're carrying Rosalind out to the lawn."

Ten feet past the patio, they set the wheelchair down. Evening dew glimmered on the grass. Stars threaded the sky in a glittering arc. Darcy marveled at the beauty of the night. The sharp scent of the grass and the sparkling heavens captured her senses and then her heart. She knelt beside her mother's wheelchair.

"Go on," she whispered. "Pick whichever star you'd like. It'll be your guiding light."

"*You've* been my guiding light these last months," Rosalind said.

The declaration nearly shook a sob loose from Darcy. On her shoulder, Michael's fingers pressed with gentle reassurance.

Something of the night's magic reached Emerson, and his pinched expression eased the smallest degree. He opened his arms wide. "Go on, Grandmother. Choose!"

On a sigh, Rosalind canvassed the sparkling night. Weighing, pondering, she sent her attention leaping across the star-studded expanse.

At last, she lifted her hand.

BOOK CLUB QUESTIONS

1. Many of us have experienced a tragic circumstance in the
    past. Discuss with your book club:

    *   Why does Darcy Goodridge feel responsible for the acci-
        dent that led to the deaths of her sister and her father? Do
        you agree with her reasoning? Was moving from city to city
        a suitable penance?

    *   Instead of self-banishment from Ohio, how might Darcy
        have dealt with her grief?

    *   If Darcy had remained in Ohio, the reader can easily see
        how Michael Varano might have helped her through the
        difficult grieving process. Have you experienced the loss
        of a loved one? Share with your book club the person
        who helped you find healing, or share a practice that
        helped you: prayer, solitary walks, a favorite pet, etc.
        Discuss how you would help a friend through the griev-
        ing process.

2. Judge Rosalind Goodridge resisted the idea of undergoing
    heart transplant surgery. Why do you believe she resisted
    the idea? Had she given up on life? Or were her reasons sub-
    tle? For example, would a controlling woman like Rosalind
    secretly worry about dying during the surgery? Or would

the need to rely upon others while recuperating prove a strong reason not to have the surgery?

3. Share with your book club examples of Darcy's emotional arc as the story progresses. She enters her nephew's life as Rosalind's estranged daughter and his mysterious aunt. What does she represent to Emerson by book's end?

- Discuss with your book club the fluid nature of family. Latrice is a mother figure to both Darcy and Emerson. Has anyone in your book club played the role of "second mother" or "second father" in a child's life?

- How do groups like Big Brothers and Big Sisters provide the element of family in the lives of children, many of whom live in at-risk homes? Discuss other groups in society that extend the beneficial aspects of family to aid children and adults.

4. Is anyone in your book club familiar with a family broken apart by tragedy, yet able to reconnect later? Discuss why tragedy can shatter familial bonds. How can grief counseling or other practices help such families before they break apart?

5. When Darcy confronts Rosalind about Dr. Jack's infidelities, does the reader feel sympathy for both women, or only Darcy? Discuss with your book club why Rosalind believed she made the best choice for her daughters. Do you agree? What other choices might she have explored instead?

6. How do the characters Samson, Michael, Nella, and Latrice serve to deepen the reader's understanding of Darcy? Of Rosalind?

7. Discuss your favorite character in the book. What did you find most appealing?

If your book club would like to discuss *The Road She Left Behind* with the author, please contact her at christine@christinenolfi.com with BOOK CLUB DISCUSSION in the subject line. Christine is usually able to schedule several online meetings per month through Skype, Facebook, or the medium of your choice.

ACKNOWLEDGMENTS

To my wonderful editor, Christopher Werner, for his brilliant suggestions and for taking the time from his busy schedule to read early drafts; to my developmental editor, Krista Stroever, for all her fabulous insights and keen eye; and to Lake Union's editorial director, Danielle Marshall, for the opportunity to write *The Road She Left Behind* for Amazon Publishing.

To my agent, Pamela Harty, for her generous advice and friendship.

To my beta readers Rebecca Frank, Jan Crossen, Pat Werths, and Robin Batterson. Ladies, thank you for your wonderful suggestions as the manuscript underwent countless revisions. Special thanks to Sergeant Kimberly Libens of the Chagrin Falls Police Department for escorting me on Geauga County's winding country roads as I mapped out the book's pivotal scenes.

To my copyeditor, Stacee Lawrence; my production editor, Nicole Pomeroy; and my proofreader, Sarah Engel, for both their patience and their careful edits. Heartfelt thanks to Caroline Teagle Johnson for the beautiful cover design.

To my youngest sister, Trish, who has always been the little piece of golden in the Nolfi family tree. From the outset, you were the inspiration behind this story about sisters.

And to Barry, for reading every review throughout the years and believing even when I entertained doubts. I love you, always.

ABOUT THE AUTHOR

Photo © 2016 Melissa Miley

Award-winning author Christine Nolfi writes heartwarming and inspiring fiction. She is the author of the award-winning Sweet Lake Series: *Sweet Lake*, *The Comfort of Secrets*, and *The Season of Silver Linings*. A native of Ohio, Christine now resides in South Carolina with her husband and four adopted children. For the latest information about her releases and future books, visit www.christinenolfi.com. Chat with her on Twitter @christinenolfi.